Praise for Jacqui Lofthouse's novels

The Temple of Hymen

'Deceptive; entertaining and unusual.' – Louis de Bernières

'A very impressive book... a superbly recreated historical period and a passionate investigation into femininity, all wrapped up in a mysterious and well-paced narrative.' – Jonathan Coe

'A remarkable, often beautiful and startling piece of writing. A considerable achievement.' – John Mortimer

'Grand fun and quite naughty in parts.' – The Times

Bluethroat Morning

'There are many elements to savour in this novel. Lofthouse has a fine eye for the bleak Norfolk landscape and how it both reflects and affects characters' moods.' – Tracy Chevalier, Author of Girl with a Pearl Earring

'A classic tale of longing.' – Time Out

'A thriller full of twists and turns that keeps the reader guessing. Every word is magical, almost luminous.' – Daily Mail

THE MODIGLIANI GIRL

by

Jacqui Lofthouse

Blackbird Digital Books

Published by Blackbird Digital Books, London
ISBN-13: 978-1503024700
ISBN-10: 1503024709
Copyright Jacqui Lofthouse 2015
Cover Design by Simon Avery www.idobookcovers.com
The moral right of the author has been asserted

'If I feel physically as if the top of my head were taken off, I know that is poetry' – Emily Dickinson

Part One

Beginning

1

'This is what I find encouraging about the writing trades: they allow mediocre people who are patient and industrious to revise their stupidity, to edit themselves into something like intelligence. They also allow lunatics to seem saner than sane.' – Kurt Vonnegut

I have often wished that I had been born at the turn of the nineteenth century, in Paris. It seems unfair to me that those lucky enough to be born in the right place at the right time had the opportunity of living a truly bohemian lifestyle, whilst those of us brought up in the eighties in Billericay are conditioned to a life of material acquisition that is hardly compatible with the pursuit of art for art's sake.

That thought again, tormenting me. I brush it aside and focus on what I see. I'm sitting before a mirror in a white dressing gown, gazing at my face but not quite recognising it. My hair is in foam curlers and my make-up is half complete: my kohl-rimmed eyes and Barbie-doll false lashes make me an airbrushed version of myself. The rest of my face is ghost-pale; even my lips are not yet painted. The mirror is rimmed by opaque light bulbs and – yes, I admit it – there's something of the *Moulin Rouge* about the scene and I ought to appreciate it, but somehow can't. I laugh out loud only there's no hint of jollity in the sound. I am not myself and I am definitely not in Paris, though the cabaret is about to begin.

Where the hell is the make-up artist, that's what I want to know? She was telling me her name is Ruby and she can't afford a down payment on a flat in Kentish Town. It was a distraction, at least, but now she's vanished to take a call and I'm left alone, staring at this new creation in the mirror, wondering what I'm doing here. In a few hours, everything should fall into place. Everything I've ever dreamed of is about to come true. If I win, I'll have it all (all the shallow stuff that is): fame, glamour and the kind of success that I always thought I wanted. My mascara is running down my face, cutting vertical lines across the pancake, but it's OK. Really, it's OK. It's only natural to cry on an occasion like this. It's stage fright. Last-minute nerves. Panic. The whole story is spinning in my head and threatens to spill out and I'm trying to keep it inside, but it's like an out of body experience. I am at once in front of the mirror and above it, watching myself, like a player in a bad farce that has become quite frighteningly real.

There's a knock at the door behind me and I stand to open it, half here and half lost in memory. Behind the door there's a young woman, pushing past me. She's holding a coat-hanger from which hangs a crumpled cream-coloured dress that looks a bit too much like a wedding frock for my liking. She's looking at me as if she wants something but I have no idea what it is that she wants.

'Well?' she says. She hangs the dress in the corner and stands back to admire it. When I don't reply, she forces the issue. 'So what do you think?'

'Of the dress?'

'Isn't it stunning? I'm beside myself with envy.'

'Why?'

She rolls her eyes as if I'm having her on. 'It's vintage Balmain?' The inflexion in her voice makes me wonder if she is Australian. Either that or she thinks I'm extremely stupid.

'Is that eco-friendly or something?'

'Sod the eco-credentials – it's a one-off piece. You're going to look incredible in this.' She is Australian, but she also thinks I'm stupid.

'It looks a bit like a doily to me.'

'Trust me. You'll own the stage.'

I try to pull myself back into the room, to really get this moment and make it meaningful. *This is it, Anna Bright.* Sadly I don't believe my own PR. *It's your time. What does it matter how you got here and what you feel inside? When you put on that dress, you can do exactly what she says: walk onto the stage and work the audience.*

2

You can become Fahy and Brown's next big thing.

But even as I say these words, I am thinking of a girl standing before a high window in Paris. I can't get her out of my mind. She has lost the only thing that matters to her and she is gazing down at the pavement far beneath, wondering if she will do it, whether the act she is about to commit is one of bravery or one of cowardice. And what would she make of me, that girl?

You are a liar and a thief.

'What the hell's going on?' Ruby is back. She takes me by the shoulders and sits me down on the stool. 'What did you say to her?' she asks the wardrobe girl.

'Nothing. She's just been insulting the dress. Does she have any idea what it cost us to borrow that for the evening?'

'It doesn't matter. It doesn't matter what Anna makes of the dress. What matters is that she wears it!' She turns to me. 'Anna – are you OK?'

'I'm fine,' I say, though my voice is no more than a whisper.

Ruby leans forward, puts a hand on my shoulder and picks up a sponge pad from her kit, repairing the pancake, before applying more glitter to my eyelids.

'Don't cry,' she said. 'It would be really helpful if you could do "internal" nerves rather than "external" ones. That way, you know, it won't mess up your face.'

If I can't cry, perhaps they will allow me to scream. I hold back, bite my lip quickly and nod. I realise it doesn't matter really. I'm not quite here any more. I'm somewhere else, driving my car, a whole year ago now. I can hear the music, the voice of Ian Dury playing my town's theme tune *Billericay Dickie* and Dury's voice takes me right back to the evening when all this madness started.

*

I was stuck in a traffic jam, en route to the Lyric Theatre Hammersmith. It was a drizzling June evening, the sky was low and a summer rain threatened. The driver's window was open and I was smoking, inhaling deeply, perhaps believing that if I inhaled quite hard enough, the nicotine rush might take away the memory of my argument with Will. But even nicotine would not do it. I kept going over the issue in my mind, trying to understand his point of view, but failing. I could not get over the fact that he had chosen to go to the *Telegraph* party rather than coming with me to support Hilary on her big night. *Had* I been too obnoxious? Quite possibly I had. Now, as well as having fallen out with my fiancé, I was also late and likely to embarrass Hils.

That was when Dury came on the radio ... His lyrics were out of tune with my thoughts, but against my will I began to laugh. I tossed the burning cigarette stub from the window and listened. Dury's voice made me think about my sister Lois: a memory of her pogoing about the kitchen to the strains of *Hit Me With Your Rhythm Stick*, tossing her head furiously to the beat, while Mum – the original Dury fan – was busy cooking our fish fingers.

The traffic ground to a halt.

It was odd to think that Hilary was about to join the ranks of the Essex glitterati. Hilary – the same girl I met at the Mayflower School. It didn't seem real or even right that she was appearing on stage that night with the much-lauded Meryl Wainwright, *Grande Dame* of British Letters. In typical Hils fashion, she had tried to play it down. *'It's just in the studio theatre, Anna. It's not such a huge deal.'* But it was impossible to miss her excitement. This was a fund-raising event for The Reading Trust and Hilary would be reading an extract from her recently published novel, alongside five other authors, including Wainwright, the notorious Harish Devan and the man that I considered the wildcard, the latest bestselling guru, James Loftus.

It had taken a while for me to adjust to Hilary's success. If I said I wasn't envious, I'd be a liar. Who wouldn't be envious of a school friend who'd just secured a six-figure publishing deal? If it had been anybody else, I'd say it was enough to make you vomit. But Hilary is my oldest friend and I was beginning to see there was some price to pay for this break. Every insecurity that ever haunted her before she signed that contract was now magnified tenfold. If she was a perfectionist before, now she was bordering on OCD. I had never known anyone more hardworking than Hilary but these days I hardly saw her; until very recently, she'd been working all hours on the sequel to her novel in a desperate bid to meet an impossible deadline. Tonight, at least, was her chance to enjoy what she'd achieved and I was furious at myself for being late.

But I was even more furious at Will. Because if Will had come along that night, I would not have been late in the first place. Will is never late. The word isn't in his vocabulary. He was certainly not going to be late for the *Telegraph* party. Having decided it was more important to network in his own little circle than in mine, he was in his dinner suit and favourite Fornasetti tie before I even got home from work.

But I had to put my bitterness behind me. It wasn't often that I fell out with Will and I vowed we'd make it up later that evening. It was likely I was being selfish. Will had been a freelance cartoonist for a couple of years now, but he got a lot of work from *The Telegraph* and if he didn't suck up to the editors at these events then somebody else would suck up in his place. In any case, I should possibly have thanked Will for his absence because being late was what caused me to bump into Meryl in the first place.

When I arrived at the Lyric, the foyer and bar were deserted. The audience had already gone into the theatre. I tried to sneak in quietly but as I stepped into the darkness of the auditorium, an usher followed me.

'You have to wait at the side,' she said. 'It's started.'

Keeping close to her, I shuffled forwards in the darkness. As I approached the stage however, I realised that Hilary was standing immediately in front of me. Harish Devan was on the podium and had just begun his reading.

'What are you doing here?' I whispered. 'Aren't you meant to be up there?'

'They screwed up,' Hilary said. 'They were meant to put out six chairs on stage but they forgot. The stage manager's in a right strop, so we've got to take it in turns.'

'Where are the other writers?'

'They managed to find a couple of reserved seats in the front row. But the others were all taken. It's full up, so I have to wait here until it's my turn to read.'

'Fabulous,' I said. 'Star treatment.'

As I spoke, I sensed that somebody was now standing behind me. I turned around and the person seemed so familiar that I greeted her.

'Oh – hello!'

She laughed and I immediately realised my error. I recognised her now, even in the gloom. It was impossible to mistake her trademark craggy features. I had seen that face in Sunday supplements, on book jackets and on TV. Yet Meryl Wainwright was smaller in the flesh.

'I've lost my damn umbrella,' she whispered. At first I thought she couldn't be talking to me, but Hilary's attention was focussed on Devan and the usher had returned to the foyer. It seemed incongruous to hear a literary legend talking about something so banal. I had only ever heard her pontificating on cultural artefacts. The umbrella clearly mattered to her. 'I put it down in the caff and now it's gone. Do you think I've got time to find it before I go on?'

'Um. I don't know,' I said. 'Do you want me to have a look?'

'Would you? Oh sod it. We've probably got hours yet. Harish is always so up himself. I'm gasping for a fag.'

'Me too,' I said. My forwardness took me by surprise. If it hadn't been so dark I might have been more circumspect. 'I couldn't cadge one, could I?'

In the end, we found the umbrella behind a sofa and I suspected its loss had been nothing more than a ploy for nicotine. We nipped out the back via a fire door and stood outside, huddling beneath a small canopy. There was a light drizzle but not enough to distract Meryl from important business. She sheltered the flame beneath her coat and ensured that mine was lit before her own. I found myself trying not to count her wrinkles; it was simply a nervous reaction, a distraction from the fear of not knowing what to say. I was determined not to sound pathetic but the sycophantic stuff must have been on the tip of my tied-up tongue because without quite knowing how it happened, I found myself praising her latest novel.

'I thought the characterisation of Ethan was so accomplished...' I said. 'Your prose is so tight. And there's something... elastic about it.' *Elastic? How can it be tight and also elastic? What was that supposed to mean?* My inarticulacy was killing me. Meryl must have thought I was a total prat but she was very nice about it.

'Thank you, my dear. That was a terrible nuisance about the umbrella. And how kind. Do you write?'

I hesitated. I had been considering the idea of writing seriously for some time. I had written fragments in notebooks, then torn them out and thrown them away. Sometimes I would scribble ideas on scraps of paper and I occasionally gathered images and kept them in an attractive polka-dotted box folder marked 'Novel', but it was not something that I ever spoke about. It had been years since I had admitted such an ambition. In our early twenties, when Hilary was at Cambridge and I at Warwick, we would write long letters to each other, professing our love of Hardy and the Brontës and our desire to write great works, but Hilary had made that desire concrete and I was still at the back-of-an-envelope stage. My answer to Meryl's question must surely be a resounding 'No'.

'Not yet,' I said.

I suppose it just slipped out.

'Fool's game, of course,' she said. 'But you could do worse than listening to this Loftus fellow.'

She cocked her head and raised an eyebrow as she spoke, as if to say 'don't underestimate the chap'. She was looking directly at me, as if issuing a challenge. I had expected her to be patronising or dismissive or abrupt but she was none of these. Meryl appeared entirely serious. The look might even have been called *encouraging*. And something about this made me feel uncomfortable. It reminded me of a look my father used to give me, a look he gave me on the day Hilary and I went up for interview at Cambridge. I did not want to remember it.

It's possible that Meryl noticed the impact of her expression. If she did, she passed no comment. I attempted to laugh it off and to continue the conversation without crying.

'You think he has a serious message?' I said.

I'd read all about the silver-haired guru in *The Observer* at the weekend (Will called my newspaper habit treason). Loftus was not such big news then as he is now, but his work was already a hit in the States and he was beginning to cause noticeable ripples here in the UK. His book, *How to Be a Literary Genius* was, as far as I could make out, an invitation to would-be writers everywhere to abandon self-doubt and to believe that they had a book inside them. I could not think of anything more depressing. The man appeared to be on a single-minded mission to convince us that "everyone is creative". It was nothing that had not been said by a thousand other gurus before him, but no one could deny the power of his marketing machine. Loftus's holiday company *Genius Vacations* had just expanded to take over half the Greek Island of Ouranos.

Yet here was Meryl Wainwright giving him a plug and challenging my cynicism. Was it possible I was missing something? According to the article, Loftus had a strong fan-base. Tens of thousands of people had used his methods to overcome chronic writer's block but that didn't give him any intellectual credibility. I had pretty much dismissed him out of hand. The last thing the world needed right now was more unblocked writers. The net result of that would surely be more bad literature. Hadn't Meryl thought of that?

'There's only one serious message in the end,' Meryl said. She stubbed out her fag on a railing.

'What's that?'

'Get black on white,' she said. Then, after a brief silence added, 'Guy de Maupassant. No one ever became a writer by thinking about it.' She shivered then, and pulled her raincoat closer across her chest. 'Come on. Devan's probably still droning on, but we'd better not miss the rest.'

We arrived back in time to see Hilary walking onto the stage. She glanced in my direction and I wasn't sure if her expression was one of relief or reprimand. I smiled back, as if to say 'of course, I never would have missed you' but I don't know if she believed me.

Beneath the brilliant light, Hilary appeared at once brittle and vulnerable. She wore a black Ghost dress, just on the decent side of transparency, the kind of dress that I could never carry off. Her hair was newly cropped and bleached. If you didn't know her, you might think her composure unnerving. Though she fixed her eyes on the audience and raised her chin and did not allow her jaw to quiver even a fraction, the small fluttering movements of her hands to her face revealed her fear to me.

Hilary need not have been afraid however. Her novel was a deeply serious one, an apocalyptic vision, rooted in science and conveyed in crisp, elegant prose. I had read a previous draft and the opening moved me now as much as it did the first time. As Hilary read, I watched Meryl leaning forward, her hand resting on her cheek, frowning and absorbed. Afterwards, Hilary told me, when she came off the stage, Meryl had whispered 'Bravo, my dear' in her ear. I had seen that moment, as Meryl placed her hand on Hilary's shoulder, her mouth to her ear and I experienced that closeness as a small stab of pain beneath my ribs.

When Meryl read, the Meryl I had always imagined reappeared. The distracted woman who had lost her umbrella receded and once again she was the literary diva, reading her work aloud in her trademark gravelly tone. Meryl spoke with authority and her talent for combining intricate research with a gripping narrative astonished me. It did not seem possible that I had just shared a cigarette with this woman. She was a legend and my friend had been on stage beside her. I remember her words in a fragmented way; perhaps I was distracted by the memory of our encounter beneath the canopy and the apparent encouragement she had given me. I was waiting for Loftus to come on; I began to anticipate his appearance as something significant. Whilst I attempted to remain calm, some small, neglected part of me would not be still; a buried voice that was now yelling out, like a spoilt brat sporting ringlets.

But I did not anticipate what happened next. The host walked to the centre of the stage, kissed Meryl on both cheeks and waited until she was seated again. He approached the microphone.

'Ladies and Gentlemen,' he said. 'My thanks to Meryl

9

Wainwright for what I'm sure you'll agree was a remarkable reading. We are honoured to have you here and deeply appreciative.' He paused for more applause, cleared his throat. 'I'm afraid, however, that I've just learned that due to unforeseen circumstances, our fourth reader, James Loftus, is unable to attend this evening's event. He sends his sincere apologies, but he has been waylaid by – a family emergency.'

My disappointment took me by surprise. There was something unconvincing about this absence. The brat inside my head wanted something and threatened to yell if she did not get it. I shook her off. I didn't really understand this feeling, nor where it came from but I knew I did not like this part of myself. I would send the brat to her room and lock the door until she came to her senses.

Afterwards, the foyer was packed. Hilary was on the other side of the room, at a table with Meryl, Devan and the others, signing books. I did not want to be disloyal, but the idea of queuing up to have my best friend sign a book was not remotely appealing. In any case, Hilary had already inscribed a copy of the novel for me. *"For Anna"* – she wrote – *"Your turn next! With love and thanks for all your support, H x"*

Hilary knew that I wanted to write. I denied it sometimes but she had known me long enough to see beyond my protests. Now as I looked about the room, I recognised a few familiar faces. These were exactly the faces I did not wish to see, the people that Hilary wanted me to meet, though I had no inclination to know them. There was the novelist Julia Claiborne, standing at the bar and laughing like a horse, surrounded by her acolytes, the small clique of women Hilary now belonged to: "the Martini Girls" they called themselves, all published novelists with varying degrees of success; their group seemed impenetrable and alien to me.

It would have been easier if Will were there. We could have found a quiet corner and had a glass of wine together. He would have made me laugh and put everything into perspective. Without Will however, I was like an uninvited guest, wondering how I might make myself inconspicuous.

In the end, I was rescued by a small display of books. There was a separate table where one could purchase the books prior to having them signed and as it was fairly crowded it was easy to browse and remain unnoticed. Though James Loftus had failed to show this evening, the display included his work. The bold lettering drew me: *How To Be A Literary Genius.* It was a crazy promise yet one which had made the man a small fortune. Will had laughed out loud when he first heard that title. 'I'm sure it must be ironic,' I said. 'If it was ironic, nobody would buy it,' he replied.

Certainly nobody about this table now seemed concerned at the stigma of the title. All around, people were handing over their cash and debit cards, as if the very fact that the book occupied the same table as novels by Wainwright and Devan made this purchase quite respectable. Yet it did not seem respectable to me. The brat inside me craved a copy but I was not about to be controlled by my alter ego. I told the brat that if she wanted one of those absurd books, she had better wait until I ordered it online, because I sure as hell wasn't going to be seen dead buying one.

I glanced in Hilary's direction. I tried to catch her eye but she didn't see me. She was speaking to a woman whose book she was signing; her eyes were shining and her cheeks lightly flushed. Then she laughed, handed over the signed book and turned her attention to the next person in the queue.

It occurred to me that if I bought a copy of this book nobody would even notice. If I took a copy of the Wainwright too, the cashier would see that I was a serious reader; she might think I had bought the Loftus as a gift – for a deluded friend perhaps. Before I could change my mind, I picked both up and paid for them. I did not look the cashier in the eye. I stuffed them in my bag and walked quickly away from the table.

As I turned, I could see Hilary still, leaning towards Devan who touched his hand to her shoulder, smiling. I felt like a bulimic who had just stuffed an entire chocolate cake into her mouth and now must find the lavatory and be sick.

2

'I really do not know that anything has ever been more exciting than diagramming sentences.' – Gertrude Stein

'What time is it?'

'It's nine-thirty.'

'Oh Jesus.'

Will turned his back to me and pulled more than his fair share of the sheet across his body, leaving my bare shins and toes exposed. Then, immediately, with no pause for breath, he began to snore again, as if he had never woken in the first place. How did he do that? It was a particular talent he had, to sleep through just about anything, even his own waking up.

I considered taking pity on him. After all, he had been out "networking" the previous evening and it was churlish of me to complain and start that argument all over again. Our wedding was only three months away now; we needed every penny we could save.

My feet were cold however. I lay very still for a few moments, admiring the fine line of Will's shoulder blades and the way his dark hair curled at the nape of his neck. Byronic – that's what I thought when I first saw him at Hilary's party. Though over the years I had become used to his good looks – perhaps even took them for granted – I was still a sucker for his physical charms and it was possible to forgive him much.

All the same, a swift tug of the sheet would do no harm. It was not my fault that Will had been knocking back the vodka the previous evening.

'An – na!' He groaned. I pulled a little harder than I'd intended. 'Give that back.'

'It's not yours,' I said, pouting.

'Yes it sodding is,' he replied. He was half-asleep but awake enough to wind me up by wrapping the sheet about his hand and removing the whole thing from my body in one fell swoop.

'Hey! Stop playing silly-buggers.'

'I love your cute little Geordie expressions.'

'I am NOT a Geordie,' I said. 'Having Geordie parents doesn't count.'

'Get-a-way man,' he replied.

'Come on, give me the sheet!'

'Geordies don't feel the cold,' he said. He wrapped the edges of the sheet beneath his feet to ensure I would be unable to budge it. 'How about a cup of tea?' he suggested, then leaned forwards to kiss me hard on the lips, which would have been very enticing were it not for the tang of last night's vodka on his breath.

'Why-aye, pet,' I said and flipped my legs over the side of the bed.

When I returned to the bedroom ten minutes later, Will still had the sheet wrapped beneath his legs but now he was snoring deeply. I took a shower hoping that the noise of the boiler starting up would wake him, but afterwards he remained in exactly the same position. He had not moved an inch. I stood beside him stark naked to see if that would make a difference, but there was no response. So I got dressed, banged a few cupboard doors, and when it was clear he was likely to be spending the morning sleeping off his hangover, I decided to start my day without him.

Half an hour later, as I walked across Richmond Bridge, a flock of geese flew overhead. The river was at high tide. I paused to lean over the balustrade and watch the geese as they settled to land on the water. The summer crowds had already begun to gather on the riverside before the fake Georgian façades and in the distance I could make out a group of people paddling in flood water beneath the White Cross pub.

Life is good, I told myself. *Life is very good.* And it was. Here was I living in a *bijou* residence, a three-bedroom cottagey affair in one of the most sought-after boroughs of London. I had a halfway decent job in a highly respected suburban theatre and I was engaged to Will Isenberg, a talented artist, a Cambridge graduate with the looks of a Romantic poet. *It doesn't get any better than this.*

Why then did I feel so uneasy? It didn't make sense to question my happiness. It was true that my job was not exactly high flying. As Senior Marketing Assistant at the Walpole Theatre, you could hardly say that I had "arrived". But I was on a career path: there were prospects at the Walpole and if I could just hang on a bit longer, I'd be sure to be in line for a promotion. Most likely, I reasoned, it was my experience of the previous evening that had unsettled me; the being-in-presence-of-greatness. When I thought about what Meryl had achieved simply through the power of words and her imagination, it awakened a sense of inadequacy. But there was only one way to counter this feeling and that was to do exactly what I was about to do. I had the Loftus book and my laptop in my backpack. I would go to a café and in the words of Meryl, 'get black on white'. If I did not begin now, perhaps I never would.

Twenty minutes later I was in Starbucks, sipping a latte and bemoaning the failure of the Wi-Fi access, a thought incompatible with my desire to have been born before Wi-Fi had ever been invented. It occurred to me that if I had been a native of Montmartre, Paris in 1910, I would by now have taken out my notebook and fountain pen and begun to write. Instead, I was trying to catch the eye of the barista and fretting about the fact that I couldn't get online.

But the baristas were busy and uninterested and in the end, I took out the Loftus book and opened it instead. Given Meryl's recommendation, I experienced a flicker of excitement, but I had no desire to be seen reading a book with such a title in public so kept the cover folded back and out of sight.

The first chapter was unexpectedly lucid. The only difference between a writer and a non-writer, Loftus wrote, was that the writer actually bothered to pick up his pen. 'If you wish to become a writer, you must take that first step,' he said, which was an obvious, but strangely mind-blowing statement. By the time I reached the end of the chapter, I was curious to attempt his methods. 'If you want to write, begin now,' he said. 'Take out a notebook and pen. Don't even stop for a cup of coffee.'

It was too late of course. Not only had I disobeyed the coffee rule, but I had no notebook and no pen. The laptop was suddenly unappealing and I reasoned that if I were to take this seriously, it would be vital to work with *exactly* the right materials. So I downed the rest of the latte and headed out to buy some stationery.

As I was walking up the High Street towards Waterstones, I picked up a voicemail. It was my Mum.

'Hello? Anna? Are you there?' Her words were followed by a pause as if she was waiting for me to pick up. 'No? I just wanted you to know that I've ordered the cake stand,' she said. 'I've put a deposit down.'

What?

'Speak soon, pet.'

The cake stand? It didn't make sense at first. Then I realised that she was talking about the wedding cake. *My mother was putting a deposit on a stand that would be used to hold my wedding cake.*

I decided not to think about it.

In Waterstones, I headed for the notebook section. There was a whole stand full of Moleskines in different shapes and sizes and I stood in front of it pondering whether the legacy of Bruce Chatwin and Van Gogh actually made these notebooks any better than your bog-standard cheapskate notebook. I decided that it did and picked up two.

At the checkout desk, clutching the books, I tried to convince myself that this was not simply another form of procrastination. It was surely more authentic to write longhand and it was possible that the right tools could make all the difference to my work.

I had nearly reached the front of the queue when I was distracted by a small display of novels on a stand to my right. It was a local author promotion: an author whose first novel I had already enjoyed.

I hesitated before stepping out of the queue to take a closer look. Will and I would be celebrating the anniversary of our first meeting next Friday and I figured this might make a good present.

Carl McGahan was a young Irish novelist, so it came as a surprise that he was living here in Richmond. I had read his first novel *Caitlin's Trial* – a novel set in Armagh at the time of the Troubles – and had been impressed. His new hardback promised much. The cover was like so many I'd seen lately, a blown-up black and white photograph of a woman's face that told us very little about the world we would encounter inside the book. I skimmed the blurb and turned to the author photograph on the back-flap of the dust jacket. It was a full-length portrait. McGahan was sitting on a metal staircase, resting his head on the palm of his hand. The overall effect was an enticing combination of boy-next-door and intellectual. His slightly scrawny physique and floppy fair hair were balanced by a sharp nose, pointy chin and eyes that beckoned me right in. I closed the book swiftly and put it back on the display stand. Will had never expressed an interest in Irish politics. It would make more sense to buy him oil paints.

It was midday when I arrived back and Will was still sleeping. He'd never slept this late before but I put it down to the many evenings he'd spent at the drawing board recently, working till the early hours, a victim of his own perfectionism.

I made tea and opened the curtains in the front room. I sat in the armchair, picked up a pen and unwrapped the Moleskine. Outside, I heard a mother calling to her child, the hum of a distant radio. I tried to ignore them, allowed my pen to hover above the page. The notebook was crisp and pristine. There was something so perfect about the leather binding, the ribbon bookmark and the slightly yellowing lined pages. I craved a cigarette. According to the recent *Observer* article, Loftus disapproved of artificial stimulants but I was convinced that like many writers, I worked better with props. It was impossible, after all, to imagine Henry Miller without a drink; or Burroughs without heroin. Would a little shot of caffeine or a single cigarette detract from my ability to write great literature?

In the absence of cigarettes however, I opened a packet of biscuits. There was a reason why I'd chosen this brand. Shortly after Hilary graduated from Cambridge, when I was temping in Billericay, she embarked on an MA in Norwich. She was studying Creative Writing and the prominent novelist Ewan Sutherland was visiting to give a talk on campus. It was a difficult time for me, entering her world when my own had reached such a dead end. I stayed for a few days and even now those days are imprinted on my memory. We stayed up late most nights, drinking cheap wine and talking about literary theory and sex, writing and ambition. The Sutherland seminar was a highlight. We had him to ourselves in a small room, just fifteen students, Sutherland and me, the gatecrasher.

We were in our early twenties then, so I like to think that my faulty memory of the talk is down to my immaturity at the time and has no deeper meaning. I have some notes somewhere – in a forgotten ring binder in the cupboard beneath the stairs. Sutherland spoke in particular about characterisation and the idea of allowing a work to grow organically; he told stories about the importance of dreaming, the necessity of reading great works. But what I remember most clearly – and I am a little ashamed to confess this – is Sutherland's statement about the importance of routine in a writer's life. He talked about the inception of his latest novel and vowed that he might not have written it at all were it not for his reliance on a particular brand of biscuits. My ears pricked up at that point and to Hilary's horror I picked up my pen to write down his recommended choice: a German brand, with a thick coating of dark chocolate on the top. Sutherland always broke his writing morning by partaking of these biscuits, he said. Nobody else in the room seemed to think this particularly significant; they laughed politely and awaited his next intellectual offering. But I underlined the words 'Choco Leibniz' in my notebook and went out and bought a packet the next day. To this day, when I eat those biscuits, I feel myself in the company of the master.

I took a bite and picked up the Loftus book again. Will was stirring upstairs but there would be time for a writing exercise before he came down, something simple to break through the block that had been holding me back.

Loftus suggested putting the word 'WRITING' down the page, like this:

W
R
I
T
I
N
G

The object of the exercise was to write seven inspirational words beginning with these initial letters – things that you must do or have, to become a writer. It seemed puerile to me and not the sort of thing that ought to sully my notebook – so I found a separate scrap of paper.

I wrote:

Wisdom
Room of one's own
Inspiration
Trust
Intuition
Nicotine
Gin

Maybe the last two weren't strictly necessary but I was beginning to think the caffeine alone wouldn't do it. The Sutherland chap was probably lying when he claimed to feed his talent on chocolate biscuits alone.

There was only one thing for it. I went to the kitchen and found a packet of Marlboro Lights stashed on the top shelf of the kitchen cupboard. I opened the back door, lit a cigarette and stood looking out at the garden. Fag in hand, there's no doubt you feel a lot more writerly. Perhaps Meryl was right. Perhaps this Loftus guy had something. All I had to do was find my subject and study hard. If Hilary had done this, why couldn't I? I closed my eyes and inhaled, raised my face to the sun and felt its warmth on my forehead. Now all I had to do was find the words.

3

'There are three rules for writing the novel. Unfortunately, no one knows what they are.' – W Somerset Maugham

The evening class was scheduled to begin at 7pm. At ten past the hour, I was rushing along a secondary school corridor that stank faintly of urine and vague adolescent yearnings. When I made it to the classroom, the door was open; the other students were already sitting in a horseshoe, taking notes and listening intently to the tutor who now turned towards me, as if mildly amused.

'Sorry I'm late.'

Carl McGahan had grown sideburns since the author shot. He stared at me, bemused. I closed my lips tightly and licked a slick of errant lip-gloss from my teeth, tried to laugh off my failure to be punctual. *Charm him* I thought. *Just brave it out.* There was only one seat left and I had to breathe in to squeeze past the broad-shouldered, white-haired chap at the end of the row who appeared reluctant to move his chair one inch.

'We were just getting going,' Carl said.

'Really sorry.'

'And you are?'

'Anna. Anna Bright.'

I knew from the look on his face that something wasn't right, but it was difficult to place it. I put it down to my own anxiety. It had been a last minute decision to take this class. On Saturday afternoon, I had Googled local writing classes and found a six-week summer course entitled "Writer's Craft". I clicked the course prospectus and a new window appeared. The tutor was one Carl McGahan.

It startled me but it was a coincidence, nothing more. McGahan was a local author so it was hardly surprising that he was teaching at the college. What surprised me more was my reaction to the idea of McGahan as a tutor. It undermined the romantic image he cut on the dust jacket. That image gave the impression that McGahan had already arrived: he was one of the literati who spent his days in a library bent over a book, too remote from the world to engage in real life. Having read his first novel and having found it both touching and inventive, I'd put him down as somehow different to the rest of us mortals. He knew how to take words beyond their separate, dull solidity, transforming them into something akin to experience. But here he was, standing in front of me, teaching creative writing in a neon-lit classroom. Perhaps, like most authors, he was on the breadline; our fees would prevent this particular poor writer from starving in his garret.

'Is something the matter?' I asked. A few of the students were giving me odd looks. Was I over-dressed? Perhaps I didn't fit in.

Carl was trying not to laugh. 'This class has been running for nearly a year, Anna. I think you're a couple of days early.'

'Oh.'

'Summer school starts on Thursday.'

'Right.'

He had a beautiful voice. I could just hear Will mocking me for falling for it, putting on his Belfast accent in bed to tease me, but this was not the moment to be distracted.

'I'm so sorry. I should go.'

Carl waved his hand in the air, dismissing the idea. 'You might as well stay now you're here. I'm sure nobody will mind. I think one or two of this crew will be coming along to summer school in any case.'

'Yeah, can't leave you alone,' said a girl on the other side of the table. I'd noticed her as soon as I walked in. She was around my age, dressed in a pink FCUK T-shirt – skinny, with bobbed blonde hair and an unnaturally pretty face that managed to look at once elfin and cutting-edge.

21

'If you're sure you don't mind,' I said. I wanted to get out of there as fast as I could. *What an idiot. I couldn't even read a date correctly.*

'Not at all.' I wasn't convinced that the other students agreed with him. The guy to my right was doodling on his notepad and there was a fury in the intense black scribblings that made his irritation clear.

'What kind of writing do you do, Anna?' *Christ, would he not just carry on with the class and stop paying me attention?* Carl was looking at me as if he expected an answer.

'I'm just a beginner,' I said. 'I don't want to write Chick Lit though. I'd like to write literary fiction.' *It was coming out all wrong; I sounded like a pretentious little shit.*

'Some of us think that Chick Lit is something to aspire to,' the girl in pink said. 'I'm not sure it's a brilliant idea to write off commercial fiction before you've written a word.'

'OK, Lucy,' Carl said, apparently anxious at the prospect of refereeing a catfight. 'Anna,' he said, 'don't listen to a word that Lucy says. She's a gentle creature really.'

At which, Lucy shot him a sarcastic smile.

'Actually I'm relatively new to this class myself,' Carl said. 'This is my first year. Some of the class members have been coming for years – under a different tutor, of course. Don, when was it the class started?'

Don looked up from his notebook and let his pen spiral above the page. His doodles had turned into an abstract expressionist hell. 'About six years ago,' he said. Don spoke with the impressive resonance of a radio presenter. 'You'd think I'd have finished a bloody novel in that time!'

Six years. What was he writing, the sequel to War and Peace?

'Don't worry, Anna.' Carl said. 'Don's a perfectionist.'

'I am *not* a fucking perfectionist,' Don said, 'I am simply suffering from Writer's Block.'

'Yeah, sure, Don,' said the only other man in the class, a bespectacled lad in a fleece jacket. 'Aren't we all?'

'Shall we get started, Carl?' Lucy said. She pursed her lips into a small "o", the painted lips of a China doll. 'You'll soon learn all about Writer's Block, Anna. Once you've got started, that is.'

Who the hell was this woman? I had obviously offended her and I really hadn't intended to. I'd never read a Chick Lit novel in my life, so who was I to judge? But it seemed I had struck a nerve and there was no going back. It probably didn't help that Mr McGahan was paying me some attention. Perhaps he was her very own Mr Darcy.

I tried to imagine what Will would do in this situation. He'd conjure up a witty comment and go right back at her. *'So,'* he'd say, *'are you trying to tell me that Bridget Jones's Diary is the pinnacle of literature?'* But then I was not Will and I had no desire for confrontation.

Perhaps I should have left the classroom, despite Carl's protestations. But the situation was too interesting to leave alone. Having read *Caitlin's Trial* I felt an empathy with Carl. There was more to him than the laddish exterior: he had depth; he cared about individual suffering and injustice and he expressed himself in prose that had left me weeping.

He was at the whiteboard now, fiddling with the coloured marker pens in an effort to avoid Lucy's eye. I watched him, anticipating his next move. It was as if I knew him, yet I had been seduced by his prose, nothing more. The intimacy I felt was entirely imagined.

'So guys,' Carl said, brandishing his pen – 'I know a lot of you feel that we haven't explored the concept of plot in enough depth this term, so I want to spend the last few weeks taking a few different approaches to story structure. If you've got time, I highly recommend you read this little tome here. It's on the handout, together with a few other reading suggestions.' He held up a bulky hardback with the word "Story" emblazoned on the jacket.

'Catchy!' I said, before I could bite my tongue.

'Robert McKee,' he said, glancing in my direction. 'This is the absolute bible for screenwriters. For screenwriters, Robert McKee is , akin to God.'

'But we're writing fiction, Carl,' the guy in the fleece said.

Carl ignored him. 'I'll draw a diagram.' He began scribbling on the whiteboard and created a lot of arcs and zigzagged lines. I tried to concentrate but it made no sense to me at all. I couldn't see how any of this related to the art of fiction. Had Carl begun *Caitlin's Trial* like this, with a diagram and graph-like precision? It was difficult to imagine. Yet Carl's hand worked feverishly as if he really believed this stuff. 'This here,' he said, pointing to a semi-circular line 'is called the unconscious desire – and according to my agent...'

'Who did you say your agent was again?' Lucy asked.

Oh perfect. Just as he was about to reveal the Holy Grail...

Carl turned and grinned. His teeth were slightly uneven; the canines crossed his incisors a little.

'Lucy, is that all you ever think about?'

'We've covered it Lucy.' Don said. 'Several weeks ago now.'

'I missed the class and keep forgetting to ask for the handout,' Lucy said.

'Lucille! You only have to look on the acknowledgements page of his book, sweetie.' It was a tall American woman who spoke. She had wild, corkscrew hair and wore a permanent frown. 'You know, my huge gratitude... blah blah... to my agent Buddy Sellers.'

'Blown my cover, Charlotte,' Carl said. 'Shall we get on?'

'The one and only,' Charlotte replied.

'So how do we go about getting an agent?' Fleece-man said. 'I mean Sellers – that's a bit jammy, isn't it? '

'OK, OK, I give in. You don't want to do plot. You want to do agents again?'

'Just a few hints and tips, please,' Lucy said. She paused, as if plucking up courage. 'What's Buddy like, by the way?'

Carl threw up his hands in defeat and took a seat at his desk, facing us.

'I'll cover this, then we'll get onto tonight's readings, yes?' The class nodded their assent but though Carl appeared good-humoured, I sensed his irritation. He leant forward and spoke slowly. 'The thing is, Buddy is a very charming man.' He paused. 'But he is very, very ruthless. I'm under no illusions about the nature of our relationship. Buddy is a businessman first and foremost and if my books stopped selling, he'd have no qualms about dropping me in an instant. And there's a problem with well-known agents too. Their books are always full and they hardly take anybody on.'

It wasn't exactly an encouraging pep talk; it made me wonder how much training they actually give you before you can become a teacher in adult education.

'Of course, Carl. I understand that,' Lucy said. 'But *Buddy Sellers*! I've heard he never takes an author onto his books unless he's convinced he'll be able to get a six-figure deal.'

'Really?' Carl said, with an expression that said '*do you think I'd be sitting here in this dive if Buddy had got* **me** *a six-figure deal?*' 'Guys, did any of you listen to a single thing I said last term? What matters is the work, right?' There were a few shrugs, but nobody spoke. 'Look, when you *are* ready, what you'll need is a *new* agent. A hungry agent.'

Carl's energy was ebbing and the atmosphere in the classroom had turned sour. Risking Lucy's displeasure, I decided to help him out.

'Carl,' I said. 'I know I'm very new to this, but I was actually quite interested in what you were saying before. About the unconscious desire?'

Carl turned, his eyes meeting mine. I looked away.

'It's very simple really,' Carl said. 'Just think of any Hollywood movie: the hero goes on a journey and there's something very obvious that he wants. That's his conscious desire and it propels his action. But everything seems to get in his way and sometimes it seems as if he'll never get it. He goes through all kinds of trials to get this thing and he overcomes the most impossible obstacles. But when in the end he does get this thing, he realises it wasn't really all that important after all. He had an unconscious desire right from the beginning – something totally different that he didn't even know that he wanted – like he's grown as a person, he's learned how to love, whatever – and it's the unconscious desire that's key.'

Carl was on autopilot. I almost wished I hadn't asked.

'Robert McKee in a nutshell,' Don said. 'That'll save us a tenner.'

'Shall we get on with it then, Don? Why don't you read?'

Was it really that straightforward, I wondered? All these neat little formulae and tricks of the trade? Did Carl really believe this stuff? I wanted to ask him, but he was already fiddling with a pile of papers and distributing Don's work to the group.

'You have to be very gentle with me this evening,' Don said. 'I'm feeling a little fragile.'

Then he waited for everyone to be ready, cleared his throat and began to read.

After class, I stood outside in the quad, looking for my car keys. I'd left ahead of the others and nobody, not even Carl, had said goodnight. They walked past me now in their small cliques and I turned away.

During Don's reading, Carl had caught my eye once or twice and I had held his gaze, just to check that I wasn't imagining this. I wasn't. Each time, I had to look away first. Carl hadn't appeared to be listening to Don at all, yet at the end of the reading, he gave a fairly incisive and generous critique. Now I felt guilty. I'd done nothing wrong, of course; a little flirtation wasn't a crime. Lucy had been looking fairly smug at the end of class, so he'd probably been flirting with her too. But if he thought I was about to be drawn in by a few lingering glances, he was sadly deluded.

I walked across the quad. In any case, I thought, even if I weren't with Will, the last person I'd want to get involved with would be a *writer*. What was wrong with me tonight? As far as I was concerned, creative geniuses should be avoided like the plague. They are almost invariably poor, with a predisposition to death by their own hand. It was hardly an attractive prospect.

It was starting to rain now and I got into the car and sat for a moment, staring into space. At least on Friday I had the day off work – Will and I would be celebrating our anniversary – it would be five years since the day we met. We hadn't had enough time together lately and the wedding preparations had become tedious. But we'd put it right tomorrow. I'd bought him oil paints in the end, a deluxe set, a selection of brushes and a large canvas. He'd been saying for years that he should take his painting more seriously.

I was about to start the engine but was interrupted by a knock on the window. The rain was heavier now; the light had faded from the sky. I rolled the window down and saw Carl, his hair a little wet already, rain dripping across his face.

'Anna – I think you left this on your desk?'

He handed me a scrap of paper. It must have fallen out of my Moleskine. I recognised it instantly and seeing it made me feel faintly nauseous. It was the Loftus exercise. *Wisdom. Room of one's own. Inspiration. Trust. Intuition. Nicotine. Gin.*

'Not a bad list,' Carl said. 'I like the gin particularly.'

I wanted to disown it but my expression had betrayed me. Carl was walking away already. Then he appeared to have second thoughts and turned. 'Are you coming along to the Summer School on Thursday?'

I shook my head. It wouldn't be fair to Will. 'Can't make it. I might be able to make Thursday next week though.'

'Perfect. The thing is, I'm not sure who else is coming yet – but it would be great if I had someone lined up to start us off with the readings. Can I put you down to read?'

'Sure,' I replied, trying very hard to sound nonchalant. I could hardly tell him that I hadn't actually begun a novel yet.

'My email address is on today's handout. You'll need to forward the work to me in advance. I'll make sure the rest of the class get a copy.'

'Oh – OK.'

I wanted to pull out, tell him that it wouldn't be possible after all, but I knew how weak that would appear so I said nothing.

'See you next week then,' he said.

I put the car into reverse and pulled out and as I turned towards the street, I caught him in the glare of my headlights. He did a strange little dance, playing the fool. I remembered that dance, afterwards, but couldn't work out why he did it or what it meant. I told myself it had no significance, even as I knew, unconsciously, that was a lie.

4

'I meant to write about death, only life came breaking in as usual.'
– Virginia Woolf

'Happy anniversary!'

I opened my eyes to see Will sitting on the bed beside me, holding a large envelope and a flat, oblong package wrapped in crisp, fuchsia tissue.

'Oh shit,' I said.

'That's a nice way to say thank you.'

'Sorry. I'm sorry. It's just – what time is it? – I thought I'd set my alarm for 6am. I was supposed to get up and write.' A small frown began to form on Will's forehead. 'But it doesn't matter. I'm half asleep. Forgive me?'

Now his lips wavered a little. 'What is this writing bollocks anyway?' he said. 'You're not serious are you?'

There was nothing unusual about his response. I'd undermined my own desire to write so many times that I could hardly blame him for not taking me seriously. I pulled a couple of pillows towards me and sat up, propping them at my back.

'Is there any reason why I *shouldn't* be serious?' He was kidding, I knew that, but it was early, I had no humour at this hour. 'Are you trying to say that I'm no good?'

'How do I know if you're any good? As far as I can tell, you haven't yet put pen to paper.'

'Have a little faith, Will.'

'OK. OK. Sorry sweetie. Look, I've brought you some coffee. Not too strong; tons of hot milk; sugar.'

'Hmmmm. I suppose you *have* got me a present.'

28

He bent forward and kissed me and lingered just a little too long, making me almost lose interest in the gift.

'I suppose you're thinking about Hemingway,' he said, between kisses.

'What?'

He leant back on one elbow, distracted now. 'He'd be at his desk each morning by 7am apparently. The perfect example of the disciplined creative artist.'

'Stop rubbing it in.'

'Apparently he'd get a thousand words down before lunch, quit when the going was good and spend the afternoon swimming in the Key West sunshine.'

'Didn't stop him from blowing his brains out with a shotgun,' I said.

'There is that,' Will replied. 'Now open your present!'

I shot him a sarcastic glance. 'Let me get yours out too,' I said.

I'd wrapped the oil paints in stylish black paper and fetched the package from the bottom of the wardrobe. These present-giving rituals had become familiar to us. I wondered what would happen when we were married. Would we continue doing this, year on year until we were withered and old, or would we one day decide that we were past such indulgence, would we settle into apathy at first and then indifference?

'Our last ever anniversary,' I said.

'What are you talking about?' Will appeared genuinely shocked.

'I just mean the last time we'll celebrate meeting. Next year, we'll celebrate the wedding date.'

'You had me worried for a moment.'

'Have to keep you on your toes.'

'You first.'

I tore the wrapping slowly, wanting to prolong the anticipation just a little longer.

'Hmmm… it's a book…'

'No surprises there.'

I tore more quickly now and liked what I saw. It was a hardback art book: *Modigliani* by Christian Parisot.

'Oh Will. This looks *fantastic.*'

'Phew. Glad you like it.'

'I always like your presents. You're infuriatingly good at choosing things.'

'Have you forgotten that time I bought you a Nigella Lawson book?'

'OK. Yes, you're right. That was a very grave mistake but luckily it was a long time ago. I think you've learned your lesson,' I paused and turned the book over in my hands. It was a beautiful object. The fact that it was second-hand lent it an authenticity that no new book could possess. 'Beautiful!' I said. It was a portrait of Modigliani's last mistress, Jeanne Hébuterne. I still had the postcard of that painting. Will had sent it to me when he went to New York on a *Telegraph* "jolly", shortly after we met. It was in the early days of our relationship. When that postcard arrived on my doormat it had seemed important. He was thinking of me when he was away: he wasn't going to vanish into thin air.

'Poor Jeanne,' I said. It was a remarkable painting, but Jeanne Hébuterne did not seem quite real in it. Her eyes were pale blue and unseeing. Her dense red hair and elongated nose were lovingly painted but they told me nothing about the woman. 'It looks like you got this from some rare book shop on the Left Bank,' I said.

Will climbed into bed again. 'Islington actually,' he said. 'As soon as I saw it, I thought of you.'

I sat up as Will put his arm around me, appearing more interested in my body than his unopened present. I was distracted by the Modigliani story. I didn't know it well but I wondered if there might be something in it, something I might write about. My knowledge was fairly sketchy but I did know that Jeanne Hébuterne committed suicide soon after Modigliani's death. She had refused to leave his bedside as he lay dying. Afterwards, she could not live without him.

Will kissed me, a little harder this time. I was tempted, but not so tempted that I could stop thinking about this idea.

'What happened to Modigliani? How did he die?'

Will pulled back. 'Can we talk about it later?'

'I suppose so. It's just I'm trying to remember the story. I'm sure you told me about it once.'

He sighed and I knew from his expression that he was cross.

'I'm sorry,' I said. 'I didn't mean…'

'Tinned fish.'

'What?'

'Tinned fish. Jeanne Hébuterne and Modigliani. He was dying of tuberculosis. She wouldn't leave his bedside. They ate nothing but tinned fish for a week apparently. When they found his body, the sheets were soaked in sardine oil.'

'Oh,' I said, trying very hard to appear contrite, when in fact, I felt rather elated. It wasn't much to go on, but it was certainly very memorable. And I was desperate for material.

'Look, Will. You're not sulking are you?'

'God, no. Why would I do that?'

We were standing on the platform at Richmond Station, trying hard to be nice to each other but not entirely succeeding. Will appeared distracted and I wasn't sure why, though I was trying to figure it out. He hadn't been impressed with the oil paints, though he'd made a show of being pleased. Perhaps he hadn't really meant it when he said he wanted to paint.

It might have been the sex of course. I'd spoilt the mood and now he was disgruntled. I fell silent, not knowing what to say. I found myself thinking of a scene in the movie *The Hours*: Nicole Kidman donning a prosthetic nose and starring as Virginia Woolf. On this very platform, at Richmond Station, she had uttered the immortal lines, "If it is a choice between Richmond and death, I choose death."

I looked at Will. *You can play Leonard to my Virginia any day*, I thought. Though Leonard, in the movie, had not been sipping Americano from a polystyrene cup. Will was more desirable in other ways. He was apparently lost in thought, but he had the kind of face that wore a frown well; if I didn't know him so well, that expression might have scared me a little.

'I love the Modigliani book,' I said, breaking the silence. 'I think I'll be able to use it, actually.'

31

'Use it?'

'You have to promise you won't laugh.'

He held up his hands in mock horror.

'Actually, I really do want to write a novel.'

Will grimaced.

'It's not a joke this time,' I said. Perhaps he had been hoping that it was. 'I'd like to read more about Jeanne Hébuterne; I think she might make a good subject.' The silence that followed was worse than laughter. 'Well, say something.'

He paused. 'You're serious?'

'Deadly serious.'

'Well then, go for it…'

'But?'

'OK. OK. It's just – it's not my subject, I might have got it entirely wrong – I'd heard that you should write what you know.'

'Sure. Everybody wants to read a novel about the Walpole theatre.'

'Give it a humorous twist and they probably would.'

'Yeah, maybe you're right. It could be a real bestseller. I could write about life as the fiancée of a workaholic freelancer who spends more time at the Groucho Club than he does at home.'

'Anna, I am not even a member of the Groucho Club.'

'You might as well be,' I said, at which point the train pulled into the station and I stormed ahead of him and boarded.

Will followed me into the carriage. I knew I shouldn't be angry with him but I couldn't help it. He was just falling into the old rhythm, talking about it in the way I always talked about it, as something impossible. *It's Hilary's domain, not mine.* How many times had I said that and was it possible I'd really fooled him?

We sat down opposite a man in a pinstriped jacket, absorbed in his newspaper and – if his tightly pursed mouth were any indication – apparently irritated at our intrusion.

'Anna,' Will said, under his breath. 'I don't know what I've done wrong.'

'Nothing,' I said. 'Please…'

The man fiddled with his mobile. I wished Will would just shut up and let it rest. It was my issue, my fault, but we couldn't fix it now, not when somebody was listening in.

'Anna, I don't know much about writing. You should never take my advice.'

'Don't worry, I won't.'

'It's a misunderstanding, that's all.'

'I thought you were quite plain.' This was a lie, of course. Will had made one innocent comment and I was tearing myself apart over it. Had he never seen beneath the self-deprecation? It seemed impossible that one could live with someone and for so long and still hide one's intimate desires so very successfully. It was a failure but I could not tell who was to blame.

Turning to the window, I gazed out at the suburban scene that once made Virginia weep. I was trying to see this from Will's perspective but it was impossible to see things clearly now. Perhaps Will was cross because he thought that I had changed. He didn't fall in love with a wannabe-writer. He fell in love with a cool-headed cynic who knew her place in life and in literature. The trouble was, I didn't know how to find that person again. So I was stuck in wannabe land without a map or compass and without a shred of proven talent to get me out.

5

'Happiness is an angel with a serious face.' – Amedeo Modigliani

'It's a shame they don't have a portrait of Jeanne,' Will said. 'We should have come to the retrospective a few years back.'

'The retrospective?'

If it had been anyone other than Will, I would have pretended that I knew exactly what he was talking about – that I had not only been to the retrospective but also absorbed the catalogue, attended the lecture and bought the T-shirt. With Will, there was no point faking it. I was as transparent as cellophane.

'Oh God, you're not being an ignorant bugger again, are you?' he said.

'Sorry darling,' I replied, taking a swig of Shiraz. This was our usual way of being, his mockery a comfortable acknowledgement of my insecurity. 'Ignorant as a flea, you know me. You do know you're about to marry a bimbo, don't you?'

'If only,' he replied. I smiled my most sarcastic smile.

I had only found three Modigliani portraits in the Tate Modern galleries – and not one of them had been of my Jeanne. Now we were in the café where Will was eating delicious but ridiculously over-priced chips and I was stealing them and ignoring the potato cake and smoked salmon on my own plate. It was difficult to maintain my earlier irritation in the face of Will's now determined charm.

'So, come on then. Get me up to speed on this retrospective. Just don't tell anyone that I cribbed my notes from you.'

'How much is it worth?' he said.

It was difficult to take anything seriously in this environment.

The restaurant was crowded and the canteen atmosphere was not conducive to talking in any depth. I considered opening the conversation about my writing again but the timing felt wrong: it was our anniversary and I felt obliged to make up for the bad start, to maintain a lightness that I did not entirely feel.

'Maybe you're right about this Modigliani idea,' I said instead. 'I mean – if Modigliani is already Mr Popular, then maybe I've missed the boat. Don't tell me – Jeanne has already been immortalised forever on a plethora of Royal Academy mugs, mouse-mats and fridge-magnets...'

Will laughed, but then – and you could almost see the thought strike him, as if so many years drawing comic strips had translated into a frame-by-frame existence – he fell silent. 'You know, I don't think that matters,' he said. 'I think it helps your case. It was just a bit of a shock earlier, that's all. Actually I think Jeanne's story would make a pretty good book. She's a relatively minor figure. It gives you a lot of scope.'

'You think so?'

'If I remember rightly there was some big row after Modigliani's death. Jeanne Hébuterne's family wouldn't collaborate with the biographers. I don't think the material was released until a few years ago.'

'God, that's perfect. I mean, if no other fiction writer has got hold of it...'

'What did you think of that Madame Zborowska portrait by the way?' he asked.

'I liked it. There was something about it; it's so austere...'

'Apparently he'd spent a lot of time studying African iconology at that point.'

'Hey, you've been reading the guidebook...'

Will narrowed his eyes provocatively. 'He was a classicist essentially. That's why Modi wasn't accepted. Not avant-garde enough.'

'I'd rather be painted by Modi than Picasso, that's for sure.'

'Jeanne painted too, you know.'

'Yes, I did know, Will.'

'Sorry.'

'I'm looking forward to reading the book, though.' It occurred to me that I could spend the following weekend studying and writing. Will was going windsurfing with his mates – something I'd not been looking forward to – but now his impending absence was more appealing.

'I'll take the laptop to work on Monday,' I said. 'I can do some writing in Starbucks again, at lunchtime. Not exactly Les Deux Magots but it will have to do.'

'I'm sure even Simone de Beauvoir would have enjoyed writing with a latte and a laptop given half an opportunity.'

'Don't get me started…'

'Seems every woman in my life is writing a novel.'

'What? What other women *are* there in your life? Have you taken some lover that you've conveniently forgotten to tell me about?'

'Ha! No,' he said. 'Phyllis.'

'Phyllis?' Phyllis was Will's mother. He always called her by her first name, she had encouraged it. 'Your *mother* is writing a novel? When did she tell you that?'

'Oh, ages ago. To be honest, I'd almost forgotten. She hasn't mentioned it for a while. Maybe she's abandoned it.'

'So what's she writing *about*? Some exposé on the New York fashion industry?'

'Probably.'

'It'll sell by the bucket-load.'

Will pulled a face and downed the dregs of his wine.

'Do you want to see a few more paintings? It's been a while since I looked at the surrealists.'

'Yup, I can take a bit of Dali. Just as long as I don't have to go anywhere near a Joseph Beuys.'

'Ever the traditionalist…'

'Dali was *not* a traditionalist…'

My mobile beeped, interrupting us. I took it out and read the message:

Martini Girls meeting Sunday night. Why don't u join us? H x

'Shit.'

'What's up?'

'Hilary's invited me to her Martini Girls evening.'

'When *will* that lot get a new name?'

'That's not the point. What the hell is she thinking? I attend one creative writing class and suddenly she thinks I'll be happy hanging out with the professionals.'

'Maybe she thinks she's being supportive.'

I guessed the others wouldn't welcome me. Even if I were experienced, I wasn't certain I'd want to go. I'd never understood why a group of mature published writers felt the need to band together and read their work aloud. It was my idea of hell.

'Maybe you'll enjoy it,' Will said.

'It's too early. This Hébuterne thing – it's intriguing but I haven't even begun the research. I'd want to write something really good before I shared it with that lot.' I paused. The waiter placed the bill on the table but Will simply nodded and took my hand. 'I think it would be a mistake; I'm not really sure I'd get along with them, they're all so...'

'... shallow?'

'No, that's not fair. I know I've said that before. They seem shallow, but who am I to judge? They can't be, can they? They've all written well-reviewed books. It's just all the frocks and obvious wealth that puts me off. They don't seem my type.'

'You know I'm away at the weekend?'

'Yes – and I can use the time to write, I know. But...'

'You could always say you're booked up?'

I shook my head.

'Maybe it's time I went along.' I thought that my resistance might be linked to my failure to write; perhaps it was time to shake things up a little. The pressure might turn out to be a good thing.

'So what will you wear?'

'Oh God, don't freak me out.'

'Just wear your Karen Millen dress and they won't notice how

37

bad your prose is.' At which point I whacked him across the face with a serviette, leaving a fragment of smoked salmon balanced precariously on his chin.

In the end, we didn't linger long in the galleries. For both of us there seemed a sudden urgency to get back home. We were buoyed by alcohol, but there was something else: Will was beginning to take my project seriously. We walked back to Waterloo along the South Bank, stopping briefly at the second-hand book stalls, scanning the rows for relevant books, anything that might add further weight to my story. Talking about Hébuterne's life, I began to feel genuinely excited at the prospect of attempting the book. I couldn't place why exactly the idea appealed to me. Perhaps it was a chance to finally get beneath the surface of my own romanticism of that period. The idea of exploring a life in fiction – and through images, half-truths and imagination – was beginning to fascinate me and Will's knowledge of the story excited me. He had given me the book but beyond that he had given me inspiration. My earlier irritation had already faded.

Back home, Will headed for the kitchen. He took out a bottle of gin and ice from the freezer and I stood behind him, wrapping my arm about his waist as he poured. He handed me a glass, but I refused.

'Slice of lime?' I asked.

'God, you're a hard woman to please.' He took a lemon from the fruit bowl, a knife from the drawer and began slicing it. 'This is as good as it gets, Anna Bright. Take it or leave it.' Then, swilling back the gin, he kissed me, but I pulled away and led him upstairs.

He undressed me in the bedroom doorway. There was an intensity about it that seemed different. The gin helped of course, as did the images of Jeanne Hébuterne and Modigliani; like ghosts in my consciousness. I wrapped a leg around Will's thigh and pulled him closer; we stumbled through to the bed. It surprised me in a way. Will's passion seemed out of character. It's difficult to pin down exactly what had changed, but somehow I knew it wasn't me. Will seemed to want me more than he usually did. That was good, wasn't it? But it was also unsettling.

He thrust his tongue hard in my mouth and I responded. *That's not how you usually kiss me.* Something felt wrong. I was trying to stop thinking, to lose myself in the experience. It was like making love to a stranger – and though the stranger was exciting, I was disappointed because I had wanted to make love to Will.

I reached out and grabbed the glass of gin from the bedside table; swigged down a little more. Will pushed me back against the bed, was inside me again. 'Will!' I whispered.

At first, he just groaned in response. Perhaps some minutes passed before he spoke. Eventually he did. 'Yes,' he said. 'Angela. Yes.'

'Wait!' I said. *I must have heard that wrong.*

'What is it, Anna? What's the matter? Did I hurt you?' He paused, looked down at me, his forehead drenched in sweat.

'You called me Angela.'

Before he could hide it, I saw panic cross his face.

'I did not.'

'Yes. You definitely did.'

I had not misheard it – I was convinced of that. I felt myself begin to tremble; tried to control it, but failed. *Will had called out the name of another woman.* And he was still inside me, having trouble controlling himself.

'Angel!' he said, half in panic, half in ecstasy. 'I called you Angel!'

'You never call me Angel.'

'Oh Anna, Angel...'

He couldn't help it. It was over, even as I was accusing him of infidelity.

*

'Anna, are you *sure* you don't know where my spare wetsuit is?'

'Haven't got a clue. Where did you last leave it?'

'If I knew that, I wouldn't be asking you.'

It was later that evening, close to midnight and Will was packing for his windsurfing weekend. What had happened, earlier, had still not been resolved. Will swore blind that I was talking nonsense. According to his story, there was no such person as Angela in his life. He understood why I was worried, but as far as he was concerned, I was inventing problems. There was nothing to discuss.

Now he had drawn up a list and was busy crossing everything off. Boomerang shades: check. Fin accessories: check. He just didn't get it. I had heard the name clearly and as it wasn't mine, it was surely somebody else's. I was trying to remain composed about it, to give him a chance to explain, but every question I asked met a wall of resistance. I tried again.

'This Angela…'

'Oh for God's sake!' It was the first time he had got cross about it. 'You're making it up, can't you see?'

He had just found the wetsuit and flung it down on a chair, on the verge of losing his cool. I thought he was about to start chucking rubber accessories at me. But instead, he collapsed on the bed, bowing his head, running his fingers through his hair. I didn't know whether to pity him or slap him.

'Don't do this,' he said. 'It's crazy. We're getting married in a few months. I love you. Why can't you accept that?' His eyes were wide in an expression so deliberately innocent that I became convinced that he was guilty.

'Because you called out somebody else's name when we were making love. It seems really very plain to me.'

'We've been over this. I know you're upset. But I've explained.'

'And I don't believe you.'

I tried, very hard, to see things from his point of view. I failed.

'I don't know what to tell you. I've done nothing wrong.' A small muscle in his right cheekbone began to twitch as his jaw clenched.

'Look, if it's just somebody you were fantasising about, you might as well tell me. That's better than me thinking it's worse, isn't it?' I'd just given him the most perfect get-out clause. He might admit to the lesser crime in order to be absolved of the greater.

'Stop it!'

I wished that I could stop. 'Is it somebody at the *Telegraph*? Somebody you met at the party the other night?'

'Oh, for God's sake.'

'A journalist?' He shook his head, shutting me out with his disdain. 'What kind? Gossip columnist?'

'You really think I'd mess up our relationship over a gossip columnist?'

'No. But getting warm, right? A serious journalist? Someone at this very moment risking life and limb in a war-ravaged country?'

'Please, Anna.'

The worst part was the not knowing. It felt as if something very solid was beginning to crack, yet I had no idea whether the ground that crumbled beneath me was the earth itself or just some stage set that I'd invented, something that would vanish if I only willed it to.

Will leant forward and put his arm around me. It was a calculated risk, I suppose, because I gave in to the sensation. It was like being rescued but it felt all wrong: the person rescuing me was the one who had caused the tremor.

'You're not going away with her this weekend are you?'

'You can take me to the train station and wave me off with Alex and Ed.'

'Maybe you all have new girlfriends...'

He could tell I was kidding now; trying to lend this situation a lightness it did not merit. 'Yeah, yeah. We're running off with a group of page three girls.'

Now that was almost funny.

'Make your mind up – are you crying or laughing?'

'Both.'

It was true. This was Will, wasn't it? He didn't do things like this. I had no real proof, only suspicion and beyond that single word, all I had was the power of my imagination: my own fear.

'What do I care about your page three girl anyway?' I said. 'I have a very important date with my laptop this weekend.'

'I'm going to expect a masterpiece on Sunday night, OK?'

'Yeah, sure.'

He leant forward then and kissed me, a kiss so tender that it was almost impossible to believe that anything was amiss.

6

'Whenever a friend succeeds, a little something in me dies.'
– Gore Vidal

There were five members of the Girl Novelists Dry Martini Club but – according to Hilary – Julia Claiborne was the richest. Of all the Martini Girls, Julia had the largest house and the most prestigious address – all of which would not really have bothered me, were it not for the fact that Julia Claiborne was also a strikingly attractive Radio 4 presenter who happened to have written a stack of bestselling romance novels.

It was not really Julia's wealth that troubled me, nor even her talent. I simply didn't feel that I belonged in her world. I'd met her briefly once or twice and she was so brittle in her manner that it was hard to imagine a real person beneath the surface.

'She's actually pretty vulnerable,' Hilary said. 'Always worried about what people are thinking; she finds it hard to relax.' Hilary had phoned on Sunday afternoon to confirm that I'd be joining her. I'd spent most of the weekend alone, distracting myself from the fear of Will's infidelity by reading the Parisot book on Modigliani. It had drawn me in and I'd become fascinated by the artist's world and his work. Modigliani had personified the word bohemian: an Italian Jew, he was an outsider and a purist. He starved rather than accepting commercial work. His genius was not recognised in his day; his one solo show was shut down by the police the day after it opened, the nudes being considered too shocking for public consumption. I had curled on the sofa, reading slowly. I was not yet sure how I would make fiction out of this, but my awareness of the evening deadline definitely had an effect. Shortly before Hilary's call, I had managed to write three pages, a single scene about Hébuterne's death.

'Are you sure Julia's expecting me?' I asked. I wanted to tell her what had happened with Will.

'Of course. She's really looking forward to meeting you. Oh, and don't bring the car. We'll share a cab home. Julia makes Vodka Martinis to die for.'

Sometimes, when Hilary went into Martini-mode I had to remind myself that this was the same girl who used to bore me rigid by quoting lengthy passages from Beowulf.

As I walked up the driveway to Julia's house, the gravel crunched beneath my feet and got stuck in the crevices of my ludicrous high-heeled sandals. I was tempted to turn back. Not only was I not ready to read but I had a nagging suspicion that Hilary had engineered this; that she had a misguided idea that it would be somehow "good" for me.

'They're dying to read your work,' she'd said.

As "my work" consisted of the three pages that I had produced in haste that afternoon, it didn't exactly constitute an "oeuvre".

Shortly before leaving the house, I'd done something stupid and now I was regretting it. Having produced a few pages of prose that I was marginally pleased with, I had emailed them to Carl McGahan. I had acted in a moment of bravado and had written a brief email, asking whether he felt the piece was heading in the right direction. Though he'd asked me to do this, I was now convinced that I had submitted too soon. The work was raw and it was far too early to share it.

I paused to admire the stained-glass panel in the door, which appeared to depict the balcony scene from *Romeo and Juliet*. I rang the bell and a hazy figure approached behind the stained glass.

'Anna, Welcome! Come in!'

Julia stepped aside. She wore a rose-patterned, halter-neck frock with a froufrou skirt and a tightly cinched waist. Her luscious red hair was twirled in an apparently effortless ponytail and her lipstick was the matt orange-red of 50s starlets. I walked past her through the opulent hallway. A vintage chandelier scattered light across embossed wallpaper; the strains of a Billie Holiday song drifted through.

'Shall I take your coat? We were just discussing Vicky's latest tiff with her agent.'

'Oh God – I thought it was all hunky-dory once you got published...'

'Don't you believe it!'

I followed her to the kitchen, a vast glass-ceilinged room with huge doors to the garden. Hilary was there and she waved and smiled her reassurance. She touched her hair, still getting used to the peroxide crop and I wanted to tell her how beautiful she looked; how only someone as gamine as her could get away with it. But I didn't feel at ease and remained silent. The other women were polite and kissed me on both cheeks as they greeted me, but they quickly drifted back to their earlier conversation. As they fussed around the canapés and paused to spear olives onto cocktail sticks, Julia drifted off to the pantry.

'So what happened next?' Hilary asked. She was speaking to Vicky, a tiny, pale-skinned woman with jet-black hair and perfectly waxed eyebrows. Vicky was an old UEA buddy of Hilary's. I'd met her a couple of times. She had attended the famous Ewan Sutherland chocolate-biscuit lecture on campus.

'It was terrible, honestly. I ended up storming out in tears. Can you imagine? How humiliating!' Everybody nodded, engrossed in the story. 'She's so selfish, that's what I can't get over. What timing! My first foray into non-fiction and she chooses a party at Soho House to break the news. Don't you think she could have been a *little* more encouraging?'

'Maybe you should drop her,' Hilary suggested. 'You deserve far better.'

'Oh, I don't know. She was pissed at the time. Maybe I should give her a chance to apologise,' Vicky said. 'I mean, I was pissed too, which probably didn't help. To be honest, I don't think it was anything to do with my book.'

'From what I can make out,' Julia said (rejoining us and proffering a bowl of nuts), 'she'd just been trying to chat up Toby

45

Larson but Toby had given her the cold shoulder.'

'But that's no reason for her to be so catty...'

'What did she say exactly?' Julia asked.

'She said I should have stuck to fiction and this book was career-suicide.'

'That's outrageous,' Hilary said.

'They're forever trying to put us in boxes. Do they have no artistic integrity? She doesn't have the right to make such judgements,' said Julia.

'What a bitch!' Claudia agreed.

'The trouble is,' Vicky said (and she appeared to be on the verge of tears), 'she's probably right. I've wasted three years of my life.'

'Oh, what does she know?' Julia said. 'Hey, Claudia, steady on the Vermouth!'

Listening to them speak, it struck me that Hilary had been lucky. Though she'd struggled enough in her personal life over the last year, her career had run smoothly, quite the rose-petal-strewn path. She had made money, had good reviews and never had a bad word to say about her publisher. Yet I'd lost count of the number of times she'd told me 'it'll never last'.

I watched Claudia now as she laid bowls of Japanese crackers on the table and handed out drinks. I'd met her only once before, at a lunch Hilary arranged to celebrate her publication deal. She was voluptuous, with doe-eyes and dark, glossy long hair. Her mouth was drawn into a permanent sulky, scarlet pout.

'There you go,' she said, handing me a drink. 'Welcome to the Martini Club!' But she appeared to look right through me.

My smile was every inch as false as hers. Hilary caught my eye and grimaced. 'Thanks.' I took the drink. I wanted to be alone with Hilary, to tell her what had happened with Will the other night and to find out how things were going with her Tom, but I knew it would have to wait till later. Determined not to be dependent, I gravitated towards Frederica.

I'd met Frederica briefly too, at a party of Hilary's. A tall, broad-shouldered German woman, with neat auburn hair and slightly crooked teeth, Frederica was older than the rest of us, in her early

46

forties perhaps. She was the author of a well-reviewed historical novel, a Victorian pastiche that had apparently disappeared without a trace. Frederica appeared to listen more than she spoke, but she had an air of authority; I had a feeling the other girls were in awe of her.

I hesitated, not certain what to say, but was saved by Julia beckoning us all to the table. Everyone picked up their bags, settled themselves and began taking out manuscripts. Their works were thick wads of paper.

'So, Anna, what are you working on?' Frederica asked.

I paused; took a breath. 'I'm writing about Modigliani's last mistress, Jeanne Hébuterne. She committed suicide shortly after his death.'

'How fascinating. And how is the research progressing?'

'It's early days,' I said. I wondered whether she noticed my folder trembling in my hand. I placed it on the table as we sat down. There was at least a sliver of truth in my words. I'd spent most of the weekend reading the Modigliani book and dipping into a few others from the library. The material was absorbing, but it was too early to tell whether I might take it further. Something drew me to Jeanne Hébuterne, but I wasn't certain I understood it yet. I was afraid of getting it wrong, of betraying her sacrifice with inadequate prose.

'Take your time – that's the most important thing,' Frederica said.

'I'm sure you're right,' I said. 'It's such an astonishing story; I want to do it justice. She was only a teenager when she met Modigliani, but she was one of the few women he took seriously.'

Frederica smiled; unlike the others she wore no make-up. She had pale skin and yellowing teeth. 'So it's a romance?' she said. I had to think about it.

'Literary fiction,' I corrected her.

'Interesting. What are you going to call it?'

'I'm not sure...'

'How about *The Modigliani Girl*?' Claudia said.

But before I could reply, the conversation was interrupted by the sound of Julia, tapping on her cocktail glass with a fountain pen.

'Girls, I'd like to officially welcome Anna to our group tonight.

Anna is working on her *first* novel, so be kind to her!'

Hilary grimaced. Everyone raised their glasses and said 'To Anna!'

'Don't worry, Anna, we won't make you go first,' Julia said. 'Claudia, do you want to kick off?'

'If nobody else is volunteering…'

I didn't warm to Claudia but I couldn't figure out why. It was probably class-anxiety: the feeling that she was looking down at me.

'What's your novel about, Claudia?' I asked.

She smiled, a broad, luscious smile and let out a sigh suggesting that she'd rather not tell the entire story all over again. 'It's my second novel,' she said. 'After the death of my mother two years ago, I found a stash of love letters in a suitcase she kept in storage. It turned out my mother was having a love affair around the time of my conception.'

'Oh, I'm sorry.'

'Don't be sorry,' she corrected me. 'My father was a shit. I rather like the idea of not being related to him.' She waved her arm delicately and pulled her lips over her teeth as if she was hiding something. 'A relief, in fact. I spent a year investigating. I suppose the book is half-fiction, half-non-fiction. There are gaps in the story. I began to invent a new truth.'

As I listened to her read, I couldn't understand why her story didn't capture me. Perhaps it was because she seemed so controlled in her behaviour. Everything about her suggested that she was minutely aware of the impression she was creating: the way she drew breath before she began to read, the low tone of her voice and the measured sorrow of her expression.

Frederica closed her eyes. I wasn't sure if she was concentrating intensely or just falling asleep. Hilary lowered her head and nodded from time to time, occasionally taking a contemplative sip of her Martini. Vicky's reaction was difficult to decipher; her eyebrows lent her an expression of permanent surprise. Julia appeared to be somewhere else entirely. She was gazing into the middle-distance, as if absorbed in some other story.

Before long, I realised that I'd made a fatal mistake. I hadn't listened to a single word. Claudia was reading something about the nature of deception; it sounded dry and theoretical, but it was possible that it would be fascinating, if only I'd had the grace to pay attention. It wasn't too late. I tried to focus on the story, in a state of mild panic in case I got the Spanish Inquisition afterwards – but there was no story, it was impossible to follow. It was as if Claudia had swallowed a dictionary and was now regurgitating it and spitting out random words.

She finished reading and fell silent. The other women glanced at one another as if nobody was prepared to speak first. Claudia fiddled with her manuscript.

Eventually Hilary spoke. 'Sometimes,' she said, carefully weighing her words, 'one gets so caught up in the narrative, it's difficult to know what to say.' She paused again, appearing to flounder. I was glad I was not the only one. Yet Claudia had published a commercial novel before, so I presumed this impenetrability of style must be a new departure.

'Absolutely,' Vicky agreed.

'It was very moving,' Frederica said. 'I like the dialectical approach; it's brave, Claudia. You have a lot of guts.'

Did she mean that, I wondered? Did she really admire it or was even Frederica just being polite? It surprised me that they bothered to read their work aloud if they weren't going to engage in any kind of honest criticism.

'"Moving" is exactly the word I would have used,' Julia said.

'Are you sure it's not too slow?' Claudia asked.

'Perhaps just a little,' I said. But as soon as it slipped out, I regretted it. All eyes turned on me. How could I possibly judge it? I relented immediately. 'Hardly at all,' I corrected myself. 'And – what do I know?'

Shortly afterwards, Claudia excused herself and went to the bathroom.

'Oh God, I'm sorry,' I said. 'I've offended her, haven't I?'

'Don't worry about it, Anna. I offend Claudia all the time,' Hilary said.

'She's going through a difficult time.' Frederica sucked in air

49

through her prominent teeth. 'We should have warned you. She knows it's not her best work, ja? She's distracted by everything that's going on in her personal life. It's just not a good moment for criticism. We have to be gentle right now.'

'Trust me to put my foot in it. I *thought* you were soft on her.'

'It's my fault. I should have warned you,' Hils said.

'So what's going on?'

The women glanced uneasily at each other across the table, as if weighing up whether it was appropriate to tell me, but their secretiveness didn't last long.

'Her husband is having an affair.' Frederica appeared to have difficulty with that word and winced as she spoke it. 'She just discovered it a few weeks ago. She's devastated.'

I thought about Will, on his windsurfing weekend in the lakes. Of course, I knew he was with Alex and Ed. They'd been planning it for months and I couldn't imagine those two putting up with any kind of subterfuge, but something stuck in my throat. I was about to get married, yet how could I get married with this kind of doubt still unresolved?

'Oh for God's sake, Freddy, it's hardly *that* bad,' Vicky said. 'She's already got her eye on another man. Actually, I think something's going on.'

'No?' I said. I felt myself being drawn into the gossip and was shocked at my own hypocrisy. I had visions of Claudia as some kind of Anaïs Nin figure; it cast her in an instantly glamorous light.

'So who is it?' Julia said. 'You're not serious?'

'She can't be,' Frederica said. 'Don't believe a word of it, Anna.'

I smiled.

Vicky narrowed her eyes. 'A film editor: Hal Jefferies. A friend of Carl McGahan. I'm convinced of it.'

The smile froze on my lips. *Carl McGahan.* I experienced a constriction in my throat, a slight light-headedness. It must have been the Martini.

'He's my tutor,' I said. 'At College.'

I should never have sent him my writing.

'Hal's gross. I have no idea what she sees in him.'

But I wasn't thinking about Hal. I was thinking about Carl. I kept remembering that moment in the car park, the little dance he'd done in the glare of my headlights. It was a meaningless antic; a piece of banal tomfoolery, that was all. How stupid of me to give it significance.

Claudia soon returned. She was smiling but her bloodshot eyes betrayed her. I wondered whether this was part of the general routine: drink Martini; read work; be damned by faint praise; retreat to bathroom and sob profusely; return in time for the next reader.

'Do you want to go next, Anna?' Julia said. 'You might as well?'

I hesitated.

'Come on, Annie. Be brave,' Hils said. She turned to the others. 'Knowing Anna, it's bound to be brilliant.'

Hilary was trying to help, but I wished she would just shut up. Perhaps Hilary had forgotten what it was like to feel uncertain. She'd been surrounded by so much hype and praise lately that she'd probably lost touch with what it felt like to not know: not knowing whether what you wrote was any good; feeling like a misfit and a fraud.

'She's already brave,' Claudia said. 'To come along and read to all of us old-handers.'

I would be kind, I decided, and assume that under the circumstances she could not help her tactlessness. Then as I turned towards her, raising my hand in a sudden extravagant gesture, I sent a full glass of Martini flying across her manuscript. It was one of those movie-shot slow-motion moments. The liquid seeped across the page and the olive, impaled upon a cocktail stick, flew in an elegant arc across the table. I thought it was about to land in her cleavage, but instead it splattered across her dress. I suppose it was all she needed.

She picked the olive up and placed it calmly on the table before us. There was a long, seemingly interminable moment when nobody spoke. It was probably no more than a second or two but it felt as if anything might happen.

'I'm so sorry,' I said. I thought she might burst into tears, but instead she grimaced, picked up a serviette and began to dab at the manuscript.

'Not to worry,' she said. 'I'll just send you the dry-cleaning bill.' She spoke in a light flurry of laughter but I imagined she was deadly serious.

Julia leapt up to fetch a cloth. I glanced in Hilary's direction and she smiled at me, but frostily. I wondered how soon I might get away.

There was a time when Hilary would have found this funny. I could see her now, in our English class, screwing up her face to stifle the laughter that threatened to erupt when our teacher, the elderly spinster Miss Thorne, launched into yet another rapture about the sensuality of the lilies in D.H. Lawrence's *Sons and Lovers*. As Miss Thorne turned to the board, Hils had been unable to hold it in any longer. Miss Thorne spun back to face the class, peering over her pointy spectacles, but it was impossible to forget Hils' face in that moment: the joy of her irreverence.

The Martini was mopped up and Julia filled my glass. I picked up my work and removed it from the plastic sleeve.

'Where were we?' Julia said. 'Your novel…'

'It's at a very early stage,' I said.

'Don't be silly. We'll tolerate no false modesty here…'

'No, honestly. It's not ready.'

I had only begun it that afternoon. I felt the full weight of my own presumption. To read now would undermine everything about the story I wanted to tell. Yet, each one of the Martini Girls was looking at me, waiting for me to read. I would have to brave it out.

'OK, so – it's a novel about Modigliani's last mistress. It's at a very early stage of development.'

Claudia stared at me, her mouth pursed in a tight grimace

'I find this very interesting,' Frederica said. She leant forwards, resting her chin on her hands. 'I've struggled to find a decent biography of Modigliani. I'll be interested to see what you make of him in fiction.'

'Wasn't he just a hopeless drunk?' Julia asked.

'A drunk – yes. But far from hopeless. The thing is, he fits so easily into the 'tortured genius' mould that it's easy not to look deeper.' I was bullshitting, making sweeping statements based on the little I had read thus far but it wasn't exactly a lie. 'The drink was only a part of it,' I continued. 'He suffered from childhood tuberculosis. His talent was unrecognised in his lifetime. He felt a crushing sense of failure.'

'Oh, I know where he's coming from…' Julia said.

'I'll just read an excerpt from Chapter One.' I took a breath. Next week I was due to read aloud – in front of Carl McGahan. This was the perfect dress rehearsal. 'Try not be too overwhelmed by my genius,' I said.

Julia bit into a Japanese cracker, cocked her head to one side and waited.

7

'But yet is merely innocent flirtation,
Not quite adultery, but adulteration.'
– Lord Byron

'Oh my *God*, that was *awful*!'

'Don't be silly, you were a total hit.'

'Come off it Hils. Did you see the disappointment on Frederica's face?'

'You're making it up. Frederica's always a bit of a sour puss.'

Hilary and I staggered out of the taxi and up my front path. It was gone eleven and I'd suggested Hilary stay over, so we could gossip till the early hours like the old days. I had work in the morning, but I didn't care.

'How do they drink so much and still manage to keep a straight face when they're reading?' I asked, as I turned the key.

'Hardened to it,' Hils said.

'Jesus, if I don't have a coffee, and fast, I'm going to vomit.'

In the kitchen, as I boiled the kettle, Hilary leaned back against the kitchen cabinets and ran her finger along the white composite work-surface.

'Still love this new kitchen, Annie,' she said. 'How come I get a big book deal and you still have a posher kitchen than me?'

'Oh you know,' I said. 'There's something to be said in marrying for money...'

'So *that's* what you see in Will! And I thought it was just his body.'

Hilary laughed, but it was the easy laughter of one who knew better. The truth was, it wasn't Will's relative wealth that drew me in the first place, but I couldn't deny that his class had played some part. The son of an English barrister and an American journalist, Will had been sent to boarding school prior to Oxford. His privileged background was the antithesis of my own; I'd been attracted by his difference. He seemed to represent something that I'd never had and was exactly the kind of boy my Dad would have wanted for me.

'I'm sorry about Claudia,' Hilary said. 'She's not exactly tactful.'

'You can say that again.'

'We're all going out again on Tuesday night. It's Frederica's birthday. We'll be going to the White Swan.' She smiled but I wasn't convinced by her jollity. I wondered what was going on beneath the surface. I hadn't asked how things were going with Tom, her new man. Maybe that wasn't going so well. 'Will you come?' she asked.

'I don't know. It'll seem a bit odd, don't you think? So soon after tonight? One minute you invite me as a guest, the next I'm living in their pockets.'

'Don't be paranoid. They'll be pleased to see you.'

'Even Claudia?'

'She's all right when you get to know her.'

'I'm not sure I want to.'

Hilary stood up and fetched her handbag. 'Want a fag?'

'Yeah. Let's go through to the front room.'

'Shouldn't we go outside? Will will kill you if he comes back to find the house stinking of smoke.'

'Serves him right for gallivanting off to Lake Windermere without me.'

Hilary followed me through, kicked off her shoes and curled her legs beneath her on the sofa. 'Need an ashtray...' she said.

'Here!' I stood up and grabbed a small clay pot from the mantelpiece.

'That's not what I think it is?'

I laughed. 'You remember?'

'How could I bloody forget? Dear old Mrs E. Can you believe they encouraged teenagers to make ashtrays at school?'

'You wouldn't get that these days,' I said, in a mock-ancient tone.

'Weren't they meant to be for our parents or relatives?'

'My Dad gave it back to me when he gave up smoking, ' I said. 'He said I could use it for paperclips.'

'Mine cracked in the kiln.'

Perhaps she didn't want to talk about my Dad. I didn't blame her. We hadn't really talked about it at the time and perhaps it was better that way.

'It seems such a long time ago now, doesn't it?' I said. 'Don't think I'd go back there though.'

'Wouldn't you? I kind of miss it…'

'*Hilary!* But your life is so glamorous now…'

'Oh yes. With Julia and Claudia and…'

'Bugger!' I couldn't help myself. As soon as she said Claudia's name, I made a connection with Carl. Perhaps I was looking for a distraction.

'What's up?'

'I've made a complete idiot of myself.'

'What are you talking about?'

'Would you mind awfully if I check my e-mail?'

Hilary shrugged but stiffened a little. Perhaps she'd wanted to stay in reminiscence-mode but it all felt a little too raw for me.

I picked up my laptop from the coffee table and switched it on. I took another drag of my cigarette but it tasted suddenly bitter, pointless and cancer-inducing.

Hilary began to flick through a magazine as I logged on and opened the mail programme. I pressed "Get Mail" and watched as a small icon whirred on the screen. This was crazy. What did it matter, after all, what McGahan thought? Within moments, his name appeared in my in-box.

'Shit.'

'What's going on, Anna?'

The message was sent at 11.17pm, which was only three minutes ago, an odd time to be thinking about a student's homework assignment.

'I sent my work to Carl McGahan.'

56

'So?'

'He asked me to send it. He's just replied.'

'I don't get it.' But then, I saw the 'ka-ching!' on her face. Her expression changed from one of confusion to one of shocked comprehension. 'You *fancy* him?'

'No,' I said. 'Well, not *seriously*.'

'Oh *God*, Anna. You *can't*. That's ridiculous.'

'Of course it's ridiculous,' I said. 'It's absolutely bloody bonkers. It's probably just pre-wedding jitters or something. Isn't that normal?'

'I don't know.'

'Anyway, I suppose I'd better open this e-mail.'

It would be something banal, I knew that. He'd be sitting there in his room, catching up on work. My email would be one of many on a long list in his in-box.

'I can't think of anybody more different than Will!' Hilary said. 'I thought you liked posh blokes.'

'I *have* a posh bloke,' I said. It sounded callous, but I didn't mean it to be.

'Come on then,' Hils said. 'Spill the beans...'

I hesitated for a moment, glad of her presence.

I opened the message and read it. Then I read it again. I read between the lines, over the lines and then under them. I wished to hell that I might lift the words from the screen and look beneath them. Next I looked for an attachment but there was none. I read the message one more time.

Ms Bright,

Good news re the Martini crowd. I trust they paid due respect to your talent? Quite unexpected.

Carl

I slammed the laptop shut and threw it down on the sofa, in a pathetic attempt to appear nonplussed. I had mentioned my visit to Julia Claiborne's in my earlier email. Why would he risk being so flirtatious? Or was I misreading it? He was suggesting he liked my work, but I couldn't allow myself to fall for that one.

'It's nothing,' I said. 'He's just acknowledging receipt of the work. I'm tired. I must have blown it out of proportion.'

Hilary looked at me, her elfin face creased in recognition that I was lying.

'It's not serious, is it, Anna?' she said. 'I mean – everything is OK with you and Will?'

I hesitated, wanting to tell her about Angela, but for some reason I held back. Perhaps speaking about it would make it seem real. And I didn't want it to be real; I wanted it to go away. In a few months' time, Hilary would be my bridesmaid. It wasn't fair to slander Will when I didn't have enough to go on.

'Of course it is. Really. This is just a minor infatuation. It's stupid. *You* know me.'

'But you seem…'

'I'm fine. Honestly.'

Hilary yawned.

'God, sorry. I'm done in. Mind if I go up?'

'Course not,' I said. 'You know where everything is.'

I was glad that she was here. Despite all her achievements, Hilary was still the same girl I went to school with. She could see right through me, but that was what I liked about her, the fact that I didn't have to pretend or explain anything. If I wanted to make a mess of my life, Hilary wouldn't advise or lecture. Perhaps it was the very fact that she didn't push things that made me feel safe that evening. When in fact, I was anything but safe. I was heading straight for the precipice.

Once Hilary had gone to bed, I returned to the sitting room and opened the laptop. What could have induced Carl McGahan to write to me in that vein? I had never mentioned The Martini Girls, only Julia's name, so presumably he knew them all.

The very idea of a flirtation with Carl McGahan was absurd. I had to forget about it; he was probably clowning around; he was not serious. I didn't even have to reply to his email. Just because he'd thrown me the ball did not mean I had to catch it.

I read his words again. *What* was "unexpected"? My talent? That's what I *wanted* him to mean, but it surely couldn't be that. It could just as easily mean my membership of The Martini Club. Or was the ambiguity his intention? There was an implication that he liked my work, but maybe he was just being sarcastic.

Having lit another cigarette, I now stubbed it out. An image of Dad came to mind, sitting on the sofa, waving his right arm about, oblivious to the ash dangling from his fag. I saw him look up at me as he ground his own stub into the small clay pot I'd made at school. He looked so large and hearty to me in those days, his red cheeks signalling robustness, his grey, wisping hair a sign of his being distinguished, not of his fading. I couldn't think about Dad now. What purpose would that serve? Nor could I think about Will because every time I thought about Will, I wanted to cry.

I wasn't drunk any more, but I felt another impulse: a desire to do something reckless, something I would probably regret. I hit "Reply". I didn't plan to send it. I was just playing with words, writing an answer that I might send if I were somebody else and not myself.

Mr McGahan,

Thanks for the compliment. It means a lot from the author of *Caitlin's Trial*. I didn't get a chance to tell you on Tuesday how much I admire your book. Looking forward to working with you at Summer School.

Anna

I was going to press "Save as Draft" but – and I'm really not sure how this happened – I pressed "Send".

'Shit!'

How could I have been so stupid? It was obsequious and over-keen. Could I not retrieve it immediately and be certain that he would never read it?

Yet a small thrill ran up my spine, between my legs. I closed the screen, sat back on the sofa. I felt at once the weight of what I had just done but I also felt the lightness of it. My guilt twisted in my stomach, even as something was released inside my chest. I felt as if small, winged creatures had hatched then taken flight inside me. They were fluttering in my chest, tickling my throat and now demanding to be released as laughter.

8

'Reeling and Writhing, of course, to begin with,' the Mock Turtle
replied, 'and then the different branches of Arithmetic: Ambition,
Distraction, Uglification, and Derision.'
– Lewis Carroll

'Morning Anna – God, did you see that *Sunday Times* piece about
the Chekhov yesterday?'

Natasha Byron-Paine, my boss at the Walpole Theatre,
approached me as soon as I entered the office. She was wearing a
funereal suit, stretched a little too tightly across her chest so that the
fabric bowed at each button. I studied Natasha's expression for a
moment before deciding that the reviewer had slated the
performance.

'Despicable,' I said. 'So ill-informed!'

Natasha pursed her lips, shaking her head ever so slightly. 'You
didn't read it, did you?'

I thought it best not to dignify that with an answer. 'Nice suit,
Natasha,' I said instead.

'Jaeger,' she replied. 'Cost a damn fortune.'

For a moment, I thought my distraction techniques might work,
but that hope did not last long.

'So what about the review?'

'The thing is,' I said. 'We get *The Telegraph*.' It did sound a little
weak. I considered telling her that I'd spent my weekend working on
a novel but quickly thought better of it. 'And *The Observer*,' I added.

Natasha paused, staring at me as if my failure to read every
Sunday supplement on a weekly basis constituted some moral failure
on my part. I knew that look well, the sharp, withering glance. I had

known her long enough now to see beneath the surface; to know that she was sometimes vulnerable, envious of my steady relationship with Will and often sympathetic at the most unexpected times. Natasha was like an expensive fondant sweet and right now it was only the candy casing I could see; the brittle, shiny exterior. Her lips were painted pillar-box red, her hair was coiffed into her trademark shiny, shoulder-length bob: the kind of hair that seemed to move as if it were a single entity. She wasn't about to let me off the hook.

'Anna,' she said, 'You are supposed to be a publicist.'

'Then maybe the Walpole should pay me a bit more? I mean – ten newspapers every Sunday doesn't come cheap you know…'

I regretted it as soon as the words came out of my mouth.

Natasha flinched. I held my breath, awaiting the inevitable bollocking.

'There's just the small matter of the Worldwide Web, Anna. Or did you forget that we're living in the twenty-first century?'

She had me there. I thought about mentioning online subscription fees, but thought better of it. I was feeling less robust than usual; fragile in fact. But I couldn't pin down why: the fear of losing Will perhaps, my lack of artistic progress, or possibly something from the past come to haunt me, a particular look in my Dad's eye, something akin to hopefulness, but that was just a memory and I wasn't even sure what it meant.

'Just make me a cup of coffee, Anna. I've put the hard copy on your desk. You could at least get in early on Mondays to check out the reviews? You know I would have liked to interview you for this new position, but I can't.' She paused. 'I'm sorry.'

I didn't know what to say. She did sound genuinely sad about it, embarrassed even, as she turned away, unable to face me. It felt like another twist of the knife but it caused an ambiguous pain. I should have wanted the promotion. I always told myself I wanted it, but I'd known for weeks that I wasn't up for the new job and I realised now it was only my pride that was hurting.

Today's interviews were an inconvenience. Natasha was interviewing for the post of Publicity Director, which meant that my day would be spent playing "tea girl" and "sandwich-fetcher-in-chief" for a series of candidates, one of whom would shortly be my immediate superior.

Luckily, the interviewees weren't due until eleven. Natasha vanished into her office, too appalled to reason with me. I put the kettle on and fiddled with my mobile. Will still hadn't called. My suspicion about Angela remained. I'd managed to hold back thus far but every time I thought about it, I felt as if I would crack. Thus far I had remained composed and whole. I had distracted myself in every conceivable way but now something threatened to break open. The smallest thing would cause this, I felt. I could picture myself going through his drawers, pulling scraps of paper from his suit jackets, delving into old suitcases in the bottom of his wardrobe on the off chance of finding evidence against him. I wanted to hold onto my dignity, but I wasn't certain that I would manage it.

I wished that Will would call and I wished that he would not. He was due back later that evening and I was preparing for another fight. I poured coffee for Natasha then sat down at my desk and turned my attention to *The Sunday Times*.

At first, it was difficult to concentrate. But I was soon drawn in by the intensity of the reviewer's bile. It tore our production of *Three Sisters* to shreds. According to the reviewer it was "an abominably outmoded, conservative and transparently cynical production designed to reinforce the theatrical status quo." I skimmed down the page. "Chekhov, frankly, deserves better." You had to hand it to this guy. The Walpole was not exactly cutting-edge.

I wanted to laugh and bowed my head, afraid that Natasha might notice. When I glanced up, I saw her glaring at me through the glass divide. There would be no breaking through to her soft centre today. I stood up and hurried to the loo in the vain hope that she might mistake my smile for a sudden bout of wind.

When I returned to my desk, my mobile was ringing. Will? I wasn't certain how I felt about speaking with him. A part of me wanted to behave normally: to pick up the phone and tell him I'd missed him; to bitch about The Martini Girls and ask about his weekend. Another part of me was left cold, still mentally ransacking his wardrobe and listening for the sound of a woman's voice in the background, except that the idea of him being unfaithful didn't exactly fit. It was hard to picture him with another woman and to fully believe in that possibility, even as a hunch told me that it was true.

There was no need to make a decision. I looked at the screen. Will's name did not appear. This was the last thing I needed. Three words: *Phyllis Isenberg calling*. Why was Will's mother calling me? She lived in the States now and we rarely spoke, though she was often on the phone to Will.

Despite my reluctance – and as Natasha was out of sight – I picked up.

'Anna, darling...'

I used to think that people didn't really talk like that. Or at least I couldn't imagine mixing with anyone who sounded so false the moment they opened their mouth. I held the phone a foot away from my ear – it was as if someone had turned up the volume.

'Is Will there?'

I pictured her, half-propped on a bar stool in her Zen aluminium kitchen, dressed from head to toe in Valentino, with her anorexic skull-face woefully undisguised by who-knows-how-many creamy layers of over-priced cosmetics. Already I could hear the distraction in her voice. She'd be looking out of her window at her pristine view of Tribeca apartment blocks, sighing. She claimed to never tire of her Manhattan existence, yet each time we visited her there, I'd noticed a wistfulness about her – as if she'd rather be elsewhere, yet had not quite figured out which elsewhere she'd prefer.

'No, Phyllis. Why would Will be here? I'm at work.'

'Oh – I couldn't get through on his phone.'

I tried not to let that fact bother me.

'Phyllis, what are you doing calling at this time anyway? It must be the middle of the night over there.'

I was regretting picking up already. Where was Natasha? She'd be furious if she found me on my phone on a personal call.

'So where's Will?' she asked. 'There's no one home.'

She hadn't answered my question.

'He'll be back tonight. He's windsurfing in the Lakes.'

I hope that's what he's doing.

'Really?'

'Yes! Really.'

'There's no need to be sarcastic, Anna. I don't know how to put this – there's a crisis.'

'What's happened?

'There's a problem with my apartment building. They've discovered dry rot. It's a disaster. The place is going to be overrun with builders.'

Thank God for that. From the tone of her voice I'd expected death or terminal illness.

'Phyllis, it doesn't sound good. I don't know much about these things, but you shouldn't lose sleep over a building job. It must be the early hours over there...'

'There's no time to sleep.'

'I'm sorry to hear that.' But not as sorry as I was to hear her next remark.

'You know, Anna, I can't stay here. And I got to thinking – hey, why don't I see this as an opportunity? I mean, it's been six months since I've seen my only son. I hope you don't mind. It's happened so quickly. I can't stay here, so I've decided to come visit y'all. I'm packing right now. The flight's booked and I'll be arriving at Heathrow around 7pm your time. It's a fine idea, don't you think?'

I decided I had better not answer that question truthfully.

'Look Phyllis, I have to go,' I said. I could see Natasha at the end of the corridor, walking towards me. 'But you should think this over... I mean...'

'I'll be setting off for JFK shortly, hon. You won't mind having me to stay for a short while, will you? I can't wait! I'll see you later...'

'Right, well...'

'Bye, Anna.'

She hung up, before I could speak. I placed the phone back on the receiver. *How the hell was I going to break this news to Will?* I felt a mild ripple of panic in my gut. I'd forgotten to open the bedroom windows that morning and had left the place stinking of fags. I hadn't washed up the previous evening either and half the contents of my underwear drawer were strewn across the bedroom floor. Phyllis was arriving at Heathrow at 7pm, around the same time that Will was due back from the Lakes. He'd be furious, but what gnawed at me most was the knowledge that we'd have no privacy. Our quiet life was ruptured.

'Anna – could you dig out the candidates' files, please?'

Natasha cut across my thoughts and I reassured her with a nod. *So how long was Phyllis planning to stay? For the entire duration of her building works?* I stood up, in an attempt to look busy, and began rummaging in the tall cabinet behind my desk.

These were our last precious months together as an unmarried couple. How could she be so selfish? Had I actually just said 'yes' to her?

But it wasn't possible. She couldn't stay with us. Why couldn't she stay in a hotel like she usually did? The spare room might be free but I had plans to turn it into my study. I could give it up for a few days, but no longer. In any case, surely she'd complain that the futon would be too hard for her bony frame and the wardrobe space inadequate. What if she didn't? What then?

I had believed that things couldn't get much worse. I was wrong. The first interviewee was due to arrive at ten-thirty. The would-be Directors of Publicity each had thirty minutes to impress Natasha and Michael, the Artistic Director. As the first candidate arrived – a balding, stick-thin chap with an involuntary tendency to lick his lips for no reason – I did my best to put Phyllis to the back of my mind, fetching coffee, attempting to put the guy at his ease. Yet my mind was barely on the job. I was still distracted by the knowledge of Phyllis's imminent arrival and I kept my phone hidden in my pocket, willing it to vibrate, longing for a call from Will, but the phone remained resolutely still.

The first candidate left, appearing even more evasive than he'd seemed at first. The second candidate was late. I scanned my checklist: Lucinda Myers-Jones. But just as I was about to inform Natasha that we had a "no show", Lucinda walked into the office, apparently unaware of her own bad timekeeping. As soon as I saw her, I flinched. She did not recognise me immediately but I knew her. She looked so different like this: still tall, blonde and unnaturally skinny, but now more composed, wearing hip, dark-rimmed spectacles, a tailored jacket and a feather brooch. It was Lucy, Miss Chick Lit, from Carl's writing class.

'Hello! Lucinda Myers-Jones. Here to see Natasha Byron-Paine.'

'Of course. She's running a little behind. Can I get you a coffee?'

She refused and blanked me. She sat down in one of our PVC armchairs, crossed her legs studiously and took out a copy of a Beckett play from her handbag. It was *Krapp's Last Tape*.

Perhaps I watched her a little too closely because before long, she looked up again from her book and this time we locked glances. This time, there was some glimmer of recognition. She smiled then: a tight, knowing smile, revealing nothing.

'Actually,' she said 'I will have that coffee.'

'Sure,' I said. 'How do you take it?'

'Do you do Espresso?'

'No,' I replied. 'Nescafé. Black or white?'

'Oh. Black then. No sugar.'

I nodded and fetched it from the kitchenette. When I returned, I noticed her eyes travelling up and down the length of my body, as if appraising my outfit, my creased linen skirt and strappy sandals that had seen better days. It was a look I recognised: it said that I would never make the grade.

'It's Anna, isn't it?' she said. Her tone remained cold. There was nothing friendly about it; this was merely a fact-finding exercise. 'Weren't you in class the other night? With Carl?'

'That's right,' I said. 'I'm the stuck-up literary one.' I barely paused for breath. It was a stupid thing to say. Lucy laughed nervously. She was the one with class and she knew it. 'Good Luck!' I said and returned to my desk.

It was not Lucy's fault that she made me feel small. Even if she hadn't put me down in the classroom, her cut-glass vowels would have shrunk me to size. The idea of reporting to her as my boss was unthinkable. I returned to the office, took out my phone and sent a text to Hilary.

R u free? Life in ruins. A x

With typically bad timing, Natasha appeared at the door and pulled one of her 'wait until I speak to you later' looks. 'Could you bring in Miss Myers-Jones, please Anna?'

'Yes, of course.'

Hilary chose that very moment to return my message. I'd put the phone down on the desk and even in silent mode, it was impossible to miss its vibrations.

'Is that *urgent*?' Natasha asked.

'Kind of, ' I replied. 'Family emergency.' At which Natasha appeared concerned but not so concerned that she was about to delay her interview.

I showed Lucy through to Natasha's office – then, knowing I had a small window of time before the next candidate, I sat down and read Hils's message:

Drama-queen. Can u speak? H x

Now that Natasha was behind closed doors, I called her.

'Oh God, it's a nightmare,' I said. 'Everything's going wrong.'

'What's the matter, Annie? You seemed fine last night. Frederica e-mailed this morning. She's raving about your work.'

'Oh that's really sweet of her. It's just…'

'What? What's happened?'

'Where do I begin?'

'It's not serious is it?'

'I don't think so. No, I'm just having a shit day.'

'So?'

'Bloody Phyllis called. She's on her way to London. No warning! Can you believe that?'

'Oh poor you. What a pain.' She hesitated. 'Is there anything else?'

'I don't know.' *Why hadn't I trusted her last night? It was stupid to hold back.* 'It's just a hunch. It's Will. I can't get through to him. And – I'm most likely being stupid, making it up – but I keep thinking he's having an affair.'

'*What?*'

'It's probably nothing. That's why I didn't say last night. I don't know… And then on top of that, there's this woman I met in Carl's writing class – Lucy. It looks as if she's about to become my boss.'

'Hang on. Slow down. The Will thing. It doesn't sound like him…'

'I don't know. He's off windsurfing this weekend. I know he's with his mates really. It's just a suspicion. And then it doesn't help that Carl McGahan sent that flirty email.'

'But Will wouldn't be unfaithful, Anna, would he? Not lovely Will. For God's sake don't do anything stupid with McGahan. You'd be an idiot to risk things with Will.'

'You think so?' I wanted to believe her. 'I need to have it out with him, but how can I with Phyllis about to descend?'

'So hang on – what proof do you have about Will?'

'Oh – it's nothing; I'm probably over-reacting. Shit. Sorry Hils, I have to go. Natasha's buzzing me. I'll give you a call later, OK?'

'All right. But I'm worried about you.'

'Don't be. I'll be fine.'

I tried very hard to take Hilary's advice. At lunchtime, I set off for the Green and sat down on my favourite bench underneath a plane tree. The sun was high in the sky and people were picnicking on the grass, enjoying the sudden burst of warmth, peeling off layers of clothing and kicking off their shoes.

I called Will again and this time I got through immediately.

'What do you *mean* my mother's coming? Didn't you stop her?'

'She'd booked her flight, Will. She was packing her case. What was I supposed to do?'

My question was met with a blank. The phone went dead. He was on the train, so I guessed it had gone through an embankment. I called back, but couldn't get a connection. I tried several times, but got the same tone, over and again. I didn't even know *why* I wanted to speak to him so much. He hadn't hung up, had he? Perhaps I thought the sound of his voice would reassure me that nothing was wrong; that the whole Angela episode was a figment of my imagination. The space between us seemed too large right now and I'd lost my chance of being alone with him.

The sky was clear and brilliant. People were walking less briskly than they usually did, as if everyone wanted nothing more than to enjoy this brief hint of summer. I swallowed hard and said the words *'Will loves me'* in my head, over and again. Yet the words proved comfortless. I wandered back to the office, hollow and raw and full of doubt.

At 5.30pm, once the interviews were over, Natasha came back into the office.

'We'll need you to stay late, Anna,' she said. 'We have to get the letters done tonight. It won't be fair to keep the candidates waiting.'

'I can't do tonight. Will's mother's arriving from the States.'

'I'm afraid that's not my problem. I promised the candidates they'd be informed of the decision ASAP.'

'But I *can't.*'

'You have no choice. We need somebody to be on box-office duty as well.'

'What about the box-office staff?'

Natasha paused and looked at me, her brow curling in incredulity. 'This is theatre, Anna.' As if that explained everything. 'There are a lot of graduates out there who would give their eye teeth to work at the Walpole.' She glimpsed over my shoulder. 'And I see you didn't get the latest programmes out this afternoon. I'd like those in the post this evening too.'

'But I've only got baked beans in the cupboard,' I said. 'Literally. And I have a guest.'

'Baked beans will be perfect, I'm sure,' Natasha said – and I cursed myself for ever letting my guard down with her, for ever believing for one instant that our pally exchanges would put me at the slightest advantage. 'It's good traditional English fare!' She laughed at her own joke, then paused; I thought I saw some hint of pity in her expression. In a moment she would break into a smile, tell me she was only kidding; it could wait until the morning after all. 'Now you know, Anna, I would type those letters myself if I could. Unfortunately however, I have a dinner date with Sir Rory Nightingale tonight.'

'Bring him to my place,' I said. 'I might manage to rustle up some toast as well.'

'I'd love to, Anna. Unfortunately I understand Sir Rory is on a wheat-free diet.'

She turned abruptly and walked to the door. She hesitated, then came back into the room.

'Anna, I nearly forgot – we've taken a decision on the candidate. Lucy Myers-Jones will be our new Head of Publicity.'

'Oh perfect,' I said. 'I can have lunch with her and we can talk about trends in downmarket fiction.'

Natasha smiled as if she were just a touch perplexed at my meaning. It was possible that I'd simply got off to a bad start with Lucy; perhaps before too long we'd be the best of friends. Such an outcome seemed unlikely however. I bit my lip inside until I tasted blood.

9

'No artist tolerates reality.' – Friedrich Nietzsche

At 8pm, at the end of an eleven hour shift, I finally made it out of the Walpole. Throughout the evening, I had tried to maintain an air of calm and a certain lightness that I did not feel, but now I was free to panic. I had already sent Will a number of desperate text and phone messages yet he had failed to respond to a single one. There was nothing from him. I wondered whether a shopping list might do the trick.

Can u get artichoke hearts? Oysters? Bollinger?

Still my phone remained deadly silent. As I hurried towards Tesco Metro, I began to worry. What if there was a genuine reason for Will's failure to call? What if it wasn't Angela? He might have been involved in a train crash…

Then it rang at last. I grabbed it, but even as I picked up, I felt a pang of disappointment. It wasn't Will. It was Phyllis.

'Oh thank God!' she said. 'I got through customs in record time, honey! A nightmare journey, wait till I tell you. The flight came in early. I'm on my way… just outside Richmond now.'

This was *not* good news.

'OK, great!' I replied. I wasn't sure whether to tell her about Will. I was probably worrying about nothing. His phone was surely out of juice. 'I'll see you at home, very shortly.'

What was I supposed to do now? I might have time to whizz around the supermarket in record time, but the idea of leaving Skinny-bones shivering on the doorstep did not appeal. I'd just have to trust Will on the food front. I turned around and headed up the

High Street towards the bridge. As I walked past the parade of designer shops, my thoughts turned to my appearance.

I remembered Lucy's expression as she looked me up and down, frowning at my creased linen skirt and grungy T-shirt. If even Lucy thought my outfit fell short, how much worse would it seem to Phyllis whose sartorial standards were the foundation stone of her personality? I glimpsed down at my bitten fingernails, fraying at the edges. Soon Phyllis would be flouncing about my home, waving her perfectly manicured nails at me, boasting at the price label on her latest handbag.

It didn't matter to me, not at all, but something was wrong. Something else. I couldn't put my finger on it.

Ten minutes later, I approached our gate and saw them in the doorway. So – Will was very much alive. The front door was open and they were standing in the hallway. They spotted me as I walked up the path.

Phyllis gave an excited wave, apparently genuinely pleased to see me, as Will helped her out of her probably-not-faux fur-collared jacket. He caught my eye before she did and his wide-eyed stare revealed his shock at her sudden presence. If I hadn't been so cross, I might even have felt sorry for him. He'd caught the sun over the weekend, I noticed, and his hair was unwashed and tousled. I wanted to hold him close, even as I wanted to slap him.

Any communication between us would have to wait. Phyllis was grinning widely, though her face appeared oddly expressionless: the surgery had ransacked all visible emotion. She beckoned me closer, holding out her arms and I allowed myself to be hugged, despite the faint twinge of repulsion.

'Anna!' she crooned. I inhaled the scent of her perfume and nearly choked. She pulled away promptly and – as expected – appeared to examine my outfit.

'Isn't it great to see her!' Will said, between gritted teeth.

I needed to be alone with him. For the first time, I was beginning to have doubts about our future. The timing of Phyllis's visit was so horribly wrong. I wanted to hold Will, to touch his hair, kiss him. It made no sense at all. If I was really so angry with him, why did I suddenly desire him like this?

But my desire was pointless.

'It's so good to see y'all,' Phyllis said. 'But hell, what a flight. I had to take economy. Such a disaster!'

Will led Phyllis through to the front room and my eye was drawn to her physique. Was it possible she'd lost even *more* weight? How far did she plan to take this? Phyllis had so distorted herself through surgery that I'd lost sight of the woman I'd first met four years ago. I was trying to work out what had changed since her last visit. Will had been to the States at Christmas, but I'd been on pantomime duty at the Walpole and had been unable to join them. Over the last year, her appearance had deteriorated.

There was a photograph of Phyllis on one of our living room shelves and that photograph had formed my most recent mental image of her. It was taken at a film premiere in Times Square; some swanky event that she'd wangled a ticket for. She must have taken hours getting ready as the photo portrayed a very different Phyllis to the one I saw before me now. It had caught her in a particularly flattering light, or else it had been heavily airbrushed. As she sat down on the sofa, I couldn't draw my eyes away.

'What's the matter, Anna?' She surveyed the room, as if something was missing.

'Nothing – nothing at all. I'm just a little tired.'

I wondered what vile, money-grabbing surgeon had preyed on her of late. A little nip-tuck here and there had lent Phyllis's face such a stretched and vapid appearance that it was difficult to decipher any expression at all. Her hollow cheekbones clashed with her very white, yet slightly protruding teeth. As she sat down on the sofa and smiled (she could still manage that at least), I remembered a conversation we once had about her pathological fear of dentists (which had however not prevented her from seeking crowns and bleaching treatment).

She adjusted her position on the sofa – perhaps it was uncomfortable, without the usual flesh to cushion you. Her hand reached to her head as if she feared her bouffant wig was about to come unstuck. Beneath it, I imagined her hair thin and greying, resembling the fur of an ageing rat. Yet she maintained some semblance of elegance all the same; she wore a calf-length black dress and a necklace – a large silver heart on a long chain and I was thankful that for once she was not baring her flesh.

'Have you been ill, Anna?' Phyllis asked.

What did she mean by that?

'No!' I trilled. 'Ah – let me get you a drink!' I regretted my words as soon as they were out of my mouth. The drink – that was the missing thing. I'd finished the last bottle of wine the previous night when drowning my sorrows after the Carl fiasco.

'Oh, just a nice, chilled white would be perfect,' Phyllis said.

I wondered whether – if I just smiled hard enough – she might forget she'd ever asked.

She was casting her eye about the living room – taking in the piles of junk that had congregated on the majority of surfaces, the empty wine glasses and coffee cups that were the remnants of my weekend alone. Even major plastic surgery was not enough to prevent her face from registering intense disgust.

Will saw it too. *Was that a reproachful look? No. I had to stop this. His look probably meant nothing at all. I couldn't let his mother cause a rift between us the moment she walked through the door.*

I felt rooted to the spot and could only watch as Will bent down to pick up a coffee cup and a congealed breakfast bowl; then more coffee cups – perhaps seven in all. He put them in the kitchen then began tidying up various cardigans and pairs of tights that had tumbled from the top of the laundry pile as I'd left for work that morning.

I had to do something, but what? Will was scrabbling about on the floor, clearing piles of papers that he'd discarded prior to his departure for Lake Windermere.

'Is everything *all right?*' Phyllis said. 'I just thought, with the mess...'

'Mum!' Will said. 'You've just arrived. Cut it out.'

She was out of order, but did he have to be so blunt in return? They were as bad as each other.

'What are you talking about, Will?'

'Can you stop this? Please.'

'Stop what, darling? I'm just commenting on the mess. Perhaps the two of you could do with a little help about the house?'

'We don't want any help.'

'Don't you? But why?'

I couldn't make out whether Phyllis was being sarcastic or whether she was genuinely confused.

'It suits us this way.'

'You're teasing me. To think anyone could enjoy living…'

'Enough. Look, what can I get you to drink, Mum? Oh – and are you going to tell me what you're doing here?'

'Hasn't Anna told you what happened?'

'No,' he said, unimpressed. 'I've only just got back from the Lake District. My mobile's out of juice and I haven't a clue what's going on.'

Will had no idea how this apparently innocuous admission affected me. *His mobile battery was flat. Of course, I guessed that, I knew it, but it was a relief to hear him say it. He hadn't been purposely avoiding me all day. He hadn't been in bed with some other woman. Perhaps there was nothing wrong at all and our only problem was Phyllis's presence in our home.*

'Your Mum's apartment has dry rot,' I said. I was trying to be the voice of calm and reason but it was difficult because I wanted to squeeze Will for information, unpick his brain for lies and find some peace again. I wanted him to myself; wished she wasn't here. If we were alone, he'd have gone straight up for a shower and would now be on his way back downstairs, wearing nothing but a bathrobe.

'Right?' Will said. He wasn't in the same fantasy as me. He just wanted information.

'The builders are in,' I said. 'Your Mum thought it would be a good opportunity for a visit.'

A small muscle twitched at Will's jaw line.

'How long are you staying?' he asked.

'Oh – I haven't decided yet. It's bound to take several weeks. But you know, as Dr. Johnson said, "When you're tired of

London…"' She stopped suddenly – as if the aftershock of his question had just hit her and for the first time she'd considered that she might not be welcome. But if she was aware of this, she didn't show it. She simply changed the subject.

'Will, darling, don't you think you *ought* to get a cleaner? You can afford it, can't you? I mean, the cartoons – I thought it was going pretty well?'

'It is going well, Mum.'

'We like it like this,' I said.

Phyllis stared at me as if trying to work out whether I could possibly be serious.

'I see. The thing is – I'm not sure I'm going to be entirely *comfortable* staying here.'

'Perhaps a hotel, Mum?' Will said, without a split-second's hesitation.

She appeared to consider this. I guessed she was tempted and I had to hold my tongue to stop myself from saying the polite thing and urging her to stay. I kept thinking about all the things I wanted to do in the coming weeks. There were the wedding preparations of course but more than that, I'd planned to transform the spare room into a study, a place where I might not only write but also curl up in an armchair to read books about Modigliani and Jeanne.

Phyllis shook her head.

'I couldn't. I belong here with you two. You probably need a little help about the house, Anna – no disrespect – and it's been a long time since I got my hands dirty; about time I did. Hell, I'm not at all tired after the flight. It must be this raw food diet. I feel better than I did in my thirties. I'll take a bath, hon and I'll tidy up a little before dinner. Now, where's my glass of wine?'

'I'll tell you what, Mum. You take the bath. I'll go out for some wine and…'

'You've run out?'

'I'll get some champagne. Then why don't we go for dinner? I know a great place in St. Margarets.'

'Oh, I don't know…' But she was standing up now – slowly, as if the movement pained her – and Will took her arm and kissed her tenderly on the cheek as he escorted her upstairs.

When he came down again, Will was shaking his head as if he'd lost the will to live. I poured a measure of neat gin into a couple of tumblers and handed him one, with ice. We clinked glasses and he spoke in a hushed voice.

'This is a fucking nightmare, Anna. Couldn't you have stopped her?'

'It was out of my control.'

'What are we going to *do*?'

'She's your mother.'

He downed his gin, not speaking. How odd, I thought, that he was related to this woman. He must have read my mind.

'She wasn't always like this.'

'I know.'

'I mean, when Dad was around – when she lived over here.' He waved his arm in the air, as if the gesture alone might bring back the past. 'OK, well, she never *fitted* in exactly, not your typical barrister's wife – but she tried, she made a real effort.'

'I can't imagine it was easy for her.'

'All the women in our village, they despised her because she wasn't one of them – how could she be? This strange Southern Belle – and a divorcée to boot. She looked so different then; curvy. Did I tell you?'

I nodded. Didn't he remember showing me the photographs? Perhaps he'd forgotten that I'd seen her change too.

'Not surprising that she went back to the States, is it?'

He slammed his glass down a little too hard on the kitchen table.

'Am I interrupting?' She was standing in the doorway, holding a bottle of champagne. 'Here – I brought some myself – Duty Free.'

'Not at all,' I said. 'Hey, you look good.'

'Just my slacks.'

Her tiny black trousers were surely far too expensive to be called 'slacks' and she wore them with a blue sequined top that for some reason put me in mind of Ali G.

'It's chilled,' she said, placing the champagne down.

'Thanks.'

78

'Now, do you possess such a thing as a feather duster?'

'What?'

'I'll make a start on the house whilst you do dinner?'

Dinner. Hadn't Will suggested we go out?

We hesitated as she began digging around under the sink; she managed to find a feather duster, still in its polythene wrap.

'Ah – perfect!' she said, as she unwrapped it and shook it hard. 'Oh, look at those cobwebs!'

Phyllis pointed to the ceiling, but I couldn't see a thing.

'Mum – I think we'd better go out for dinner,' Will said. 'We didn't know about your raw diet. We're not really prepared.'

Phyllis had dragged a chair from beneath the kitchen table and was about to step up onto it.

'I'm sure I can make an exception for one night,' she said. 'What do you think I am, Will, a fanatic? I'll eat a cooked meal tonight and we can stock up on something more suitable tomorrow.' She paused and peered down at me. 'Anna, do you have an apron I can borrow?'

'I'm not sure.' When she was out of earshot, I beckoned Will over and whispered, 'There's nothing in. Beans on toast is about as good as it gets.'

'Fuck.'

'Not our fault. We had no warning.'

He fell silent, considering his options. At first he seemed uneasy but then defiance crept back in. 'Sod it,' he said. 'Let her slum it.'

He marched through to the lounge. 'Mum – Haricots Napolitanas – is that OK?'

'Sounds delicious, William,' she replied.

As Phyllis got friendly with the polish. I rummaged around in the freezer and found a carton of Ben & Jerry's.

'Do you think this will help soften the blow?' I asked

'Perfect. Do you think she'll eat it though?'

'I hope so. She's in need of some decent nourishment.'

'I wish she wouldn't starve herself,' Will said.

I wanted to say something to comfort him, but I couldn't find the right words. Instead I turned away, dug beneath a couple of old potatoes in the fridge and found a few stray coriander leaves. I chopped them as garnish, heated up the beans and put the toaster on.

'God, how long is she going to stay for?'

'It'll be fine.' Of course, I didn't mean that. 'Aren't you a tiny bit pleased to see her?'

His pause told me all I needed to know. Their relationship was so ambiguous, it would probably take years of therapy for Will to get to the bottom of his feelings and here was I, asking demanding questions that seemed to require no more than a sound bite in response.

'Yes, but that doesn't stop her from driving me nuts.'

'So much for starting work on my novel…'

'Tell me about it – I've got deadlines coming out of my ears.'

I wondered whether the comment about my novel had actually registered. Just as I was beginning to think about Jeanne Hébuterne, as I was ready to plunge into research, the possibility of working on this idea was snatched away.

'You know I haven't even asked about your weekend,' I said.

Will leant forward and kissed me.

'Missed you.'

Did he? Did he really? His kiss almost convinced me, but we must have lingered there too long.

'I smell something burning...'

Phyllis stood in the doorway, holding the feather duster aloft like a trophy. Will pulled swiftly away.

'Dammit,' I said. 'The toast!'

Before Phyllis could get her head around the idea of us dining on toast, Will grabbed the bottle of Veuve Cliquot. 'Stand back, everyone!' Phyllis let out a happy whoop as the cork bounced off the ceiling. Will distracted her by leading her through to the dining room, just as the smoke alarm went off.

'Shit, shit!' I abandoned the toast and went to open the back door, to release the smoke. But the noise was deafening and wouldn't stop. Will began wafting his hands beneath the sensor, as Phyllis made her way outside to avoid the high-pitched squeal.

'Where's the 'off' switch?' she shouted.

'There isn't one,' I replied. It had to stop eventually, didn't it?

'Perhaps the restaurant is not such a bad idea…'

Great! Now that I've bloody made it!

'It's fine,' I said. And for a moment it was. The alarm stopped as suddenly as it had begun. I returned to the kitchen, scraped the toast and plated up, then carried the food to the table.

As I placed the beans down however, Phyllis's face began to crumple; her bottom lip quivered. It couldn't just have been the beans. Perhaps it was the stress or some form of early jet lag. It was such an extreme response that my first instinct was to assume that she thought this meal was intended as an insult. A small tear formed in the corner of her eye.

'I know,' Will said, 'Look, Mum. I know it's not up to your usual standards. I know you're on a raw food diet, but you did say…'

'You don't remember?'

'Remember what?' he asked. 'Mum, what are you talking about? I mean, this is the kind of stuff we like.' Something seemed to snap in him. 'Anna didn't have time to pop to Fortnum and Mason, for Christ's sake. You gave us no warning. This is all we had in. All right?'

This didn't feel right. He was losing it, but he'd got it wrong. I sensed it.

'You came at really short notice, Mum. I've been away and Anna had to work late. If you're going to stay here, the least you can do is be gracious for once.'

I looked from Phyllis to Will and back to Phyllis again. He was staring at her – the kind of look I imagined he'd given her as an adolescent, but it seemed churlish; he wasn't giving her a chance. Phyllis pushed her chair back from the table.

We were missing something.

'Have you forgotten what day it is, Will?'

He'd forgotten her birthday! No – that was in April. I looked at Will and like me he appeared to draw a blank.

'Haricots *what* did you call them?'

'It was just a joke, Mum.'

'A sick joke!'

'Oh come off it!'

My mind was working overtime. I could almost see the machinations of Will's brain. He paused, stood very still. His anger dissolved all at once.

'Shit!'

I wished somebody would let me in on the secret. Was this a medical problem? Gluten intolerance? A sensitivity to coriander?

'I'm sorry. Mum, I'm really sorry. This has nothing to do with the beans, right? It's Dad.'

She was twisting a napkin about her fingers, muttering beneath her breath.

'It's the anniversary of Dad's death today.' Will said, turning to me. 'What an idiot to forget that.'

'How could you?' she said. 'Baked beans. Your father's favourite dish.'

She looked away, attempting to hold back the tears, but they dripped into her champagne. Will put his arm around her and kissed her forehead. She was so frail, all her bravado gone. Beneath that curious façade, was it possible that Phyllis was mourning still? Will didn't talk much about his father but his head was bent and they were locked in an embrace, crying for a man I'd never met. These people were about to become my family. Yet it felt as if I didn't know them at all.

10

The men who really care for their art, who wish above all things to do the best that is in them, do not take the way of the world and the regular salaries of the newspaper offices. They stay outside, reading, writing, painting for themselves, and snatching such golden crumbs as fall within their reach from the tables of publishers, editors and picture-buyers.' – Arthur Ransome

It was Tuesday and dank, heavy clouds threatened rain. I braved it all the same and headed to the Green. I'd promised to meet Hilary and so, armed with sandwiches and coffee, I sat alone beneath a tangled oak tree, awaiting the arrival of my friend.

Hilary, however, was late, so I unbuttoned my bag, took out the Loftus book and began to read. I half hoped I might find an answer there. Perhaps the book contained a miracle formula that would enable me to conjure vast swathes of time from thin air. Yet whatever Meryl Wainwright had said, I was finding it difficult to take this book seriously. I had reached Chapter Three and so far I'd learnt precisely nothing. The book was full of confidence-boosting quotations and earnest, empty phrases. I flicked to a random page: "People around you, even those closest to you, may not be comfortable with the idea of your creative growth." Did one have to be a genius to work that out?

I took a sip of coffee and let the warm, milky froth dissolve on my tongue. Was it possible that I was missing something?

'Any good?'

Hilary had crept up on me while I was reading.

'Na,' I said. 'Not really.'

'Budge up.'

She sat down beside me and lit a cigarette. It occurred to me that Hilary was the kind of person who might appear in a cigarette advertisement, if such things still existed. With her waif-like proportions and closely cropped platinum-blonde hair, she reminded me of a modern-day Jean Seberg. Hilary would look very good in black and white.

'Smoking at lunchtime?'

'I'm depressed,' she replied.

'You're not allowed to be depressed. You have a massive publishing deal and you look like you just stepped out of a Jean-Luc Godard movie.'

Hilary leant back against the bench and as a light rain began to fall, she frowned, thinking about it.

'Can't help it,' she said, reflective. 'Nothing's good enough.'

'Hils, what are you talking about?'

'My publisher doesn't like my new novel.'

'Bastards.'

'No, they have a point.'

'Course they don't.'

'You haven't read it, Anna.'

I paused. She was right about that but I still thought they were bastards.

'Anyway, that's not it.'

'What do you mean?'

'That's just the icing on the cake.' She shook her head. 'Tom dumped me last night.'

'What crap timing.' I'd only met Tom twice, but I'd been hopeful that this time Hils might have found someone who'd stick around.

'Didn't like him anyway.'

'I didn't either,' I agreed.

'You never said.'

'Well I couldn't, could I? You were infatuated.'

'Only for a while.' She smiled but it was unconvincing. 'He was rubbish in bed anyway.'

'At least you'll have more time to write.'

'Yeah, there is that.' She fell silent. Sometimes when Hilary was like this, I wondered whether she regretted divorcing Ben. Maybe her mum had been right and she'd married too young. Her mum said it was bound to end in tears – and it did.

'Are you OK?' It was lame, but the best I could come up with.

She took another puff of her cigarette and pouted. It struck me that being beautiful might sometimes be inconvenient, because Hilary's misery only seemed to intensify her beauty. If I didn't know her better, I'd have found it difficult to believe that she was suffering.

'No,' she said. 'I'm very shit. But I don't want to talk about it. Anyway, how are you?'

'Apart from my mother-in-law-to-be dossing down in my writing room, you mean?'

'Yes, apart from that.'

'Apart from my pathetic attempts to flirt with my creative writing teacher?'

'Apart from that too.'

'Did I mention that Will whispered another woman's name in my ear when we were making love?'

'So *that's* what made you suspicious…'

'I probably imagined it,' I said, even though I could feel tears welling up and it took every ounce of my energy to stop them.

A small cloud of smoke escaped from Hilary's mouth. 'I don't know what to say.'

'You don't have to say anything. But it doesn't seem real, you know? I mean it was "Angela" which does sound a bit like "Anna".'

'Not. But he wouldn't do that, would he? I'm sure he wouldn't be unfaithful.'

'Well you wouldn't have thought he'd be such an idiot, would you?'

She laughed. 'Cigarette?'

'Thanks.'

I left my sandwich untouched and lit up.

'Sodding rain.' Hilary pulled her cardigan tighter about her body. It was a pretty, dove-grey mohair thing that she probably bought at a jumble sale, yet she made it look chic and expensive. 'You know, I bet you'll find a publisher before I get my latest into print,' she said.

'Yeah, right.'

'I wouldn't mind my publisher rejecting this draft if Tom hadn't dumped me too.'

'Tom will regret it.'

'Course he will. But by then it will be far too late.' The rain was getting heavier but we were sheltered from the worst of it by the canopy of leaves above us. 'The problem is, I'm still lusting madly after him.'

I didn't know what to say to that. Lust had a lot to answer for. As the rain broke through the leaves and we stubbed out our cigarettes, I found myself thinking about Jeanne Hébuterne lying naked in Modigliani's bed, sewing her torn underwear before she could go home to the dull, bourgeois existence she had led before she met him. I thought about Carl McGahan too. Why was I lusting after him? It must be pre-wedding jitters, nothing more. It was just idle curiosity, a final indulgence, like the last drag of a cigarette before you put on your first nicotine patch.

I was shivering.

'We can't stay here – we'll get soaked.' I began to gather my things, putting the untouched sandwich packet in my bag for later.

'Can you make it to Frederica's birthday tonight?'

I shook my head. 'Don't want to gatecrash.'

'You wouldn't be gatecrashing. Honestly. It's only the pub – she asked me to invite you.'

'I can't,' I said. 'Phyllis, remember?'

'McGahan's going to be there…'

'Stop it! Anyway, since when did he become part of your crowd?'

'Not part of my crowd: Julia's crowd. Julia knows everyone, you know that.'

'So do you these days.'

Hilary laughed, but her laughter was cut short as the sun broke through a cloud, dazzling her.

In the old days, when we were at school, there was nothing we couldn't say to each other. Now I knew that I was holding back. I didn't want to speak my fears out loud. I was afraid they might come true.

11

'Be regular and ordinary in your life like a bourgeois, so that you may be violent and original in your work.'
– Gustave Flaubert

By the time that Phyllis came downstairs dressed for dinner, I'd almost forgotten that we were supposed to be going out. I was ensconced in front of the TV screen, wearing a little black dress and heels, sipping a glass of chilled Sauvignon and watching a DVD about Francois Truffaut when she swanned into the room and paraded herself before me.

'You know,' she said, 'I always preferred Renoir myself.'

I flicked the TV to stand-by mode and gave her the attention she demanded.

'You look fabulous, Phyllis.'

She looked like an emaciated version of Barbara Cartland. Phyllis twirled before me in a low-cut turquoise evening dress, revealing a broad expanse of her bronzed and scrawny chest. Even at this distance, her pungent perfume near choked me.

'You two ready then?' Will appeared briefly in the doorway before returning to the hall where he stood before the mirror adjusting his tie.

'Do you think this dress is too much?' Phyllis asked.

'It's perfect,' I said, and she followed me out to the hallway.

'You both look gorgeous,' Will said, then paused as if waiting for me to return the compliment. But there was something empty about his flattery. In any case, the way he flicked the tip of his tie through the knot had irritated me. He seemed... what... smug? A little too slick? Too perfect?

I laughed out loud at my own stupidity.

'What's the joke?' Will said.

'Nothing. Come on.'

But I was thinking about a photograph I'd seen in the Parisot book, a photograph of Modigliani, dressed in a scruffy corduroy suit and a chequered necktie. Amedeo Modigliani was the archetypal artist. Will looked like your archetypal television presenter.

'I'll have a Clementine Bellini,' Phyllis said.

She was the kind of woman who would choose a vulgar aperitif, just because it was there.

'Make that two,' I said.

Phyllis began to smile and chatter like one who had arrived home after a long absence. Something about the delicate shade of grey that adorned the walls, the dark oak floors, the mirrors and the sparkling glasses must have appealed to her sensibility. The opulence of this environment suited her very well.

'Well, this is nice!' she said. 'Isn't this nice?'

'Glad you like it, Phyllis,' Will said. *She ought to bloody like it. It was going to set us back two hundred quid!*

'It's one of our favourite restaurants,' I said.

She picked up the menu and perused it slowly.

'No raw food.'

'I'm sure they'll accommodate you, Mum, if you want to eat rabbit food.'

'You're such a philistine, Will.'

'Oh, have a steak, won't you? I'm sure they'll do it rare.'

'That's not such a bad idea...' she said.

I tried to concentrate on the menu too, but was distracted by Phyllis's appearance. Her wizened chest reminded me of chicken skin and I found myself unable to face anything containing even the slightest trace of poultry.

The waiter arrived with our cocktails.

'I'll have the octopus,' I said. 'Followed by rigatoni.'

'Good choice!' Will said. I shot him a look that said: *"Could you please cut out these stupid platitudes?"* Since Phyllis's arrival, so much of his energy had gone into sparring with her, I felt as if I'd ceased to exist; but was I merely self-dramatising or was there a truth in my perception?

As Phyllis placed her order, my phone beeped. It was a text from Hilary.

Can we tempt u 2 White Swan? H x

I considered my options. Toothache? Sudden vomiting? Diarrhoea?

'I'll have the rib-eye steak,' Will said. 'Well done.'

The waiter nodded. 'Excellent.'

Why had I still not challenged Will? Was it because I had so little to go on or because I knew he would deny it, no matter what? It was possible I'd never get an answer about Angela but the more Will uttered banalities that evening, the more convinced I became that something was not right. I knew I had to speak to him and soon. I needed to hear him tell me it was crazy and I needed to believe his words.

He was conversing with the sommelier now and Phyllis was joining in. I replied to Hilary's message.

Sorry. Am at Groucho Club with Martin Amis. Next time maybe? A x

'I can't get my head around technology,' Phyllis said. 'My friend Maggie keeps sending me texts but I haven't a clue how to reply. Look!' She took out her phone and handed it to me. 'Will you help?'

'Same phone,' I said. 'That makes things *much* easier.'

'Oh God, you two are primitive as each other.'

'Will thinks we should get iPhones,' I said.

Phyllis shook her head. 'All that tweeting?' she said. 'I don't think so.'

'See!' I said. 'Nothing wrong with our Nokias. Who wants to be permanently connected?'

'Who's Maggie?' Will asked.

'Charming lady. She recently joined my book club.'

'Ah, the infamous book club!' I recalled my last visit to New York, at dinner in her apartment, when she'd regaled us with tales of her friends in high places. She'd boasted about a whole host of authors she'd apparently lined up to attend their evenings. 'Are you still attracting celebrity guests?'

'There aren't many authors who'd be short-sighted enough to turn down an invitation to speak at our group. A couple of the major magazine editors in New York are members, Anna. Think of the publicity.'

'Surely they don't *need* the extra publicity?' I said.

'Ha! Famous authors are the biggest whores around – forgive my language. And the longer I'm in the club, the more I realise the truth of it.'

'I'm surprised to hear that,' I said. I took a sip of Bellini and thanked the waiter as he placed my octopus down before me.

Phyllis pursed her lips, narrowed her eyes and shook her head as if she pitied me. When she spoke, her voice was quiet and measured.

'I'll just say this,' she said. 'Of all the living legends we've invited thus far, not a single one has turned us down.'

I raised my glass, humouring her, certain that she could not be serious. Maybe she had a quirkier imagination than I'd thought. Or maybe there was some truth to it and she was hoping that I would try to pump her for information and names.

Will had ordered a bottle of Barolo and the waiter filled his glass. He picked it up, sniffed it, sloshed it around in his mouth and declared his approval. Phyllis appeared momentarily distracted and Will winked at me which I assumed meant that she was deluded and to be humoured.

My phone beeped again and Will flinched but was obviously not in the mood to challenge me. Phyllis shrugged and tucked into her chicken liver salad. She seemed to have conveniently forgotten her raw diet. Will bit into a morsel of smoked mackerel and gave me a disdainful glance as I picked up my phone to read.

Martin a bad influence. Get your arse over here. Carl

I stuck my fork into a spiny tentacle and raised it to my mouth. I concentrated all my energy on pretending that nothing at all had changed. I even managed to bite into the octopus and chew its rubbery flesh. It seemed to me that if I continued to smile and to eat, they would not notice how the text had at once shocked and excited me. The octopus tasted delicious but I could not swallow it. The thrill I felt was sexual and it worried me immensely.

Yet it made no sense. If I was in love with Will, then why did Carl McGahan's behaviour have any impact at all? *It's a test, that's all. Sexual desire means nothing at all; it's just a biological response.* But what about McGahan, why was he doing this? He'd only met me once. He was my *teacher*. How did he know I'd respond like this? How did he expect me to respond?

'So Phyllis,' Will said. 'What are you planning to do tomorrow?'

'I thought I'd take in the V&A; meet an old pal for lunch.'

I imagined Carl McGahan standing outside the White Swan, snatching Hilary's mobile from her hand, swigging beer from a bottle.

'Who was that? Your new boyfriend?' Will said.

Had he acquired psychic skills on Lake Windermere? Now I understood what was at stake. I was toying with my own future.

'Don't be stupid. It's just Hilary.' *He can't know...* 'I'll just say goodbye, OK?' I keyed in a quick message.

Sorry, Kingsley's just arrived. Mustn't be rude. Anna.

'Welcome back,' Will said, as I put the phone down.

'Shit,' I said, as I realised my mistake.

'Anna, is something the matter?'

'Oh, you know Hilary; just man trouble.'

Carl's retort came quickly and despite Will's displeasure, I couldn't stop myself from peeking.

A séance at the Groucho? Am I invited?

Now Carl must think I am a total airhead. Kingsley Amis was dead. I knew that, right? I put the phone off and attempted to save the only relationship I had left.

'Sorry. Really sorry. That's it. Phone off. No more interruptions.'

Phyllis held up her hands as if to say 'I'm not getting involved!'

'How is your mackerel, Will?' she asked.

'Ummm,' he said. 'Superb!'

Nothing that Will did this evening seemed right. I couldn't put my finger on it. In his mother's presence, he seemed different: more obsequious, less himself. Will said that Phyllis had many saving graces, which was true, but it was sometimes easy to miss them. Her surgically reconstructed face didn't help – it was difficult to see past that level of self-mutilation in the name of beauty – but I had tried. I'd listened to everything Will told me about her difficult years in the Suffolk village, how she was ostracised by the locals, an outsider. It wasn't until Tobias's death that she had her first surgical procedure; the year before I met Will. I had watched her face change, yet I could not remember the way she used to be.

'Now, Anna...' she said. She paused between bites of fresh-baked bread roll and butter and I had a sudden fear that she might be bulimic. How else could she eat like this and remain so skeletal? '... You're being very coy about it, but Will tells me you're writing a novel?'

A dab of butter had lodged on her chest.

'It's in the very early stages.' I hoped that might shut her up.

'Will tells me it's about Jeanne Hébuterne.'

She pronounced Jeanne's name perfectly, as if she was familiar with her: one of her saving graces, her education. She had originally majored in art history and started her career as a reviewer for a number of minor New York art magazines.

'That's right,' I said.

'Did you know, I'm writing too?'

'Yes, Will told me.'

'Such a fascinating story though, Hébuterne's.' She paused and drained her glass. She tapped her fingers on the table, whilst her eyes drifted to the middle-distance, as if she were searching for some memory there. Then, at once, she seemed to find what she was looking for. 'Have you read Jeanne Modigliani's account?' she asked.

'Jeanne who?' I was confused, but only for a moment. I knew Jeanne's daughter by Modigliani was also called Jeanne, but I had no idea that she'd written a book.

'It's next on my reading list,' I said. *It was now.*

'Such a shame that it's only published in French.'

Phyllis's breadth of knowledge was not new to me – but it always caught me by surprise. Her face and her intellect were mismatched. As she placed her cutlery down on her plate, I looked at her hands – the age-spots, the prominent purple veins – and wondered what her face might have looked like if she had simply allowed herself to grow old.

'How is your French, Anna?' It was this insistence on her own right to judge other people that bothered me. She lacked subtlety and it was difficult to forgive her for that.

'It's rusty,' I said. 'But I'll get by.'

'I met Will's father in Paris.'

'Yes, Will told me.'

'I was doing a placement at the Jeu de Paume.'

A black and white photograph of Will's parents hung in our hallway at home; I knew it well but had never been able to connect the Phyllis I saw before me with the fleshy girl wearing flares in the photograph, leaning against her boyfriend in front of the Eiffel Tower, her head thrown back, her mouth wide open, laughing.

I was beginning to wish that we'd continued to discuss the mackerel. At least a mackerel could not be intimidating.

'I suppose it was the Patrice Chaplin book that inspired you?' she said.

Would she not shut up? Change the subject?

'No,' I said. 'It was a picture postcard.' A picture postcard that her son – now looking distinctly sheepish – had once bought me, as if his fascination with this Modigliani painting was his own, whereas in fact, it was possibly his mother's.

Phyllis leant forward across the table. 'Isn't it wonderful?' she said. 'We share so many common interests. I'm thinking all that dry rot in my apartment was there for a reason. This is such an opportunity for us, Anna.'

'I suppose it is.' Yet I was still wondering whether it was too late, after all, to broach the subject of hotels, because at that moment, I would have given anything – truly, anything – to escape her earnest stare, her unnatural face, her knowledge of art and her chicken liver

94

breath.

'Shall we have another bottle?' Will had drained the last glass of wine and was about to call the waiter.

'Maybe we should just have coffee?' I said. I'd had enough. I wanted to be alone with him.

Will's jaw hung loose and he appeared to have difficulty focussing.

'Oh, come on, Anna, have another. It's not as if we're driving.'

'I don't want another – really – but if you and your Mum want another bottle…'

'Phyllis?'

'Well, I wouldn't say no to another glass…'

I didn't want Will to still be drinking. *Why did he want to prolong this?*

'But hey, Anna, if you want to be a drag…'

'Oh right – it's like that now, is it?'

Well, screw him! Really – screw him. This didn't even sound like Will. Was it just the drink talking? I didn't recognise him. And something else – Will no longer seemed irritated by Phyllis's presence. He appeared to be *enjoying* this cosy threesome. He was probably picturing Phyllis and I spending long evenings together in earnest literary conversation, thickening our plots over tall G & Ts.

'Another bottle of Barolo?' He didn't look me in the eye.

'And a cappuccino,' I said.

'So, Mum. How's your novel going?'

So, he was calling her 'Mum' now…

'A slow business,' Phyllis said.

Will glanced in my direction, as if he expected me to say something but all I really wanted to do was scream at him. I managed to compose myself. I *knew* that I was being totally unreasonable. Would I like Phyllis more, I wondered, if her appearance was different? I wanted to take her words and divorce them from her Texan drawl, the lurid dress and the glossy poppy-coloured lipstick spilling from the wrinkles that still remained about her mouth. *Was* I in fact prejudiced against her?

'You know, Anna,' she said, 'the reason we have so many gaps in our knowledge of Modigliani is that he wrote so little down.' She paused to take a sip of wine and appeared to contemplate this. 'That's why we know so much about Van Gogh. He couldn't stop scribbling. Modi was more private. He put it all into the painting. That's his appeal, you know – the drink, the drugs and the failure to truly succeed in his lifetime, the early death. It takes over. People see nothing else. They cease to see the art, Anna. They're judging the art by the life.'

'Are you saying his life doesn't matter?' I asked. I imagined there was some criticism here, a suggestion that my novel was encouraging this philistinism.

'Not at all. It's a fascinating life; of course we're interested. His life influenced the choices he made in his art. If his health had been better, if he hadn't had TB, he'd have continued sculpting, so much of his later output as a painter wouldn't exist. It's far from simple, don't you agree?'

'Yes. Of course you're right.'

Why was I so cross with her? It made no sense. How could I *not* be engaged in this conversation? It was exactly what I needed. Phyllis knew more about the life of Modigliani than I did and so it figured that I should stay here and listen to her speak. Yet I felt small in her presence. I wanted to discover this for myself. I didn't want to be spoon-fed. I acted quickly and almost without thought:

'I'd love to talk about this some more, Phyllis…'

'Absolutely.'

'…but the trouble is – I promised to meet up with Hilary later.' I didn't dare look Will in the eye and turned to Phyllis. 'She's my oldest friend; she's going through a bit of a tough time.'

'Oh! Well, yes, of course…'

'It's nearly ten,' Will said – as if that was his final word on the matter. But there was no hint of concern in his comment; just cold disapproval.

'Plenty of time,' I said. I hesitated. *Just ask me to stay,* I thought. *That's all you have to do. Say 'please Anna, why don't you stay?'* But Will said nothing. So I stood up very quickly and kissed Phyllis on both cheeks.

'Bye, Will,' I said. It was madness. He should have asked me where I was going and how I was going to get there, but he just looked baffled and a bit cross.

'I'm sure you two need a little more quality time together,' I said. Then I turned around, picked up my coat and left.

12

*'Do I contradict myself? Very well then, I contradict myself; I am
large, I contain multitudes.'* – Walt Whitman

Will was drinking red wine on the first evening that I met him. It was
Hilary's birthday and she'd invited a lot of her old Cambridge
chums. By midway through the evening, Will and I were ensconced
in a corner of the sofa, our intimacy accelerated by alcohol, leaning
towards one another, our foreheads nearly touching. A kiss surely
wasn't far off. It was then that he threw the death of his father into
the conversation.

I didn't know what to say but as I pulled back, he misunderstood
my response.

'I'm sorry,' he said. 'That killed the mood.'

It had all happened fairly recently, but having lost my father too,
I instantly felt closer to him.

'No. 's OK,' I said. 'I've been there.'

That evening seemed such a long time ago now. The
conversation that unravelled between us then formed an immediate
bond that went deeper than physical attraction or the imbibing of too
much red wine. That Will had such conventional good looks might
usually have made me wary. I associated physical beauty with
arrogance and vanity. There was a little of that, as I expected, but
there was more too. As Will spoke about his father's death, I admired
his openness, his lack of guile. It might have been premature but I
remember thinking 'so – this is it – this is him, "the one".'

Now, as I walked alone along St. Margarets Road – looking for a
cab, cursing my high heels and taking huge gulps of air to stop
myself from crying – I wondered if it was possible that I had got it

98

wrong about Will. What if I had made a mistake? Marriage was such an enormous thing: so final. How could one ever feel utterly certain about another person? And how was it possible that somebody that I loved so much could suddenly seem so alien and unknowable? Could the guy who wrapped his arms around me so tenderly on the night we met, be the same one who now let me walk out into the darkness away from him – and didn't stop me?

It was already too late to turn back. I was approaching Marble Hill House. Not a single cab had passed. They were probably paying the bill by now; perhaps they had already left the restaurant and were on their way home. I was wrong to hate her, I knew that; I was being unreasonable. I turned to look behind me – he might be running up the road towards me, full of regret – but there was nobody there.

We had talked about everything that night at Hilary's, before we ended up in bed together in his college flat, wrapped up tight in his duvet, with the heating turned up high and frost on the window-panes. Will was studying in London then, doing an MA at St. Martin's but he'd been reading a lot of French literature too and he was going through his Victor Hugo phase. We even talked about love.

'Of course, you know what Victor Hugo said,' Will murmured, as he lay naked beside me.

'Yeah, course I do,' I said. His words seduced me, but I was still marvelling at his physical beauty too. 'I'm an authority on Hugo, but tell me again.'

'He said "Life's greatest happiness is to be convinced that we are loved."'

'And what do you think about that?' I asked.

'Na,' he said. 'Not convinced. I'd rather be rich.'

'Me too,' I said and pulled his face towards my own.

I had reached the river now. I walked along the towpath, gritting my teeth, determined to keep putting one foot in front of the other. The full moon was high over the water and the river was calm, a low mist suspended above the surface. If something happened to me here, Will would probably never get over it. Did that attachment – the guilt he'd feel if some crazed axe-man leapt out and bludgeoned me to death – amount to love?

Across the water, lights gleamed in the warehouses of Eel Pie Island. A lone rower made his way along the river and it occurred to me that if I tried to live my life according to Victor Hugo's dictum, chasing this illusive "perfect love" like a holy grail, I might risk throwing away something infinitely deeper and more lasting than a fragile, intangible concept that was, in any case, destined never to be permanent.

I approached the pub, pausing for breath. The chill air caught my throat. The pub appeared busy; a few of the outside tables were full. Standing beneath a lamppost, I took a mirror from my handbag and reapplied my lipstick. Once inside, I headed for the bar.

The barman brought my gin and tonic and I spotted Hilary waving at me from the other side of the room. Next to her was Carl – he must have come along after class – and a few of the Martini Girls, together with another guy I didn't recognise. Carl caught my eye and I felt an unnerving rush of pleasure that made me want to turn around and run and not stop. Instead, I took a large gulp of gin and walked towards them. Carl flashed me a large, uncompromising grin.

'Anna, hey! Have you met Hal?'

I shook my head. So, this was the man Claudia was apparently toying with. He was a huge, broad-chested guy, with a ratted beard and a weak chin. He wore a grubby, once-white T-shirt, shorts and trainers.

'Hal, this is Anna,' Carl said. 'She just got back from a séance at the Groucho Club. Got in touch with Kingsley Amis apparently.'

'Don't envy you,' Hal said.

'Oh, he was pretty witty actually,' I replied. Hilary was on the other side of Hal, dressed in a shimmering bronze dress. I wondered why she was so tarted-up, then remembered that it was Frederica's birthday. I hadn't even brought a card.

'Happy birthday, Frederica!' I said, across the crowd.

'Thanks, Anna. So glad you could come,' Frederica said. I wanted to join the girls, but couldn't get past Hal's bulk.

'Where's Claudia?' I asked.

'No idea.' Hal said, but his mouth shuddered a little. 'So who else deigned to appear at this literary séance?' he asked, apparently keen to change the subject. 'What about Graham Greene? Any sign of him?'

I attempted to laugh flippantly but something about Hal made me uneasy. It was years since I'd read a Graham Greene novel and I couldn't think of anything to say. I should never have left the restaurant.

Frederica saved me. 'That's so funny you should mention Greene, Hal,' she said. Frederica's accent made her sound so formal; there was an earnestness about her and she spoke slowly, emphasising each word. 'I was reading a book of his literary criticism only yesterday. It was most interesting – an attack on "modern literature". He said literature had lost its way because it had no religious context. He said that most modern novels were populated by characters who – now what was it? I wrote it down...' She pulled a spiral notebook from her capacious black handbag and flicked through pages of scribblings to find the note that she was looking for. 'Here it is...' She peered at the page. '...superficial characters who "wandered about like cardboard symbols through a world that is paper-thin."'

I wondered if I'd ever become the kind of writer who would read literary criticism as a hobby and carry a spiral notebook to my birthday party.

'Well,' Hal said, 'that describes the characters in *The Quiet American* just perfectly.'

'Don't talk shite, Hal,' Carl said.

'I'm not talking shite. Anna will back me up, won't you, Anna?'

The Quiet American was one of the only Graham Greene novels that I *had* read. It was a long time ago and I could barely remember the plot, let alone the characters. Hal was a stranger to me, but I was wary of him and couldn't understand what Claudia might see in him. I found him physically repulsive – but it was not the overgrown beard, nor the body odour that put me off the man – but my suspicion that he had the capacity for humiliating me very deeply.

Hal must have seen the expression on my face. He read my silence too. 'Don't tell me, you haven't read it?' he said. So, my instinct had been right.

'Sorry – did I *miss* something?' He had chosen the wrong moment for a fight.

'An interesting response?' he replied.

'Oh – fuck off.' Who was this guy? Was he a *friend* of Carl's?

'Hey, Anna – seems like I met *you* in a good mood.'

'Absolutely,' I said. 'You should see me when I turn nasty.'

In a strange way, I was enjoying this. I was wound up and ready for it. Hilary was making faces at me as if to say: '*I'm so sorry, nothing to do with me.*' But she was stuck in a corner, barely able to squeeze past the other Martini Girls to rescue me.

'Do you *know* this girl, Carl?' Hal said. 'She's got a mean tongue.'

'Shut up, arsehole,' Carl said. 'Another drink, Anna?'

'Yes please.' I realised that I was trembling and tried to hide it. Carl was right; I could keep arguing or just walk away. I had achieved precisely nothing by coming here. Will would be furious at me and Phyllis would have been better company than this idiot.

'Come on, you can help me choose the peanuts,' Carl said.

I followed him to the bar and couldn't help but notice that despite his slight build, he was compact and muscular. He was casually dressed in jeans and T-shirt and he wore a strange yellow webbing satchel across his shoulder; I suppose it was meant to be 'preppy'.

'I'll have a Jack Daniels,' Carl said to the barman. 'Anna?'

'Bombay Ice with lime.'

As I picked up the glass, I promised myself it would be my last. I glanced across the room at Hilary and gave her a small, casual wave. She looked back at me, her expression anything but casual.

'God, I could do with a fag!' Carl fingered the packet of Marlboros that protruded from his pocket. 'This smoking ban does my head in.'

'Me too. Can I nick one to smoke on the way home?'

'You should buy your own.' His voice was delicious. The Belfast accent got me every time. He smiled directly at me, meeting my eyes and daring me to flirt back. I felt a little out of control, a little reckless. He beckoned me to an empty table on the other side of the room and I hesitated, but followed. *It's not as if I'm actually **doing** anything. I'm just having a drink with a mate, that's all.*

'Sorry about Hal,' Carl said, as he sat down. 'He's a good lad actually. But you wouldn't think it from first impressions.'

'No. You wouldn't.'

'He just split up from his wife.'

'Good for her,' I replied and despite himself, he laughed.

'Look, Anna, I know you've been out with Amis tonight,' he said. 'So you've probably had enough book talk, right?'

'Can never have enough book talk. And to be honest, Mart can be a bit of a bore.'

'I'll try not to be too dull then,' Carl said. 'I wouldn't want you to tar all of us literary types with the same brush.'

'Would I?' I wanted to touch his hair. *Whoa! Better stop right there. Too much to drink.*

Carl bent down, opened his satchel and pulled out a book. 'This is brilliant. Have you read it?'

He handed me a thin black paperback with a red title: *Stealing the Mona Lisa*. I shook my head. On the cover was a black and white photo of five people standing behind a rope barrier at an art gallery. They were leaning forward to gawp at an image that was out of sight.

'That looks like a *Doisneau*,' I said and immediately regretted it. It was a pretty obvious assumption and I was bound to be wrong.

'It is,' Carl said. 'It's not a well-known one though.'

'Yeah, makes a change from that couple kissing on all the Athena posters.' I wished I hadn't said that. I looked over my shoulder and saw Hilary on the other side of the bar; she beckoned me over and I nodded as if to say "OK, I'm coming" but didn't go. 'Anyway, what's the book about?'

'Oh,' Carl scratched his head. 'You know, it's a kind of philosophical tome on the meaning of emptiness.'

'Sounds pretentious.'

'Nah, 's me that's pretentious. The book's cracker.'

I smiled.

He leaned forward and took a swig of whisky. 'It's a fascinating premise,' he said. 'In the 1920s, the Mona Lisa was stolen from the Louvre…'

'Really?'

'It's true. It was a sensation, you can imagine. But listen to this: people came to look at the empty space.'

'You're kidding?'

'No. I mean, thousands came – folk who'd never bothered to even see the painting. Don't you think that's amazing? The space was more popular than the Leonardo.'

'Bit before its time then?'

'Aye, Martin Creed eat your heart out…'

Carl looked me in the eye again and I looked away. I was enjoying myself too much. It was so tempting to stay and talk, but I'd barely spoken to Hilary and the landlord would be calling last orders soon.

'We'd better join the others,' I said.

'Pity.' He was being blatant now. He bit his lip, stared harder at me, waiting to see what I'd do.

The worst thing was, I was tempted.

'Um. I have to go the loo,' I said. 'I'll be back in a minute.'

In the Ladies', I stood before the mirror and stared at my own reflection. I'd felt fine at the restaurant but those last couple of drinks had pushed me over the edge. *Thank God I walked away. If I'd just stayed a moment longer I might have messed up big time. Had I really considered going there, even for a second?* Carl was charming, of course – and if I'd been single, it would be pretty obvious where this was heading – but I was not single. I had Will.

I leant closer to the mirror; I should have looked washed out under the fluorescent lighting but I could see the flush of my cheeks. *Was I actually tempted? I ought to slap myself.* This was nothing but mindless lust, an idiotic urge for self-destruction. Or did I just want to get my own back? Was it the suspicion that somewhere Will had his Angela tucked away, that he was making a fool of me and that something was horribly wrong?

I placed my hand to my forehead and the person in the mirror followed suit. I wished that I could leave her there – faithful and forever questioning her lust. *Forever* – now that was the word that bothered me. Was I more afraid of marriage than I realised? Did the idea of walking up the aisle actually terrify me? "Til death us do part" and all that. And Will might have his Angela but what would I have? How would I know that this was right? How does anyone ever know?

I turned away from the mirror. I knew what I *ought* to do, but there was a nagging voice in the back of my mind. What if I was wrong about Will? What if Carl was the person I ought to be with? What if this was one of those vital moments where the decision you made would affect everything that followed – so if I made a mistake, the rest of my life would go spinning in some totally wrong direction?

Slowly – and without any idea what I was about to do – I walked back into the pub. Carl was at the table, waiting. I looked across the room, saw the Martini Girls, but Hilary was not with them.

'They're going back to Frederica's,' he said.

He was right; they were leaving the pub, not giving us a second glance. *Had Hilary given up on me?* Perhaps she was simply treating me like a grown-up.

'I think I'd better join them,' I said. 'I mean, there's so much I'd like to talk to you about; writing and stuff. But maybe it can wait until we're a bit more sober. I'm not sure that this is wise.'

'Definitely not wise to walk away right now. Sit down.'

'Well, just for a minute.'

'Good.'

'I'm getting married in September,' I said.

'Well, you're not about to be late for that.'

I laughed. 'I have to go. Really I do.'

He paused. 'He's a lucky lad, your boyfriend.' He held the silence for what seemed like a long time. I didn't move. 'Not too late to change your mind though.'

'That's outrageous!'

'I mean about leaving the pub.'

'Oh.'

'You don't look like somebody about to go. Look, you're taking your shoes off.'

I looked down at my feet. I'd kicked off my high heels, without thinking.

'It's very fetching.'

'Fetching?' I laughed. 'Isn't that a little Victorian?'

'I'm quite a fan of the Victorians actually.'

'Time please!' The voice of the landlord interrupted us. The lights in the pub flickered on and I looked away. The light was unforgiving.

'You know you have a habit of taking your shoes off,' he said.

'What are you talking about?'

'You did it in class the other day. It's very sexy.'

Really? Did I do that?

'What are you?' I said. 'Some kind of pervert.'

'Yes, probably.' He smiled and stood up. 'Come on then, I'll walk you back to the High Street.'

He stood up and I slipped my feet back into the heels. I followed him to the door.

Outside, the mist had risen over the river; I was reminded of a Whistler painting I'd once seen at the Tate, where everything was hazy and indistinct. The Martini Girls were already out of sight. Carl was so close, we were nearly touching; I could see his breath on the air.

'I don't know what Hilary would have made of that,' I said.

'Of what?'

'Us ignoring them.'

'We were just having a private conversation.'

'She didn't look impressed.'

'Is Hilary your keeper?'

'No, just my best friend.'

'Hey, look!' Three swans swam past. The fresh air hit me and I felt sick but didn't want Carl to know that. I hoped I wasn't going to do some mad teenage thing and puke.

He followed me to the water's edge.

'I told you how good I thought your work was, didn't I?'

'It's a few pages. I'm totally inexperienced.'

'I wouldn't have guessed.'

'Sure.' I wasn't going to fall for that one. How stupid did he think I was?

'I'm not certain I should come to your class,' I said. I started walking again and he followed.

'What are you talking about?'

Did I have to spell it out?

'Look, Anna.' He took my hand; it was absurdly thrilling. 'I don't play games. Yes, I find you attractive and it's against the rules to flirt with you, but it's done now. OK? But I wouldn't lie about the work. I wouldn't bullshit you on that. Ya have a talent, girl. Honest to God.'

'Beginners luck,' I said.

'I don't think so. Actually, you've got a week or so to think about it. I forgot to say I won't be teaching on Thursday. I wasn't thinking. There's a stand-in.'

'Oh.' *I must be out of my mind.*

'It's my book launch that evening. I haven't invited the students, but I'd like you to come.'

'Congratulations. But maybe I should just go to class.'

'It's your choice. I invited your pals earlier too. They seemed keen, so maybe you can all come?'

We were nearly at Eel Pie bridge again. Carl stopped; turned towards me. For a moment I was tempted.

'Hey – a cab!'

He lurched off towards the road, held out his hand and a black cab pulled up beside us. 'Here!' He handed me a small piece of card, an invitation, and I hopped inside, closed the cab door and smiled at him through the glass. *Why did I feel so disappointed?*

'Nice evening?' the cab driver asked.

'Yes,' I said. 'Very nice, thanks.'

I was going home to Will and Phyllis, to real life. But the idea of marrying Will – an idea that had seemed so ordinary before and so solid – now seemed a strange and almost difficult concept, a possibility that I could reach out and take or simply release.

13

'A writer is a person for whom writing is more difficult than it is for other people.' – Thomas Mann

'Cup of tea, Anna.'

'What?'

'I've brought you a cup of tea.'

I groaned and turned away. Surely, it wasn't time to get up yet? And where was Will? Why was Phyllis waking me?

'Will told me to wake you at seven.'

'He should wake me himself.'

'He's gone for a jog.'

'Oh God.'

She obviously wasn't going to leave me alone so I forced myself to sit and propped myself up with two pillows. Phyllis was dressed in a white seersucker dressing gown; her hair was tucked into an olive green scarf, like a hospital patient about to go into theatre.

'How come you're up?' I asked.

'Couldn't sleep. Jetlag. Will's been gone for an hour. Is he in training for a marathon?'

'No, just a bloody show-off.'

I had vague recollections of a dream; something sexual that did not involve her son. I turned to the clock.

'It's only half past six. Will left at five thirty?'

'Said he was on some new fitness programme.'

'Why are you waking me earlier than he said?'

'There's a funny smell in the kitchen. I wondered if you knew what it was?'

'You've woken me about a smell? It's probably Will, burning the bacon.'

'No. He had porridge.'

'A dead body perhaps?'

'I thought it would give us a chance to have a chat before you have to rush off to work. How was last night?'

It all came back to me in a rush; walking along the riverside with Carl McGahan, his arm around my shoulder, half hoping he would kiss me. That was the last time I would ever drink gin. 'It was lovely, thanks.'

'Will seemed a little upset at you rushing off like that.'

Oh, fuck OFF! 'Did he? I had warned him. He must have forgotten.'

'Well, never mind.' She appeared hesitant. 'What's that you're reading?'

'A biography of Modigliani. I'm about half way through.'

'No, this one.' She picked up the Loftus book from my bedside table. 'What do you make of it?'

'It has some useful ideas, but it's difficult to take it seriously.'

Phyllis bent over and clasped my hand; hers felt fragile and clammy.

'You know,' she said, 'Loftus is an old friend of mine.'

'Don't tell me. He visited your book group?'

'No. You don't understand.' She stood up and walked to the window, remained still, gazing out at the street below. It struck me as melodramatic, but I understood that she was serious. When she turned to face me again, her expression was vacant. 'I haven't seen him for some years.'

It was possible I was reading too much into this.

'He's a wonderful man. Such charisma.' She picked up his book again and ran her fingers along the spine.

'I think I'll take a bath,' I said. I got up and walked right past her. I noticed there was a tear in the corner of her eye but I ignored it.

I locked the bathroom door and began running a bath. As I undressed, the sound of running water lulled me. I sat on the edge of the bath, watching the steam rise. I was hung over and couldn't think straight.

The water was so hot, it near scalded me. I lowered myself in, made myself bear it; picked up the soap and lathered it across my arms. I still couldn't kill the paranoid thoughts. Where was Will going at this time of day? He'd always enjoyed jogging, but to leave at 5.30am? In all the stories I'd ever heard about other people's love affairs, I'd never known anyone eager enough to get up at 5am for it. What if Will was the exception? What if his subterfuge knew no bounds? I lay there for a long time, watching the colour of my body turn from pale fleshy white to a delicate pink.

'Anna! Anna!'

'Yes – what is it?'

'Are you OK?'

'Yes, 'course I am.'

How long had I been in there? I jumped quickly out of the bath – too quickly. I unhooked my silk kimono from the hook on the door and wrapped it about me. The speed of my movement had left me dizzy.

'I thought you might have fallen asleep,' Phyllis said, as I opened the door.

'No, no. Just wallowing.'

'What's that you're wearing?' Phyllis asked. 'That Geisha look really doesn't suit you.'

'Thanks. It's vintage actually.' I didn't care what she thought, it was my favourite. 'Got it from Oxfam, still in it's packet. Paula Yates. Late eighties.'

Phyllis grimaced. 'We don't wear garments designed by notorious suicides, darling.'

I didn't reply, determined not to sink to her level.

'Let's make a deal,' she said. 'If we ever take a trip to Ouranos, you and I, you must promise to get yourself a new bathrobe?'

'I *don't* think so.'

'Anna, a white bathrobe is hardly going to cost the earth, even on your salary.'

'I was talking about Ouranos. Isn't that Loftus's Greek resort?'

'You'd love it there, Anna.'

'Sure.'

'I mean it. What do you think? We should have some girls' time, just the two of us. I mean, why not? Couldn't you do with a break? And I'd love you to meet James!'

'James? You mean Loftus?'

'So what do you say?'

All I could think about was breakfast. 'I can't justify another holiday. We haven't even paid for the honeymoon yet.'

'My treat!' Phyllis said. 'I mean how on earth do you expect to get a decent run at this novel you're writing if you're always working at that God-damn theatre?'

The first rays of morning light cut through the curtains as she spoke and I sat down on the bed and pulled the kimono tighter. Phyllis had a point of course. On a Greek island, I would have time to read; I'd take a stack of books about Modigliani. If I could sort things out with Will before I left, it might be good for us to have a little time apart.

'I don't know. I do have a week's holiday in lieu. But...'

'Perfect; that's decided.'

She stood up and began pacing the room, her arms flapping in excitement, her sarong wafting about her body, revealing her bony limbs. 'You'll love Ouranos. We must make sure we stay on the right side of the island.'

'The right side?'

'There's Molos Bay and the Loftus Centre. We avoid Molos Bay at all costs.' She came closer, leant conspiratorially towards me. 'Tree-huggers. You know the type: sweat lodges; crystal healing. I've heard he's going to sell that side of things. Don't know how he allowed it to happen in the first place.' She shook her head. 'They share showers.'

'And the Loftus Centre?'

'Decent apartments. You wouldn't believe it was the same concern. Why don't we go online and check it out?'

I hadn't seen Phyllis this animated since her arrival; her eyes appeared brighter than usual and she couldn't sit still. This crazy idea had taken hold. I was humouring her.

The laptop was upstairs in Will's study and we were halfway up the stairs when I heard the front door opening below. That sound was followed by another: an odd, straining howl, as if someone had dragged a wounded animal into the hallway.

'Anna? Muuuum? Are you up there?'

'Will? Is that you?'

'I need some help. Fuck this hurts!'

I ran downstairs, fearful. We found Will slumped on the doormat. He'd taken off his right shoe and sock and was clutching his bare foot, wincing in pain.

'Christ – what happened?'

I wasn't sure how severe this was. I couldn't see anything wrong with his ankle. It appeared grazed and slightly swollen, but when he glanced up, his face was pale and wretched.

'I think I've broken my ankle,' he groaned. 'Oh God, Mum.'

Thanks Will. Nice one. You fall over in the playground and immediately you want your mother. Phyllis bent down by his side.

'How did you get home?' she asked.

'I walked. It's been fucking agony.'

'Mind your language,' Phyllis said.

'It's taken over an hour.'

'Didn't you consider hitch-hiking?' I asked.

I didn't know why I was being so spiteful. Had I really not forgiven him for last night? The man I loved was suffering and all I could do was play it down and be sarcastic. If he'd broken his ankle, how could he have walked all the way home?

I'd taken it too far. Will's face crumpled and for a minute I thought he was going to cry. I really hoped he wouldn't. This was divine vengeance for my flirtation with Carl.

'We'd better get you to casualty,' I said. 'What happened anyway?'

He sniffed and gritted his teeth; his nose crinkled. After a gasp or two, he managed to get a few words out. 'I fell off a kerb.'

Oh Jesus, I thought. It's hardly *Touching the Void*.

I dressed quickly and left a message at the office, telling them I'd be late. Natasha would be furious – she'd probably ask why his mother couldn't do the bloody hospital trip – but I'd worry about that later. En route to the hospital, my thoughts were vile and selfish. All I could think about was the wedding and whether he'd be walking up the aisle in plaster. We still hadn't spoken about last night and I put my coldness down to our disagreement. Phyllis took over and I let her. When we arrived, she spoke to the receptionist whilst Will and I took a seat beneath fluorescent strip lighting on moulded plastic chairs. He found a sailing magazine, which seemed to function as a powerful painkiller, whilst I was left reading posters about rheumatoid arthritis and testicular cancer. By the time Will limped in to see the doctor – insisting he go alone – I was ready for coffee.

'Shall I get you something from the machine?' I asked Phyllis.

'Does it do green tea?'

'I don't know what kind of vending machines you have in New York – but no, not on the NHS.'

'Double espresso, then,' she said. 'With sugar.'

I returned with two identical cups, handed one to Phyllis and sat down beside her.

'You know, Will would be a fool to let you slip through his fingers,' she said.

I wasn't sure of her meaning but decided not to ask. 'I'm sorry, I've been a bit useless today; I must be tired.'

'Or hung over?'

'That too.' I took a sip of lousy coffee. 'Maybe that's why Will fell over. Too much alcohol still in his system.'

'I did tell him,' she said. 'But he's a big boy now.'

I was about to reply when my phone beeped. 'Oh damn. I forgot to switch it off. I'd better go outside,' I said.

As I walked out to the car park, my stomach churned. I hadn't eaten since I woke up, which probably explained my tearfulness. I opened the text.

Thanks 4 last night. Hope u can make my launch? C x

I experienced a tightening of my gut, as if a piece of fishing twine had got tangled inside and was caught on something; each time I moved it just became more knotted. I had hoped last night might go away and the small flirtation would have no consequence. Should I ignore the text? That would be the most sensible thing to do. Yes, definitely, I would ignore it. Carl would get the message then. I didn't have to join Summer School. I could walk away from the whole situation.

Except that it would be impossible to avoid Carl. He was too friendly with the Martini Crowd and unless I wanted to cut myself off from them too, I had no choice but to see him. It was only an attraction and I would have to deal with it. I'd just reply as if he were a mate. It was extremely simple.

Hope so too. Will let u know, A x

I hesitated before adding the kiss. I removed it, but the message seemed a little callous without it, so I put it back on. As soon as I pressed "Send", I regretted it. I might not be asked to launch parties every day, but I should forget about this one right now.

I got back to the waiting room just in time. As I arrived, Will was limping out of the consulting room on crutches. His left foot – exactly as I'd dreaded – was clad in plaster.

'Oh, poor you.' I hugged him. 'You really *did* break your ankle?'

'My foot. Metatarsal bone. I'm going to have this on for six to eight weeks. At least I'll be out of plaster in time for the wedding.'

'You walked for an hour with a broken foot! God, what a bitch I am. I should have taken it more seriously. Who would have thought you could break your foot falling off a kerb?'

'I did tell you.'

I probably ought to kiss him, I thought, but I wasn't in the mood and I suspected he wasn't either. As we walked out to the car park again, a woman and her teenage daughter passed by. The girl was holding a bloody rag against a gash on her forehead, but despite her injury, she turned to look at Will and I recognised her expression, the intrigued smile that crossed her lips at the mere sight of him. Only I couldn't see his beauty today. Everything about him irritated me. And the worst thing was, I didn't even know what had gone wrong;

115

something had changed, but I had no way of grasping what it was.

14

'Reimagining implies some measure of forgetting. The actual or factual has to lose definition, become fluid, before the imagination can begin its task of reconstruction. Data transferred straight from the research area to the book will simply remain data. It will be imaginatively inert.' – Rose Tremain

PATHWAY TO EMOTIONAL EQUILIBRIUM
('HOW TO BE A LITERARY GENIUS' – APPENDIX A)

In order to thrive as a creative individual, it is first necessary to shed those habits that are harmful to creative growth. Emotional Equilibrium is a prerequisite for artistic development. Contrary to popular belief, artists do not thrive in an environment of pain, addiction, struggle or poverty. Artists who work and succeed in such emotional environments, do so in spite of circumstances not because of them.

Answer the following questions to determine your current Emotional Equilibrium Level.

Upstairs in bed, I turned the Loftus book over and picked up the glass of chilled Muscadet at my side. Phyllis and Will were still awake. I'd left them bonding over *The Real Housewives of Beverley Hills* on the sofa. Will said that being an invalid gave him an excuse to watch trash. He'd been in front of the TV most of the evening, his foot propped up by a pouffe and several cushions. He didn't appear bothered by the accident; he even seemed mildly amused.

The Loftus book had drawn me in at last. It was trashy too, in its way, but I had to admit that he asked good questions. Modigliani had his share of "pain, addiction, struggle and poverty". Did his success stem from his suffering or did he succeed despite it? I placed my glass down at the bedside and leant back against the pillow. I was thinking about a painting of Jeanne, one of Modi's last works: her head tipped to one side, her auburn hair, the elongated neck. Jeanne's existence was more tragic than magnificent I thought, yet there must have been moments in her life of sheer, unadulterated pleasure. She was the muse of a devastatingly attractive, undiscovered genius. She had abandoned her bourgeois family to be with this "debauched derelict", to become a painter herself. *Would she have been a better painter had she not experienced the extremes of passion that he surely drove her to?* Perhaps not, but she might at least have lived.

I turned the story over in my head. Modi had promised to marry Jeanne – just as soon as he found his identity papers. She was the mother of his child, the only one he ever recognised as his own. He was as faithful to her as he'd ever been to anyone; but that was not the same thing as fidelity. Zbrowski, his dealer, couldn't stand her; he believed Jeanne distracted Modi from his work. It was Zbrowski who should have come as Modi lay dying. She wanted Zbrowski to save them. It was Zbrowski she was waiting for.

I turned off the bedside lamp and lay down. I wished that Phyllis wasn't here, that Will had not broken his foot, that he had never called me Angela. There was something so *romantic* about the liaison between Modi and Jeanne; they were the archetypal doomed lovers. Yet if the narrative held a certain glamour, the reality must have been very different. Jeanne spent the last week of her life with a dying man spitting blood, stinking of sardines and alcohol. Modi lay there cursing himself for filling the world with pictures that nobody wanted, yet within weeks of his death, art dealers were making a small fortune from his work. Soon Jeanne was also dead. She walked backwards out of a Paris window.

I must have fallen asleep thinking about Jeanne because the next thing I knew was a banging sound on the stairs. Will wasn't in the room and I leapt up, disorientated. Who was that? The noise was unfamiliar and it was getting louder. An intruder? But where was Will? I didn't even have a weapon. The heaviest object in the room was probably my hair straighteners.

Whoever it was, was just behind the door. I froze. There was nothing I could do. When the door opened, I let out a small scream.

'Fucking hell, Anna – you having a nightmare?'

'Will! Oh God, I thought you were a burglar.'

'Do I look like a burglar?'

'Sorry, I'm half asleep.' I propped myself up on my elbow. He stood in the doorway on crutches. 'You were noisy.'

'You try getting up the stairs with these things.'

He limped over to the bed, sat down and bent to kiss me.

'God, what a day.' I watched him as he undressed, unbuttoning his shirt and tossing it at the foot of the bed. He unbuckled his belt and I saw him hesitate.

'Do you want some help?' I asked.

'Do you mind?'

I got up and came round to his side of the bed, helped him with his shoe, then unfastened his jeans and slid them over his hips and the plaster cast. I hadn't expected to be turned on, but Will reached down and stroked my hair and there was something erotic about the act of undressing him. Before I knew it, I was going down on him.

It was a mistake, of course. I began enthusiastically but very quickly I regretted it. I knew I was trying to prove something; that last night's flirtation with Carl McGahan was meaningless; that Phyllis's presence in our home was irrelevant; that I was wrong to ever suspect Will of infidelity. What had begun with passion now became mechanical: the physical act of fellatio.

I tried to hide my lack of pleasure but Will was not stupid. He was barely responding. He pulled away.

'What's up?' he asked.

'Nothing. What are you talking about?'

'Something's the matter, Anna.'

'Nothing's the matter. The only thing that's the bloody matter is the fact that clearly my blowjobs aren't up to scratch.'

'Your heart wasn't in it.'

'Does one's *heart* have to be in a blowjob? Oh for Christ's sake.'

I wanted to go to the bathroom and brush my teeth, to wash the scent and taste of him away.

'This isn't a one night stand!' he said.

'You've been reading too many *Telegraph* editorials on family values.' *Call me sexist, but what bloke ever complained at his girlfriend being too sluttish with him?*

'What the hell is up with you, Anna?'

'I might ask you the same question.'

He turned away then and reached for his crutches. He stood up, pulled his shirt on and hobbled out of the room, muttering *'I'm not listening to this'* under his breath.

'And the honeymoon hasn't even begun!' I called after him. He didn't turn, but even if he had, it was dark, so he would not have seen my tears.

I heard Will go upstairs to the study. It was too late to work, but I knew that's what he'd be doing; I often thought his drawing board could save him from anything.

I couldn't sleep, so I put the lamp on and sat up. Will had left his iPhone next to the bed. *Why hadn't I thought of that before?* Until now, I'd never taken much interest in it. I imagined his calendar to be full of dull appointments with art editors and links to websites about obscure French comic books. I picked it up and keyed her name into the search field:

A n g e l a

I held the phone in my hand, stared and waited. The calendar icon appeared and I clicked it.

June 27th

8pm Angela and Co

Not just a single Angela, but a whole bloody troupe of them. *Tomorrow. The date of Carl's launch party. Angela and Co. Like an eighties dance troupe, all sporting legwarmers.*

It was like watching a movie on TV when something dramatic happens and you don't believe it because it seems too far-fetched. I closed my eyes and opened them again but the words on the screen didn't vanish.

When I heard Will on the stairs again, I couldn't even pretend. He limped in, still wearing only the shirt and his pants, revealing more flesh than was strictly necessary. All I could do was hold the phone up, accusing him.

'What is it?'

But he knew.

'Angela.'

He didn't even flinch.

'Don't look at me as if you don't know what I'm talking about!' He managed a smile, as if this amused him.

'Maybe that's why you couldn't keep it up just now.'

'All right,' he said, and sat down beside me. 'You're right. I should have told the truth.'

'Spill it out!' I clenched my teeth hard. I didn't want him to see me trembling.

'Angela is just a woman I met on an exhibition stand a couple of months ago. You remember? At Earl's Court?'

'I don't care where you *met* her Will. Who is she, a journalist or something?'

'No. God, no.' He laughed. 'Do you remember, I was approached to do some cartoons for that Lads' Mag *Glam-Go*?'

'How can I forget?' *Was the mention of Glam-Go supposed to cheer me up?* 'Do you want to dig yourself a deeper hole?'

'I visited the *Glam-Go* stand. Angela is a *bunny girl* for Christ's sake. Angela and her mates were employed to attract punters to the stand.'

I did my best to smile but it took every ounce of my energy.

'So you have a date tomorrow evening with a *bunny girl* and the fact that she's only a *bunny girl* is supposed to make it all right?'

He appeared perfectly calm as if I had absolutely nothing to worry about. Did he not really *fathom* why I was angry? His shirt was open. He was holding out his foot at an odd angle and wincing.

'You've got it all wrong, hon. 'Look, *Glam-Go* was right next to *The Telegraph*. I was chatting to the editor just to pass the time when some PR person from *The Economist* came over and handed us free tickets to a party. Angela's going to bring her boyfriend. And I got a ticket for you too.'

'But it's tomorrow – and you hadn't mentioned it.'

'I'd kind of forgotten about it. Anyway, isn't it your writing class tomorrow?'

I shrugged. 'Actually I'm invited to a party as well.'

'Great!'

'What do you mean 'Great!'? I hate that about you.'

'What?'

'That you're not even slightly jealous.'

'Why should I be jealous? More to the point, why are you? You can't be jealous of a porn star!'

'Oh, so now she's a 'porn star'…'

'Same difference.'

'You're forgetting one small fact.'

'What's that?'

'You called out her name when we were making love.'

I saw the giveaway involuntary movement of his Adam's apple. Such a small, unconscious sign but it revealed so much. He didn't speak at first and it frightened me. The silence seemed too intense.

'It was just a fantasy, Anna,' he said at last. 'A stupid fantasy.'

'I'd be more impressed if you were fantasising about somebody with half a brain.'

'Oh, *come on!*'

'Don't tell me, she's also a member of Mensa?'

He stood up and walked to the fireplace, began fiddling with a small stone paperweight on the mantelpiece, as if engaging with any inanimate object were an improvement on speaking to me. 'I don't believe this, Anna,' he said, under his breath.

'*You* don't believe it? I can't believe I'm about to marry someone whose sexual fantasies are so bloody predictable!'

Then it occurred to me: he might not be telling the truth. The "porn star" business might be an elaborate deception.

'What's her full name?'

'What?'

'I want to know that you're not making this whole thing up.'

He laughed.

'What are you laughing about?'

'I couldn't make up a name like hers. Look, if you don't believe me, pass me my wallet.'

I picked it up and gave it to him. I watched as he rifled through business cards.

'Here…'

He pulled out a bright pink card and handed it to me as if this were a perfectly normal occurrence – as if this sort of thing happened every day. Her name was embossed in silver letters.

Angela Crystal – Actress
http://www.angelacrystal.com

'*Crystal*?' I said. '*Crystal*? An actress?'

'She's just somebody I bumped into at a conference.'

'Yeah, right.'

His face fell. *Good! I wanted him to feel bad.*

'You're making a mistake,' he said. 'There's nothing in this.'

Of course there wasn't. *Was he having a mid-life crisis twenty years too soon?*

'Sure,' I said. 'Nothing at all.' I stood up to go.

'*Fucking fantastic*,' he muttered, to my back. As if it was me who had done something wrong.

I left the room, slamming the door behind me.

Upstairs, the yellow glow from the streetlights shone through the Velux windows. It was late, close to midnight, but sleep was the last thing on my mind. *Angela Crystal*. I sat down at Will's desk and Googled her. My hands were shaking and I was finding it difficult to type.

Contrary to popular fucking belief, I thought, *artists do not thrive in an environment of pain, addiction, struggle or poverty*.

I did not want to enter her website, but if I was to have a hope in hell of fighting back against this woman, I'd have to face the truth. *How bad could it be, after all?* Whatever she revealed, I was ready for it. I took a deep breath and double-clicked.

15

'To cure jealousy is to see it for what it is, a dissatisfaction with self.' – Joan Didion

I saw it first in the way she walked. I had agreed to meet Hilary on the concourse at Waterloo and I caught sight of her before she spotted me. Even from a distance, there was something about her – the way she held her head, the swing of her arms – that revealed a change in her. As she came closer and noticed me, she gave an exaggerated wave. It was years since I'd seen her like this; she reminded me of the old photographs of herself, the sixth-form Hils, bursting with confidence and enthusiasm, not yet knowing the meaning of doubt.

I had dressed up too, but confident was the last word I'd use to describe myself. I'd found a strapless fifties-style frock in my wardrobe – just the kind of thing that Julia Claiborne liked to wear. I played it down with my denim jacket and a faux-ruby brooch.

'Bloody hell, Anna,' Hilary said, hugging me, 'is something the matter?'

Trust Hilary to see right through me.

'You don't look so bad yourself,' I said. 'Apparently the God of Literary Agents will be attending, so I thought I'd better make an effort.'

'Buddy Sellers is not God,' Hilary replied. 'But on the other hand, George Lagana…'

'What? What are you talking about?'

'You won't believe this. I've just sold my film rights for the new book!'

'No?'

She nodded.

'I thought your publisher rejected the draft?'

She kept jiggling about, as if she was unable to stand still in one place, like a bottle of champagne about to pop.

'Weirdly enough, the publisher has mysteriously changed his mind.'

'Thanks to George Lagana?'

'It doesn't seem real, Anna. I met him this afternoon...'

'You didn't tell me!'

'I only found out myself this morning. I got a call from my agent and was summoned to a meeting in Bloomsbury.'

'My God – my friend the Hollywood scriptwriter.'

'Somebody else will write it. And it'll probably never get made.'

'It probably will. That's so brilliant, Hilary. Well done.'

I could hear the flatness in my own voice. Hilary probably heard it too, but it was nothing to do with her good news. I could not get the image of Angela Crystal out of my mind.

'I was really worried about telling you,' she said.

'Why would you be worried? I'm really pleased for you. You so deserve it.'

Hilary was not stupid. She could tell something was bothering me.

'Let's get you a cup of strong coffee,' she said. I nodded meekly and followed her to the café.

I had prepared for the worst: explicit, shocking images or hard porn. Most likely, I thought, it would be something garish and predictable. But what I had not prepared myself for was how delectably beautiful she would look; the unmistakeable look of innocence in her eyes.

I could see her still: an apparently natural blonde with entirely unnatural breasts, dressed in a bubble-gum pink basque. Her beauty transcended the clichés. In spite of the heavy make-up, her face commanded attention. She had a long nose, delicate bone structure and perfect almond eyes. Modi would have adored her. I felt only a desperate, aching envy.

I waited at the table. Hilary was carrying two steaming mugs of

125

coffee and placed one down in front of me.

'So what's the matter?' she said, as she sat down.

Angela's website was polished and professional. She must have spent a fortune on the design. Her logo was a stylish abstract shape, suggestive of a bunny's ears. I spent a few minutes there, briefly checking out her blog and her availability for corporate functions. I glimpsed at the "private area" for "members only" but I had no intention of joining the *Crystal Club*.

I shook my head.

'You seem a bit upset.'

'I'm fine – but what about you? Hollywood beckons...'

'You must be kidding. Remember what happened to Frederica?'

'Not a clue.'

'The film rights to her first novel were bought for half a million, but the film never got made and now the paperback's been pulped.'

'Brutal.'

'Yeah.'

'At least she's wealthy now,' I said.

'There is that.'

'You're not really all right, are you?'

'If Will wants to go out with a bunny girl, that's his problem, I suppose.'

'What? What are you talking about?'

'Exactly that. He claims they're just good friends, but he's out with her tonight.'

'You are kidding?'

'No, absolutely not.'

'Why didn't you stop him?'

'He has to stop himself, Hils. He says it's nothing. Maybe he's telling the truth.'

I tried to convince myself that this was the right thing. I'd leave Will alone to do whatever Will was going to do – I'd test him. Wasn't that the best way? If you love someone, set them free? But if it was the right thing to do, why did I keep bursting into tears at inconvenient moments? If it was the right thing to do, why did it hurt so much?

As we descended the stairs to The Medici Bar, the partygoers burst into applause. We had missed Carl's reading. I could see him on the other side of the crowded basement, placing a book down on the table, smiling with affected coyness.

An underground bar, with raspberry red walls and an absurdly low ceiling, the room felt more like a torture chamber than a prime literary venue. Somewhere, on the other side of London, the *Economist* party was in full swing. I imagined a light, airy ballroom with bright chandeliers and cocktail waitresses offering Campari and soda to the guests. I pictured Will, sidling up to Angela Crystal, whispering something that nobody else could hear.

Now I regretted coming here. I opened my mouth to say as much to Hilary. Perhaps I could go, before anyone noticed me, but it was too late. Frederica had spotted us and she was leading the rest of the Martini crowd in our direction. Before I knew it, Hilary was telling the others about her film deal and I was nodding, yet trying to make myself inconspicuous. I wondered if it might be better, under the circumstances, for me to avoid Carl altogether. In any case, he'd surely be far too busy with his publishers to bother with me. It was so noisy here. It would be easy to get lost in the crowd.

But no! He was onto us already. He too was weaving his way across the room, fixing on me with what I could only assume was the coolest expression he could muster. Behind him was a tall, bespectacled man who looked familiar, though I couldn't place him. As Carl stopped to whisper to him, Hilary nudged me.

'It's Buddy Sellers,' she said. Hilary was slightly allergic to Buddy – he'd rejected her work earlier in her career. She backed off, out of his way, as Carl came closer.

I immediately felt uncomfortable. Carl approached me. He stopped and looked at me – stared, as if he'd never seen me before. If he noticed that Buddy and the Martini crowd were observing him, he didn't seem to care. A small smile crossed his lips; he nodded.

'Anna Bright,' he said.

He was looking at me as if he were Hamlet gazing at Ophelia, as if at any moment he might ask if I were honest and fair, as if he was about to suggest a nunnery was the best place for a girl like me. I could think of nothing to say.

He turned to Buddy. 'Don't you think she's beautiful?'

Buddy nodded. 'Very.'

It occurred to me that Buddy looked exactly as you imagined somebody called Buddy would look: like an American high school sweetheart type. He was muscular with a broad face and a strong jaw, but there was something weird about his eyes, half-hidden beneath old-fashioned horn-rimmed spectacles. He was slightly cross-eyed which was surprisingly disconcerting.

'I haven't formally introduced you to Anna, have I?' Carl said.

'Well, it's always good to meet a new girlfriend of Carl's,' he said, archly.

I laughed. 'Ha ha. Do I *look* like Carl's girlfriend?' I addressed my question to the rest of the Martini crowd, most of whom seemed faintly amused by this scene. Only Hilary was not smiling.

'Yes,' Buddy said. 'Yes, I think you do. What are you drinking, Anna?'

'Campari and soda,' I said. 'If you can't beat them, join them.'

'Perfect!' Sellers said.

'I'm going to get a beer,' Hilary announced and moved towards the bar, not looking back. The other girls trailed after her and I stood, divided between my friend and my ambition.

'Actually, I think I'll just go get a beer too,' I said.

'Nonsense,' Buddy replied.

Then Carl took my hand and held it tight. Nobody noticed, nobody was looking, except Buddy – and he didn't seem to care. I remembered how I'd felt when Carl hailed the cab, when the cab door closed.

'I'll get you that Campari,' Buddy said and followed the Martini Girls to the bar.

Carl was still staring at me. I looked away.

'I mean it,' he said.

'Mean what?'

'About you being beautiful.'

'You're pissed.'

'Only a bit.'

'I'm taken.'

'I know.'

He put his arms around me all the same and kissed me, he pressed his lips hard against mine and for the briefest of moments – I let it happen, I responded.

Then I pulled away, but it was too late. The damage was done. Carl looked at me, his intense blue eyes demanding more.

I shook my head. 'I can't.' *What the hell had I been thinking of? Had I gone totally mad?* I wanted to turn around, find out who'd seen. Maybe nobody had. That was wishful thinking. I caught a glimpse of Hilary, her expression of blank astonishment.

'I'm sorry. That was stupid,' I said.

'Don't say that.' Carl curled his fingers about mine; his lips quivered a little. 'You can't pretend it's not happening.'

'Can't I? I'd better go find my friend. You have a lot of people to talk to.'

He shook his head. 'Not interested.'

'Yes, you are.'

'Really. Not in the mood.'

'Campari and soda!' Buddy was back already. 'Sorry? Did I disturb anything?'

'What's that?' Carl said, as Buddy handed him a beer.

'You on the spirits too?' I said to Buddy; anything to avoid talking about what he'd probably just seen.

'It's mineral water,' he said.

'You had enough?'

'No. I don't drink. I'm a Buddhist. It's against my faith.'

'Oh, I forgot. Of course! I read that profile of you in *The Telegraph*.' He nodded, unimpressed. The article was coming back to me now; that explained why I'd recognised him in the first place. 'But I know Buddhists who drink...'

Buddy leant closer. Beneath the thick lenses of his glasses, he widened his eyes. 'I wasn't sure whether to do that interview,' he said. 'I think it paid off. Some people regard me as a bit of an oddity.'

'Part of your charm,' Carl said.

He turned to me. 'My faith is at the core of who I am,' he said. It was difficult to be heard above the music; he had to raise his voice. 'Why don't you come to the Temple, Anna? Get Carl to bring you along.'

I hesitated. Some people would kill for an invitation like that. Carl put his hand against the small of my back; I couldn't go there. 'Well, thanks,' I said.

'You should read Anna's novel, Buddy.'

'Really?'

'*The Modigliani Girl*,' I said.

Buddy nodded, considering it. It was not every day that one had the opportunity of pitching one's novel to one of the most eminent literary agents in the country. I should have had an elevator pitch at the ready but I was entirely unprepared. The warmth of Carl's palm against my back distracted me. It felt like stepping into somebody else's life – and if only it really were somebody else's life, I might have enjoyed it, but it was not. It was *my* life and I was making a mess of it.

'I'd love to read your work,' Buddy said. 'Carl has good taste.'

Is Carl going to tell Buddy all I've written is one lousy chapter?

'Here's my card, Anna,' Buddy said. 'Give me a call.'

'Thanks.'

Buddy's phone beeped then and he took it out and glimpsed at a message. It was obviously good news; his teeth fair dazzled me.

'Carl, there's someone here I must introduce you to,' he said and he gave Carl a little shove, at which Carl blew me a kiss and was gone.

'Are you OK?' Hilary was right behind me. I couldn't work out whether her expression was disapproving or merely sad.

'Not really.'

'You're not falling in love with him are you?'

'I barely know him.'

'That's normally a prerequisite for love!'

The music was getting louder now and it was becoming increasingly difficult to hear each other speak. I beckoned Hilary over to the far side of the room where it was quieter; we found a plush velvet sofa and sank into it.

'Oh God, I'm sorry. It's such a *mess*, Hils. I feel a bloody idiot. I shouldn't have come here; it's only lust, I'm sure of it; I'm so confused.'

'Maybe you just need to stay away from him for a while?'

'What if I'm mistaken? What if he really is 'Mr Right'?'

She shook her head. 'No such thing. You don't believe all that crap do you?'

'Cynic!'

'Don't you think you should just give Will a chance?'

I didn't know anything any more.

'You haven't slept with him, have you?'

'No! It's just I'm suddenly questioning everything. I mean, when I think about Will, I feel weirdly empty. I keep imagining him with this bunny girl and it makes me wonder whether I even know him at all. I keep thinking that it can't be happening and he can't possibly be out with her and I didn't just kiss Carl and...'

I couldn't speak any more. Hilary leaned back into the sofa and took a long swig of beer. Her lipstick had faded and I noticed the dark roots of her hair just starting to appear. She said nothing but her silence was enough.

'It's OK, I'm not going to do anything stupid.'

'Buddy seemed to like you,' Hilary said. Perhaps she thought distraction was the best idea.

'Buddy doesn't know that I've got nothing to offer him.'

I turned away, not wanting to look her in the eye. Sometimes it felt as if Hilary knew me better than I knew myself. Close by, I saw Julia, waving as she approached.

'*There* you are!' she shouted, over the music. 'I thought we'd lost you. Oh nice dress! It's too noisy here. We thought we'd head over to the Groucho; celebrate your film deal, Hils?'

She was kidding, wasn't she? This was a joke? Yet nobody else was laughing.

We went upstairs and outside, in the porch, we bumped into Carl again. He was standing at the top of the stairs with Buddy. Buddy was introducing him to somebody; they were shaking hands and when I saw who it was, I nearly choked. I looked around, expecting to see a swarm of paparazzi, but there were none. Obviously. He might be a Literary Icon but that didn't make him a "celebrity".

Rashid Sulyaman was unmistakable. His hooded eyes glanced in my direction and briefly held mine. Carl's back was turned and he didn't notice me. It was better that way. Julia was hovering, hoping for an introduction, but Sulyaman was engrossed in conversation. Carl was nodding his head, leaning in; their body language suggested an instant rapport. Ten minutes ago, Carl had eyes for nobody but me. *"How fickle!"* I thought as I tugged on Hilary's arm and walked away.

We headed up St Martin's Lane, past the Opera House and onto the Charing Cross Road; we cut past the edge of China Town where ugly red ducks hung on vicious hooks in shop-windows.

'Poor duckies,' Julia said.

Will and I hadn't given much thought to the ducks when we had our first official date, just down the road, in the Golden Pagoda. We had met at Hilary's party and behaved like intimates from the beginning. That night we ate our way through a great pile of crispy duck, plum sauce, spring onions and pancakes. I'd started off drinking mineral water and nibbling at the dim sum but Will had mocked my feeble appetite. Before long I was slurping Tiger Beer and stuffing my face, trying to eat crunchy seaweed with chopsticks and ordering sweet and sour pork balls for main course.

I wondered whether Will was eating out this evening. Or whether the Will who shared that Chinese meal with me five years ago would recognise the Will who was toying with a porn star on the other side of town? The thought was painful and I blocked it out.

By the time we reached Dean Street, I was shivering. It was only then that I realised my mistake.

'Damn!'

'What's the matter?' Hilary asked.

'I've left my jacket at The Medici Bar.' It was my favourite denim, fraying in all the right places: irreplaceable. My dad had bought me that jacket and the idea of losing it was unthinkable. 'I'm going to have to go back.'

'I'll come with you.' Hilary seemed a bit too eager.

'Why don't you text Carl?' Julia said. 'He'll look after it for you.'

'Carl will probably be distracted by Sulyaman, don't you think?' Hilary said.

'No. Julia's right. Maybe he can look after it.'

I took out my phone. I didn't want to call Carl now. It would make more sense to go back and get it myself, except that the girls were eager to get to the Groucho and we were close now. I'd try texting him first.

Carl, Sorry, left my denim jacket on the back of sofa; the velvet one by the fireplace. Has ruby brooch on collar. Can u retrieve? Anna. x

I felt uneasy. Carl would be discussing literary theory with Sulyaman by now. My request barely stood a chance. Why did I say it was a ruby? Wouldn't he be able to tell it was a cheap paste trinket from Accessorize?

'Come on,' Julia said. 'Let's go in and get a drink.'

I hesitated. I needed to be sure I wouldn't lose the jacket.

'Perhaps I should go back.'

There was no way that Carl would reply. He had better things to do and I was not in the mood for more drinks. What did it matter that I'd met Buddy Sellers when the whole "writer" thing was nothing more than an idea, a fragile dream? I should go home and read about Jeanne, put a few words down. It was a waste of time being here. I wanted to be at my desk.

Instead my phone was buzzing. It was Carl.

I have the jacket hostage. Just figuring out the ransom.

'Shit.'

'Can't he find it?' Julia said.

'No. It's safe. Let's go inside.'

Julia flashed her membership card, signed us in and we meandered through the crowded bar and followed her up the staircase. Hilary grabbed my arm.

'You're not going to do anything stupid, are you?' she whispered.

'Course not.'

I knew Carl's meaning but it was a flirtation, nothing more. It didn't have to lead to anything. We followed Julia upstairs, found a table adorned with huge white lilies and sat down. The flowers were almost indecent.

'What do they remind you of?' I said to Hilary.

'Bloody hell – *how* much have you had to drink?'

'No – I don't mean that. Well, I do – but think about it…'

She shook her head, drew a blank at first. Then she got it.

'Miss Thorne! Ha ha…'

'What's this?' Frederica asked.

'D.H. Lawrence,' Hilary replied. 'We studied *Sons and Lovers* at school together.'

'I didn't know you two went back that far.'

'The famous lily scene,' Hils said. '"*The tall white lilies were reeling in the moonlight…*"'

'Now I'm impressed.'

'Drinks anyone?' Julia said, handing out the menus.

I leant back, gazing at the rows of spirits behind the bar, the long glittering mirrors.

'God, it's all there,' Hilary said. 'How scary. "*She touched the big, pallid flowers on their petals, then shivered…*"'

'Now I know why you made it to Cambridge and I didn't.'

'Oh, rubbish. Rote learning means nothing.'

Maybe she was right. What I remembered most of all about that time was the words themselves; words had magical properties in those days. They conjured up whole worlds. Mrs Morrell's garden, the intensity of the blooms in the moonlight. I had my issues with Lawrence – Hilary and I had spent hours debating it.

A waiter placed several little pots of Twiglets on the table and hovered. 'Shall we just get a couple of bottles of Pinot Grigio?' Julia asked.

Everybody agreed.

The scent of the lilies was overwhelming. I reached out and touched the stamens, rubbing the pollen between my fingers.

'Careful! That stuff stains,' Frederica said.

We had lilies at Dad's funeral too. Not this type of course – the Lawrentian type, the Arum lily, austere white blooms with violent yellow stamens. Hilary was there too that day. She watched as the flowers were laid out on our front lawn and held my hand when the hearse arrived.

'So, Vicky, what's the latest on your agent situation?' Frederica asked.

'Oh don't ask. I am *incapable* of making a decision.'

There was no point in being maudlin. Dad would have liked to see me here – he enjoyed a good party himself. I could hear Mum's voice. *"Your Dad would have been proud of you."* But would he? I wondered. Would he really? I suppose he would have enjoyed the idea of me mixing with the right people in the right places; the idea of my literary success. But he knew as well as I did that being with the right people didn't amount to bugger all if you didn't have the substance behind it.

The waiter delivered the wine and Twiglets and Julia offered them around. I should have been grateful. I had just attended a glitzy party where London's brightest literary agent had singled me out for attention, given me his card and asked me to get in touch. A celebrated young novelist (who now included Rashid Sulyaman amongst his friends) had recently kissed me hard on the lips. Now, I was sitting in the Groucho Club about to eat premium quality Twiglets and drink Pinot Grigio with a crowd of published novelists who had accepted me, almost without question, as one of their own. Why then did I feel so hollow inside? Was it just the alcohol, emptying me of all verve and ambition? Or was it the knowledge that I had done nothing to deserve this good fortune, the feeling that there was no real connection between the women about this table – and that even Hilary felt suddenly distant and out of reach?

'Come on Vicky, spill the beans,' Julia said. Julia looked so contained and perfect in her scarlet cowl-necked dress, with the handcrafted silver choker that snaked about her collarbone. The worst thing about Julia was that it was impossible to hate her. You really wanted to hate her because she was so beautiful and accomplished and successful and rich, but she was also so incredibly nice that you would feel churlish finding fault with her.

'The problem is, now that I've decided to leave Clemmie, I have two other agents interested. I just can't make up my mind between them!'

'Two! How wonderful!' Frederica said. I wondered what envy simmered beneath the surface. According to Hilary, Frederica was finding it impossible to find a new agent. She'd suffered several recent rejections and was still raw about it, but her open expression revealed no hint of malice.

'Yes, there's Rita Kapoor and Violetta Brown.'

'Violetta Brown! Oh she's *lovely*. Wasn't she the one who represented that really obscure book about Surrealist Cinema? What was it again?' Julia said.

'Automatic Cinema,' Frederica replied. '*The Observer* devoted a whole page to it last weekend.'

'God, get me that guy's publicist!' Vicky said.

I racked my brains for any vestiges of knowledge of Surrealist cinema. I'd seen *Un Chien Andalou* once, but my memory of it – beyond the slitting of the eyeball – was vague.

'I've been having sleepless nights about this agent business,' Vicky said. 'I've been pacing about the kitchen in the small hours; it's driving me insane. Violetta or Rita? Violetta or Rita? Michael is sleeping in a separate bed, says he can't stand it a moment longer!'

I couldn't either. Back at The Medici, Carl McGahan (a man known to read philosophical tomes on the meaning of emptiness) was conversing with Rashid Sulyaman. Did I belong there any more than here? I downed my glass of Pinot Grigio in one.

'Guys,' I said. 'Look, I'm really sorry. I'm going to go back for my jacket. I know it's only an item of clothing, but – my Dad bought that jacket for me when I was seventeen.' I told Carl about a ruby. It was at least a half truth. 'It's Carl's launch night, so I can't possibly expect him to stay sober enough to look after it. I hope you don't mind?'

136

'Course not,' Julia said.

'Do you want me to come with you?' Hilary asked.

'No, it's OK. I don't want to spoil your fun. I'll be fine, really.'

I could tell she was confused; wanting the best for me, but knowing the argument about my Dad trumped every other bit of good sense that she might throw my way.

'Take care,' she said.

'Course.'

I stood up, hurried downstairs and made a dash for the door.

16

'Whores and writers, Mahound. We are the people you can't forgive.' – Salman Rushdie

The crowd at The Medici Bar was thinning by the time I returned. I hovered at the top of the stairs, not wanting to go in alone, but knowing that I had no choice. The loss of the jacket had triggered memories. I leant against the wall as people brushed past me. Dad's face was there; the day the letter from the exam board arrived. His cheeks were flushed but his watery, grey eyes should have warned me of his illness.

I tore open the envelope and slowly pulled out the form.

'Two As and a B,' I said. I hadn't yet been interviewed at Cambridge. I planned to take a year out, so had not yet received an offer.

'What did I tell you?' He was chuckling and wheezing all at once. 'Here – treat yourself.' He fumbled in his inside pocket for a chequebook and wrote me a promise of fifty pounds.

'Don't be silly, Dad. I don't need that.'

'I didn't say you needed it, pet. Get yourself something nice.'

'Are you sure?'

'You want me to take it back?' he teased.

'No, OK. I'll keep it.'

The next week I bought the denim jacket.

'You're on your way to Cambridge with that,' he said.

'I suppose I am.' The funny thing was, neither of us ever doubted it. Nor did we doubt that within the year he'd be driving me and my belongings up the motorway to my new life. I was blind in those days; too in love with life to contemplate that it could ever end.

Buddy Sellers put his arm about Carl's shoulder, as if consoling him in some way. There was no sign of Rashid Sulyaman. As I came closer, Carl turned around and spotted me; he snapped out of whatever funk he had been in.

'Hi,' I said.

I was trying to be nonchalant; as if wandering into bars alone was something I did every night of the week. Carl wasn't fooled. He must have sensed my confusion, the way the alcohol blurred my thoughts. I was giddy, but trying to hold it together and make sense of the images in my mind: the ruby brooch made only of paste, the lilies, Angela Crystal; the coldness of Dad's face as...

Carl locked eyes with me and slid his arm about my waist. He pulled me closer and I didn't protest. He smelt faintly of aniseed.

'Are you OK?' he asked.

I nodded, though it wasn't true. 'What about you?'

'I had a row with Sulyaman.'

'Ah.'

'It wasn't exactly a row,' Buddy said.

'What was it?'

'I said I thought his fiction was becoming derivative.'

I laughed. 'What made you say that?'

'Well it is.'

'That's your opinion, Carl,' Buddy said. He wasn't laughing. 'Anyway, it's done now. I'm sure it's nothing we can't smooth over.'

No doubt Buddy had had an entire PR team working for months to ensure Sulyaman's appearance tonight and Carl had screwed up within ten minutes of the Great Man's arrival.

'I don't want you to paper it over,' Carl said. 'I'm not going to apologise.'

Buddy shook his head, his strange fish-like eyes appearing to wobble slightly. I got the impression there was nothing on the PR front that Buddy could not manage, except, perhaps, uncooperative authors. Somehow, Carl's rebellion drew me.

'So,' I said, 'my jacket?'

Carl manoeuvred his fingers through my dress straps and was

now caressing my shoulder blades.

'Did you forget the ransom part?' he said.

I closed my eyes. I wasn't in the mood for playing games.

'Anna?'

'I'm sorry.'

'What's the matter? Oh God, don't cry on me.'

'Sorry. Really sorry.'

'Have I been insensitive? I usually am.' Buddy raised his hand in a half-wave. He knew when he wasn't wanted. 'Do you want me to lay off?' Carl pulled away.

'No.' I paused. 'Yes. I'm very confused.'

'I can see that.'

'You have got the jacket though, haven't you?'

I didn't want to tell him about Dad; that was how Will and I first bonded. It was not exactly romantic.

'It's not a ruby though, is it?'

'Nope. Just the jacket: sentimental value. I should have said.'

He whacked the air before my face, mock slapping me.

'Don't worry; it's perfectly safe. I'll get it for you.'

'Thanks,' I said. 'Sorry to be pathetic. Must be the drink.'

'I'll take advantage of you then,' he said and kissed me. 'You're so bloody beautiful,' he murmured.

Nobody else seemed to notice us. Nobody cared what I was doing. Why should they? Our kiss would damage nothing, except me.

Perhaps, somewhere, on the other side of London, Will was doing exactly the same thing. Will would not let the small matter of a foot in plaster get in the way of anything that he desired. And if it was true – if he really did desire Angela Crystal – then he would have her, no matter what. I used to think that I could trust him, but now I couldn't count on it. He might have his tongue deep in her throat. He might be outside, in the street, pressing her against a wall, her legs wrapped around his waist, her collagen lips sucking the life from him.

Carl pulled back, but I clung onto him again, to steady myself.

'Come on, let's get out of here,' he said.

'But it's your party.'

'So I can do as I please.'

He took my hand and led me to the cloakroom, where he handed over a ticket and reclaimed my jacket. He unpinned the ruby brooch and dangled it before my face, then put it in his pocket. He wrapped the jacket about my shoulders as if it were a precious fox fur. He didn't have to say it. The brooch remained his hostage. I was going back to his place.

On the train, Carl leant forward to entwine his fingers in mine. I pulled back, convinced that somebody would spot us – some mutual friend of Will and I was probably lurking further up the carriage, waiting until the moment when we were in a deep-tongued embrace before leaping out to accuse us. I wasn't prepared to risk it. Carl didn't seem to notice the people around us. He stared at me, not flirtatiously but rather teasing me. *You can't fool them* his look seemed to say. *You're coming home with me and you can be as coy as you like, I know exactly what's going to happen next.*

'You know,' he said, flicking his hair out of his eyes, 'you can thank God you missed Buddy's speech tonight.'

'Why's that then?' I was pretending to be light and casual when what I was doing terrified me.

'He was talking a load of crap, Anna. Said my novel was going to "permanently alter the literary landscape" or some such other bollocks.'

From this, I gathered that Carl was actually desperately annoyed that I had missed the speech. I wondered whether he was, even now, working out ways of quoting Buddy's every other superlative at frequent intervals throughout the evening that lay ahead of us.

'Maybe he's telling the truth?'

'Yeah, probably,' he replied. 'Like sure – I wrote the new Ulysses or something. I'm just being humble about my vast talent.'

'It's why Sulyaman didn't stick around. Couldn't bear the competition.'

'There is that,' Carl said, cuffing his palm to his forehead. 'Why didn't I see that he was just jealous?'

This was the kind of banter that Will and I engaged in. *Where was Will now? Was he swilling champagne with Angela – or worse? And what if my suspicion was unfounded?* It struck me – as my eyes skimmed the line of his shoulders, the thin curl of his lips – that I knew nothing about Carl at all. My instinct was all that led me and it was likely that my instinct left much to be desired. I had read *Caitlin's Trial,* yes, but so had thousands of others before me and those other readers weren't contemplating jumping into bed with the author on the pure strength of his words alone. Except, perhaps they would, if they were given half an opportunity? So what was this about? Pure desire? Revenge? That sounded far too dramatic, as if my life was about to dissolve into some Jacobean tragedy. *And was it?* Would all this end in an array of dead bodies heaped in bloody piles upon the stage?

No – I told myself – it was more than that. There was an affinity between us, a mutual understanding, a possibility. Will's betrayal seemed a solid thing; a small boulder lodged in my gut. Love should be about lightness, shouldn't it? It should make one feel weightless, like an astronaut floating in zero gravity.

We left the train at Twickenham and walked down the hill together. He took my hand and this time I didn't pull away. I was tottering slightly on the high heels I wore; they were rubbing at my ankles, causing pain.

'Tell me about your childhood!' I said. I laughed as I said it, but it's possible he recognised it for what it was: a hopeless bid for intimacy; a justification for what I was about to do. There was no point in lying now.

We rounded the corner by the traffic lights, passed the neon-lit convenience store and opposite The Bear pub we headed through the streets behind the library.

'There was hardly a single book in the place when I was growing up,' Carl said. 'We lived in a flat above a launderette and I was kept awake at night by the sound of the dryers spinning – incessant it was; it was difficult to sleep a wink with that racket going on so I took to reading any junk that was on the shelves: horror and gore for the most part.'

I had the vaguest sense of having heard this story before; he seemed to have it off pat, giving nothing of himself away. He led me through a small courtyard as it started to rain. My high heels slipped on the wet pavement and I stumbled and nearly fell. I forced myself to think of Angela Crystal, imagining Will wrapped in her arms. When I did that, everything seemed easy and uncomplicated.

'Take your shoes off, for Christ's sake, hon,' Carl said. 'You'll break your fecking neck in those things.'

'I'm not falling for that one again,' I said. 'Bloody fetishist.'

But he was right – my feet were killing me – so I bent down and removed the stilettos and walked barefoot down an unlit alleyway.

We came out beneath a flickering lamppost and Carl led me up a rusting iron staircase. It was not bohemian Paris but it was about as close to the *Bateau Lavoir* as you were likely to get in central Twickenham.

Carl put his key in the lock but it stuck and he had to toggle it before the door, eventually, gave way. I told myself it was not too late to change my mind. Having coffee didn't have to lead to sex.

The hallway was unlit and I waited for Carl to put the light on. Instead he pushed me against the inside of the door, crushed me against it in the darkness. His tongue snaked into my mouth, overwhelming me. I couldn't imagine Will ever behaving like that. If he did, he'd probably ruin it by apologising afterwards.

I was fixated on the idea of coffee. Even as his groin was grinding into mine, a small part of my brain remained detached: the part of my brain that thought this was not irreversible – I could still politely decline his advances. I kept thinking: *in a minute he'll take me upstairs for a coffee. I could murder a cappuccino.* But of course, Carl had no intention of showing me his cafetière or any other kitchen appliance. He intended to have me right there, against the door.

He reached inside my skirt, unzipped his trousers and yanked them down. I wanted him too and wrapped my legs about his waist. He paused, took my face in his hands and gazed at me, a kind of lunatic gaze, half-tender and half-cruel.

'Don't speak,' he said, as he thrust himself into me. He didn't take his eyes away. 'Don't… say… a word…'

Was it like this for Jeanne Hébuterne, I wondered? '*Not without a certain horror*,' she had said.

My desire appalled me. I didn't even know *what* it was that I desired, only that it seemed necessary somehow, like a persistent thirst.

'Don't bite me!' He wasn't thinking about the evidence, but I was.

Carl crushed my shoulder against the wall as he grasped me tight. Another bruise I'd have to explain. Then he pulled back. *Was that it?* He made no noise.

'Come on, let's go inside.'

So, I had not – as I had imagined – just had sex against the door of Carl's flat, but against the door of the communal hallway. My eyes were adjusting to the light and I could see two further doors – one immediately in front of me, from which, presumably, the neighbours might emerge at any moment. *Good evening, Mrs Cuthbert, we were just having a quick meaningless fuck; you will excuse us?* Another door, ahead of us, was Carl's.

'Sorry,' Carl said. 'You're just too gorgeous, girl.'

I slipped my shoes back on, bent down to fasten them and fumbled for my underwear. Carl led me inside and now I was grateful that we skipped the coffee percolator and headed straight for the bedroom.

'Christ, how can I still want you?' His kiss tasted of salt water.

We wound our way across to the bed, clinging limpet-like, lips entwined; I tripped over a pile of books and slid onto his mattress. He tossed a book onto a bedside table; a thin layer of dust shifted.

I leaned back on the bed, propping myself up on my elbow. On the bedside table, an ashtray was full to the brim of old butts. The stupid tears threatened again.

'It's OK,' he said. 'I'm not as bad as I seem.'

'I know, it's just…'

'You have a boyfriend; you're feeling guilty.'

'Yes…'

144

'You're free to go, ya know. You don't have to stay.'

'Well fuck you!'

'What? What did I do?'

Did he have no idea?

'You've had your way with me and now you want me to go?'

He laughed.

'You bastard.'

He laughed some more. 'No, no, you don't get it. Stay! Stay all night. All week. Forever... I haven't even begun with you yet.'

Forever?

'No?'

'I want to kiss every inch of you.'

'Is that what you say to every gullible girl who comes in here?'

'You're not the tiniest bit gullible, Anna Bright.'

He edged closer to me then and slid his fingertips beneath the edges of my jacket, at my collarbone. He edged the denim from my shoulders, gently, as if he were undressing a china doll. I reached out and touched his face and he paused, let himself be held. His pointy chin had a slight cleft in it, I hadn't noticed earlier.

Carl nudged his head to the side, whispered in my ear.

'Let me kiss your dirty feet.'

My turn to laugh now; anything to cover up the unexpected thrill his words sent up my spine.

'What?' I'd heard him perfectly well.

"How ridiculous!" I thought, but I didn't have much time to think about it because Carl was already playing with my ankle straps. *So, he was serious about this.* He seemed to want to do it all over again. He was leaning over me, flipping the stilettos off, putting his mouth to my toes. I closed my eyes. It was too late to stop it. Given the way I felt at that moment, I'd probably have indulged in any number of mildly perverted sexual acts, so long as they were legal.

Carl began working his way up my legs with his tongue. I was thinking about Modigliani again. Modi slept with pretty much every woman who became his muse. According to Modi, sex was a necessary stimulus, without which, he said, he couldn't create. Carl

145

was kissing me between my thighs. I turned my head. The pillow beneath me was stained with what looked like another woman's mascara, but that was surely my imagination. I should stop it, of course I should stop it. Only perhaps I was not like other lovers. Perhaps I was his Jeanne and he was Modi – the tormented genius, the incorrigible alcoholic, the prodigious seducer of women, the naked dancer in the street...

Carl came up for air and whispered in my ear.

'I'd like to see you in a pair of those long, black boots...' *Now he was taking it too far.* 'Do you have a pair?'

As it happened, I did possess a very attractive pair of black suede boots that I had bought last January in the Hobbs sale.

'What if I did?' I said.

'Just wear them, next time we meet.'

Next time? I wasn't certain there should be a *next time*, but then he kissed me, far too tenderly for me to ever consider that this was the last time we would be intimate. Something about that kiss convinced me that there was more to this than lust alone. I kissed him again. And again. Again. I was lost in it, so lost that Will vanished, nothing mattered – not even the fetishism – only the kiss itself, the perfection of the sensation. *It must have a meaning, surely?* It had to be more than physical. There was love in that longing. There must be. Then, half way through a particularly intense embrace, he paused, lifted his head and waited until I opened my eyes and met his.

'You're not serious about marrying that boyfriend of yours, are you?' he said.

It terrified me. 'I don't know. I'm confused.'

He kissed me again, half smiling.

'Oh, I love you, Anna Bright,' he said. And in that moment I believed him. In that moment, I believed I felt it too.

When I awoke, I saw Carl's face beside me, oddly beautiful even in sleep, with his mouth slightly open, his cheek squashed against the pillow. The room stank of cigarette smoke and I remembered smoking with Carl afterwards, laughing at a joke that I could no longer remember. My eyes wandered across the objects on his bedside table: a plastic contact lens container; a packet of Marlboro Lights; a few loose pills; a rubber band. I smiled. The unfamiliarity of the scene gave me a stupid thrill. Then something shifted. I opened my eyes wide. *What time was it? What was I doing here? Why was my mobile flashing in my handbag?*

Perhaps it was the phone that woke me. I reached over and pulled it out, moving slowly, taking care not to wake Carl. It would be Will.

But it was not. Will had clearly not noticed that I'd stayed out half the night. His mother, however, had. I listened.

Anna darling, it's Phyllis. Where are you? Will's asleep now, but I'm worried about you. Bloody jet lag, I can't sleep. Are you OK? I wonder whether I should wake Will? Anyhow, let me know. I've just been online by the way. I booked us a week at the Ouranos Centre. You said you had some holiday left, didn't you? We leave next Tuesday. Don't worry about William. He'll be just fine. Do call, Anna. It's nearly 3am. Do you usually stay out till this time? Bye sweetie.

She had booked a week on Ouranos? I was half asleep. *Booked it, without asking me?* She could at least have waited until the morning. This was out of order. It was the last thing I should have cared about but at that hour my brain was barely functioning.

I lay back, breathing fast, trying hard to calm myself but failing. My thoughts were circular, chasing one another in a hopeless pattern that would allow no resolution. I wanted to move, but was either too tired or too confused. Carl shifted beside me, his eyelids fluttering in a dream. He kicked his legs out, enacting some drama in his sleep, pushing the sheet from his body. His naked back stretched out before me and I wanted to run my hand up his spine, to explore each vertebra slowly. The knowledge that I might walk away from here and never see him like this again pained me.

But the thoughts returned, the stupid, everyday practical concerns that made a farce of my desire and of his beauty. His

147

throwaway declaration of love was exactly that, a casual line that meant nothing at all. I needed to focus on the things that really mattered: the man who wanted to marry me, and the novel that I had not yet written. I closed my eyes, hoping that if I simply waited, clarity would come. I turned away from Carl. If I looked at him for a moment longer, I would reach out and touch him, pull him out of sleep and into my arms and that might prove disastrous.

I can't say how long I lay there in that indefinable state. It might have been an hour, maybe two. Eventually, a brilliant chink of light appeared in the corner of the window, glancing across the wall, reflecting in the opposite mirror. *How long had Will stayed out last night?*

Carl stirred again. He pouted. A few strands of fine hair fell across his eyes. My breath surely stank and my mascara would have hardened into gritty lumps. He must not see me. Naked, I stood up and quickly picked up my clothes, the vintage dress scrunched on the floor, a crumpled rag.

In five days' time, I would fly to Ouranos. Natasha would have to agree. Soon, surely, everything would become perfectly clear.

Part Two

Middle

17

'The real voyage of discovery consists not in seeking new landscapes but in having new eyes.' – Marcel Proust

As the plane circled, waiting to land above Ouranos airport, I leant across Phyllis to catch a glimpse of the Mediterranean beneath us. The sea glimmered, a perfect shade of azure.

'These anti-thrombosis socks are so uncomfortable,' Phyllis said.

Phyllis was wearing airline pyjamas that she must have picked up on her flight from the States and she now resembled something out of an alien-invasion movie, as if she had dressed to avoid contamination. 'I don't know how you can eat that airline food,' she said. The entire flight had irked her.

Almost as soon as we got on the plane, Phyllis had complained about the lack of male flight attendants. Next, it was the faulty earphone socket that made the in-flight movie redundant. To add insult to injury, the duty-free supplies were running low and her favourite Clarins moisturiser was out of stock. We had barely spoken during the flight. She had spent half of it in a semi-inclined position, plugged into her iPod, pausing from time to time to spray her face with a fine mist from a travel canister of Evian water and to apply another coat of lip salve with her index finger. Now she opened her handbag to retrieve a sachet of face pack, which she applied without a trace of embarrassment.

I had hoped to see the best of Phyllis in Ouranos – I had imagined picking her brain about Modigliani, sharing ideas with her and treating her with the seriousness she deserved. But now she seemed to want to shut me out. Her agitation made her a caricature of herself. It was impossible to reach her.

This holiday was a mistake. I should not have left Will at home, not with his foot in plaster, not with so many questions left unanswered. Since the night I spent with Carl, there had been an uneasy truce between us. He had been home and sleeping when I returned at 6am that morning and he never mentioned my failure to come home. I could only assume that his not asking was due to his own guilt and that his failure to question me revealed a total lack of interest. He had been as reluctant to talk as I had been, as if neither of us were willing to shine a light on recent events; we preferred our separate secrecy. It was no foundation for a marriage.

Carl, too, had been worse than useless. Since we had spent the night together, I had received only a few short texts: a few worthless pornographic syllables, no more. It was possible I had hurt his feelings by vanishing without saying goodbye, but somehow I rather doubted that. Most likely he had been relieved.

Phyllis pulled her seat upright for landing, prematurely removing the face pack with damp cotton wool.

'You did send that synopsis off to Buddy Sellers, didn't you?'

I nodded, unconvinced that it had been a wise move. Phyllis had encouraged me to follow up the contact immediately, but I had known at the time it was short-sighted. Sellers was not stupid. He would not have the patience to nurture a beginner and very soon my inexperience would become clear to him. I would be revealed as a fraud.

We were still circling the airport, though there was no other plane in sight.

'I think it was a mistake,' I said.

'He has the synopsis, Anna. And he *liked* you. You'd be out of your mind to miss an opportunity like that.'

I fiddled with a packet of peanuts that had been proffered several hours ago and absent-mindedly took one.

'Nuts aren't good for your metabolism,' Phyllis said.

'I don't think you're taking this seriously.'

'Of course, I'm taking it seriously. You're an artist for God's sake. I'd be worried if you didn't have doubts. That's normal, hon. Get used to it.'

'Thanks for the sympathy.'

She shrugged. 'James understands all of this. You'll come back a new woman.'

'Does he? Is Loftus really all that?'

'The man is a genius. Trust me.'

If Phyllis was joking, there was no hint of humour in her voice.

'Oh yes,' I said. 'I nearly forgot.'

I paused at the top of the stairs overlooking the iridescent tarmac and shaded my eyes with the cup of my hand. *I had been lulled by the promise of a space in which to write, but was I, rather, merely running away?* I looked up towards the flawless sky, then across the concrete expanse of the airport to the violet mountains beyond. The heat gripped me and I was relieved to feel giddy with something other than desire.

Phyllis gave me a nudge, I blinked and descended the staircase. I took out my mobile and switched it on. It beeped instantly. *Carl?* It was only a Greek mobile network, informing me of their services.

As we crossed the tarmac to the main building, it struck me that something was wrong here. I was reminded of all the holidays I'd had with Will in the past, stepping out of a plane with him at my side – and the pleasure I used to take in small things, the ephemera that I'd pack in my suitcase: cute, oversized shades; a brilliant red bikini; a trashy novel for the beach; a snorkel that I'd never use. It wasn't the items themselves that mattered but what they promised – the time alone together. How uncomplicated that used to be.

We made out way through passport control, policed by a thickset man with a handlebar moustache, like a character from one of Will's comic books. We had left Will alone with a broken foot, hobbling about the house on crutches. I should be there, I thought, challenging him, facing my own failings, not running away to some Greek Island utopia on a vague promise of solitude that would probably never materialise. But it was too late. Phyllis and I were standing by the carousel, yanking our luggage through the crowd, walking across the polished, tiled floor that stank of cheap disinfectant. Already a woman wearing a white linen dress, black leggings and pretty patent sandals was taking an interest in the labels on our suitcases.

'Loftus Holidays? Yes? Excellent. Welcome. Welcome. A pleasure. I'm Elspeth, your representative.'

Elspeth spoke with a warm Edinburgh accent, the kind of voice they use in commercials to make you feel safe and comfortable and ready to take out credit. She wore lipstick the colour of blood oranges to complement her tan; her eyelashes reminded me of exotic caterpillars. Elspeth sported a huge diamond ring on her finger and her nails were immaculate and fake.

'It's good to be back. I'm Phyllis Isenberg and this is my soon-to-be daughter-in-law, Anna Bright,' Phyllis said. 'Virtually an Isenberg,' she added.

I swallowed hard.

'Wonderful. Isenberg and Bright? Good. Ah yes. You're in the Writer's Centre. Fabulous – oh you're in for a treat. Have you visited Ouranos before?'

'Absolutely,' Phyllis said, irritated that Elspeth hadn't listened the first time. Elspeth's sing-song tone was that of a patient nursery schoolteacher. Perhaps she had been warned that most writers are a few sandwiches short of the picnic. 'I was here in the early years,' Phyllis continued. 'When you were still in the first grade, I imagine. I'm an old friend of James Loftus's.'

'How very fortunate. You know he's leading a group this week? We're so privileged to have him on the programme. He's taken a step back from the hands-on work in recent years, so you really are tremendously privileged.'

'He's fucking privileged to have us,' Phyllis said, then smiled her usual disingenuous smile.

'Ha ha!' Elspeth's laughter failed to conceal her shock. 'Do take one of these folders,' she said. 'The folders contain a little background information about your holiday. Just along the pavement, you'll find Coach 275, which will take you all the way to the Centre. Yours is the second stop. The first is for Molos Bay.' Elspeth seemed to forget to breathe between sentences. She couldn't wait to get rid of us. 'Make sure you don't get off at Molos Bay or you'll be spending the week under canvas,' she trilled. I got the feeling that Elspeth would secretly like to see us suffering in a tent, preferably one with a leak.

We made our way along the pavement, past the taxi rank where drivers with bags under their eyes snoozed at the wheel, past the flowerbeds overflowing with bougainvillea where powder blue butterflies hovered. Ahead of us, a couple of middle-aged women in flowing cheesecloth dresses seemed to be heading for our coach. Their hair was plaited with small coloured beads and one of them reached up to scratch her head, I noticed her hand was decorated with henna tattoos that formed a bizarre contrast with the large diamond ring on her finger.

'*Molosiers*,' Phyllis whispered.

'What?'

'The well-heeled, hippy crowd. Typical of the Molos Bay lot. They just come for the yoga. High-flyers recovering from nervous breakdowns, you know the type.'

'Isn't that a bit reductionist?'

'I *know* these people,' Phyllis replied. 'Some of the fiercest, most screwed-up women I've ever had the displeasure of meeting were Molosiers.'

'But that doesn't mean...' I couldn't gather the energy to continue. I half wished that I *were* clad in muslin, with long beads about my neck and brand new Birkenstocks on my feet. It might be quite nice to sleep under canvas, to spend the week hugging trees and singing Joni Mitchell songs about a campfire.

We stepped onto the coach and the cool air enveloped us. The driver was picking his fingernails and avoiding eye contact. At the front, a young couple were engrossed in conversation: the woman threw the word "Nietzche" at the man, who replied with the word "Borghes" stated very loudly mid-sentence, in the hope that the entire coach might consider his intellectual credentials superior to hers. Behind them was a guy around my age, on his own, with cropped black hair, sideburns and trendy-geek glasses. The two girls on the other side of the passage appeared to crouch, like small rodents that would prefer to avoid attention.

Phyllis however, could not avoid being conspicuous. It was easy

155

to forget how odd she appeared to strangers. Now I felt protective towards her and as Elspeth arrived and the coach started up, Phyllis, fussing with the overhead locker, lurched forward, which gave everybody a chance to ogle her one more time.

'You OK?' It was the guy in glasses. He stood up to help but he had the kind of physique that I thought could only hinder; he must have been about six foot three and he had to crouch to avoid knocking his head on the ceiling.

'We're fine.' I steadied her and helped her to her feet. She was like a newborn bird, a poor broken thing, whose shell had prematurely cracked.

The coach set off and the driver fiddled with the jangling worry beads suspended in the front window. He switched on the radio, releasing a stream of traditional music. I could picture myself standing on a table, dancing, as plates were routinely smashed by waiters and the whole room clapped encouragement.

'Welcome, Ladies and Gentlemen, to the beautiful Island of Ouranos!' Elspeth's smile revealed a large globule of lipstick on her front teeth. Her hips were gyrating almost inconspicuously, to the music. 'We wish you a most inspiring experience on the Island and we hope that in the week ahead you will become truly connected to your innate creativity.' She paused, quietly beaming. 'Ouranos is one of the greenest and least discovered of the Greek Islands and I can tell you from personal experience that you cannot fail to be moved by your time here. In this splendid setting, you will be able to write and create in absolute peace. Most exciting of all this week is the fact that we will be joined, for a rare visit, by the *Literary Genius* himself, James Loftus.'

I noticed the infatuated sparkle in Elspeth's eye when she uttered Loftus's name; her look made it plain that in her opinion Loftus was nothing short of the status that he claimed for himself.

'We trust you have packed the essentials recommended in the pre-holiday reading, but if you have forgotten anything, rest assured that you can purchase the Genius™ brand of Notebooks, Writer's Journals and Yoga Mats in the Loftus village shop.

'Your Welcome Meeting (for those staying at Ouranos Bay) is

tonight in the bar of the Writers' Centre. For Molosiers, this will take place tomorrow morning. James Loftus himself will be present and he'll be at the Ouranos Hotel this afternoon on your arrival. In the meantime, we wish you a pleasant journey. Please sit back, allow the music to wash over you and take a little time to reflect on the insights you have yet to have, here on the idyllic island of Ouranos. '

Elspeth placed her microphone down, pursed her lips and shrugged her shoulders. She had the air of a slightly demented game-show host who had just come off camera but had forgotten that the reel was still running. She yawned, failing to cover her mouth and moved to the front of the coach where she picked up a small tray of baklavas from a built-in trolley and proceeded to walk along the aisle to hand the local delicacies to the guests. As we careered along the potholed road, Phyllis took three and scoffed them fast. With a dribble of honey still trickling from her lips, she drifted to sleep again, leaving me to admire the austere, rocky coastline that now opened up beyond the window.

I felt a pang of dislocation then. It might have been the distance that the air-conditioning and the glass put between myself and the landscape, or it might have had something to do with the tacky gold-embossed folder that lay in my lap, reminding me of glitzy wedding stationery, the like of which I hadn't seen since my sister Lois got married in Billericay in the late nineties. I watched the glitter of light on the sea, the constantly shifting kaleidoscope. I felt a bitter constriction in my throat.

The invitations to my own wedding had already gone out. The replies were in and had been counted. Some of the guests would have already bought their outfits. My mother's two-piece suit took pride of place in her wardrobe. Mum had made a special trip to Lakeside to find a "mother of the bride" outfit that would flatter her physique; she had chosen an elaborate hat in a delicate shade of apricot.

Marriage had been part of the mythology of my childhood, not something I'd ever questioned. I'd spent hours poring over Ladybird books, examining each fairytale princess and the dresses they wore: yellow silk; pale blue chiffon; white satin – wondering which one I

157

would choose and how I might look with such voluptuous fabrics wound about me.

But that was before I grew up. It was before Will uttered the word *Angela* in my ear, before Carl McGahan did the small dance in the car park, before he held my jacket ransom and kissed my dirty feet. It was before I ever came to Ouranos and before I imagined a woman standing at a window in a Paris suburb, about to die for love.

18

'Dr. Octavius: If you want to get a woman to fall in love with you,
feed her poetry.
Peter Parker: Poetry?
Dr. Octavius: Never fails. '
– from "Spiderman 2"

'Are you all right, Phyllis?'

'I'm fine and dandy,' she said, in a tone that revealed she was anything but. I hadn't seen Phyllis so unsettled since the day I'd served her beans on toast, unaware of its emotional significance. 'OK, so I'm a little nervous,' she said.

'What's there to be nervous about?'

She shrugged. 'Nothing I can't handle.'

We had been on the coach for over an hour. The Molosiers had all left. Phyllis had been awake for about ten minutes but had barely said a word. She had spent that time staring into a tiny, circular mirror, applying thick bronze make-up and a dusting of shimmering face powder. She painted her lips again and when she had finished, she unbuttoned her blouse to uncover a low-cut, black, halter-neck top that revealed an expanse of scrawny flesh.

We rounded a tight hairpin bend at an inadvisable speed. Phyllis stood up and hitched up her bra before settling back down again and nudging me, cocking her head at the view beneath. Beneath us was a sheer drop to the sea.

'Oh – my – God!' I had visions of the coach toppling down the hillside.

The cliffs fell away beneath us to a turquoise bay, a landscape uninterrupted by any man-made structure. The late afternoon light

159

lent a particular glamour to the view: a sharp, orange-tinted light, with long shadows thrown by the vegetation. Just as the coach drew to a halt, we rounded the last part of the bay and only then did The Writer's Centre come into view. I stood up and gathered my bags, trying to block out Elspeth's voice as she chanted instructions about leaving our suitcases for the porters.

'Echoes of the Guggenheim, don't you think?' Phyllis sighed as we stepped outside. The heat was immediate and all-embracing; it clung like shrink-wrap to my skin.

'It doesn't seem possible,' I said. The Writer's Centre was a circular, modernist building, a whitewashed concrete construction, hidden halfway down the cliff face. Its isolation made it surreal, like an Escher print made material. 'But it's so small.'

'Look again...' Phyllis appeared unaffected by the sun; she pulled down her shades but seemed entirely comfortable.

Even with shades, it took a while to get used to the light. At first glimpse, I had believed the building to be no more than a few storeys high – I saw only the central spiral that was immediately visible. But now I realised that hidden levels were built into the hillside below, making the building almost a part of the landscape.

'You have to hand it to him!' Phyllis said. 'Those are the writing rooms. Each one is designed so that when you're inside a room, you can't see any of the others.'

'Absolute solitude?'

'As close to Proust's cork-lined walls as you're ever likely to experience.'

Now I understood why I was here. I had only to endure this first evening, then I could refuse to go to class and spend my days in one of those rooms. A week should give me enough time to get to grips with Jeanne's story. I could read two or three books about Modigliani and get a few chapters down. I could figure out why this story attracted me and where I might now take it.

I closed my eyes. The air was oppressive and briny. The sea whispered in the distance. It might have been perfect, had not my peace been interrupted by an incoming text.

Shit.

Seven syllables.

Can't stop thinking about you

Seven darling syllables. But not from Will. I didn't know what exactly Carl was playing at, but I did understand the effect of his words. I was thrown into confusion. My legs trembled a little; perhaps it was the heat. I knew these words meant nothing, even as I longed them to have meaning. But how could I imbue them with anything? Carl's communication was pathetic. All he had to do was raise his thumbs and tap in a few clichés. What kind of fool was I to think that this could ever be a prelude to anything deeper? I was surely no more than a plaything that he would chew up and spit out – just as soon as he got the satisfaction that I was falling for it.

I switched the phone off and gathered the contents of my handbag. As I stood up, I found myself face to face with a tall Greek whose physical perfection was marred only by the size of his ears. He proffered a tray, replete with glasses of lightly fizzing champagne. Phyllis, never one to turn down free booze, moved fast, grabbed two glasses pronto and thrust one into my hand. I wondered why – when I could have been observing his perfect square jaw-line or pondering the precise shade of blue of his eyes – all I could look at was the waiter's ears, unlikely growths with protruding lobes.

I downed the champagne fast and followed Phyllis into a wide, white foyer, backed by a panoramic glass window that revealed the long, unspoilt bay of Ouranos. A large, metal fan whirred slowly, above our heads, wafting a strong, sweet scent across the room.

Phyllis whisked my glass away and handed me another as the waiter passed by us once again. She held her glass up and chinked it with mine.

'Champagne for my real friends,' she said, 'And real pain for my sham friends.'

I laughed, perhaps too loudly.

'Francis Bacon,' she said. 'God rest his soul.'

'Are you a fan of Bacon's work?'

'You'd have to be a philistine not to be,' she said.

'The trouble is…' I began. But I realised then that Phyllis was entirely distracted. The room was full of reps milling about with clipboards, with new arrivals and waiting staff. Phyllis appeared to stumble; she grasped my arm and dug her fingernails deep into my skin. She hardly noticed my small cry of pain. Her eyes were fixed on the other side of the room. A red flush crept up her chest and I turned to see the object of her attention. A silver-haired man was descending the central staircase. He was dressed in a dazzling white suit and, given the sudden silence in the room, it seemed I was the last to recognise him. James Loftus was shorter in the flesh.

When he reached the bottom of the staircase, he was joined by two almost-indecently-tanned women, carrying garlands of blossom, which they placed about his neck. Around me, everybody began to applaud and Loftus smiled graciously, baring his over-large bleached teeth beneath his white moustache.

Phyllis's mouth hung loosely open.

'Actually Anna,' she said, gathering her dignity, 'I think the journey has been a little too much for me. I feel a bit nauseous. I'll go outside for a moment, but you stay here… enjoy…'

I considered following her but sensed she did not want me to. It was obvious there was history here. I looked closer. It made no sense to me that any woman could find this man attractive. Whether his face was reddened through too much sun or too much alcohol, I couldn't tell. His thick white hair was coiffed back, his eyebrows far neater than would be natural in a man of his age. A queue was forming already, as if everyone in the room desired his company. I hung back but remained close enough to observe him in action.

At the front, a broad-faced blonde woman approached him, plucking a copy of his book from her handbag. He touched her shoulder proprietarily and rather than pulling back, she seemed to lean into it, then came closer still as he bent his head to sign his name on the title page.

'Of course, of course,' he said. 'Who should I dedicate it to?'

Loftus's calm expression suggested he had seen it all before, been there, done that, knew it all and had it all. But I imagined him without the suit, without the bling (an enormous gold ring on his finger, a gold chain about his neck), with unruly eyebrows and decaying teeth. He had the face of an alcoholic; the kind of person you wouldn't like to bump into in a dark alleyway. Yet the woman was giggling, touching her hand to her hair.

I shivered. The air was artificially cooled and the fragrance from the garlands choked me. Phyllis had come back inside.

'I'm not sick any more,' she said. 'Just gasping.'

'Aren't you going to say 'hello'?' I asked.

She shook her head. 'Let *him* speak to me,' she said.

The crowd was converging about him now, but however strong her resolve, Phyllis could not stop herself from glancing in his direction. She caught his eye and for the briefest of moments, he lost his composure. It couldn't have lasted more than a second or two, but when he saw her, a look of blind panic crossed his face. All his attention, his poise and charm seemed to waver. But then, just as quickly, he recovered and the recovery was so complete that I wondered whether I had imagined what I had seen. The show continued as if nothing whatsoever had happened.

Phyllis gasped. I reached out, took her arm and led her back to the balcony outside where she grabbed the decorative cast-iron railing, making an effort to slow her breathing. *This isn't right.* I tried to hold my fury inside. *She enticed me with the promise of solitude; time to write. But she was just chasing an old flame. I'm an accessory, entirely dispensable.* The sunlight was too intense and there was no shade here – but there was nowhere else to escape to. Phyllis appeared blanched and exposed, her skin as delicate as rice paper.

'Are you OK?'

'Of course I'm OK,' she snapped. 'Look at this view. It's perfectly serene.'

'I just thought you seemed a little uneasy.'

'It's the heat. I'm not good with the heat.'

'You don't want to talk about this?'

'Oh for God's sake, Anna – what is there to say?'

'I'm sorry,' I said. 'But you did bring me here.'

'You're right. It was a mistake. I'm a fool.'

19

'In relation to a writer, most readers believe in the Double Standard: they may be unfaithful to him as often as they like, but he must never, never be unfaithful to them.' – W.H. Auden

On the other side of the room, Loftus disentangled himself from his admirers. He was approaching us now, armed with more garlands of blossom and his dazzling, fraudulent grin.

'Felicity!' he said. It happened very quickly. He did not give her pause for thought, but grabbed her in a tight, unreservedly sexual embrace. As he pulled back again, I caught her expression. It was like seeing the adolescent within; a yearning that was impossible to miss. Loftus's eyes by contrast were opaque. How could one discern anything in such bulbous orbs? I looked closely, the small blue irises swimming in the whites, revealing nothing.

'What a wonderful surprise!' he said. 'Here – orange blossom…' The accent was difficult to place. Most likely it was Californian. 'You look more beautiful than ever, Phyllis.'

'Thank you!' she trilled, as he placed a garland about her neck. 'James, this is Anna Bright. She's Will's fiancée. My Will, can you imagine – getting married already?' Phyllis's voice had raised two octaves. 'Anna is writing a novel about Modigliani's last mistress. She already has interest from Buddy Sellers.'

'Buddy Sellers? Well, well… It's some time since I've seen Buddy. How is he?'

'I barely know him,' I said. 'I met him at a party. I sent some work to him before I left.'

'Good girl! You don't want to miss an opportunity like that.'

Girl? The patronising little shit…

'It's not every day that Buddy Sellers takes an interest in a female author,' he continued. 'He normally goes for the boys…'

I laughed, disguising my surprise. *How stupid I'd been.* I recalled Buddy's body language, the way he leant towards Carl, placed a hand on his shoulder.

'I see you don't really know Buddy,' Loftus laughed. Phyllis joined in, although I got the feeling she would have laughed at anything Loftus said.

'Well, I have to say, it is so good to see you, Felicity. Do you remember the early days? Over at Molos Bay? Impossible to forget, no? You looked magnificent then darling.' He paused, then appeared to realise what he had said. 'Not that you don't look magnificent now. You do. Of course you do.'

Phyllis flinched.

'Yes,' she said. 'You were quite a gentleman in those days.'

Loftus grimaced and I considered leaving them alone but as I turned to go, Phyllis grasped my hand as if it were a line thrown by a lifeguard.

'You should have told me you were coming,' Loftus said. 'I was shocked when I saw your name on the guest list this morning.'

'Shocked?' Phyllis said. 'In the old days, you would have checked the guest list weeks in advance. Are you losing your edge, James?'

'I have a team these days. I'm a busy man.' He kneaded his moustache, as if the action would fend off the criticism.

'Clearly,' she replied.

'No matter. I'm thrilled to see you here. Anna, it is my pleasure to meet you too. You'll both be at the Welcome Drinks tonight, yes? Good. I look forward to that. I nearly forgot – your garland, Anna. Here.'

I stepped back to stop him from placing it round my neck. I took it in my hand.

'Please yourself,' he said, and his smile was closer to a sneer. 'I have to dash now. All these folk to check in. I'm sure you understand?'

'Of course,' Phyllis snapped. 'All those eager beavers.'

165

'No rest for the wicked,' he said and turned away.

As soon as he was gone, Phyllis ripped the bouquet from her neck and tossed it aside.

Loftus strode towards his minions and the queue of writers waiting patiently to meet him, with a sense of purpose that I assumed was not entirely literary.

We made our way to the lift and Phyllis turned to smile at me. Her smile was rigid: a rigor mortis grin. But as the lift doors closed, her expression crumpled (so much as it was capable of crumpling) into a pout, a tremble and finally a sob.

'A shock?' she said, her voice a wired, high-pitched squeal. 'Is that what he calls it? The puffed-up little idiot, is that the best he can do?'

'I'm sure he didn't mean it in that way,' I said, but I was certain that he did.

'I looked magnificent *then*, did I? Does he think he's so invulnerable? Fucking men – they think wrinkles make them look *distinguished*. He could do with a sodding face-lift himself. When's he going to learn not to spend so much time on the sun bed?'

'He does seem a little vain.'

'A little? If you made electricity from his vanity, it'd light up the Golden Gate Bridge!'

The lift doors opened and I turned quickly so she might not see my amusement. If Phyllis couldn't get the irony of her words, I was not about to enlighten her. The complexity of her desire confused me however. How was it possible that an educated woman who exhibited intelligence in other spheres could be so blind in the matter of love? If she was unhinged enough to fall for this jumped-up little would-be guru, she possibly deserved every last morsel of humiliation that he deigned to toss her way.

But who was I to speak? We walked along the curved, whitewashed corridor and it struck me that if I could get Phyllis to see Loftus for what he really was, then I might also learn disenchantment. In saving Phyllis, perhaps I could save myself.

Our room was a clean, white minimalist box. It smelt of fresh linen and sandalwood – *or was it amber?* There was something too clinical about it, too measured. Phyllis made a dash for the balcony and could not conceal the sound of her sobs. Our suitcases, delivered by a valet, were the only out-of-place items in the room. The few adornments included a cuboid white vase filled with pale roses, a huge, shallow glass bowl and a stack of leather-bound books. I picked up a wooden bird and ran my fingers across its carved feathers, as my eyes were drawn by two framed black and white photographs that hung above the beds.

The photographs were of Durrell and Hemingway and I had to stifle my laughter. It was all far too predictable, too engineered. Hemingway was bent over a small, wooden desk, his forehead leaning towards the page, his solid arm embracing it; his lip was curled towards the work, as if nothing in the world had meaning beyond his words. Durrell, by contrast, was in close-up, staring beyond the viewer, his eyes narrowed, his shirt unbuttoned to reveal a few stray hairs on his chest. He was clutching what appeared to be a thin tree trunk. Both images conveyed an urgent masculinity. The Hemingway bed would be mine.

Phyllis had fallen silent. Outside, on the balcony, I found her spread-eagled on a brilliant red sun-lounger, like an exotic lizard. Her shades were pushed back onto her forehead, and she appeared unaware of her streaked mascara; she stared into space, barely blinking, conveying no expression at all. Even her self-pity was now repressed.

I stood in silence, looking out across the swimming pool to the placid Mediterranean, the horizon and the sky. Down below, in the pool, a lone woman performed perfect breaststroke. Phyllis sighed and there was something about the sound that suggested a world-weariness that no words could easily fix. I crouched down, wondering whether I should attempt to comfort her, but my mobile rang, interrupting me. I checked the handset and the name onscreen was one I had keyed in the previous week at The Medici Bar.

'Fuck,' I said. '*Fuck*!'

'Is somebody dead?' Phyllis asked.

'It's Buddy Sellers. What shall I do?'

'Remember he needs you more than you need him,' she said.

I picked up the phone and took it inside.

'Hello?'

'Anna – darling. It's Buddy.' *Darling?* I imagined there were people on this island who would slaughter their pet cat to be the recipient of that "darling".

'Buddy. What a nice surprise.' *I didn't intend to be so facile.* 'I'm in Ouranos.'

'Yes. Carl here mentioned that.'

I was finding it difficult to hold the receiver steady. *Carl was with him?* It made sense. Literary agents weren't supposed to *call* you. They were supposed to avoid you at all costs – for weeks and months; if you weren't careful they'd leave you alone for a lifetime.

'I've read the extract you sent,' he said. Then he fell silent. I wasn't certain whether he was thinking in the silence or whether I was supposed to say something. He let it hang and so did I. It seemed to go on forever. *How strange! Carl, in that room with him, but I can't reach him.* I could hear the hiss of the sea in the distance, imagined the phone like a conch to my ear, the distant roar, the imagined echo of the waves. Buddy broke the silence by laughing. *Perhaps I'd won.* 'It's very short,' he said. *Don't speak.* I willed myself. *Don't say a word.* This conversation shouldn't be happening, I thought. *He doesn't have enough to go on. He's playing for time.* 'But it's not bad,' he said in the end. 'I think you have something.'

Phyllis had wandered inside as he spoke. She sat down on the Durrell bed, straining to hear his voice.

'Thank you,' I said. *Something. Was that enough? Was something worth anything at all?* I must not qualify myself, I thought. I must not show I care.

'The trouble is – ' Buddy said, ' – there's nothing here that shows me you can go the course. A synopsis and a single chapter, Anna. Very difficult for one to judge from a single chapter. And it's a little raw. Can you sustain it? That's what worries me.'

'Yes,' I said. *It had to be yes, didn't it?* I was hardly going to say *No, you're right, I'll probably quit next week; you're wasting your time with me.* 'Absolutely.'

'We'll see. But let's have tea, shall we? When are you back?'

'Umm. The 2nd.'

'Good. Afternoon Tea on the 4th then.'

'I'll just check my schedule,' I said.

'Sure, sure. Call me back if it's a problem.'

He hung up and left me staring at the receiver. *Such breathtaking arrogance...* Yet I had waited for this moment for so long.

Phyllis smiled. 'Congratulations Anna,' she said. 'You've nailed it.'

My good fortune seemed to rouse Phyllis from her previous dejection. She stood up and began pacing, making small moth-like movements with her fingers, her eyes lively once more. She began exploring the room, stopping off at the bathroom for a pee, closing the door behind her.

'Have you seen those tiles?' she said afterwards. 'Titian blue!'

'You still have a little…' I pointed to the mascara streaks on her cheeks.

'Did I miss a bit? My eyes aren't what they used to be. Had them lasered, but the surgeon was a quack, I tell you.' She paused and fell silent and I wondered whether she was contemplating an aspect of her surgical history, whether she regretted what she had done to herself in the name of beauty. It was something she never talked about. *Verboten.* She acted as if stretched skin were a natural consequence of the ageing process. 'Why don't you order a bottle of champagne?' she said, suddenly. 'The last glass has worn off.'

I called down to Room Service while she went to the bathroom to shower. We had a couple of hours until the official Welcome Meeting. I picked up my bag and returned to the balcony where I took Phyllis's place on the sun-lounger, beside a succulent aloe vera plant. I ran my fingers along a smooth leaf, holding back from the temptation to crush it. It was so perfect, it might have been plastic too. How was it, I wondered, that my whole life had taken on this air of artifice? Only a few weeks ago, everything seemed very settled. My life was ordinary. I knew who I was and where I was going. The

169

objects and people that surrounded me were solid and familiar. But here I felt out of place. The vibrant colours, the dazzling whiteness, it was like some perfect pop-up book and I was a paper character on the page. At any moment, some malicious God might snap the book closed with me inside it.

Carl was a part of the invented world too. He was new and shiny and did not seem quite real. He was playing games with me and what was between us was surely worthless; his affection was shallow and misguided and could not be compared to what I felt for Will. Why then, was I even contemplating returning his text? Perhaps it was because I'd read his novel. I knew that however playful our liaison had been, there was more beneath the surface that I hadn't seen, that I hadn't even begun to explore. His writing was serious and convincing. But would he let me come close to the person who wrote those words? Did I even want to get to know him better? Was it possible that if I let this relationship develop, I'd get beyond the initial façade and discover a very different Carl; an intimacy that neither of us had yet conceived of, something far more complex than Will and I shared or could ever dream of sharing? Or would I, by contrast, get nowhere?

I attempted a few responses to his text, each time deleting what I wrote. He couldn't stop thinking of me? In the end, I settled on a single line.

I haven't thought about you once.

I'd toyed with a few lines before that, but nothing came out right. This was surely wrong too. He could see it as a brush-off or a flirtation, depending on his mood. But it didn't commit me to anything. I might offend him, but I imagined he was thicker-skinned than that. He'd get that I was joking, wouldn't he? If I wrote anything else, anything vaguely encouraging, I'd be no better than Phyllis. I'd end up on the shelf, wasting thousands of pounds in plastic surgery clinics and shedding copious tears for the sake of some idiotic, short-arsed man with a fake tan and a mouthful of porcelain veneers. I pressed "Send".

The champagne arrived as Phyllis emerged from the bathroom.

She had already applied a few spadefuls of Estée Lauder: her skin was satiny and her lips shone like newly-set jelly. She wore a white bathrobe and her hair was wrapped in a pristine white turban.

'What must you think of me?' she said. 'I'm so sorry. I hadn't anticipated this.'

I supposed she was talking about Loftus. 'I thought I'd prepared myself. After so many years...'

'It's only natural,' I said. The man was patently absurd but I wasn't in the mood to challenge her.

'Well, are you going to pop that cork, or am I?' She was already taking the bottle from the cooler and fiddling with the wire mesh. I wasn't certain that I wanted another drink, yet a part of my brain said *what the hell* and laughed as the cork flew from the bottle and hit the ceiling, as the champagne trickled over her bony fingers.

I grabbed a glass, as Phyllis poured. I wondered about sending a P.S. to Carl, to soften what I'd written but knew that would be a mistake. The politics of text-messaging were very simple: so long as you do not reply to any message you have received, you are in a position of power. Once you relinquish that power by responding – no matter how witty, intellectual or apparently disinterested the text in question may be – you are in a position of weakness, reduced to the status of *one who is waiting.*

'To you, Anna!' Phyllis declared. 'To you and your literary success!'

'It's only a tea,' I muttered, but after a sip or two, that tea with Buddy already seemed a far more promising affair.

'To you and Will!' she added. 'May your marriage be long and happy!'

'Thank you.'

'So good to see you two exchanging so many messages,' she said.

I nearly choked on the champagne.

'It's just so lovely to witness, you know. I mean, whatever my own situation, it's good to know that Will has someone he can rely on.'

I sat down on the edge of the bed, gripping the glass tightly. Did

Phyllis suspect my infidelity? I doubted it. She was behaving as any mother would, protective of her son, wanting the best for him. I tried to quash my guilt – *he* was the one who had sown the seed of doubt, *he* called out another woman's name. But how could I blame Will now for anything? I didn't know the truth. I'd gone on suspicion and anger and my own infatuation with Carl had surely played a part in this. I felt faintly sick but had no idea if it was the alcohol or self-disgust that caused it. I might vomit all I liked but I couldn't take back what I had done. Yet I could stop the madness now. Even if Carl replied to my message, I could ignore it, quit his class, marry Will and never see McGahan again.

'It's disgusting!' Phyllis said.

You're right, I wanted to say, y*ou're so right.*

She picked up the champagne bottle, examined the label. 'Bloody Cheapskate.'

I realised my mistake immediately. 'Not a good year?'

'If I know James, he probably bought a job lot at the discount store. Where's the f'ing mini-bar when you need it?'

The mini-bar was concealed inside the wardrobe. On discovering it, Phyllis took out a couple of tiny bottles of vodka and poured them into tumblers. She fetched a bottle of dry Martini she'd bought in the Duty Free shop at Heathrow and added a slug to each tumbler, together with a few cubes of ice from the champagne bucket. She handed me a glass and chinked hers with mine, then sat back on her bed, cross-legged, her legs so frail I thought they might snap.

'I think I owe you an explanation.'

I shrugged. Her feet were deeply tanned, the veins standing out like macramé, the toenails painted fuchsia pink.

'I thought I could handle seeing him, Anna.' She laughed, a hollow hoot. 'I know! I know he's not everybody's cup of tea and I wish to hell and buggery that he wasn't mine. I thought I got over it a long time ago.'

Not knowing what to say, I said nothing.

'He was my lover, Anna.'

'I guessed you had history.'

'I was married to Will's father at the time.'

So… infidelity was something she understood. I took a first sip of Martini.

'I didn't betray him intentionally.'

Nobody ever does, I thought.

'It crept up on me.'

Like a plague. Something vile and unstoppable.

Phyllis perched on the side of my bed and leant in, too close. Her breath was sour and I caught the gaudy stink of her expensive face powder. It took every ounce of my strength to remain still and not recoil.

'I rather lost my head,' she said.

'It can happen to anybody. You shouldn't feel bad.'

'Oh, I don't. I could never regret it, not really. Of course in those days he wasn't the bestselling author he is today. He was no more famous than you or I: just a hack, like any other. A Nobody, an utter Nobody!' Phyllis threw her head back in disgust and took a large swig from her glass. Her head appeared to be rolling a little – like a plastic nodding dog in the back of a car window. 'I was Fashion Editor at *La Vague* in those days; everybody wanted to know me. For a tacky little journo, he was onto a good thing.'

'So why did you fall for him?'

'Ha!' She spat unintentionally in my face but did not apologise, merely stood up and went to fetch her cigarettes. She stood at the bedside, her hand trembling as she lit up and inhaled. Pulling her bathrobe more closely about her, she appeared to be fending off an invisible predator. Her bottom lip trembled spasmodically, as if she had a piece of glass lodged in her mouth.

'Tobias and I were both workaholics,' she said. 'We hardly saw each other. I had the occasional weekend off, but when I did, Tobias was never there; if he'd thought, for one minute, to drag his scrawny backside out of that office…'

I wondered then if I should stop Phyllis from speaking. Will wouldn't want me to hear the secrets of his parents' marriage. And where was he at that time? Off at boarding school already? Surely he knew nothing, even now, of this liaison with Loftus. But I sensed that Phyllis needed to make this confession. I wished that she would stop drinking; I wished she'd stop talking. But there was nothing I could do to arrest the flow of words.

'I took a break, Anna – time for myself. It wasn't Tobias's fault, not really. I came to Molos Bay. Never expected to meet a fellow American in a place like that – there were no tourists on the island in those days. But Loftus was here, checking out locations for his new business venture. He was different then, believe me: less *glitzy*. His plans impressed me.'

'How many years is it, since you've seen him?'

'Must be fifteen… twenty… I haven't been counting.'

'But why now?'

She winced a little, as if the speck of glass in her mouth had dislodged and shifted, as if she was trying to find that small shard with her tongue, but could not. 'A whim,' she said. 'Just a whim.'

I ought to have been furious at her. Instead, I felt only pity.

'He understood me,' she said. 'But he never took me seriously. I couldn't forget him though, Anna. I never forgot him.'

Phyllis paused and downed the rest of her Martini in one. She slammed the glass on the bedside table and the stem cracked beneath the pressure. She released it, then shook her head, barely seeming to notice the small trickle of blood that ran down the side of her palm.

'Let's get ready, shall we?' I said. Perhaps I couldn't bear to hear any more. 'Isn't the Welcome Meeting soon?'

'There's no hurry. We should at least finish off the champagne.' She poured a fresh glass, apparently no longer concerned at the vintage. I knew I ought to stop her from drinking, but how could I? Phyllis opened her suitcase, pulling out a number of garments, considering each one before discarding it on the bed. She came across a pile of underwear, intricate lacy confections, but tossed these aside too. 'You know Tobias was distinctly average in the bedroom department,' she said.

I decided to pour myself more champagne after all. I was going to need it.

'Whereas James…'

'I get the idea.'

Phyllis appeared not to notice my rebuff. She had chosen a

flimsy cerise frock and – still clutching the nearly-spent cigarette – she removed her robe to dress. Her emaciated frame gave her the look of a death-camp survivor. It scared me suddenly. She had done this to herself in the name of fashion, but seeing her now, all I could think of was the damage done. Did she have any idea how she appeared to others? I doubted it. She was unselfconscious as she pulled the dress up her spindly legs, across her empty, sagging bosom. Did she never miss her old self – full-bodied and ripe? She appeared so comfortable with self-starvation. It had become – at least to her – unremarkable.

Phyllis slipped her feet into jewelled flip-flops and crushed her cigarette on the balcony, beneath her rubber soles. A brilliant green gecko skittered across the wall and she jumped a little on seeing it. Feeling my eyes upon her, she looked up, but her look revealed nothing at all, only the mask-like tightness of her artificial face which made her appear suddenly invulnerable.

'I've made a mistake. I'm sorry, Anna. I shouldn't have brought you here.'

'Don't be silly,' I said, though I was wondering whether she was right. 'It's the first night. You're bound to be feeling jittery.'

'Do you think so? Sex is such a distraction.'

'Sometimes I think the whole of life is a distraction.'

'It's just a chemical reaction, isn't it?' she said. 'Perhaps we should rise above it.'

'Personally, I'd rather talk about art and philosophy.'

'I'd rather talk art and philosophy with an immensely attractive single man!' Phyllis replied. She paused in drunken contemplation. 'And don't tell Will that you prefer philosophy to sex.'

She had a point there. "*Sorry darling, not tonight. I'd rather discuss Kierkegaard.*"

Phyllis must have read my mind because for no reason at all, she started to laugh and before I could say 'Fear and Trembling' the two of us were creased up in alcohol-induced hysterics, like hyenas on acid, clutching our stomachs, bent double, hardly able to string words together, yet somehow bonding in a way that was anything but intellectual.

175

20

'But you know, I think I could probably have written better if I'd been a little more comfortable.' – Katherine Anne Porter

The large, square courtyard was bedecked with scarlet geraniums. We sat with a small crowd of other would-be writers, on separate tables, beneath the great Ouranos Vine. Phyllis was sporting a floppy orange sun hat and over-large, dark shades – a kind of Jackie O look that was almost fetching.

Already I suspected that Phyllis was right: it was a mistake, coming here. It was picturesque – with the illuminated pool to our left, the sun setting over the Mediterranean ahead of us and tea candles burning in glass lanterns, strung across the pergola. Somehow the aesthetic beauty of the scene did not soothe my unease. I placed my mobile down on the table as a heavy-jawed waiter offered us a glass of ouzo. I guessed we would spend more time talking about writing in the week ahead than engaging in the act itself.

As Phyllis raised the glass to her lips, I spotted Loftus strolling towards the courtyard. His physique was odd, his legs too short and a little bandy; his chest was overly broad. He wore a pale blue shirt and white jeans, tight about the crotch. As he paused to converse with his guests, he threw his head back and smiled. *Stop judging people on appearances. Grow up.* He strode about like a cockerel, fluffing his feathers, eliciting attention. Wherever he turned, people fell for it. He promised everything they desired. They wanted to believe in him.

'He's adorable,' a woman on the next table said. 'Not at all stand-offish!'

'We've paid close to two grand a head for the pleasure of his company for God's sake,' Phyllis hissed. 'He's just making sure we get our money's worth.'

Now he stood up to the microphone. He took a breath and everybody fell silent.

'Good evening,' he said.

'It was good until you showed up,' Phyllis muttered.

'I am honoured to be here tonight and it's my pleasure to officially welcome you to the Ouranos Centre in this, our twenty-first anniversary year.' His voice had a studied suaveness; I was trying to place his accent still but couldn't get it: it had an unfamiliar lilt. 'When I set up this centre, I could not have imagined that the Ouranos Group would grow so quickly. Today, The Ouranos Centre is without doubt the most successful holiday company of its kind and that gives me a thrill, not least because being part of this enterprise has allowed me to support thousands of people in their creative pursuits.'

'Doesn't it make you want to puke?' Phyllis leaned back in her chair and yawned.

Loftus began outlining practicalities: breakfast times, meditation classes, yoga. He didn't mention writing.

'Where's he from?' I asked Phyllis. 'California?'

'In his dreams,' she whispered. 'He's from Hicksville, Tennessee. He could have bought a small ranch with the money he's spent on his voice coach.'

'I trust you've all received your complimentary Ouranos Centre notebooks?' Loftus asked. 'Good.' He was responding to a nod or two. 'The other workbooks are all available at the Centre shop, as I think you're aware. These are all such fantastic tools for your personal development. You know, many of the notebooks and pens are manufactured here in the Ouranos Mountain Village Workshop – we've arranged an excursion to the workshop midweek and also one to the Ouranos Vineyard tomorrow afternoon. One of my proudest achievements is the effect this centre has had on the local economy and I'm thrilled to have played a role in that.

'But I want to talk to you now about the reason you're here. You know, ever since I created this community in Ouranos, I have come to understand that creativity is at the core of all humanity.'

'Bollocks,' Phyllis said. 'He doesn't give a fuck about creativity. All he cares about is getting screwed and his damn profit margin.'

'*Phyllis*,' I said, under my breath. Her voice, loosened by the alcohol, was louder than before. I heard laughter behind me and turned; it was the guy I'd first noticed on the coach, the geek. His laughter was louder than it ought to have been – and he didn't seem at all self-conscious, despite the fact he was alone. I couldn't work out whether those dark spectacles were meant to be stylish or whether he'd just picked up the first pair he saw in the optician's. At least somebody appreciated Phyllis.

It occurred to me that if Phyllis had told me, in the first place, that she considered Loftus to be a narcissistic fraud, I might have stayed at home. I might be with Will now: we might have sorted out the almighty mess we were in. Instead I had to listen to Loftus, spouting something about *the unique voice of each individual writer*. He was quoting the American dancer Martha Graham but the effects of the alcohol were hitting me and I was finding it difficult to concentrate.

All around me, rapt faces looked up to Loftus. He did not have to work to convince his disciples. Perhaps there was some complex subtext to his utterances that I had failed to understand. More likely, I was wasting my time. And I was missing Will. If Will were here, he would probably go further than his mother. He would be heckling Loftus, giving him a hard time. And imagining that, I felt a sudden, desperate longing to go straight back home. I wanted to get away from this bad salesman, to be away from Phyllis and to be alone on the sofa with Will, talking things through, making sense of the mesh of lies that now seemed to surround us.

I was about to stand up, but as I budged in my seat, Loftus turned towards us. Phyllis lowered her head beneath her hat, but he kept staring, willing her to look. His gaze was insistent, but when it was finally clear he would get no joy, he turned away. On the other side of the courtyard, Elspeth was circling the tables, handing out leaflets. As she came closer, I took one and was about to read it when

Loftus turned to a projector screen and began fiddling with a laptop. Behind him, an image appeared, a photograph of Ouranos Bay and beneath it, a quotation:

"Other countries may offer you discoveries in manners or lore or landscape; Greece offers you something harder – the discovery of yourself." – Lawrence Durrell

The geek was in eyeshot now, trying to amuse me, poking a couple of fingers down his throat. I laughed but quickly turned away. *Not a good idea. Flirting. Stupid.*

I tried to focus on Loftus again.

'I want to tell you about a unique opportunity,' Loftus said. He ran his fingers backwards through his silver hair. His was a sleazy charm, but a charm nonetheless. 'I've realised in recent years that many visitors to the Ouranos Centre gain so much from this experience that they wish to repeat it – not just by returning here on vacation, but taking a much bolder step: by choosing to make a second home on the island.'

He paused and all about the courtyard people appeared absorbed in his spiel. Even Phyllis appeared momentarily distracted by this pitch.

'A second home on Ouranos can work as both a personal retreat and, of course, an investment property.'

Phyllis leant forward, appearing suddenly interested. There was clearly some cultish aspect to Loftus's personality that was lost on me, because she wasn't the only one.

On the next table however, the geek was shaking his head in incredulity. He seemed to be the only other person to find Loftus's performance amusing. So I was not alone, not the only sane person in the asylum.

'With this in mind,' Loftus continued, 'I took the bold step of embarking on a new construction venture. It is with great pleasure that I can reveal, in this our twenty-first anniversary year, the full range of properties that are now available for purchase. First, I am proud to present –' He paused for effect and clicked the gizmo in his hand. '– The Sappho Villa.'

I burst out laughing, but managed to half-suppress it, disguising the laughter as a coughing fit.

On the screen before us, an impressive villa appeared.

'The Sappho Villa,' Loftus said, 'offers the ultimate in luxury and comfort. No expense has been spared in creating a Greek Island home that is also the perfect Writer's Retreat. Named after the great Greek lyric poet, this Villa comes equipped with a stunning kitchen/breakfast room, three bathrooms, a courtyard garden, a swimming pool, a full library and a study overlooking the sea. I'm sure you will agree, the perfect spot for any writer...

'The Sappho is our top-of-the-range property. However, we have also created the Durrell White Houses. These outstanding three-bedroom properties are situated in the heart of Ouranos Town. They have the same luxurious facilities as the Sappho but on a smaller scale. They each boast an outdoor spa tub and, naturally, residents will have easy access to the Ouranos Writer's Centre. The White Houses – you'll be pleased to hear – are complete and available for immediate purchase.'

I shouldn't be here. I might just as well have come on a week-long belly-dancing retreat for all the good this would do me. It was madness to be wasting my time like this when I had a relationship to repair, a novel to write and a wedding to organise.

Loftus continued his sales pitch, describing the very affordable "Miller Complex", perfect for the budget-conscious and available both for purchase and for rental; the Kazantzakis Cottages and the Aristotle Lodge. And why stop at that? There was also a new onsite Literary Consultancy with online access to trained editors, ready to assess your finished manuscript at the drop of hat. Loftus's belief in the financial viability of this project was proof of my hypothesis that there is not a soul on this planet who is not actually writing a novel.

'I think I'm going to be sick.'

'Oh shit!'

Phyllis had begun to sway very suddenly to one side: the alcohol had finally got the better of her. She slumped over the table and I began to panic. I was responsible for her; I should have stopped her. In the semi-darkness, nobody seemed to notice us, but we needed to move and swiftly.

'Come on, Phyllis,' I whispered. 'Let me take you back to the room.' I put my phone back in my bag and tried to budge her. But she resisted.

'Nonsense,' she said, raising her head briefly, her voice slurred. 'I'm perfectly fine.'

'You said you were going to puke. Come *on*, we have to move. Stand up slowly and nobody will notice.'

She slumped back upon the table.

'Do you want some help?'

The geek was right behind us. What kind of accent was that? Mancunian? He towered over us. He appeared curious, most of all, and vaguely amused.

'Thanks. I just need to get her back to the room.'

Phyllis looked up again, pushed herself to her feet, still swaying woozily, but now making an effort to appear sober, as she gathered her belongings from the table.

'I don't know what all the fuss is about,' she said, though she took his hand as she stood up, to steady herself. 'Who are you?'

'I'm Joel.'

'Hmph.'

Loftus glimpsed briefly in our direction.

'What's he going to think?' Phyllis said, as we left the courtyard.

'He's too busy thinking about profit margins to worry about us,' Joel replied.

He held Phyllis's arm almost tenderly, helping her up a step, chatting to her to distract her from her own inebriation. When we got to the lift, he hesitated, as if not sure what to do next.

'It's OK. We'll be fine.'

'If you're sure.'

He scratched his head.

'Absolutely.'

Joel shrugged, gave a curious wave and returned to the bar.

Inside the lift, Phyllis finally removed her shades. Beneath the fluorescent light, her skin appeared a distinct shade of green and her frailty was all too apparent. She leant against me, her head nestled in the hollow of my shoulder. I craved the familiarity of Will's presence then, his voice. Perhaps the Angela story was just a bizarre fiction that I'd invented, an extreme form of self-torture.

We made it to our room just in time. Phyllis staggered to the bathroom like a circus clown feigning drunkenness. She closed the door behind her and I headed out to the balcony. The night air was still humid. The illuminated swimming pool appeared to hover, a turquoise lozenge of light. I stood staring out, looking up at the stars.

Behind me, I heard footsteps, and turned to see Phyllis, significantly paler now.

'I'm going to bed,' she said. 'You should go back downstairs.'

'No, I'm done.'

'You haven't eaten, Anna – and the buffet is still open. Go on.'

But I didn't want to go.

'You OK?' I asked.

'I'm fine. I'm tougher than you think.'

Was she? I couldn't be sure. I wanted to call Will, to tell him what had happened, but how could I discuss her in her presence?

'I'm fooling myself,' I said.

'What? What did you say?'

I hadn't meant to speak out loud. *About your son*, I might have said, if I'd dared to speak the truth. *Fooling myself that everything's fine, that everything is just as it used to be, when nothing is as it used to be, everything has changed and we've messed it up, there's no going back, it can't be done.*

'I'll make an idiot of myself,' I said. 'If I go back down there. I'm pretty drunk. I need to sleep.'

It felt good simply to *imagine* being with Will. When I thought about being in his presence, I could bestow on that relationship a perfection that in reality it did not possess. So long as I imagined our conversations, those conversations could be intimate and passionate, whispered pillow talk and wordplay. His best qualities – his artistic brilliance, his wit and his perceptiveness – would shine through and I could ignore the parts of him that irritated me: his inability to support me when it mattered; his inexplicable interest in a porn starlet; his work obsession and his pig-headed, right-wing politics.

'You don't look drunk to me,' Phyllis said.

My mother-in-law. How would it feel to call her that?

'Goodnight Phyllis,' I said. 'It's been a long day. I think I'll crash.'

She turned to me, frowning, as if disapproving that I should bail out so soon when the party was only just about to begin. I took no notice. Within minutes I was in bed, whilst Phyllis still shuffled about in the darkness. I was vaguely aware of her rifling through her suitcase, but my eyelids were heavy, my limbs relaxing into torpor and I could not make any sense of it.

'I'm sorry, Anna,' she whispered. 'I have to go back downstairs. I can't leave it like this. I have to talk with James.'

I fell asleep and was not troubled by a single dream.

21

'The writer is either a practising recluse or a delinquent, guilt-ridden one; or both. Usually both.' – Susan Sontag

I took the long route to the breakfast room, across the bridge that overlooked the swimming pool. The early-risers had already secured their sun-loungers and a group of women in varying states of undress were engaged in a yoga class, stretching their limbs in unnatural postures that appeared to defy the laws of gravity. The sun had risen behind us and if you listened carefully, you could hear the hum of cicadas and the trill of a goat bell, but there was something unusual about the sound.

'It's shite, isn't it?'

I turned to see Joel – who must have come from the breakfast room – dressed in a loose white T-shirt and shorts. He blinked in the bright sunshine.

'What is?'

'Seen any goats around here?' he said. He cocked his head upwards towards a discreet speaker over the bridge. 'It's canned!'

'Oh Jesus.'

'How's your Mum this morning?' Joel still wore the trademark oblong specs. He blinked in the bright sunshine.

'Oh, she's not my Mum. But she's asleep,' I said. 'Snoring with her mouth wide open like a Venus flytrap.'

'I'm sure she'll thank you for that.'

I laughed.

'She your mate then?' he said.

'No, not my mate exactly.' *Did she look like a mate?* 'The mother of a friend. Phyllis.'

Oh hell. It would have been so easy to say 'my fiancé's mum' or even 'my boyfriend's mum'. *What was that about?*

'You both doing Loftus's class?'

I nodded.

'Well, nice to meet you.' His sudden formality took me by surprise, as he held out his hand to shake mine. I expected him to continue the conversation, but he seemed stumped for words. He just stood there, putting his hands back in his pockets, grinning somewhat sheepishly.

'Well,' I said. 'Breakfast.'

'Avoid the mushrooms,' he said. 'Ghastly.'

He said "ghastly" with a mock public-school accent and it made me laugh. I was about to reply when his phone rang. At least, I assumed it was Joel's phone because I didn't recognise the ring tone. But Joel was staring at me, wide-eyed with an expression that clearly meant 'why aren't you picking up your phone?' and I realised that the phone in my bag was indeed ringing. It looked like my phone, it just didn't sound like my phone. I went to answer it.

'What's up?' Joel asked.

'Nothing. Just the ring tone. Technical error!'

The name on the screen was Will's.

I picked up.

'Hi, Will!' I could hear my own voice; it sounded cool and delicate; at any moment it might crack or break.

'Oh, Anna.' His response was brusque, as if an irritation hovered beneath the surface. He had called me, but didn't sound happy to hear my voice.

'So how are you?' There was so much that I wanted to say, but there were too many miles between us, the timing was all wrong. Joel, having no idea of the significance of the call, appeared to hesitate, uncertain whether he should stay or go.

'I'm fine,' Will said. 'Where's Phyllis?'

No 'I've missed you' or 'why haven't you called?' Like speaking to a stranger.

'She's still sleeping, I think.'

'You think?'

Why was he so combative? What had I done?

'I've come down for breakfast,' I said.

'So why have you got her phone?'

'*Her* phone?' The penny dropped. This was not my phone; it was Phyllis's. She had the same model and I had picked up hers by mistake. That part of the equation was easy to fathom. It might explain his tone. 'Oh, sorry, Will. I've picked up your Mum's phone by accident.'

'Brilliant!'

'What's that supposed to mean?'

'It's not supposed to mean anything.' Will seemed absent, as he had no desire to communicate.

Joel was pulling a face that said 'I'd better go' but I held up my hand to stop him, only he didn't get my gesture. He gave a small "catch you later" kind of wave and left.

'If it's your mother you want,' I said, unable to keep the barb from my voice, 'why don't you call my number?'

'Fine. I will.'

*Why was he doing this? Why were **we** doing this?* It didn't seem possible that in such a short space of time, everything we'd built up over five years was dissolving. Or was I too quick to read his voice? Was this nothing but a misunderstanding that being in each other's presence again would solve?

'We'll speak later, yes?'

'Sure. I'll call you later this morning. Love you.'

'You too.' But the words were flat and meaningless and I knew that neither of us believed them.

22

Dear Sir, I am in a Madhouse and quite forget your name or who you are.' – John Clare

After breakfast, I returned to the room. As soon as she saw me, Phyllis, who had been sitting on an armchair in the corner, stood up and began to throw things into a small satchel. She was dressed in a long, white kaftan; her hair was pulled back with a white bandana. She appeared to be packing her notebooks for class, but there was a fury in her movements and she was studiously ignoring me.

What the hell was going on here? First Will, now Phyllis. They had clearly been talking about me, but why? I decided to be calm. I sat down on the edge of my bed, and picked up the Parisot book. I flicked through it, trying to appear uninterested in the vagaries of Phyllis's behaviour, as if everything were completely normal. The page fell open on a subtle nude, resting her hand lightly between her thighs. It was not Jeanne, I knew that much. Modigliani never painted Jeanne nude; it marked her out from his other models. With Jeanne, he was more interested in the woman he knew, capturing her essence, yet still abstracting it. In Jeanne's face, often, he caught a sense of her, but you could also see the Cycladic figure, the ancient stone face beneath her modern beauty.

I tried to focus on the image, but Phyllis was determined to make a scene. She was attempting to squeeze a large folder into a bag that was far too small for it and she'd clearly had enough.

'Oh for fuck's sake,' she said, flinging the satchel across the room.

Silence no longer seemed an option. I closed the book.

'What's the matter, Phyllis?'

She was ready for me.

'The matter? The sodding matter! As if you don't know, Anna!' She spat the words and her face appeared contracted and pinched; her bandana had slipped across her ear like Van Gogh's bandage.

'I'm sorry, have I done something wrong?'

'I'll see you in class!' she said. She bent down and picked up her bag before flouncing from the room, her kaftan trailing like a bridal gown behind her.

As I entered the Writer's Centre, I half expected to see the Guggenheim spiral staircase rising above me. In fact, the interior reminded me of nothing so much as corporate America, with soulless corridors and slightly scruffy white walls adorned with uninspiring photographs in chrome frames. I took the lift to the third floor and entered the classroom, expecting more of the same. Instead, I entered a gigantic semi-circular space with floor-to-ceiling glass windows, overlooking the bay.

Phyllis was already at the table as was Joel and about ten other students. Nobody was speaking. Phyllis was leafing through her notebook; her eyes flickered up to meet mine but she hurriedly returned them to the page. I looked away too and took in the room and the peculiar silence. The tables were arranged in a horseshoe formation with leather chairs for around twenty students. They were set with glass tumblers and carafes of water. At the front, a few red gerberas stood in an opaque black vase. The air-conditioning system whirred.

'Hi Phyllis,' I said. I sat down next to her, determined not to sink to her level. She raised her head and gave me a venomous stare. 'Hi Joel. You met Phyllis?'

'Not officially,' Joel said. He held out his hand. 'Pleased to meet you.'

But Phyllis merely smirked, narrowed her eyes and turned away.

The silence was briefly broken as more students came into the room; but the mood of the room infected them and they soon fell quiet too, exchanging whispers and muted greetings, pouring water and arranging their books.

189

When Loftus entered however, there was a distinct rustle of excitement. He emerged from the lift with Elspeth, held his head up high and strode in. Yet despite his self-conscious strut, he seemed smaller today; except that his eyes protruded even more than I remembered.

'Good Morning,' he boomed. 'I trust you've all slept well!' He smiled, displaying his brilliant dental work. His eyes scanned the room, taking in the women in particular, before finally settling his attention on Phyllis. Her head was bowed but she raised her eyes slowly, giving him the full Lady Diana, which oddly he appeared to appreciate. He sat down, allowing Elspeth to take the floor.

She cleared her throat and smiled.

'Welcome,' she said, 'to your first class at the Ouranos Bay Centre. We are so excited this week to have our Founder, James Loftus on site. I'm sure you'll all agree that we are privileged to have James here.'

As everyone applauded, I took in Elspeth's studied perfection. She was tall, large-boned, all gloss and polish, her face thick with creamy make-up. She wore a pale, exquisitely-tailored linen suit and delicate jewellery that complemented her flawless skin.

Loftus stood up again, nodding his appreciation. He swaggered a little and gave a little mock bow.

'Thank you. I'm honoured to be here.' He paused. 'There's little need for me to introduce myself, but I will say a few brief words about my favourite subject – that is, myself.'

Joel glimpsed in my direction; I wondered what had brought him here, how the cult of Loftus had sucked him in. I was still rattled from the events of the morning, regretting not calling Will back, wondering if my worst fears were about to become manifest. Loftus had launched into a lengthy spiel: he explained how he had begun life in a working class suburb of Tennessee, living with his mother and stepfather, having lost his father at the age of six. He was influenced, naturally, by the Beat poets, by Hemingway. He talked about a successful career in journalism and extensive world travel, mentioning, in passing, the titles of a whole raft of his earlier published novels, none of which I had ever heard of. And of course, he gloated at the recent bestsellerdom of the Literary Genius book, which had surely earned him more than his entire oeuvre to date.

'And now – before we begin… ' Loftus added. 'I'd like to introduce our special guest, Joel Beck, a journalist from *Beauvoir* magazine.'

Now he had my attention. Joel looked skywards, as if the attention was not merited. *A journalist? Hell.*

'Joel is here to write about the emergence of Creative Writing Retreats as an industry. There's a form on the table here where you may give your consent to be photographed and included in Joel's article. I'm sure you'll all get to know Joel and co-operate with him in the week ahead.'

I was still taking this in. *The bloody Beauvoir.* Joel didn't look like the kind of guy who worked for the *Beauvoir* and he certainly didn't act like it. And if Loftus thought this was a great PR stunt, he might be about to get an unpleasant surprise. Nothing Joel had said thus far suggested any kind of approval of this enterprise.

But what must Phyllis be thinking? This was the guy who saw her to her room last night when she was vulnerable and inebriated. Was he about to make a story out of *her?* He was avoiding my eye now. I should have seen it a mile off. Those specs were simply screaming '*media type*'. Now that I thought about it, he was not so different to the rest of the boy hacks that I'd encountered at Will's *Telegraph* parties. As for the consent form, I had no intention of signing it.

The other students – encouraged by Loftus – now began to introduce themselves. This was a room full of jostling egos, a peculiar mix of earnest women and pushy men, a few absolute beginners and several hardened pros. When it was Phyllis's turn, she made a determined effort to address each person, meeting everybody's eyes but mine.

'I first came to Ouranos in – it must have been 1989,' she said, 'in its first year of opening. I was a magazine editor at the time; I featured the resort in an editorial.'

It was true, of course, but were Phyllis's words merely an attempt to gain status within the group? Loftus was nodding his approval.

'Phyllis was one of our very first guests,' he said, 'so it's perfectly fitting that she's here today. I'm thrilled.'

She smiled with an affected coyness, but when I placed my hand on her shoulder, she pulled sharply back. I turned to the window, the expanse of glass dividing us from the elements and making the idealised blue of the sea beyond seem a fantasy, a mere trick of the light. Loftus was giving instructions now for a warm-up exercise, instructing us to free write on the subject of "what it means to be a writer" and I watched as the others bent their heads to the page with an enthusiasm that I could not muster. *I don't want to be here. I don't want to be here, falling out with Phyllis, scribbling the first nonsense that comes into my head.* Was I was the only one who could not engage with this?

In three months time I would be getting married. That gave me three months to get a headstart on the Hébuterne story. It might be ridiculous to think of marriage as some kind of deadline. Before I knew it, I'd be getting pregnant and giving up my job at the Walpole, joining an NCT group and practising panting between contractions. Soon I'd be spending my days bouncing a demanding fat baby on my knee and my evenings would be spent peeling sweet potatoes to make puree. The worse thing was, this was not the work of a sick imagination. I had actually seen it happen to people. How would I write a novel then, my brain reduced to soup?

'Wonderful. If you could now put down your pens...' Loftus said.

I had not written a single syllable.

Elspeth used the interlude between writing and reading aloud to broadcast a quick advertisement. 'Straight after class there will be a coach tour, leaving the Ouranos Centre at noon for a trip into the mountains. You'll all have an opportunity to take lunch in a secluded village before touring the Ouranos vineyard and sampling the local wines.'

At the mention of wine, Phyllis's mouth twisted into a semblance of a smile.

'Felicity,' Loftus said. 'Would you like to be the first to read aloud?'

'Absolutely,' she said. There was no trace in her voice of the vitriol she had reserved for him the previous evening. I glanced in his direction. He was looking her straight in the eye, his upper lip trembling with a kind of simpering lust that made me feel faintly nauseous. Had something happened between them after she returned downstairs? Was that it, some kind of desperate romantic encounter that had robbed her of all sanity? Is that why she had turned on me, was it simply the knowledge that I had witnessed her rants against him and that left her feeling vulnerable?

Phyllis cleared her throat. Everyone fell silent. She stood up, swooshed her kaftan in front of her and adjusted the white turban on her head. As she began speaking, I noticed the lipstick on her teeth and I wanted to tell her but could not.

'Being a writer, she said, 'is not a job but a vocation.' Her voice was clear, her manner intense. She glimpsed down at her notebook but I got the impression she was half reading, half improvising; giving it her best Glenn Close. 'You see, it's not *what* we do, but *who* we are.' She paused and looked directly at me. I couldn't interpret her look, didn't know if it was anger that I saw there or some immeasurable sadness. 'A writer who does not respect the word is something of a whore. To disrespect the word is an act of infidelity and what can be worse than that?'

Phyllis was accusing me, clearly, but what was the charge? That I was guilty of poor punctuation and grammar? *If only.* I desperately willed these to be my crimes, even as I was certain that it was more than this. Now there could be no doubt that she *knew*.

My phone was ringing. The word *infidelity* still hung in the air. Phyllis continued to read, she had moved on, but her accusation left me breathless. And she was right to accuse me. She let the phone keep ringing, its fake jangly ring-tone taunted me and though I wanted to pick it up, it was not in my possession.

Phyllis paused in her reading, smiled benignly at the other students, then bent down and reached into her handbag to take out my phone.

'Perhaps you should answer this, Anna?'

'You have my phone...' I said, stating the obvious.

'It might be –' she paused, narrowing her eyes, '– your boyfriend?'

'Will never calls from work,' I said. *How long was she going to continue with this farce?*

'Excuse me for breaking up this little family party...' It was the mousy girl from the coach, stepping outside the role I had consigned her – 'but could we possibly get on with the readings?'

'It's your mother.' Phyllis said, looking at the handset. 'How disappointing.'

My Mum. That was all I needed. I grabbed the phone and left the room.

'Hello? Mum?'

I made my way downstairs, placing my hand against the glass partition to steady myself. I had answered the phone on instinct: an excuse to get out of there, away from Phyllis. I did not have to re-read Carl's text messages to know what they said. I had them word perfect. If Phyllis had read them – and of course, she had read them – then she knew enough to piece it together. She knew that I had betrayed her son.

'Now Anna,' Mum said, not pausing for breath, 'the thing is this. It's about bridesmaids.'

Oh no, not this, anything but this.

I wanted to tell Mum everything: to cry into the telephone and confess every single mistake, every unfounded suspicion that I'd ever harboured. *She couldn't talk about the wedding now. Surely, she could **tell**?* I could feel my future slipping away from me, not just the wedding day itself (it didn't matter, did it, the façade of perfection, the satin dresses, the scent of roses, the tin cans tied to the back of the car as we left the hotel and drove towards our future) but everything that I had assumed to lie beyond it: waking up next to Will – his scent on the pillow – every morning forever more; the idea of Will as the father of my children; the family I'd half imagined who now were evaporating before my eyes, dissolving before they even had a chance to exist.

'Mum, is this important? I'm on holiday, remember?'

'The thing is, I'm at Lois's place – we're having a chat... and we've been looking at one of the bridal magazines.'

'Mum...'

'And Anna, little Freya is with us too and – I know you're not going to like this, but, well, she's seen the pictures of bridesmaids; you know, all the pretty little posies of flowers; the headdresses.'

'I know what a bridesmaid looks like,' I said. 'But who's been showing her the pictures, Mum, that's what I want to know? I'm not having bridesmaids. I've told you that.'

Couldn't she hear it in my voice? Had she been my mother for so many years and was she still so terrible at reading me?

'This is what we're thinking, Anna. You don't have to have *official* bridesmaids. But we could just let Freya have one of these dresses, you know? And perhaps she could walk up the aisle behind you. Make her *believe* she's a bridesmaid.' She paused, waiting for my response but the problem was, I was crying, and I couldn't speak. 'You wouldn't really want to disappoint Freya, would you?' she said.

'Of course not,' I said. I spoke in a half whisper but I don't think she was listening for the tone. Her head was full of other things: of Freya, of the swish of my bridal train, the family day that would be perfect, surely, even given Dad's absence. I leant against the wall in the corridor of the Ouranos Centre and slid down it, to my haunches, still holding the phone to my ear. Mum had it all worked out. Perhaps she thought that if we did it all well enough, we wouldn't notice. If the flowers toned with the dresses, if the maiden aunts made it to the church, if the harpist played sweetly enough and the sugared almonds were not too brittle – then the fact that it was my uncle walking me down the aisle and not my Dad might slip past us, unnoticed.

There was so much that I wanted to tell her. How could I say it? *There might be no need for a cake stand, Mum. And hold the bridesmaid dress, OK?* That dress might be destined to a life of no purpose, stashed in Lois's wardrobe inside a pretty floral box, lined with scented tissue paper. It would be too sentimental to be discarded, too beautiful to be worn.

'You've done the right thing, Anna. Really. Lois will be so

pleased.'

'Of course,' I said. 'I've been selfish.'

'Now you're sure about this,' she said. 'You're not going to change your mind?'

'No. Buy the dress,' I said. 'I really do think you should buy one.'

23

'Nothing is allowed to be nice any more; everything has to be sordid.' – Barbara Cartland

The Ouranos Vine Bar was deserted. It was only mid-morning but the waiter had barely raised an eyebrow when I ordered a double vodka and tonic. The truth of what had happened was only just beginning to sink in.

After class, I had taken a walk along the cliff top. I stood, gazing down at the rocks beneath, half waiting for someone to come running up to me, begging me not to jump. But of course, they would have been wasting their time. My feet were miles from the edge and my tragedy far too minor to merit the contemplation of suicide.

Instead, I'd hoped that the natural beauty – the sun at its zenith, the haze over distant mountains – might prompt a sudden revelation or even some perspective on this God-awful mess that was my life. The worst part was the knowledge that this was surely (if I looked at the greater picture) entirely trivial. After all, if I stopped to consider all the atrocities in the world, the real tragedies that I witnessed each time I switched on my television set to watch the news – then the small matter of Anna Bright's infidelity to her fiancé really did not matter a jot.

Now, tossing the purple cocktail umbrella that graced my glass aside, I picked up my phone. I plucked up courage to flick through the list of messages that Carl and I had exchanged. There were a couple more than I remembered. I opened the first.

Want 2 have u again. Miss u babe.

Was that the best he could manage? I thought Carl had forgotten me and now I rather wished he had. I had never seen this message before, yet it had been marked as "read". So – Phyllis had received this message on my behalf.

Anna Bright is losing Will Isenberg. I spoke the words under my breath. Yet it was nothing really – that's what I told myself. People fall in and out of love every day. People suffer, more than I could possibly imagine. Some people were tortured and died horrible deaths. But even so, as a small tear fell into my vodka glass, it felt like everything to me. Enormous and earth-shattering and final.

'What's with the tears?' I turned to see Joel, glass in hand, behind me. 'Mind if I sit down?'

'Go ahead.'

'I take it that's not water?'

'Smartarse. Is yours?'

'Sadly, yes,' he said. 'I obviously need to live a little.'

'Where are the others?' I wasn't in the mood for conversation. Phyllis was probably upstairs in the bedroom by now, telephoning Will to spill the beans. The whole thing seemed inevitable. I ought to rouse myself from self-pity; I ought to go and beg her not to tell him. But I was to blame. I had set off a train of events and there was nothing I could do to stop my world from tumbling about me.

'They've all gone on the excursion,' Joel said. 'The Ouranos Vineyard.'

'Shit.'

'Did you want to go?'

I laughed: a dull, empty sound, more like a sob. So, Phyllis was probably halfway up the mountains. But had she told Will? Was she planning to?

'What's the matter?' Joel asked.

'Let's just say I've messed everything up.' I paused. 'I mean, really messed everything up. Big time.'

'Sounds serious.'

'Yeah, well.'

'You want to talk about it?'

'Not really.'

198

'OK.' He paused, looked across at me and sucked his lip. He stood up, putting his hands in his pockets. There was something a little oafish about Joel; his movements were lumbering, as if he was uncomfortable in his large frame. 'I'll go then.'

'Fine.'

'I'll leave you to stew in your own misery.'

'Fuck off!'

'Can I get you some more vodka before I do?'

'You know, for a journalist, you seem like a halfway decent bloke.'

'No, I'm a real bastard,' he said. 'Just like all men.'

I met Joel's eyes very briefly, then I burst out laughing. His flirtation was the worst thing that could have happened under the circumstances which was why it seemed suddenly so hilarious. But then something caught in my throat. One moment I was laughing, the next I was choking. I couldn't stop coughing. My body was racked with unattractive convulsions. Joel leapt up – like a grasshopper – and whacked me hard on the back.

'Here, have some water.'

After taking a few sips, I finally managed to catch my breath. He looked at me and I had the impression that he could see me from a great distance even though he was right next to me.

'I'm sorry about that.'

'S'OK, I often have that effect on women.'

'Oh shut up.'

'You don't believe me?'

I shrugged.

Joel called to the waiter. 'An ouzo please,' he said. 'Anna?'

'The same.'

'Two ouzos. Thanks.' He turned his attention back to me. 'So, what did you make of class?'

'Apart from wondering when Phyllis was going to pull a dagger from her pencil-case?'

'Apart from that.'

'This is not for *Beauvoir* right?'

'Strictly off the record.'

'I don't believe you.'

'You're right. Actually anything you say about the course definitely counts as material. So tell me the interesting shit instead...'

'I can't.' I was trying to imagine Will's face when Phyllis told him about Carl. *Because she would, wouldn't she?* She could hardly let her son marry me, knowing what she knew. 'Why don't you tell *me* something instead?' I said. The waiter placed the ouzos down on the table and I picked up the glass, poured in some water, swirled it and watched the liquid turn opaque.

'Cheers,' Joel said, clinking my glass. He took a large gulp and I followed suit.

'So you've only just met me and already you're after some murky story from my dark and dismal past?'

'Absolutely.' It felt surreal to be indulging in this conversation, when simultaneously, everything was falling apart. 'I need some ammunition in case you ever decide to print stories about my personal life in a national magazine.'

'Well, I don't know how to tell you this,' Joel said, archly, 'but I'm actually a transvestite. I do a brilliant drag act in a Soho strip joint at weekends.'

I smiled and instinctively elbowed him, then immediately drew back; even that touch had felt too intimate.

'So what's up with you and Phyllis?' he said.

I hesitated. It seemed wrong to share the intimacies of my relationships with this stranger I'd only just met. But there was something in his manner that made it seem ordinary. He leaned back in his chair, but in his swaying away from me I sensed that he was in fact giving me a space. I garbled at first of course, about Will, the wedding, Carl, the texts that Phyllis had read. Joel wasn't joking now, he was listening intently, nodding. I didn't know why I felt so relaxed and whether it was just the alcohol loosening my tongue, but nothing felt taboo, until he looked away suddenly, stared out to sea.

'Sorry,' I said.

Joel shook his head. He took a breath. I thought he was going to make his excuses and leave. Instead, he said:

'Why don't you do this properly – from the beginning?'

'What do you mean?'

'It's like listening to an express train. You're thinking we're still in London. We've got all day, right? '

'I thought you were meant to be working here.'

'I missed the coach. Should've been up in the mountains.'

I stared at him then, trying to work him out. There was something bearish about him, but I also sensed a rawness, an openness that made me unafraid. It might have been crazy to trust this man whose face was half hidden behind Jarvis Cocker spectacles, but I had no one else to trust and the alternative was to sit and cry into my ouzo. It took a while, but Joel appeared to be in no hurry. He sat back and listened silently, nodding sometimes or offering encouragement, but never appearing to judge me. When I got to the end of my story, I started talking about the Modigliani novel too and I realised, as I spoke, that I hadn't really talked about it before – at least, not like that, not with somebody who was really listening.

'I think Will thinks it's just a whim,' I said. 'He thinks I'm writing about art because I can't think of anything else to write about. Maybe he's right.'

'How can you tell what Will is thinking?'

'God, d'you know, sorry, but I'm starving. I can't concentrate.'

'What do you want?' Joel asked. 'Some taramasalata or something?'

'Yeah, good idea.'

Joel called the waiter again and ordered. 'So – Modigliani?'

'Perhaps it is romanticism,' I said. 'I mean, I so admire his work, the lines in his sketches, those beautiful caryatids, I adore those.'

'But what makes you want to write about this Jeanne?'

'It's just a hunch. An image that draws me and I want to know why.' I paused and downed the rest of the ouzo. We were in the shade but the heat was making me giddy, blurring my thoughts.

'That sounds good enough to me.'

'Really? Sometimes I feel like a fraud.'

'Why?'

'When I was eighteen, my Dad wanted me to get into Cambridge.' I paused as the taramasalata arrived. I took a hunk of bread and dunked it in the milky pink paste, took an enormous bite. 'I came top in everything at school, so it seemed like the logical next step.'

'And?'

'I went up to interview at St Catharine's. What a disaster.'

'What happened, love?'

Love? Did he call me "love"? It must be a Northern thing.

'They hauled me over hot coals.'

'Meaning?'

'I wanted to speak about Plath and Larkin. They wondered why I hadn't read Tennyson.'

'Oh, give me Larkin any day.'

'The worst part was feeling stupid, you know? And I can't even blame my school or my background. My friend Hilary – she got in.'

'Do you really care what the dons think?'

'No – no, of course not. It's just – something happened, a few weeks later.'

'What?'

'My Dad. He was the one who really wanted it for me.' I was used to telling this story. It shouldn't have affected me like this. 'He died the day before I got my rejection letter.' I bit the flesh of my cheek hard, tasting blood; I didn't want to make a fool of myself. 'So of course, Cambridge meant bugger all in the context, but actually that wasn't true. It was what he wanted, so it seemed to mean everything.'

Joel leant forward and placed his hand over mine. Instinctively, I pulled away.

'It's all a long time ago. Only – I never made that connection before – I've spent most of my adult life feeling not-quite-good-enough, the "nearly girl".'

I'd said enough. Joel must have sensed that the conversation was closed.

'What do you want to do about Phyllis?' he asked.

'She's half way up a mountain and if she has a mobile signal she's probably been on the phone to Will already. There's nothing I can do to stop her.'

'Does it matter?'

'Christ, who do you think you are? Of course it bloody matters.'

'So this Carl bloke...'

'I'm not *in love* with Carl. It's just sexual obsession for God's sake, something I need to get over. Whereas with Will... I feel safe with Will.'

'Aside from the issue with the porn star...'

'I told you to forget I ever said that.'

'Even so – "safe"?'

'It's none of your business.'

'So what you're saying is that Will is definitely the right guy for you?'

I hesitated. I had no idea why Joel was pushing me like this; I barely knew him.

'Yes,' I said. 'Absolutely.'

Joel nodded, as if taking this fact in, absorbing it. 'Then we need to call you a taxi. You need to get yourself up to the Ouranos Vineyard, find Phyllis, get down on your knees before her and tell that walking corpse of a woman that you're so desperately sorry, you will never again be unfaithful to her son. Tell her that you've realised your terrible mistake and beg her not to call him.' He paused, as if contemplating his own brilliance. 'That should do the trick.'

'Walking corpse is a bit much.'

'Whatever. Just take the advice.'

'You're not serious?'

'Perfectly serious. If you want to marry this man you don't actually love, then really, Anna, you have to do everything in your power to get him back.'

'I never said I didn't love him.' *What right did this guy have to make these assumptions?* It wasn't surprising that I snapped. 'I do love him. It's just...' And then I realised it was the "just" that Joel was talking about. 'It's just that I didn't realise it earlier,' I protested.

'OK,' he said. 'If you're sure. I'll go up to reception and call a cab.'

He looked me straight in the eye as if daring me to stop him. He held my gaze for longer than was strictly necessary and it felt at once interesting and deeply uncomfortable.

'I'm sure,' I said.

Joel stood up and headed towards the main building, while I remained in the bar, wondering what I had just done.

24

'Never go on trips with anyone you do not love.'
– Ernest Hemingway

Within half an hour, I was ensconced in the back seat of a clapped-out Greek taxi, with Joel at my side. Joel was making a brave effort at understanding the driver's pidgin English, while I sat back, enjoying the strains of tinny bouzouki music that blared from the radio. I felt like Jeanne Moreau in *Jules et Jim*. The driver tooted his horn as he hurtled around blind corners and like that other Jeanne, my heart was divided.

Up here, amongst the umbrella pines and the bare, white rocks, it was difficult to imagine any other reality. The windows were down but in the sticky heat, my legs were adhering to the car seat.

'So what's your article going to be about?' I asked Joel. I was flicking through a magazine that the driver had left on the seat.

'You still don't trust me, do you?'

'I didn't say that.'

'But you're thinking it.'

I shrugged.

'Why don't you just come out with it?' he said.

'OK. You're a journalist writing an article about Genius Vacations. I've just told you half my life story and we're now chasing my soon-to-be-mother-in-law up a mountain where I'm going to beg her to keep my infidelity to her son quiet.'

'Hmmm…' Joel seemed to consider it, a half-smile gracing his lips. 'It's not a bad story.'

I thwacked him about the head with the magazine.

As we rose higher into the mountains, my anxiety began to recede. It seemed to me that I had a choice. I could go through life in a perpetual state of paranoia or I could trust my intuition. Joel didn't seem like the kind of guy who would stitch me up, so I refused to proceed with caution. He seemed to sense my nervousness and tried to draw me out on the subject of my novel again, but I was suddenly reluctant so we eventually fell silent.

The closer we got to the Ouranos Vineyard and Phyllis, the more I began to realise what was at stake. My stomach churned. The cab bumped over rocky ground. I focused my attention on the mountains and wound the window down. We had reached a plateau that was unexpectedly verdant but the driver was still accelerating, as if he wanted to climb yet higher, in defiance of the fact that there were no more peaks to climb. We rounded another corner at high velocity before he screeched to a sudden halt causing a colossal cloud of white dust to fly up from the road. He turned and grinned, self-satisfied, as the dust caught in my throat.

'Here,' he said – displaying tobacco-stained teeth and a couple of dulled silver fillings – 'Ouranos Vineyard. You want to taste wine?'

I shook my head. 'We're just looking for my friend.' I was relieved to see the Genius™ coach still in the car park, alongside several other tour buses and numerous hire cars. Now the fear cut in. *Was I serious about confronting her? Was it too late?*

'You wait,' the driver said and signalled for us to remain seated. We watched as he got out of the car and pressed on up the hill.

Beads of sweat were running down Joel's brow and he wiped them away with the back of his hand. He was about to get out of the car when we were interrupted by a familiar beep.

'Sorry,' I said to Joel.

'You sure you have the right phone?'

I ignored his quip. My response to the noise told me something. I wanted it to be Will.

I picked up. There were two texts; I must have missed the first. The first was him.

In Moss Bros with Hils. Can't decide on suit. Do you like double-breasted?

I should have been overjoyed. The message told me what I needed to know: Will knew nothing about the Carl affair. If he did, he wouldn't have turned up for the shopping trip with Hilary. He wouldn't be texting me about trivialities. But it was difficult to say what, exactly, about this message, was most irritating. Was I just tired of being the oracle on wedding attire? Was it *all* that anybody ever thought about? Or was it that the very phrase "double-breasted" conjured up something unpleasant and old-fashioned? Having a mother who used to be a fashion editor was obviously no guarantee of personal taste.

Then I remembered the second message that had been hidden on the home screen. It might be from him too. There could have been a time lag between the arrival of the two messages. Phyllis might have got through in the meantime. Perhaps Will was now sobbing inconsolably on the floor of the Moss Bros changing room.

But no – Will was safe. The second message was from Carl and could not have been more predictable.

Want u badly. When r u back?

I threw the phone down. How was it possible that a guy capable of writing such astonishing prose thought he could woo me like a Neanderthal? I would not dignify it with a response.

I did, however, reply to Will.

Miss you. Yes, avoid d-b. Single-breasted, two buttons is best. xxA

Turning to Joel, I arranged my lips into a semblance of a smile. I had done nothing wrong but even the act of reading Carl's message made me feel deeply culpable. The expression set rigidly on my face. The ease with which I had responded to Will felt wrong. There was some rot at the heart of our relationship, like a vile fungus, eating away at everything that had ever made it seem important. But we were both refusing to see it. Beneath the surface, everything was crumbling. If we did not acknowledge it, perhaps we both thought that it would repair itself or vanish. Yet if we could not repair it, what then? What kind of life were we about to live if all we had was surface beauty, good suits and shiny shoes?

'You look a bit peculiar,' Joel said.

207

'I presume that's not a compliment.'

'Distracted. You look distracted.'

'Oh, you know,' I said, 'it's just all these men who won't leave me alone: the perils of being desirable. You wouldn't believe how difficult it is.'

Joel brushed my sarcasm aside; he seemed to see the rot that lay beneath my laughter. 'I can imagine,' he said, as if considering this seriously. 'It must get in the way of your writing.'

'Being so gorgeous? Oh yes, it really does.'

'When are you going to cut the crap, Anna?'

I turned away. I barely knew Joel. 'That driver's been gone a long time,' I said, refusing to meet his eye. 'Do you think we should follow him?'

'No. Answer the bloody question.'

'OK, so I'm not getting much writing done.'

'Thank you,' Joel said. 'Now at least you're being honest.'

'What difference does that make?'

'A huge difference.'

'Really? I suppose you're now going to lecture me on the direct correlation between my misguided libido and my failure to produce 'great work'.

'I never said anything about libido,' Joel said, raising an eyebrow.

'Oh yeah, it's out of control.'

'Fabulous,' he said. 'Fancy a shag?'

I wasn't sure whether to laugh or cry. Joel looked away, perhaps regretting his words and our driver appeared at the corner of the hill, shaking his head and muttering. He approached the car and leant over to speak through the open windows.

'You look for James Loftus, yes?'

I nodded. He pursed his lips and I had the impression he was about to break some serious news.

'You have no luck. Rest of party is at vineyard. Mr Loftus, he already leave.' He paused, as if he wasn't certain he should repeat what he had heard. 'With a lady.'

Damn.

208

'What kind of a lady?'

'Yes. Of course. Dimitri say skinny lady. Skinny old lady. With plastic bag on face,' he said.

'Plastic bag?' I had to laugh. 'You mean plastic surgery?'

'Ah – surgery. Yes. I think.'

'Bugger it. Do you know where they've gone?'

'Oh yes. They go to Sappho.'

'Where is that?'

'Yes. It's very nice villa. Very expensive. You know?'

'No,' I said. *Why had they left alone?* 'I can't say that I do.'

'I think you had better take us there,' Joel said and gave me a look that I could not quite decipher.

I thought we had already reached the highest point of the island, but now I realised I was mistaken. We drove for another twenty minutes during which time I caught occasional glimpses of the plateau that lay beyond the peaks. The sun was high in the sky and the taxi had no air-conditioning. Again, for some time, we didn't speak.

'How are you?' Joel said eventually. He seemed awkward, as if the seriousness of what we were doing had just struck him. I shrugged. 'You know, she'll be too interested in Loftus to call Will.'

'Maybe,' I said. 'But just because she hasn't told him yet, doesn't mean I'll be able to influence her.'

'What were the texts?'

'You don't want to know.'

'Actually, I do.' But he didn't look at me this time.

'What do you think? Will and Carl.'

'You're one popular girl.'

'Not for long...'

It was just typical, I thought, that even when I tried to escape the web of my recent relationships, I ended up becoming more deeply enmeshed. I'd wanted to crawl away and hide in some dark spot but instead I was still stuck and struggling, unable to make sense of the threads that bound me. I felt an urge to confess.

'The thing is,' I said – and even as I hesitated, I knew that I was twisting myself into ever deeper and stickier knots – 'there's a small part of me that wonders if I'm doing the right thing.'

There. I'd said it. It was out there, no way of taking it back.

'What do you mean?' Joel turned to me now. He was sitting close to me; too close.

'I'm trying to rescue a relationship, but a tiny part of me wonders if I really want to rescue it. I'm not sure I want a relationship with anyone right now.' I looked down at my knees. 'Does that sound awful?'

'No,' he said. 'It sounds very human.'

'Honestly?'

'Marriage is a big deal,' he said. He must have sensed how uneasy I was as he sat back and leant against the window. The car was straining against the incline and the driver was struggling to get it in the right gear. 'It would be a little idiotic to rush into marriage if you didn't feel completely sure,' Joel said. He smiled, very briefly, touching his hand to his hair.

This was bad. Very bad. We rounded another corner and at last had a clear view of the promised plateau: lush, green and somehow unexpected. It was difficult to be certain what had changed during the course of this journey, but something had just shifted.

'You could still stall her,' Joel said.

'What do you mean?'

'Ask her not to tell Will. It wouldn't commit you to anything. It would just give you... thinking time.'

He turned away to gaze out of the window. I tried to look past him, but his hair fell against the nape of his neck and I caught myself staring.

'You know what's really bothering me?' I said.

'No?' He turned to face me again.

'The writing.' As soon as I said it, I understood the significance of that admission. It frightened me a little. 'I came here to escape all the drama at home: the love affairs, the literary soirées, the bitching at the office. But I can't get away from it; sometimes it feels impossible to ever find a moment when I can focus on putting words on a page. Even now, I should be in one of those writing rooms down at the Ouranos Centre, thinking, keeping my head down, but instead I'm chasing Phyllis up a mountain. Why is that?'

Close to tears, I could hear the sound of my own voice, the high-pitched, slightly hysterical tone.

Joel frowned, worrying his forehead with his fingertips, 'Perhaps you create the drama, Anna?' he said gently.

'What?'

He was kicking me when I was down. How did he have the right to make assumptions like that? Was it my fault that my boyfriend lied to me, my fault that Phyllis came to stay, that Lucy came for an interview at the Walpole?

'You know, like a self-distraction technique. So long as there's some crisis in your personal life, some man on the horizon, then there's no need to focus on what you really want.'

'That's not fair.' *But was he right?* 'It's a bit bloody patronising, don't you think?'

The driver rounded another tight corner and pulled over at the roadside before Joel could reply. He turned the engine off and twisted his body to face us, pulling aside the plastic window that separated us from him.

'The Karpathian Plateau,' he said. 'We arrive.'

Joel stepped out of the cab and I followed him to the edge of the path where the plateau spread out beneath us, a blanket of green and straw-coloured plots, scattered with small windmills. It was so quiet here; such an expanse of space. The landscape should have been scorched, yet the farmers had kept it verdant.

'Sorry,' he said. 'I've been an arse.'

'Must be the heat.'

'You want to take a photograph?' The driver was standing too close behind me.

'No thanks.'

'You know the Venetians make ditches here?' he said. 'For good harvests. You understand?'

'Yes. Thank you,' Joel said.

'You see windmills? For irrigation, yes?'

'I see,' I said, not seeing at all.

'You should come in the spring. The almond blossom...' the

211

driver went on.

If he would just be quiet for a moment, I might take it all in.

'Yes, that sounds lovely.'

We had to find Phyllis. Before I changed my mind.

'Where's the villa?'

'We get back in car. This photo stop. Five more minutes.'

'OK,' I said. 'In a moment. I just need to think.'

Beneath his words, I could sense the silence. I closed my eyes and listened. Perhaps the driver knew that silence only too well. Perhaps he had been here too often and knew the sound of emptiness – the echo of the wind against the mountain. It was possible he wanted to avoid it. That silence, I thought, might drive a person mad.

25

'Life is the farce which everyone has to perform.'
– Arthur Rimbaud

'Christ, is that it?'

We had reached the highest point on the island but it was not the view that attracted Joel's attention. The Sappho Villa was impossible to miss. A gargantuan, dazzling white building stood on a promontory, overlooking the plateau, like a fairytale castle, complete with battlements and pointed towers, enclosed behind a tall security fence.

'We arrive!' the driver said.

We drove closer and parked outside a perimeter fence. The building seemed to bask in its own artificiality and faux-grandeur.

I stepped out of the car and Joel followed. 'It makes me feel claustrophobic. It's so sterile.' I wanted to turn back, to be close to the sea again.

'You like?' the driver said.

I shook my head. 'Not my kind of place.'

Who would want to live here, in such isolation? I wandered to the edge of the promontory and could make out the sea, just visible on the horizon, but the glimpse did nothing to soothe me, it merely intensified my longing.

Beyond the security fence, I could make out the large, empty swimming pool and the formal garden, replete with structured, tropical plants in otherwise barren beds.

I turned to the driver.

'Can we go in?'

'Yes. You get back in car. We drive through.'

I needed to get inside and quickly. I wasn't certain what Loftus and Phyllis were doing here, but I had a strong suspicion. Phyllis might be able to afford the Sappho but she couldn't exist out here on her own. Was it possible that Loftus was trying to persuade her otherwise? Or was he more genuine than I suspected? Was this indeed a love tryst and were we about to intrude on an intimate moment? Whatever the reason for their presence here, I knew they would not welcome an interruption.

'What's the matter?' Joel asked.

'Just nervous, that's all. But let's get it over with.'

We drove up to the security gate and the driver pressed a buzzer. A gruff voice answered and a conversation ensued in animated Greek. There seemed to be some disagreement. Our driver sighed heavily and turned to us.

'He says Mr Loftus busy. You must wait.'

'Tell him it's urgent. It can't wait.'

'I tell him already. He said no good.'

'My mother-in-law is in there. I must see her. It's a family matter.'

'I try. OK?'

After another short exchange, the driver spoke to us again.

'He says Mr Loftus do business. Important business.'

That resolved it. Loftus intended to swindle Phyllis into making this ridiculous purchase. I had to stop it.

'The thing is...' I was stalling for time, but needed to think fast. Joel stepped in to rescue me.

'Mrs Isenberg is also my business partner,' he said. 'She can't conclude any deal without us.'

Our driver seemed to consider this an important fact and relayed it to the disembodied voice. At last, the voice was convinced. The door swung open and we drove into the courtyard of the Sappho villa.

The high, white walls loomed above us; the light was unforgiving. We followed the driver to an enormous porch, framed by two palm trees. The wooden door was embellished with a carving of a gigantic mandolin.

A short, burly man in uniform opened the door. His eyes were peculiar: heavily hooded and lopsided. He muttered something to the driver and stepped aside to let us in. We entered an impressive, sunlit atrium, graced by a wide white staircase curving up to our right. It was a bleak space, embellished with tasteless accessories: brilliant chandeliers; gilt mirrors adorned with prancing cherubs; golden finials on the banisters.

'This way,' the burly one said.

Our driver stood aside and Joel and I followed the man to the foot of the staircase. The security guard beckoned us up the bare stone stairs, which echoed beneath our feet. This was a comfortless space. Nobody in their right mind would choose to live here. Joel reached out and touched my shoulder. Our earlier laughter in the Ouranos Bar seemed like a distant and unconnected memory.

At the top of the staircase was a long corridor, from which led several doors. One, at the end, was slightly ajar and we approached it. The guard knocked and within moments, a thin, besuited Greek wearing half-moon spectacles opened it. The man – whose suit was particularly sharp and whose shoes were particularly shiny – appeared shocked.

'Excuse me?' he said in perfect English. 'What's going on?'

'This is Mrs Isenberg's business partner,' the guard said. I winced.

The man looked over his shoulder. As far as I could make out, nobody else was in the room. He frowned; appeared confused.

'My name is Tomaras,' he said. 'Come in.'

Joel glanced at me. I could tell that he needed to speak.

We stepped into a bedroom. To our left was an ornate four-poster draped in white voile. The room was large and bare, painted white with a black and white chequered floor. To the side of it was a life-sized sculpture of a muscular, naked man leaning back against a column.

'It's a faun,' Tomaras said. 'Hellenic style.' Tomaras glanced towards a pair of open doors at the far end of the room. 'Mrs Isenberg made no mention of a business partner.'

I hesitated. Somebody was standing on the balcony: Phyllis.

'Business aside,' I said, 'I need to speak with Mrs Isenberg on an urgent family matter. I'm her daughter-in-law.'

'And you are Mrs Isenberg's son?' Tomaras asked Joel.

'No.' Joel's mouth twitched a little at the corners; it was only just perceptible but I saw it.

Tomaras tutted. 'I hope it's important.'

'Of course.'

Close to the balcony, I noticed a table decorated with champagne glasses and an empty bottle of bubbly together with a tray of local delicacies that had not been touched. I followed Tomaras to the balcony. Joel hung back.

At first, Phyllis didn't see us. Loftus was there, standing beside her. His arm was about her shoulder and her fingers were playing with his. They stood just beyond the windows by a muslin curtain, contemplating the view. Phyllis half-turned but did not see me. She was flushed and swayed slightly on her feet. She had changed into a pink chiffon dress and the skin on her shoulders was lobster red – she must have been in the sun over lunch.

Now, as we approached, she turned and looked over her shoulder. When she saw me, her expression changed: her eyes widened and started darting about, like a child caught in a forbidden act. Loftus's face hardened, his jaw clenched so tight I thought he might crush his own teeth. Tomaras began fiddling with his spectacles and talking quickly, his voice rising in pitch.

'This is Mrs Isenberg's daughter-in-law. She says…'

'Anna,' Phyllis said, cutting him off. Then to Mr Tomaras. 'This is NOT my daughter-in-law.' Her glance shifted to Joel. 'And who is THAT?'

'You met Joel earlier, in class,' I said, concentrating every ounce of my strength on keeping my voice steady. 'He has very kindly accompanied me here.' I sounded like a character from Jane Austen.

I steeled myself against her response, waiting for the inevitable rant. The worst part was, I hadn't even prepared an argument. But she made no noise. She hesitated, turned to Loftus; he simpered back at her and they shared a long moment of mutual adoration.

'Well, never mind that now,' Phyllis said. Her eyes skimmed Joel from head to toe. She must have decided he was no threat because her voice softened. 'It's all right,' she said to Tomaras. 'She can stay.' She turned to me. 'Anna, we need to have a serious talk.'

'I know,' I replied. 'That's why…'

'Not now. You see the thing is – I have news…'

She paused and my head spun with my own preoccupations: the uncertainty I felt about Will; the need to stop him finding out about Carl; but beyond that, something more, the knowledge that Joel was right to doubt me.

'It's so exciting,' Phyllis said.

'Sorry – what is?'

Loftus watched me, his brow contracting. I sensed a quiet threat.

'I'm going to buy it!'

'No.' Even as I'd guessed it, I had not fully believed that this would happen. *How could she even contemplate it? At her age, to live here, in the middle of nowhere?*

'The villa.' She beamed. 'I'm going to be the proud owner of the Sappho.'

'Yes. I see.'

'Come and look! Look at these windows!' She stepped inside and picked up a remote control from a small coffee table. She proceeded to demonstrate how, at the push of a button, windows slid slowly across the balcony making a peculiar and extremely irritating whirring sound.

Was she mad? Did she really think that electric windows would provide good company in her old age?

Tomaras picked up one of the trays and offered it. I took a small skewer of calamari and promptly choked.

'And look at this!' Phyllis appeared not to notice my sudden bout of asphyxiation. She handed the remote to Loftus and approached the bed. She sat down on the edge of it, then leant back against the white satin sheets, revealing her scrawny, fake-tanned thighs. I longed to scream at her, to force feed her, anything to stop her wasting away any more. Instead, I looked about the room for something to cover her up with. I wanted to stop Loftus from looking at her as he did, with that expression halfway between lust and disgust. *What had he done to her?* I had always thought she was so strong, hard as marble, yet when it came to this man, she was clearly putty. He moulded her and she yielded. 'It's a beautiful bed, don't you think?'

'For God's sake, Phyllis…'

I couldn't help myself. Somebody had to bring her to her senses. She was consumed by her infatuation.

'Oh Anna,' she said. 'Can you *imagine* writing here?'

I shook my head. If Loftus had brought her to a modest, whitewashed house, overlooking the sea, a place with peeling paintwork and rickety shutters, I might have understood her temptation. But *this*?

'You must be out of your mind, Phyllis. You'll be cut off here; its madness.'

Tomaras shifted his weight, his hands flapping slightly at his sides. He was making eye contact with Loftus and I got the feeling that if they had their way, they'd call the security guy to hurl me out, but their latent fury made me all the more determined to act.

Phyllis was out of her depth. Will would never forgive me if I allowed her to be duped like this.

'Look,' I said, 'I need a moment alone with Phyllis.'

Loftus smiled, a slow, smug grin. 'Phyllis, my dear?'

'Yes, darling.'

'Are you going to tell them? Or shall I?'

Phyllis's eyes appeared to shine, coy and girlish. She held out her left hand and waggled her finger.

An impressive diamond was sparkling against her knuckle. It must have been there all along yet I had failed to notice it. But it was too big to be real: it was probably some cheap little trinket that she'd picked up in a trashy gift shop that sold snorkels and sponges and fluorescent pink flippers.

'James and I are going to live here together, Anna,' she said. 'We're getting married!'

The impact was physical, like a harsh blow to my gut.

'We've waited a long time for this,' Loftus said. 'Years.'

I tried to get my brain into gear. *What would Will do now? What*

218

would Will want me to do? The idea of my own impending marriage felt less real than ever now. I had come here to rescue that relationship, but this was more urgent. Phyllis was an adult, capable of making her own decisions – yet everything about this situation seemed wrong. There might be history between them, but *love?* Loftus turned to me, his mouth curled in a sneer.

'Miss Bright,' Tomaras said. 'I'm afraid we have important legal business to complete. So, if you'd excuse us?'

'What?' I turned to Phyllis. 'You're getting married *here? Today?*'

Phyllis laughed. 'We're finalising the contract on the villa purchase. I just have to sign on the dotted line and…'

'There's a problem!' I said. I had no idea what I was about to say, but I had to stop her from going through with this purchase. I could not stand by and watch Phyllis be swindled out of her life savings for the sake of some out-of-date love affair that had obviously been doomed from the beginning.

'Miss Bright came here on personal business,' Joel said. 'It's vital that she gets an answer.'

I glanced in his direction. He was thinking on his feet.

'I really don't think this is the time or place for this conversation, Anna,' Phyllis said.

'Trust me, it is.'

'I don't want to talk about it.'

'How can you wave your diamond ring in my face and expect me not to talk about my own wedding?'

'Anna…' She lowered her voice and I could sense her mood deflating. 'I don't know what to say about your wedding.'

'What do you mean?'

My mouth had turned to dust. Tomaras coughed, breaking the silence.

Imagining this loss was one thing; experiencing it was something else.

'What have you done?' But I didn't even know if she could hear me.

We should have been alone together. Joel looked away. Loftus and Tomaras stood firm; they had no intention of leaving.

'You betrayed him.'

'You've misinterpreted…'

'Those texts speak for themselves.'

'I can't imagine life without him.'

'Which doesn't mean it's not possible, Anna.'

'Please.'

'Do you think I could do it?' she said. 'Stand up in the front row of the church and not speak up when the vicar asks about "any just impediments"? You think I'd stand there in a Philip Treacey hat and just let it go?'

'What's the hat got to do with it?'

Phyllis began pacing back and forth, as if questioning her own motives. Loftus tried to hold her hand, but she pulled swiftly away. Her lips seemed to hang loose on her face. Her make-up was beginning to melt in the heat and was now streaking across her cheeks.

'I made a mistake,' I said. 'I thought you'd understand.'

'And what is that supposed to mean?'

I shrugged.

'I should never have married Tobias, Anna. That's the thing,' she said. I wasn't certain whether she was talking to me or to herself. 'That's why I'm here now, with James.' She sat down on the bed again and I perched beside her, but the white satin sheets and the voile drapes about us made our conversation seem farcical. 'You think you can waltz in and interrupt us, for your own selfish little reasons…'

I took a deep breath. 'Can't you think of Will?'

'I *am* thinking of Will, believe me.'

'Just give me a chance,' I said. 'Please Phyllis. Don't tell Will. I think he's been unfaithful too, but give us time to work it out.'

How could a life that was so perfectly ordinary, so stable, atrophy like this?

'I'll have to think about it,' she said. 'I can't promise anything, Anna. I'm terribly confused.'

As she spoke, I sensed that this was the most I could expect, the best outcome, under the circumstances.

'I'd better go. I should never have come here today.' The urge to leave was overwhelming. I had wanted to dissuade Phyllis from this purchase, this marriage, but I was beginning to realise the futility of that desire.

Loftus stood up and was approaching us; he placed his hand on my shoulder.

'Get off me.'

'Anna,' Phyllis said. 'Show a little more respect.'

'You want to leave?' Joel said.

'Tell her about the competition,' Loftus said.

I didn't know what he was talking about. All I could think about was the possibility of losing Will. *What was he talking about?*

The idea that it might really be over had never, until that day, seemed a possibility. Perhaps I had never allowed myself to believe that I was risking anything at all. That night with Carl McGahan – I had honestly never thought that it would alter anything. It had seemed like a separate reality. *What a fool.*

'James is going to be hosting a literary competition,' Phyllis said. 'It's a big deal. It's going to be televised.'

'Is this relevant?' Joel asked.

'It's going to be *very* high profile,' Phyllis said.

'What's it called?' I asked, hardly caring. *The Slush Pile?'*

'*The Lit Factor*,' Loftus replied.

'You are kidding?'

'We're looking for someone special,' he continued. 'A nationwide hunt for a new literary star. The producers were inspired by my book and got in touch. I can't begin to tell you how humbled I am by that.'

'Ha!' Joel couldn't help himself.

'Can you believe it, Anna?' Phyllis said. 'My future husband on prime-time television!'

'You can't find writers on a TV show,' I said, irritated at myself for even being drawn into the argument.

'You can do anything on a TV show,' Loftus said. 'Anything at all.'

It was time to go, but Tomaras was standing by the door, giving the distinct impression that he expected me to stay and give Loftus's vanity an audience.

'Why don't you sit down, Anna?' Loftus said, indicating a large, white leather armchair at the far end of the room. 'Let me fix you a drink. What's your tipple? Scotch?'

Yes, Scotch – please – anything to numb me – make it a double.

The armchair was soft and yielding. I took the drink and knocked half of it back in one gulp. Joel refused the Scotch and helped himself to a glass of water.

'Literary agents can submit three first novels in progress,' Loftus said. 'Unpublished authors can submit directly. We'll shortlist twelve authors and those twelve will take part in filming.'

I downed the rest of the whisky. The room began to sway and I must have closed my eyes. Behind closed eyelids I saw a woman walking down the aisle, a woman, not me, but wearing my wedding dress. Only it wasn't exactly my dress because this one had a bigger bust-size and her unnaturally rounded breasts were spilling out over a white corset. She had a cinched-in waist and matchstick-thin arms. Her marigold hair cascaded across her shoulders. Phyllis and Loftus stood at the front of the church, their plastic faces glowing with pride. Will turned to see his bride: his Angela, walking towards him.

I opened my eyes. Joel stood on the other side of the room, close to the balcony.

'So how are you supposed to film this?' he said. 'Surely writing doesn't make riveting television?'

'We'll just film the important stuff,' Loftus said. 'Video diaries; literary soirees; meetings with agents and publishers – the human side.'

'So the act of writing – in itself – isn't human any more?' Joel said.

'It may be human,' Loftus replied, (his expression akin to that of a man talking to a chimpanzee) 'but it is not televisual. The agents and publishers are going to be key here. We have several bidding for sponsorship. It's going to be *huge*. We want to find a literary genius who can succeed on a world stage.'

'I thought most writers were fairly private people.'

'The writers of tomorrow need to know how to present themselves.' Loftus came closer, sat on the edge of the armchair and patted my arm. 'We need marketeers: writers who can speak to large audiences and leave them gasping for more.'

The black and white chequered floor was beginning to shift; I felt vertiginous. Loftus came closer; his breath stank faintly of garlic.

'When you find yourself sitting in Buddy Sellers' office, Anna, that pretty face of yours won't be enough. You have to be tough; entertaining; entrepreneurial.'

'Is that so?' I said.

'Why don't you ask Buddy Sellers to put your name forward?'

The room was spinning uncontrollably. I wanted to lie down and wait for the feeling to subside. Everything was melding together: the chandelier, the faces, the gilded cherubs: a glittering mosaic of meaningless fragments. I stood up to leave.

Joel's face was the last thing I saw before I felt my eyelids closing again and my legs giving way beneath me. My head cracked against something hard as I gave in to the lure of exhausted oblivion.

26

'He who desires but acts not, breeds pestilence.' – William Blake

On the train home from Clapham Junction to Richmond, I gazed out at the muted English afternoon. The light was not grey but a dull yellow; even my white linen trousers had an ochre tint. I rummaged in my handbag for a mirror and found a small powder compact. When I held it to my face, my skin looked ashen; there were dark circles beneath my eyes.

Since landing at Gatwick, I had not yet plucked up courage to call Will; he would not be expecting me until next week. I pulled my oversized shades down over my eyes and shivered. My head was throbbing. It had been throbbing ever since the previous day when I blacked out in the Sappho villa. The local doctor had insisted that, despite the egg-shaped bump on the back of my head, I was not concussed. I was perfectly well and there was nothing to stop me from travelling home.

Phyllis had argued against my early departure. No doubt she felt responsible for my accident and she encouraged me to sleep on it before making any decisions. But I woke at dawn and in a fit of pique, I dressed, went outside and called a cab to take me to the airport. I felt guilty at not saying goodbye to Joel, but I was determined to avoid further complications. I didn't know if I'd find a flight but as it happened, a London departure was imminent and a few seats remained unoccupied. Before I knew it, I was in the air, flying home to an uncertain destiny.

Now I needed to confront my future. It was like trying to solve a particularly difficult puzzle when the essential piece that would allow me to see the whole was missing. I needed to know whether I had a relationship left to salvage.

I tugged my suitcase across Richmond Bridge. Looking out across the mock-Georgian development that overlooked the river, I found it difficult to imagine a life other than the familiar one that I was living before I went to Ouranos. I walked past the restaurant where, just over a week ago, I'd dined with Will and Phyllis. That was the night the whole Carl fiasco was set in motion.

I turned into Cresswell Road and stopped just before I reached our house. I looked up at the window to Will's studio. It was most likely that he was inside, at his desk, working from home. After a long day at the drawing board, his fingers and shirt would be ink-stained, his upper lip just a little moist. He would look up, surprised, as I entered. Perhaps a delighted smile would cross his lips and I would realise instantly that Phyllis had kept my confidence; I was perfectly safe. Within a couple of months he would be walking up the aisle with me, looking every inch the ideal man and I would become something else: Anna Isenberg, the wife of the celebrated *Telegraph* cartoonist, not, admittedly, so bohemian a match as Jeanne Hébuterne's, but my story, at least, would not end in sardine oil and certain tragedy.

Damn. I approached the door and put the key in the lock, only to discover that it was double-locked. So – Will was out. I turned the key and stepped inside. There was an odd smell in the hallway, a musty, unfamiliar odour. I ignored it, dumped my bags in the hallway and went upstairs to the bathroom.

I was about to enter the bathroom when I noticed that the bedroom door was closed. That was unusual. I might have dismissed it, if I hadn't heard voices behind the door. My stomach turned. I hesitated, but I was not mistaken: a woman's voice. I stood, very still, unable to think or act. It was difficult to believe this was happening. *Had I stepped straight from one farce into another?* I thought about turning to run but I had not flown half way across Europe to escape the truth.

Trembling, I pushed the door open. It was the only way. There was nobody there. The bed was empty and remained unmade. Will had left the radio on. I was alone in the room. *How stupid I was!*

How bloody stupid! I sank down on the bed, exhausted. *I must not cry. Don't cry.* I had to gather my thoughts, make sense of this mess. The trouble was, I had half expected to find them there. For a moment I'd really believed that the uncertainty would be resolved and I would discover that Will had been as unfaithful as I had been and I would know, at last, that it was over. The not knowing that had plagued me ever since he called her name would be over.

Her absence did not prove that he was faithful. Perhaps it was time to let it go. So what if he had betrayed me? I had done the same, so we were quits. But if that were so, we were about to enter into a marriage that would be built upon two lies. One lie, my own, was enough. Didn't that tell me all I needed to know?

I bent down to the chest of drawers on Will's side of the bed and started rifling through it. I knew it was wrong – the actions of a crazy woman with no pride or self-control. There were more important things in life than my own little dramas. But knowing that somehow made this all the more important. If I were to live a calm life (some small part of my brain was telling me), if I were to devote my energies to my work, attempting to look beyond myself, to be less self-obsessed, then first I had to create a calm space in which to live; I had to know the truth.

Was I ready in that moment, to understand the contradiction in my own reasoning? Did I see that I had to trust or not trust, that ransacking Will's belongings was no basis for a beginning? Of course not. I looked beneath his socks and in the drawer where he kept loose papers. If I looked long and hard enough, I would surely find something to satisfy my curiosity – an old hotel receipt, a banana-flavoured condom, a private journal where all would be revealed. When I found nothing in the drawer, I hesitated, but only briefly. I had come this far and had abandoned logic. I looked beneath the bed, in the wardrobe, in every pocket of every jacket, but I found precisely nothing: only a brand-new, single-breasted suit, its label still intact.

Everything was calm: perhaps too calm. I could have stopped there. So what propelled me to continue? Was it desperation or fear or was it, rather, some misguided need to lay the blame for my own

226

monumental idiocy on anybody's shoulders but my own?

I went back to the hallway and climbed the stairs to Will's study. His desk was neat as ever, the ink bottles lined up in a row, his pen nibs in a labelled transparent box. This room represented a part of Will that had nothing to do with me; a part of him I ought to have understood but did not. What would happen if I simply sat here and did nothing? Might I remember why I fell in love with him in the first place? I could forget about Carl, about Ouranos, the crazy shenanigans at the Sappho villa. Phyllis would come back and we would get married and then she would leave and I could choose to write, quietly and in obscurity. I could abandon ambition; like Jeanne Hébuterne yoking herself to an artist far greater than herself. I could choose love and devotion, a life in his shadow.

I laughed out loud. If Jeanne had lived, she might have made a name for herself, become an artist in her own right. That was what I wanted to uncover: the person she might have become. And besides, Will was talented but hardly a doomed and thwarted genius. He was a jobbing cartoonist on one of the most conservative newspapers of the day.

I sank to the floor, beside the bookcase. Will kept his postcard collection here: a small library of fifteen leather-bound albums that he'd treasured since his teens. He had collected postcards from every exhibition he'd ever visited and he ordered them precisely in carefully labelled books. I surveyed the spines: *Renaissance portraits; Dutch masters; Neo-classicism; Gothic architecture.*

At first glimpse, *Dutch Masters* did not seem to be the most promising volume. I reached for the *Renaissance* instead but as I pulled at it, it got stuck on an object that must have been behind it. I tugged harder but still there was no give so I bent low, pressing my head against the sisal flooring. With my left cheek squashed flat, I could make out an obstruction at the back of the shelf. It appeared to be a small, leather suitcase. *How strange! I didn't know there was a space behind those shelves.*

I reached my hand in, but the gap was too narrow to reach it. With a little manoeuvring, I managed to get the *Renaissance* volume free and after that, the other albums came out without difficulty.

Now the space was big enough and I slid the suitcase out. I stared at it a while. It was shabby, very sturdy but battered at the corners: a 1950s design probably, the kind of suitcase a young Phyllis might have carried about Europe in her youth.

Claudia's story came to mind: the tale of her mothers' love letters. *This is none of your business.* But it was far too intriguing to ignore. Will had never seemed like the kind of person who would keep secrets. In all my desperate ransacking, I had not really believed that I would find anything.

But what if he came home, right now? If I heard his key in the lock downstairs, would I have time to shove this back under the bookshelf, replace the albums and make my way downstairs before he made it up? Given his foot in plaster, it would be easy. The catches of the suitcase pinged aside and I opened the case.

No love letters then. I opened my mouth and felt my gut twist. The suitcase was virtually empty, except for a few magazines: porn magazines. I didn't have to touch them to recognise the identity of the woman who graced the cover. It was *her*: Angela Crystal. She leant towards the camera, her wide, doe-eyes in a 'come to bed' stare, her pneumatic, surgically-enhanced breasts filling the palms of her hands, her legs spread out gymnastically on either side.

It is difficult, even now, to revisit that moment. To imagine it was one thing, but to see this evidence impacted me in an entirely new way. For a moment I wanted to laugh – perhaps I wanted the numbness of mockery – I wanted to be able to shrug and say, '*Well, I've had a lucky escape'*. It would have been so easy to conclude that I now knew everything I needed to know about my fiancé (or should I say ex- fiancé?). But I was incapable of cynicism. The truth was visceral, wringing my insides like a wet rag, leaving me empty, almost devoid of emotion. A part of me wanted to reach out and touch it, yet at first I held back as if it would contaminate me. It was not evidence of infidelity of course, but to me it seemed enough. I knew one thing. Will was not the man I thought he was. Call me naïve – but he had never struck me as the kind of man who would find this type of thing even remotely titillating. I had him down as the type who got his kicks from watching mildly erotic French

228

Arthouse movies.

But there was nothing Arthouse about Angela. Now I picked up the magazine – one of several in the case. I turned the page to discover a whole feature about her and another revealing photograph. Beneath the image was an inscription.

For Will, with thanks for your encouragement, Angie xx

Encouragement? What did that mean? I recoiled, shoved the magazine back in the suitcase. I had seen enough. And yet it made no sense. I flicked the locks and put the suitcase back under the shelf, carefully replacing the postcard albums. *How can a man who collects postcards of Dutch Masters get off on something as tacky as that?*

Still shaking, I stood up. I was not exactly blameless. *Where is he now? With her?* Modigliani, of course, had other lovers beside Jeanne. Jeanne did not like it but she accepted it. But I couldn't live like that. Nor did I desire to throw myself from a second floor window for the love of him. That was her game, not mine. I was standing in the doorway at the top of a high staircase but was not even vaguely tempted to take the plunge. I probably needed to cry for a while. For quite a long while actually.

I walked slowly downstairs and as I did so was once again aware of the musty odour in the hallway. *Probably a dead body*, I thought. Like I said to Phyllis. *More likely Will hasn't emptied the dustbin since I've been away. If I left Will for good, he would have to learn to empty the dustbin by himself, or else teach Angela to do it.*

I decided to go out, take a walk; I needed to make sense of this. But I was interrupted by the sound of a key in the lock. I held my breath as if that act would make him vanish.

He opened the door and limped in. I looked at him.

'Shit,' he said.

What kind of greeting was that?

'That's nice,' I said. 'You're pleased to see me then?'

'Oh Anna, I'm sorry. It's just…'

I must not cry. He did not deserve my tears.

'You don't have to explain.'

229

'Yes, yes, I do. But what are you doing here? You're supposed to be…'

'In Greece, yes. How inconvenient.'

'Anna, I don't know what you're talking about.'

Will was still using crutches to walk, his foot remained in plaster. He took a step towards me, as if he were going to kiss me. I was trying to conceal the fact that I was trembling. He was wearing the shirt I had bought him last summer, a pale blue linen number, cut to perfection. He looked exactly as he always did. But he sensed something was wrong; instead of kissing me, he placed an arm on my shoulder and his eyes kept darting about the hallway, fixing on anything but me.

If I allowed myself to feel even a tad tender, I was lost.

'Why are you home early?' he said. 'Is everything OK?' Then his expression changed. 'It's not Mum, is it?'

'No, Phyllis is fine.' That wasn't strictly true but the story of Phyllis and Loftus could wait.

'So what?'

'I don't know where to begin.'

'There's something I need to tell you too.'

I wasn't sure that I was ready for it.

'Let's sit down, shall we?'

I moved towards the kitchen, but he stood in front of me and stopped me from going any further.

'What's the matter?' I asked.

'You can't go in there.'

'What do you mean, I can't go in there?'

'Let's just talk here.'

'Why can't we go in the kitchen? What are you hiding in there? Or who?'

'I'm not going to dignify that with an answer.'

'Well it's not my birthday and it's not Valentine's Day, so I'm assuming you haven't been baking a surprise cake.'

'You don't understand.'

'No, you're damn right I don't. What's going on?'

The vehemence of my anger surprised me. Yet even in the midst

230

of it, there was a small part of me that wanted to discover a perfectly logical explanation for all of this. I wanted the magazines to have been placed there by some malevolent third party, intent on destroying us. I wanted the kitchen to be full of guests who were about to leap out and congratulate me on an anniversary that I'd forgotten all about.

Will did not reply. The silence deepened, a great yawning chasm between us. *What was he hiding?*

'OK – fine!' I said. 'Let's go in the front room then.'

'No. Let's not.'

'What?'

The door to the front room was closed too. We never closed the door to the front room.

'I don't know what this is about, Will,' I said. 'And you know, I'm not even sure if I care any more.' I had a strong feeling that afterwards I would very much regret what I was about to do, yet all the same, I heard the words coming from my mouth, as if they belonged to somebody else. I couldn't stop myself. 'I found the magazines. The ones with Angela in – behind your bookshelf.'

He winced. I watched his reaction very closely. He was internalising it, trying to work out how to respond.

'What were you looking *there* for?'

'Why? Did I miss something in some other hiding place? Just looking at your postcards if you must know. *Taking an interest.* What does it matter?'

Everything was beginning to crumble. It was not the fact of his deeds nor of mine, but our admission of them.

'A lot of guys have those magazines.'

'Oh God, Will. You can do better than that.'

Was this really the same man who had made me happy and for so long? I wasn't even sure that I still liked him.

'It doesn't mean anything.'

'Not even when you're shagging the centre-fold?'

'I am NOT shagging Angela.'

'Well if you're not, you soon will be.'

His expression was more revealing than his words could ever be.

'I won't dignify that with an answer, Anna. You haven't been listening. There's something else I've got to tell you.'

'It gets worse?'

'It depends on your perspective.'

'OK. Hit me with it.'

'You're not going to like this. I have no idea how it happened.'

Something in the kitchen. If it was not Angela, then what?

'I don't get it, Will. You had a takeaway and you didn't clear up last night? There's been a flood?' He said nothing. 'I can cope with a little bit of mess, Will. Really. I assume you don't have Miss Crystal in there, else you might be a little less blatant about it? You don't have the look of a man who's just been shagging on a granite work-surface.'

I'd had enough and pushed him aside. I flung open the kitchen door.

It's difficult to remember the exact order of events. There was a loud voice; it must have been my own.

'Oh my God. What?'

Will was standing behind me, muttering. 'I'm sorry. I didn't know how to tell you.'

I hadn't thought that anything could be worse than finding Angela Crystal here; but perhaps I was wrong.

'Will, *get it out of here*. Please.'

At the far end of the room, cowering at the edge of the skirting was the most enormous mouse I had ever seen.

'It's a rat, Anna,' Will said. It was typical of him to correct even my thoughts.

'You're damn right, it's a rat,' I screamed. 'But what the hell is it doing in my kitchen?'

Its damp fur was on end and it was staring at me with what looked like malicious intent.

'I don't know how it happened. There are several of them.'

'*Several?*' And then I understood. The smell. That explained the smell. '*Then where are the rest?*' I was suddenly terrified lest the rats escaped to the rest of the house. 'Close the door, for Christ's sake.'

Will went to close it behind us. '*With us outside,*' I said and once again barged past him as I left the room.

Will followed and once we were in the safety of the hallway, I tried to take it in. I was shaking. *An infestation of rats. In our home. It was biblical. First pornography. Now rodents. It would be locusts next.*

'I noticed the smell shortly after you left,' he said. 'I didn't know where it was coming from.'

'Didn't you put the rubbish in the wheelie-bins?'

'It must have already happened, Anna, before you left. We just didn't notice. I saw the first one last night.'

'But why did you go out today? And leave them the freedom of the kitchen? They're going to colonise the place.'

'I've been over to the VerminoKil office. I was waiting at home for them, but they were being slow, so I thought I'd give them a kick up the arse.'

'When are they coming?'

'In about an hour.'

'Thank *God*. So they'll be able to get them all out today?'

He winced.

'They *won't?*'

'Apparently they have to find the entrance; how they got in,' he said. It's most likely to be a hole in the brickwork or something. That's what they said on the phone.'

'Right,' I said. I was trying hard to calm myself. I had to put the Angela thing aside and focus on this. We could talk about her afterwards once the emergency was over. 'So they have to block their entrance, is that right?'

'No. They say they can't block it. Otherwise they'd shut the rats in. Even if we didn't see any, there's no way of knowing whether they're under the floorboards.'

'I don't get it, Will. If they don't block them out, what do they do?'

'They poison them.'

I paused, as the implications of what he said filtered through. Surely, I wasn't understanding this correctly?

'And while they're being poisoned, they just roam free in our kitchen?'

Will nodded grimly. 'That's just about right,' he said.

It was the '*just about*' that gave it away. 'Why is the living room door closed?' But I didn't wait for an answer. I had worked it out. I didn't want to look, yet I felt a sudden compulsion.

It's possible I knew what I would see. Perhaps I imagined it fully even before I saw it; as if what I saw, improbable as it was, was somehow meant to be: a sign or signal that I had no choice but to follow.

In the living room, there was not one rat but two. I felt the same revulsion as before, but this time I did not shout or scream. The smaller rat appeared aimless. He scurried from where he had been sitting in the centre of the room. The second however was intent on his purpose. I looked up to see my wedding dress, hanging high above the dresser, wrapped in opaque cellophane where I had left it. Perhaps, if I'd been more romantic, if I had kept it hidden, out of Will's sight, this would not have happened. Something had fallen down and the second rat was worrying that thing. He held it between his claws; it appeared so very small and white and fragile. The creature looked at me and I looked back, open-mouthed, barely able to comprehend it yet at the same time understanding it entirely. The rat was chewing my wedding veil.

27

'Have you thought of an ending?'
'Yes, several, and all are dark and unpleasant.'
– J.R.R. Tolkien

It is not every day that you discover a stash of porn magazines behind your fiancé's Renaissance postcard collection. Neither would I describe the discovery that one is living with an infestation of rats as an everyday occurrence. Yet the Bulgarian man, who was now pacing about our front room, did not find our rat situation at all unlikely.

Verminokil had cancelled their visit at the last minute, so Will had called an independent expert. As he entered the house, he thrust out his hand to shake Will's,

'Gabriel Dimitrov,' he said, as his long, keen nose sniffed the air.

'Thanks for coming so quickly,' Will said.

'I smell RAT!' Gabriel replied, perhaps a little too keen to prove his credentials.

Now, having drunk a cup of tea and examined the house outside, he was explaining how this had happened.

'You have created *perrrrfect* conditions for rat,' he said. 'That little shed; good nesting spot. And the hole in the brickwork – that's where they scuttled in.' And I'd been right about the wheelie-bins; like a fool I'd trusted Will to organise the rubbish and he'd left the black sacks out the back with no protection.

'You might as well leave a *Welcome Mat* for Rat!' Gabriel said.

'So how do we get rid of them?' I asked. 'That's the important thing.'

Gabriel smiled as if killing rats were his greatest pleasure in life.

235

'You give rat poison,' he said. 'Rat *very* confused. Rat have headache. Like migraine. Rat seeks fresh air. Rat goes in garden, Rat lies down and Rat dies.'

'And we can't just block them out?' I asked. I wondered whether Verminokil had been wrong. *We couldn't just let them stay here, roaming freely about our home.*

'Ha ha. No. But don't worry. Rat more afraid of you than you of Rat.'

'Very reassuring,' I said.

'You seem pretty passionate about your job,' Will said. 'How d'you get into a line of work like that?'

Oh, shut up, Will. Just let the man get on and put the poison down.

'I fall in love,' Gabriel said, the smile at last wiped from his face. 'In Bulgaria. But she betray me, I have – how you say it? – heart is broken. So I leave Bulgaria and come to England. I work in building trade for several months but it very boring, and then I meet my friend Keith. Keith is expert in pest control. He tells me it very sociable. He is right. I meet very nice people.'

Afterwards, once Gabriel had deposited small blue pellets about the house and garden and left, it struck me that I would like to be as passionate about my job at the Walpole as Gabriel was about his rats.

'I have to get out of here, Will. I'll call Hilary and see if she's free for a drink. I can't stay. I won't be able to *sleep* here.'

'I've looked it up on the net,' Will replied. 'Apparently, rats don't generally climb stairs. You'll be safe in the bedroom.'

'It's that word "generally" that bothers me,' I said. 'We might not have "general" rats, Will. We might have quite extraordinary rats with great fat hind legs and extreme agility.' I tried to laugh, but the noise that came out of my mouth sounded thin and strangulated. 'If you want to risk it, fine. That's up to you, but I'm not going to even contemplate the idea of waking up with a rat on my pillow. I'm going to ask Hils if I can stay at her place.'

Will was silent. The door to the kitchen and lounge were both closed, but I wondered if any rats had escaped to other areas of the house. Perhaps I might send one up to the attic to have a nibble at his magazines.

'We need to talk,' he said.

Given that the rat had so enjoyed my wedding veil, I was seriously considering feeding it the dress as well.

'Do we?' I replied. 'I don't know. I just need a bit of time to take this in.'

'The rats will be gone in a week or so.'

'I'm not talking about the bloody rats!'

'OK. OK. Look, I know you're upset, but please don't get things out of proportion.' It was almost touching. 'But you're right. We can't put things right between us when we're in this situation. I'll find us a hotel for the week.'

'No. I don't want to share a hotel room with you, Will. I'm too upset. I'll go to Hilary's place.'

I'm not sure what I was expecting. Perhaps I was hoping that he would break down and tell me how much he loved me, that he had made a dreadful mistake: Angela Crystal meant nothing to him; he would never see her again. Yet my own hypocrisy swamped me. He was no more at fault than I was. All the same, I longed for some sign of regret or sorrow, however remote – if he'd weakened just a little, I might have paused and listened. I might have realised that he was, after all, *the one* and as he so clearly adored me, I should forgive myself too, put my doubts behind me and finally commit.

Will did not break down however. He did not even look sad. He just looked cross.

'Fine,' he said. 'Whatever.'

'Whatever? Is that it?'

'Well what am I supposed to say?'

'I dunno,' I said. 'Goodbye?'

'Right, fine,' he said, clearly not getting it. To be fair to him, I was only just getting my meaning myself. 'Goodbye,' he said. 'See you tomorrow.'

His face was a little bit twisted, but all the same, I tried to remember what I used to feel when I looked at his face – to reach out and stroke my hand across his cheek – but for some reason, I could not conjure that tenderness.

I shook my head. 'I'm not coming back tomorrow, Will.' *Did I mean that? It was a joke, wasn't it?* I had a suitcase packed. If Hilary wouldn't have me, I'd have to go down to Essex and stay with Mum.

'Oh don't be so fucking melodramatic, Anna. It's just a few rats. It's not the end of the world. We can buy you another headdress-thingy.'

'No, Will,' I said. My voice sounded very measured. 'It's just the end of us.' But I wasn't at all calm inside. I knew that I had to leave and quickly else I would start to cry and he would try to comfort me in some terrible ham-fisted manner and that would make it worse.

Will stood very still, open-mouthed. I couldn't tell whether it was shock or relief. It's possible it was a little of both.

'No wedding?' he said.

I couldn't speak. If I spoke, I might find words to deny it, explain it away, excuse myself or make half-hearted promises I could never keep. Instead I bent down and picked up my suitcase, not yet unpacked, still standing by the front door. I wrapped my jacket about me, knowing that this moment might always haunt me; it was the pivot on which my future turned. I glimpsed at him. It was his last chance to say he loved me, to beg me to change my mind.

But he said nothing, so I turned quickly and dashed outside. I closed the door with a quiet click behind me and I strode down the path, breathing, taking huge, desperate gulps of air. I heard his voice, the door opening, him calling my name – but the moment had passed; it was too late. I rushed down the street, away. It didn't seem possible that the streets of Richmond should look exactly as they had done a couple of hours earlier. The tall red-brick buildings remained solid and unaltered. People seemed to be going about their business as usual, as if nothing untoward had happened.

I was still holding back the tears, sucking in my cheeks in the hope that this would stop my grief. I might have got over the small things; we might have overcome pornography and even rats, if that was all we had to worry about. But I knew it went much deeper. I sensed that I had lost Will – or rather that I had never really had him in the first place.

I stood on Richmond Bridge, looking out across the Thames. Only that morning, I had been woken by a pack of disturbed, barking dogs and a cockerel who began his crowing long before dawn. I had crept to the balcony and quietly opened the doors while Phyllis still snored in her bed. A gauzy, lilac mist half obscured the mountains and I had stood there, no longer certain what I wanted.

Yet surely, I had not wanted this. It was not too late to turn around and walk back to the house, tell him I'd overreacted and it wasn't serious. We could stay in a hotel together tonight, he could put Angela behind him. I'd forget all about Carl McGahan and we could live happily ever after.

The river, beneath me, looked cold and uninviting. Virginia Woolf had once stood above a river like this. She had loaded her pockets with stones before walking into the Ouse. Jeanne Hébuterne, too, had been unable to bear her grief, when her beloved Modi died on the sardine-oil-soaked bed. But the idea of *Anna Bright committing suicide* was the most ridiculous thing I'd imagined in a long time. There wasn't much point in self-sacrifice – and somebody should have told Jeanne that. This was simply the end of a relationship.

To an outsider, I must have looked eccentric: a young woman standing alone, gazing out across the water and laughing. The laughter came from nowhere and it saved me. In the distance, a pair of swans took off and flew closer. I watched as they descended, landing softly with a poise and grace that made me feel inadequate and humble. What I was about to do was frightening. But the alternative was worse. No doubt, fear was good sometimes. Especially for a coward like me, who will usually do anything to avoid it.

Part Three

End

28

'All I could do was to offer you an opinion upon one minor point – a woman must have money and a room of her own if she is to write fiction; and that, as you will see, leaves the great problem of the true nature of woman and the true nature of fiction unsolved.'
– Virginia Woolf

When the telephone rang, I hesitated and wondered whether to answer it. It was April and for days I had been ignoring every call, letting the answer-phone cut in. *"You're through to Anna Bright. I'm not taking calls at the moment but please speak after the tone and I'll get back to you in the spring."* Now the spring was here, but I couldn't bring myself to change the message.

Sometimes I felt uneasy about the situation. I knew I wouldn't be able to keep it up for much longer. But the answerphone had served a purpose. I had almost completed a draft of *The Modigliani Girl* – that message had protected me from the world.

It had all been decided, that day on Richmond Bridge: I would quit my job, move away from Richmond and cash in my wedding savings. I'd figured I had enough to keep me going for six months and in the end I had managed to eke it out a little longer. Now I was living in Barnes, renting a studio flat above a shop and the savings were fast running out. When I first moved in here, I had stuck to my original plan. *No email. No telephone. No relationships.* But everything changed, of course, when I got accepted for *The Lit Factor*. The producer had insisted I checked my mobile regularly; it was either that or quit the show.

Hilary was the first person that I told about the competition. It was New Year's Eve and I was feeling guilty, having avoided her for several months, just as I'd avoided everybody. I don't like to think how my behaviour affected the people around me. Christmas was the worst part – not showing up on Christmas Day.

I knew, of course, that Lois and the grandchildren would distract Mum, but I still felt bad about it. The truth was, it had very little to do with my resolution and everything to do with Will. I had no doubt that if I'd turned up, their insensitivity would have known no bounds. Mum would have tried at first, of course. She would have kept schtum until half way through lunch – just long enough to devour the turkey, pull the crackers and play a short game of after-dinner charades – but with a few glasses of bubbly Rosé in her, she'd eventually cave into curiosity, asking *why* I did it. Why leave a lovely man like Will? And for what? A book without a publisher? By the time of the Queen's speech, Mum would be sobbing quietly about her lost son-in-law and my impending spinsterhood and Lois (still simmering at Freya's disappointment in the bridesmaid stakes) would be making snide remarks about the ticking of my biological clock.

On New Year's Eve however, Hilary turned up unannounced. It was around 11pm. Her lipstick was smudged and she was clutching a pink paper bag tied with a profusion of white raffia.

'I thought I'd find you here,' she said, slurring her words a little. 'What a waste.'

'I'm fine,' I said. 'I've been writing. Are you coming in? What are you doing here anyway?'

'Come to stop you working,' she said, as she followed me inside.

'Shouldn't you be off at a party somewhere?'

'I was at a party. It was crap. There was some awful bloke who worked at the Council who was trying to get off with me.'

'Grim.'

'So I thought I'd come here and cheer you up.'

She was in my kitchen already, beginning to rifle through the cupboards.

'Do you have a cocktail shaker?'

'As if…'

244

'What are you doing here on your own? If you don't join the human race soon, you'll wither and die for God's sake. I'm going to fix you a drink...'

I shrugged. What could I say? Did she even want to know what was going through my mind, the many contradictions of the previous months? I *had* been lonely, true. I also now had half a manuscript sitting on my desk.

I found a glass jug and a couple of cheap wine glasses. She took a bottle of fizz from her bag and another, a sickly pink colour.

'What's that?'

'Rose liqueur.'

'Ew...'

She slugged the liqueur into the glass, popped the cork and poured.

'Cheers!'

'Cheers.'

Hils leant against the kitchen surface and smiled, but I caught the tremor at the edge of her lips. I guessed what might lie beneath it, but wasn't sure that I wanted to ask. What are you supposed to say to a friend that you'd neglected for over five months? And how would she take my news?

'Let's sit down, shall we?'

In the front room, we put our drinks down on the coffee table.

'God, my ears are still ringing from that party.'

'I'll put some music on.'

As I fiddled with the iPod, I came across a Jacques Brel track which Will had downloaded. *New Year's Eve and he wasn't here.* The small, familiar pain beneath my ribs stung me. But it was the pain of loss, not regret. If I was looking for lost intimacy, I didn't find it. New Years Eve with Will always involved a party with his mates from *The Telegraph* and last year I'd been alone at midnight in a room full of strangers, while Will had been catching up with a mate at the bar – he didn't quite make it across the room in time.

'*Good riddance,*' I muttered, under my breath. I had done my mourning and couldn't face going there again.

'What was that?'

'Nothing. Sorry.' I put on Nina Simone and joined her on the sofa. 'So what's going on in your life?'

'Nothing much. Just been living vicariously through the Martini Girls.'

'So how are *they*?' I wished I hadn't asked. Talk of the Martini Girls would surely lead, before long, to Carl McGahan and that was a subject I wanted to avoid.

'Well, Julia has made us all sick with envy – she's just bought a holiday home in San Gimignano. Vicky has a new agent, thank *God* and there's an auction under way, but she's now being totally unbearable about it and everybody's pissed off with her for all sorts of reasons; there's talk about dropping her from the group.'

'Perhaps I'm lucky to be out of it.'

'Oh and Claudia's husband has come home with his tail between his legs, but Claudia – typical – isn't sure that she wants him any more. Frederica's finally finished her latest novel and it's fucking brilliant but nobody seems to want it.'

'What about you?'

'Still single.'

'And the book?'

She shrugged, non-committal.

'That means you've sold over 100,000 copies.'

'First they have to publish it, remember?'

She hesitated, looking at me oddly as if there was something she wanted to say but she couldn't bring herself to say it. It was getting closer to midnight and I sensed that all of this talking had been merely a prelude to a more important conversation, as if we were both skirting around the things that really mattered. She held the silence and I imagined that something was wrong. It had to be more than my *faux pas* about the book. Perhaps if I had been comfortable in that silence, if I had just waited, let it be, she would have spoken. Instead, I filled it.

'I think I've done something stupid,' I said.

'Aside from leaving Will you mean? You still haven't told me how you are after that?'

'I'm fine – and yes, aside from that.'

'*So what?*'

'I've been selected as a contestant for *The Lit Factor.*'

I watched her expression, the way her eyes flickered and her mouth twisted in distaste. I said nothing.

'But that's Loftus's thing, right? The TV competition?'

I nodded.

'I don't get it. I thought you didn't want anything to do with Loftus.'

'I don't. Buddy entered me. He said it was a good commercial proposition.'

'Well maybe it is, but that doesn't mean that you have to do it. I mean why would you put yourself through that? And anyway, you *know* Loftus. Isn't that unethical?'

'Thanks for the vote of confidence.'

'But just on a practical level – surely that's breaking the rules?'

'You're trying to say I'm a nepotist?'

'I didn't say that.'

'Actually, it's not. Only "friends and family" of judges are ineligible. I'd hardly call myself a "friend". And as I didn't marry Will, they can't call me "family".'

She paused and when she spoke, her voice was subdued. 'Is is really what you want, Anna?'

I knew what lay behind that question. She thought it was somehow beneath me, that all that commercial exposure was a bad thing – or rather that it was the *wrong kind* of exposure. It was one thing getting reviewed in the broadsheets or being short-listed for a prize, but something else to expose oneself to the glare of publicity that was reality TV.

'Absolutely.' Why should I tell her I'd had the same doubts? That I understood her reservations entirely? 'It would be crazy to turn it down. Filming starts in January.'

'Oh hell...'

'You don't approve?'

'It's just...'

'What?'

'I mean, you've been avoiding everybody. You haven't answered anybody's calls for months, not even mine. You left you fiancé and you didn't even lean on me, your best friend. Christ, Anna, you've been a total recluse and yet now, all of a sudden you're going to appear on national television. So you're quite happy to be going to parties and meeting publishers but you can't even pick up the telephone when I call.'

Her face crumpled, her lower lip trembling like blancmange.

'Shit.' I didn't know what to say. I hadn't even thought that my absence would affect her. 'What an idiot I've been.'

I might have said more, but outside in the street, a firework exploded, then another, huge cracking explosions, a cacophony of noise. We had missed the countdown and the New Year had begun, without us even noticing. Hilary moved to the window and pulled the blind aside. I looked over her shoulder and we watched as the sky was filled with bright galaxies of light.

'Happy New Year' she said, and her tone remained a little steely as she raised her glass.

*

Now it was April and the telephone was ringing. Hilary was firmly a part of my life again, but I was not ready to resume a full social life. These days, I only picked up the phone when it was Hils, my Mum or a member of the production team. My diary was full of filming commitments, parties that related to the show and interviews. Every week, I submitted two thousand words of my work to the *Lit Factor* and within hours those words appeared on the *Lit Factor* website, to be read and judged by the reading public. On Friday evenings, the show was broadcast on live TV. I sat on stage, after hours in hair and make-up, to face the "constructive criticism" of the judges: Loftus, his new best pal Meryl Wainwright and a young Bengali first-time novelist, Urmi Somayaji, whose family saga novel had just secured the largest transatlantic deal in publishing history. At the end of each programme, the host, Helena Hyssop would formally (and tearfully) announce the latest casualty of the reader vote. I always expected my name to be called but weirdly, it never was. I had seen nine other contestants eliminated, one by one.

Tomorrow was the final. It was just beginning to sink in. The prize – a lucrative publishing deal with Fahy and Brown – was the very thing I coveted. Yet all the same, this seemed like a joke that had gone too far.

"You're through to Anna Bright. I'm not taking calls at the moment but please speak after the tone and I'll get back to you in the spring."

'Anna, it's Joel.'

Joel? Joel? How did he get this number? At first, when I left Will, I used to think about him. After the fiasco with Will, the rats and the porn magazines – and having taken a decision to have nothing to do with Carl McGahan – I *had* indulged in daydreams about Joel. But I had quashed such thoughts at source. That was one of the rules too – *no men!* So I hadn't even tried to work out how to contact him; he reminded me too much of the past.

Yet now, I knew – in that split second that I heard his voice – that I had been hoping to hear from him. The solitude had felt crippling at times and there had been moments when I had allowed myself to imagine what it would be like to know him better, to at least give our potential relationship a chance. I could not separate myself from the world forever – the money would run out and my friends would lose patience, or else I might simply go mad, if I had not already. And yet, while it lasted, it seemed a delicious madness. For the first time in my life I was taking my work seriously. I had spent many long days in the British Library, first reading all the standard works on Modigliani, then moving on to more obscure publications, catalogues from long-forgotten exhibitions, essays in minor publications and original documents. The research itself could have gone on forever and I thought, if I were to do it properly I should learn Italian too, so that I would not miss a fact or a potential revelation in my search. Yet in the end, I had reminded myself that I was not a biographer; I was trying to write a pretty good novel and it would be wrong to allow research to get in the way of writing this story. I'd come to realise that there were gaps in this tale, but it was the gaps themselves that were important. It seemed to me that if there were not gaps, a novelist would have no role. Jeanne's story obsessed me.

And here was Joel, threatening to interrupt it all.

I would not pick up the call.

'Anna, please pick up. I've been talking to Hilary. She wouldn't give me your mobile number; but she gave me this one.'

How did he know Hilary?

'And in case you haven't noticed, it is already the spring, so you have no excuse not to pick up.'

Had I mentioned him to Hilary? Perhaps I had. Would she have tracked him down?

There was a long pause and for a moment I thought he had gone away. Then – he spoke again.

'I was really sorry to hear about you and Will.'

*He didn't sound sorry. I wasn't even sure that I **wanted** him to be sorry.*

'OK. Well, you don't have to pick up if you don't want to. It's just – well, I'm in London – in Barnes actually. And I thought you might like to have a coffee or something?' He paused and it took every particle of my strength not to pick up. 'Well, I guess you're not in. It's just a little urgent, that's the thing. And I'm actually in Sonny's.'

He knew where I lived? He was outside? Sonny's café was opposite my flat. Hilary must have told him my address. *I was going to **kill** her. Or kiss her, one or the other. But why didn't he just knock on the door?*

My instinct was to duck beneath the window pane. Instead, I approached the window and looked out. I could see him, standing in the doorway of the café. He was just as I remembered him: the familiar oblong spectacles and slightly lanky gait. He wore a long wool scarf about his neck and a woollen hat; he looked up and waved. I raised my hand and gave a small wave back.

'So pick up the phone!' His voice almost came as a surprise. I did as he asked.

'Hello.'

'What took you so long?'

'What took *you* so long?' I might have replied, but thankfully, I had the good sense to keep quiet.

In Sonny's, I sat down opposite Joel, carefully placing my coffee cup on the table. It was lunchtime but I told him I wasn't hungry. He shrugged and ordered a panino.

'So – you left pretty swiftly last time we met?'

I liked his directness. I couldn't have handled small talk.

'I'm sorry I didn't say goodbye.'

'S'OK,' he said, pursing his lips in mock disapproval. 'You'll just have to make it up to me.'

I smiled. This was interesting. I didn't remember him being quite so flirtatious on Ouranos. I found it disconcerting. I knew that I was staring at him now, but I couldn't help myself. He was so different, physically, to Will: taller, broader and less controlled in his movements. There was something chaotic about him, the way he moved his limbs, the lack of co-ordination that was somehow immensely appealing.

'I see you've sold your soul,' he said.

It did sting but I tried not to show it. 'You're talking about the show, I presume?'

He nodded.

'Yeah, well. I had to find some motivation to finish the book.' It was weak, I knew that.

'What *possessed* you, Anna?'

If it had been anybody else, I would have been offended. But there was something about the way he said it. It wasn't an attack; he was just telling the truth as he saw it. I happened to agree with him.

'I obviously wanted to be famous more than I wanted to get married,' I said. But I instantly regretted that comment. It was a callous half-truth.

'Hey, I'm very *glad* you didn't get married. But you know – if that's really what you want – there are other ways of getting famous.'

I took a sip of my coffee and felt the froth against my upper lip.

He reached across to wipe it away. This was exactly what I'd been trying to avoid.

'Yeah?' I said, pulling myself together. 'Like what?'

'Oh, you know, like the traditional slow, hard slog, taking years to write the book, being rejected by fifty or so agents, rewriting several drafts, submitting again, then eventually finding a small, obscure publisher who will print a thousand copies of your first book which in the end never sees the light of day; writing a second novel, getting a little more successful with that one but seeing it pulped in the end. You know how it goes, you'd have a break-through book around novel number five and suddenly they'd bring out your backlist – you win a major prize for the novel they pulped and all the years of suffering in obscurity would suddenly be justified.'

I smiled. 'Mmm. That sounds really appealing.'

'You look beautiful on-screen, by the way. The content might be shit, but I can't stop watching.'

'You've been watching?'

He nodded.

'If you had any idea of the hours it takes to get tarted up like that you might appreciate it even more.'

He shrugged. 'Seriously though, why didn't you go the traditional route? Didn't you have some agent that was interested in you?'

I nodded. 'Buddy.'

'I'm surprised that Loftus shortlisted you, after that fiasco we witnessed.'

'To be honest, I'm not convinced he even got involved in the shortlisting; he looked pretty shocked on the first day of filming.'

'I think it gets you votes actually. His antipathy makes good television.'

He held my gaze for just a little longer than was necessary and I felt a familiar, aching weakness. I'd felt it in the Ouranos Vine Bar too but I hadn't allowed myself to acknowledge it. If I hadn't met Joel – if he hadn't pointed out the flaws in my thinking that day – I might have married Will. *Was that true?*

'I've been reading your work online,'

'Oh.'

It shouldn't have come as a shock. I still wasn't used to this feeling of exposure. It was one of the things that I most hated about the competition – that thousands of people were reading my work-in-progress and I knew in my gut that this was wrong; it wasn't the way it should be. I didn't want Joel to read it when it was still so raw; it should be honed to perfection before he saw it.

'It's really strong, Anna. You're getting to the heart of it.'

I shrugged. 'Thanks.'

'You don't believe me?'

'It's a first draft. I'm forced to put it out there…'

'Forced? What particular method of torture do they use?'

'OK, OK, I choose to be in the competition. But I can hardly pull out now… I can't bear it that everyone's reading my first drafts.'

'It didn't bother Dickens…'

'Stop being so bloody clever.'

'I just meant it's OK. There's a literary heritage.'

'Well, it's very kind of you to make my selling-out a little sweeter…'

'Anna…'

I sensed that whatever it was – this urgent matter he'd earlier professed – was not going to be pleasant. I wanted to stall it. The café was getting noisier, the ice-crushing machine cut across his anxiety. I jumped in.

'There's a party tonight,' I said. *I wished I didn't have to be there; that I could have a social life of my own again, beyond the false whirl that had been created by the show.* 'It's on a riverboat: the pre-final bash. Hilary's coming. And I managed to get tickets for all her cronies.'

'Have a great time…'

'Yeah, I understand,' I said. 'Not your thing.'

'Oh!' he said. 'You're inviting me? Why didn't you say?'

'I thought it might be a bit beneath you.'

'It is,' he said. 'But you're not.'

'Thanks.'

But he didn't look pleased.

253

'Anna,' he said. *Here we go.* 'There's something I have to tell you.' In the brief pause that followed, a thousand possibilities crowded my brain. Perhaps he would tell me that he was married. He had a kid. Or maybe it was something unexpected: he had an STD or an incurable disease that meant he only had three months to live. 'I left my job at *Beauvoir.*'

'Oh.' *Was that it?* 'God, I thought you were going to tell me something serious.'

'I am. I'm freelancing now: articles for other magazines, a couple of websites and the broadsheets.'

'Freelancing's not exactly a tragedy.' I couldn't work out where this was going. *Was he thinking I might have concerns about his career path?*

'Hang on. You might change your mind about the party. I've got a story appearing tomorrow. It's about Loftus.'

'Right.' I didn't like his tone. 'What is it?'

'That day at the Sappho place – something didn't seem right. I had a hunch and I followed it up.'

'What are you talking about?'

'The wedding thing, the lawyer and all. It was just too much of a hard sell.'

'I'm sorry, I don't get you.' Had my first suspicions been right? Perhaps Joel had written an article and he'd used our private experience as part of it. I might be estranged from Phyllis, but I still felt protective towards her. Who was I to judge her marriage to Loftus? If it made her happy—

'He's married, Anna.'

'Yes, I know.'

'No, I don't mean to Phyllis.'

'But he did marry Phyllis. I saw the pictures in the press.' I didn't want to talk about this; didn't want to think of the images of Will at his mother's wedding, wearing a white rose in his lapel. His lapel of THAT suit. The suit he bought for OUR wedding.

'He's married to someone else. He has an estranged wife who lives in Texas.' I drew breath. 'There's more. About a year ago, he married another elderly woman who has recently purchased one of the Durrell White Houses.'

I placed my coffee cup down. I felt a little sick. 'Fuck!'

'Exactly.'

I was still taking it in.

'So hang on… you said you've got this story appearing tomorrow?'

He nodded.

'The day of the final! Oh marvellous.'

'It's my job, Anna.'

'Yeah. Of course it is. But why the hell are you coming here to tell me?'

'I thought you had a right to know.'

'Yeah well, you've told me now. Thanks. See ya.'

I told myself I was angry on Phyllis's behalf, for what Loftus had done to her. But if that was true, why was I taking it out on Joel? Did I really care, I wondered, about the publicity? Did I think it would detract from my own big moment? Of course not. I was beginning to regret ever entering the competition, yet how could I walk away when the big prize that I'd coveted for so long was now so close? No, it wasn't that.

'It had to come into the public domain, Anna. The guy's a crook.'

'I get that. But why are you here? Why didn't you just write your story and put it out there?' His expression was one of curiosity and bafflement.

'I didn't want you to find out second-hand.'

He paused and fiddled with his specs. 'And I wanted to see you.'

I was surprised to discover that this mattered. 'Poor Phyllis…'

'Yeah, I pity her.'

'Does she know yet? Or is she going to read about it in *The Guardian* tomorrow?'

He flinched. 'I'm not sure that she's aware of it yet, no.'

'Great.'

I looked down at my hands and saw that I'd been rolling a serviette into a ball and had now pulled it into shreds that were scattered across my saucer. I couldn't really pin down the source of my emotion. Was I angry at Loftus for plotting bigamy and swindling old ladies of their life savings? Or Joel for finding him out? Who did I most pity? Phyllis, who was about to have the rose-tinted glass cruelly ripped from her spectacles? Or myself – for finding myself at the centre of this media circus, my book a mere commodity, with viewers voting as much (or possibly more) for the dresses I wore as for my prose?

'I suppose it's a good thing,' I said. 'You finding out I mean.'

'Somebody had to shop him.'

'The bastard… '

'I didn't think you cared that much for Phyllis.'

'No. Neither did I.' The last time I saw her, she was asleep, that morning on Ouranos. The memory of the afternoon at the villa returned to me, when I'd travelled up the mountain with Joel, in the back of the taxi, wanting to reach out and touch his hair, yet hardly able to make sense of that desire. Now I was about to cry. 'I think I'd better go.'

'Don't. I should have got in touch earlier. My timing is crap.'

'It's not your fault.' I stood up to leave. 'I have to get back to work,' I said. 'Thanks for letting me know.'

I didn't know why I was doing this. *Because I have a novel to write.* I can't afford to get involved. I knew I'd made a mistake as soon as I'd stood up, but I was too proud to change my mind. I didn't look over my shoulder as I left and no sound followed me. I walked out into the street, turned left and stood there for a moment, watching the passers-by.

29

'She was not accustomed to taste the joys of solitude except in company...' – Edith Wharton

I found it impossible to write that afternoon. The harder I tried to find the right metaphor or the perfect line of dialogue, the more I struggled to find the words. Occasionally, forced to admit the extent of my distraction, I'd get up from my desk and wander to the bedroom to try on a dress. I'd stand in front of the mirror and twirl an ironic pirouette, forcing my mouth into a contorted smile.

This farcical performance continued for most of the afternoon. I kept thinking about Phyllis and how she would react when she discovered that her new husband was not the man she believed him to be. But it wasn't just that. I couldn't get Joel out of my head. I knew from all-too-bitter experience that the moment I got entangled with a man, my writing suffered; I told myself that this was an absolute truth, and no amount of reasoning should shift me. But I was beginning to fear it was too late. I'd lean towards the screen, squint my eyes, attempting to focus on Jeanne and Modi; but all I could think about was Joel: his large hands on the table, so close to mine; his slightly clumsy grin coupled with eyes that were anything but; his stare had been so intense, I thought his eyes alone might swallow me.

At around six thirty, I finally conceded defeat and trashed the document I'd been working on. The study floor was littered with versions of the scene I'd printed out and discarded; the bedroom floor with dresses. I took a shower, thinking that might help, but the hot spray on my shoulders only served to intensify what I now conceded was desire: a physical longing that had crept up on me, almost without my noticing it and over which, it seemed, I had little control. How stupid of me to think that celibacy could be so simple.

I stepped out of the shower and wrapped a towel about myself; as I did so, the doorbell rang. I froze. If I was silent, I thought, whoever it was might go away. But it rang again as I pulled on a dressing gown and tugged a hairbrush through my hair. The buzzing continued. When the irritation of listening to that sound started to feel worse than the potential pain of being seen without make-up, I gave in and went to the door.

I had not expected it to be him. I had not thought it would be so simple. Joel was standing there, his expression open, as if it was not me who had been caught unawares but him. He was dressed in the same T-shirt he'd worn that afternoon, the same brown suede jacket. I guessed he had not been home.

'So we're going to a party, right?' he said.

'Ha!' I just grinned back at him, for a moment forgetting the dressing gown, my bare face. I stared at him, not certain which of us was most astonished.

'Your timing really *is* bad. I look a wreck.'

'You have no idea how untrue that is.'

I tried not to reveal how his comment affected me.

'You'd better come in and wait while I get ready.'

'I'm not good at waiting.'

'Then you'd better learn some patience,' I replied.

The party was due to start at 8pm. The production team had told me I must be punctual. We walked from Waterloo, beneath the bridge and past the statue of Nelson Mandela. As we crossed the Hungerford footbridge over the Thames, Joel took my hand; I turned, very briefly, to face him and saw the grin that hovered beneath his apparently calm expression. His fingers entwined with mine and as I looked out across the skyline towards St Paul's, the lights of the Festival Hall reflecting in the river, I felt suddenly resentful of the evening that lay ahead of me: the cameras; the people; the whole damned party; everything in fact, that wasn't just Joel.

As we walked along the Embankment and came closer to the

dock, we could see the party guests, waiting to embark.

'Damn,' Joel said, as we approached.

'What? Have you seen Loftus?'

'It's not that...'

'What then?'

'All the blokes are in black tie.'

I laughed; I suppose he was underdressed, but his presence was comforting. I was shivering in a thin, shimmering mac and instinctively moved closer to him for warmth.

I recognised a lot of faces: my fellow finalists, Maud and Antony and Loftus too, chatting to Urmi Somayaji. Joel averted his eyes as we walked past them, muttering 'the little shit' under his breath. Then I spotted Hilary. She was with Julia Claiborne, waving and coming towards us. Hilary's hair had been newly bleached and Julia was wearing a sea-green sheath dress that glittered like the scales of a mermaid.

'You look stunning!' Hilary said to me. She glanced at Joel. 'Where's your dicky-bow?'

'Yeah, well, it was a last minute thing,' he said. I kept wanting to touch his face. 'I spent the afternoon walking the streets of London doing penance for pissing Anna off.'

'Oh God, you didn't cross her did you?'

He laughed and shook his head. 'I'm Joel, by the way.' He held out his hand. 'We spoke on the phone.'

'Well who else would you be? Good to meet you.' They indulged in a playfully formal handshake.

'Oh sorry... Where are the others?' *How strange to see them again, as if nothing whatsoever has changed.* 'God, it's cold, when are they going to let us on that boat?'

'Vicky can't make it. Frederica's somewhere or other. She's here to celebrate; she sold her novel at last.'

'Oh that's brilliant! I'm so pleased for her. Is Buddy here yet, by the way?'

But as I said it, I spotted him on the far side of the crowd, wearing a starched white tuxedo, nodding and frowning and deep in conversation with Meryl Wainwright.

'It's easy to take it all for granted, don't you think?' Joel said.

'What?'

'This.' He held out his hand to indicate the view. 'The river at night. London.'

'I don't think so,' I said. I turned to see the neon-blue brilliance of the London Eye reflecting in the water. 'At least not tonight; I'm taking nothing for granted.'

'I haven't been to the National in ages. We must go.'

'Are you asking me on a date?'

'I *might* be,' he replied.

'Oh, *come* on, you two. There's no time for all this flirting. They're letting us on.'

People were beginning to walk up the gangplank, picking up glasses of wine from the table at the top. I grabbed a glass of red as I passed and raised it at the waiting cameraman; it was becoming second nature.

'So let me get this straight,' I said, as we walked along the deck. 'You two have been plotting. I don't get it. How did you get in touch?'

Joel widened his eyes at me; there was something beautifully irreverent about him. He wasn't doing anything he shouldn't be, but his demeanour gave me the impression that he might.

'It's my fault,' Hilary said. She grimaced, as if there was something she would rather not say. 'I was reading a copy of *Beauvoir* at the hairdressers.'

'And?'

'I just *saw* something and it made me feel uncomfortable.'

'Something Joel wrote?'

'No. It wasn't one of his.'

'Sorry?'

'Well – there was a bad thing – and a good thing. Unconnected.'

'You're talking in riddles, Hils.'

'The bad thing was a photograph. But the good thing – well, just seeing the magazine reminded me about this guy you mentioned, Joel – when you first came back from Ouranos. I remembered you said he worked for *Beauvoir*. And – well – I just thought I should put you two in touch with each other again, that's all.'

'Matchmaking.'

'If she hadn't emailed, I would have called you again – eventually,' he said.

'What do you mean, eventually?' I asked.

Hils shrugged. 'SO – I Googled him, found his website, emailed. Seems it wasn't such a bad idea.' She looked down at Joel's arm, now resting almost casually around my shoulder.

'And the bad thing?'

'Oh God – here comes a bad thing.'

I turned to see what she was looking at. She was right: it was bad. I felt my throat constrict and reached up for Joel's hand, squeezing it so hard, he must have thought I was trying to extract juice from it.

Carl McGahan was walking up the ramp, hand-in-hand with Lucy Myers-Jones.

'Damn.'

I hadn't anticipated this. *Who the hell had invited him?* He hadn't seen me yet and I fixed on him, hardly knowing what to feel. This was the first time I'd seen Carl since returning from Ouranos. The last time we were in touch was some filthy text that I'd failed to reply to.

'Who's that?' Joel asked.

'It's Carl.'

'Right.'

I watched as Buddy now approached Carl, touched his hand to Carl's shoulder, then kissed Lucy on both cheeks as she stepped onto the deck beneath the bright fairy lights; she kissed him back, smudging magenta lipstick across his cheek.

'You don't have to talk to him,' Joel said.

'He's right,' Hilary agreed.

'No, it's OK. I can handle this.'

It was just then that Carl spotted me. I noticed the small quiver of his lip and the way his hand instinctively rushed to his forehead to flick his fringe back. I hardly knew what to feel. Whatever had happened between us, we'd let it go; it hadn't really mattered. It should have stung me but I felt strangely empty.

All the same, I walked towards him, determined to appear strong and in control. Joel came with me, curling his arm around me, so his hand rested on my hip. Lucy spotted me and I watched as her eyes quickly scanned my body. I could feel the flashbulbs lighting up around us, as if every pap on the boat had sensed the drama of this moment. Bright shocks of light making me squint. Lucy was so skinny, in a thin, pale pink silk mini dress, though her appearance was ruined by legs clad in high-heeled patent boots, shiny like the carapace of a stag beetle.

'Hello Carl,' I said. I kept my voice steady.

'Hi Anna.'

'And Lucy. How's The Walpole?'

'It's fabulous,' she said, pulling her lips tightly over her teeth as if she were concealing something.

'Anna – hi!' Buddy came up from behind, leaning towards me. I air-kissed him, avoiding the lipstick stain. 'Good luck for tomorrow, darling.'

There was something different about Carl's expression: a seriousness that I hadn't expected.

'I was sorry to hear about you and Will,' he said.

Him too? Why did they all appear to care? They were just going through the motions. I barely knew him. I remembered the intimacy though and as we stood there, surrounded by other people – maybe it was the same for both of us – I felt a sense of mutual understanding of the kind you only get when you've had physical closeness with a person. Perhaps we both wanted everybody to melt away (Lucy dissolving into the air leaving only the shiny boots as a memento, they might shrink down and scuttle off) so that we could, however briefly, exchange a few words that would make sense of what almost happened between us.

'It's OK,' I said. 'It was the right thing. *Je ne regrette rien.*'

Lucy grimaced then. My fault, talking in clichés.

My legs were trembling but nobody could tell. I didn't want him. This wasn't about wanting at all. Joel was silent but I could feel his presence beside me. Carl looked so slight beside him, insubstantial, like a twig in the presence of a great tree.

'It's freezing up here,' Lucy said. 'Shall we go below deck, Carl?'

'I would have thought those boots would keep you warm,' I said.

I couldn't help myself. Carl's lips broke into a half smile; he was trying to stop himself from laughing.

Buddy was looking on, hovering behind Carl, as if seeking an opening in the conversation. Despite Joel's presence, a part of me wanted to stay and talk, knowing that if Carl and I were alone together, I might at least be able to get some explanation. We might piece together what happened between us and find… what? A portion of nothing was nothing after all. It didn't matter.

The bad thing. That mattered more. *What was the bad thing Hilary had mentioned?*

'I must get another drink,' I said. My glass was clearly full. But I knew that I had nothing to say to Carl. I half turned but Joel stood still for a moment, looking at Carl, really looking at him, as if trying to figure him out. 'Hilary, you coming too? See you, Carl.'

'Yeah, see you,' he said.

As we wove past Buddy, through the crowd, back towards the gangplank, Hilary grabbed my arm.

'You OK?'

'I'm fine,' I said. 'Hey, Joel, slow down.'

He was walking fast, a few paces ahead of us. 'Just need to get as far away from him as I can,' he said.

'You allergic?'

'Just jealous,' he conceded.

'Nothing to be jealous of.'

'Right, I'm going to leave you two lovebirds alone,' Hilary said. 'SO many people I need to talk to.'

I almost took her at her word, but as I was about to wave, I hesitated. I couldn't ignore the sarcasm in her voice. It seemed to come from nowhere. Had I done something wrong? Joel looked from one of us to the other; he could tell what was going on.

'Hilary, what's the matter?'

It didn't make sense. She had set me up with Joel, hadn't she?

263

'He's jealous of Carl. I'm envious of you. Who are you jealous of, Anna?'

It came from nowhere. There was a piece of this puzzle missing, there must be. But even as I paused to try to figure it out, the party photographer must have sensed an imminent row. He was lurking behind us, pointing his lens straight at Hilary. Hilary, however, hadn't noticed him; whatever had been building up inside her was clearly now threatening to erupt.

'Nobody,' I said. 'I'm not jealous of anybody.' Did she think I had a secret that I refused to share with her? 'And *you*, envious of *me*? I don't get it.'

'Huh!' She looked skywards, as if despairing of me.

But this was Hilary Stevenson we were talking about: the beautiful girl who went to Cambridge, graduated with a first, got a six-figure publishing deal and now a film deal with George Lagana. Even now, the flashlight was exploding in her face, capturing her perfect elfin looks, ready to share with the readers of some glossy magazine.

'You might have to explain,' I said, gently. 'Joel…'

'Sure. I'll go fill my glass,' he said.

We slipped down a staircase, out of sight and found a quiet corner where the other guests had not yet invaded; the photographer had enough grace not to follow us. He already had his tearful shot. We sat down on a low banquette.

Hilary sniffed hard and dabbed the corners of her eyes with her index finger.

'Do you think you can make this simple,' I said, 'because I'm clearly being a bit
thick here?'

Her face looked very pale suddenly; I hadn't noticed that earlier.

'It's just that nothing seems to touch you,' she said.

'What?'

'Men fall at your feet and you seem to just take it for granted. Your wedding gets cancelled and you bounce back and suddenly you're a TV celebrity. I mean, you're quite capable of going months without seeing your friends. Will does what he does and it seems like oil on water; like nothing touches you.'

'What do you mean 'Will does what he does'?'

She shook her head. 'Sorry.'

'Sorry for what?'

'I shouldn't have said that.'

'But now you have?' I paused. 'You said there was a "bad thing".'

'Stupid of me to mention it. Fucking stupid.'

'Just spit it out.'

'A picture of Will at some media party; in the *Beauvoir*; Angela Crystal was on his arm.'

'Oh,' I said. I couldn't think what else to say. 'That doesn't surprise me.'

'I'm such a twit,' Hilary said.

I closed my eyes tightly, sucking my lips between my teeth.

'Of course it hurts you,' she said. 'I was telling myself lies.'

'Like the lies I tell myself about you,' I replied. 'I mean, I thought everything was fine?'

She raised her glass to her lips and drank the rest of the wine down in one.

Will with Angela. Imagining it was like looking through a mirror. It didn't seem possible.

'Well, first of all I got back together with Tom. Then I broke up with him again in October. Then in November, I found out I was pregnant – and to top it all I had a miscarriage just after Christmas.'

'But you didn't say anything... on New Year's Eve...'

'You were so keen to talk about the show. I was so angry at you for disappearing.'

'I thought you wouldn't notice. I mean you had Julia and the Martini Crowd.'

'Great.'

'And then there was the Lagana deal and...'

'Oh yeah, I forgot, I have a film deal and that makes my whole life perfect.' She stood up. 'Look, I think I'm going to go home.'

'You found Joel for me,' I said. 'Why?'

She shrugged. 'A hunch.'

'Thank you.'

But she didn't acknowledge it. She walked out, not looking back. I had no idea whether I was forgiven and when Joel found me, ten minutes later, wandering about the lower deck of the boat, talking nonsense to anyone I happened to bump into, I was so relieved I started to cry.

'What is it,' he whispered? 'What happened?'

'Just too many things in the course of a single night,' I said. 'It's not fair on you. `I can't begin to explain.'

'Try.'

'I've just made a lot of mistakes.' I gestured to the room, the people milling about. He seemed to get me.

'You mean this little merry-go-round?'

'The important people,' I said. 'I thought this was important.'

'They're just a lot of tossers,' he said.

I laughed. 'What everyone in this room?'

'I'm sure they're all fine as individuals,' he said. 'But collectively they're tossers.'

'Is that your philosophical observation for the evening?'

'Yeah,' he said. 'What's yours?'

'I've been so busy being a media tart that I forgot to take care of my real friends.'

He must have counted himself in that latter category because as I said it, he wrapped his arms around me.

'You know, Anna, it'll all be fine. It'll all be over tomorrow; whether you win or lose.'

'I thought if I won, that might just be the beginning?'

He shook his head. 'Wishful thinking,' he said. 'If you win, you get another 24 hours of stardom and then you sink into obscurity like the rest of us.'

'Thank God for that,' I said. And then he kissed me.

30

'One may smile, and smile, and be a villain.'
– William Shakespeare

When my alarm woke me the following morning, the first thing I noticed was his absence. Joel was not in my bed and it troubled me. I turned over, half burying my head in the pillow, running my fingers across the space where he should have been, the space he had occupied for at least half the night. I attempted to remember: some conversation in the middle of the night; it was all a blur, because the part that I remembered more clearly – the imprint of his body on mine, the surprise of physical connection after so many months in the confines of my own space – was more insistent. He had said something about going, an explanation; I must have been half asleep.

It took all of two minutes to work out that he wasn't in the flat. It didn't have to mean anything bad. He had explained, surely. Only I'd been too drunk on proximity to listen, too hung up on the taste of his skin, the sensation of his kisses to notice what he'd said.

Today. It was today. I sat up, leant down to pick up my discarded underwear from the side of the bed. If all went well tonight, if I won the competition, *The Modigliani Girl* would find an audience. I'd have a publishing contract with Fahy and Brown. And that was good, wasn't it?

Yet something had shifted, as if all of my nerve endings had been shaken up and rearranged. A shower didn't alter the feeling. The lovemaking had increased, not diminished my longing for Joel.

As I emerged from the bathroom, the newspaper came through my letterbox.

So. This was it.

Joel's story had made the front page – at least it occupied the header that directed me towards the supplement: *TV's Literary Guru in Bigamy Controversy.* There was a photograph of Loftus: it must have been taken in an unguarded moment. His nose appeared red and swollen, his eyes more bloodshot than usual. On the front page of the supplement there was a photo of Phyllis accompanied by Joel's by-line.

I put it down. It was too disorientating. Too complicated. And I was late for the lighting rehearsal. I had to get dressed, brush my hair, gather my things. I wanted to hate Joel for exposing Phyllis – except that I couldn't hate him. The memory of his mouth on mine was too intense; and he was also saving her.

I telephoned the production office and got through to a woman called Ruth.'

'So what's happening?' I said. She must be the new PA. 'This story? Is everything still going ahead?'

'It's a bloody nightmare. But don't panic, OK? We've got a replacement lined up.'

'What? What are you talking about?'

There was an uncomfortable pause.

'There's some talk that Loftus might be arrested.'

'Arrested? You are kidding?'

'Anyway, we have somebody else. We're in negotiations.'

'The show can't go ahead without Loftus…'

What had Joel done?

'It's just a rumour.'

'But who have you got lined up?'

'It's Vernon Chandler.'

'Chandler? No way!'

'It'll be fine. It's just going to cost us an arm and a leg.'

'So…'

'That's confidential, of course. Don't say a word to the press.'

'I wouldn't dream of it,' I said.

I didn't look at the newspaper until I was on the Tube. I thought it might normalise it, that the act of reading in a public place would ensure that I considered it calmly.

The story had made quite a splash. I'd glimpsed the tabloids and even they had picked up the "exclusive". The combination of bigamy, fraud and TV celebrity was too good for any gossipmonger worth his salt to resist. I half expected people to start staring at me and prodding me saying 'hey, aren't you the girl in this show?' But nobody did.

Loftus was the star. But as I turned the pages of the supplement, I found his co-star too: a photograph of Phyllis, in her prime, in the 60s. I marvelled at her delicate features, the perfect jaw-line, and her enormous, bright eyes. Even with the false eyelashes and kipper collar, she looked the epitome of effortless chic.

What was she thinking now? She was in love with him. I had no doubt of that. Yet he had swindled and humiliated her.

As I approached the studio, I shrank beneath a huge, black umbrella, almost comforted by the encompassing greyness and the rainwater that bounced at my feet. Everything was changing too quickly. Hils had lost her baby and I hadn't even known about it. I had neglected my best friend – and for what? Will was really with Angela Crystal now and Carl with Lucy. Nothing seemed solid. Nothing was predictable.

'Anna!'

I was nearly at the studio entrance, but a woman was rushing towards me on stiletto heels. *Some nutter* I thought. I saw her in the periphery of my vision: a woman in a black raincoat, a patterned headscarf and oversized scarlet sunglasses. I turned to look properly and then of course, I knew her: the slightly hunched form, the shrunken head.

'Anna, for God's sake, I need some help.'

'Phyllis. What are you doing here?'

This was the last place she should be; she should be a million miles away from James Loftus today. He couldn't justify his actions and hers were those of a desperate woman.

Behind her, a skinny, bearded guy with a nose-ring, sweating profusely, followed. He raised his camera and the zoom lens shifted towards us.

'I didn't know what else to do,' Phyllis said. 'He's not answering my calls.'

'That's hardly surprising,' I said.

It wasn't tactful, but it was difficult to focus with this pap in our face. I turned and marched towards him. I shoved my hand across the lens. I had always wanted to do that.

'Hey! Fuck off,' he yelled.

'Can't you see she's upset?' This was about as clever as telling a hangman that his actions will kill the guy standing in front of him.

'Get your hands off my lens,' he said. He pulled back, away from my grasp and zoomed in on Phyllis once again.

'You little shit!' I grabbed hold of Phyllis's arm and hurried her to the entrance hall.

'He's only trying to make a living,' she said. I hurtled her through the revolving doors and we landed safely in Reception.

Phyllis's presence was, of course, the last thing I needed. She pushed her sunglasses up onto her forehead; her face was streaked with mascara and her meagre frame appeared pitiful. I wondered how a person could live so long with so little flesh upon their bones. She leant forward and grasped my hands. Hers were so frail, I thought that they might break.

'How *could* he, Anna? How *could* he?'

There was no restraint in her voice. The receptionist gestured that I should remove her but I didn't give a damn about the receptionist. Phyllis's hands were clammy too and she clutched me tighter as she sobbed. She managed a few, faltering words.

'A wife in sodding *Texas*!' she said. '*And* another…'

'I know,' I said. She had every right to sob; nobody deserved this. 'The bastard. God, this sucks.'

A security guard approached us, but I waved him back and for the moment he was appeased.

'I can't live in that villa by myself. I *can't*, Anna! We were going to move out there, just as soon as the show is off the air. But I can't go alone; it's miles from anywhere. I even sold my time-share in Turkey. That was the deal. We'd live together. We're married, for

God's sake. At least, I thought we were.'

'You're right. Of course you can't live there. Come and sit down.'

She followed me to the sofas where she took off her raincoat and headscarf and threw both in a pile on the beige velvet. Her sober black dress was clearly funeral attire. Her body was hunched and her skin almost transparent; I wondered if she was about to pass out. Perhaps she suspected that too because she sat down very quickly.

'Are you OK, Phyllis? I mean, are you well?'

'Of course, I'm not well. I'm never bloody well.'

'You should eat something.'

'Ha!' Her features creased together, she held her eyes tightly closed for a moment, then she opened them suddenly, and despite everything else, her eyes remained bright. 'You were *there* that day, weren't you?' she said. 'He seemed totally genuine, didn't he? He always does. There was *nothing* I could have done to prevent this. I mean, did *you* see this coming, Anna?'

'Of course not.'

'I was so in love with him … I am in love with him… but I can't be, can I? He thinks I'm a gullible old woman. That's what it said in the article, *preying on susceptible older women.*'

'That's ridiculous.' I silently cursed Joel.

'You don't have to be tactful, Anna. Spare me.'

How had I got mixed up in this? I felt as if I'd been dragged onto a merry-go-round that I'd never wanted to go on in the first place.

'Do you think it's a good idea, coming here?'

'I have to see him.' Her head appeared too large for her body; it lolled.

'I don't think that's wise, Phyllis. Anyway, it's possible that Vernon Chandler's going to step into his shoes tonight.'

'What? Chandler?'

'From what I've heard they offended him when they didn't ask him to do it in the first place, but they seem to have placated him.'

'Well, Vernon Chandler is better looking,' she said. 'I should have fallen for bloody Vernon. You can get me in though, can't you? I don't want to ask James. You can get me tickets for tonight's

271

show?'

'Why do you want tickets? That's madness.'

'I want to watch.'

'It's not a good idea.'

'Not a good idea?' Her voice had modulated into a high-pitched shriek. The receptionist stood up, her mouth skewed into a lopsided contortion. 'Not a sodding good idea? You're talking about the man who quite literally screwed me out of my money, made a public idiot of me and broke my fucking heart in the process. And now I'm not even worthy of sitting in his audience?'

'No, Phyllis. It's not that. But what good would it do?'

'I'll be the judge of that.'

She pushed past me and headed for the reception desk. I imagined for a minute she was going to punch the receptionist, but she thought better of it and turned her rage back to me.

'He needs a showdown, that's what he needs. I'm going to tell the whole world what that man has done to me.'

The photographer was still outside. I thought about calling Will but I hadn't spoken to Will since the day I left him in the summer; I realised that I was shaking; I stood very still and closed my eyes. I knew that I could not change the past yet the knowledge of my impotence seemed to freeze me in the present.

It took a little courage to open my eyes, knowing I had to face her again. Phyllis was still pacing the atrium and the security man was hovering, as if about to escort her from the premises. I had to stop him. She'd had enough trauma for one day, enough trauma for a lifetime.

When I touched her shoulder, she turned and searched my face for answers. She spoke, but so quietly I had to strain to catch her words.

'Talking of broken hearts: you broke Will's too, you know?'

That wasn't fair. However much her words hurt me, I had to remind myself of the truth. We were both guilty; I was not solely to blame.

'So what about Angela?' I said. My throat felt tight and constricted; I was surprised I could get the words out.

'Flash in the pan,' she said.

'I'm so sorry…'

Why was I crying? It would never have worked with Will. In spite of all this pain – which was the pain of loss but not in fact of regret – he was not right for me. I had not left Will for some imagined or actual affair. It was far more complex than that.

Phyllis put her arms around me and held me and there was an unexpected comfort in her bony embrace that made me cry all the more. Had she forgotten her behaviour on Ouranos? She had seemed to despise me then. But now, at the height of her own suffering – the last person on earth who should have cared about my grief – she was offering me comfort. Here was the mother-in-law that was never to be, the victim who had momentarily forgotten her victimhood: a woman who should by rights have hated me still – yet somehow, I knew, did not.

31

'Then on the shore
Of the wide world I stand alone and think
Till love and fame to nothingness do sink'
– John Keats

'You must be pretty shocked, Anna. That was your ex's mother, wasn't it?'

It was Antony who spoke, one of my fellow finalists. He was a Scottish academic who had begun writing fiction during a sabbatical and had never returned to his post. We were in the Green Room, half an hour after Phyllis's departure, and Antony appeared to be distracted, flicking the kettle on as he spoke. Yet I wondered if there wasn't some implied criticism behind his question. Having worked out my relationship to Phyllis, was he now accusing me of nepotism?

Perhaps I was reading too much into it. Maud, the other finalist was there too and we were all on edge as we awaited the arrival of Vernon Chandler. Nobody seemed certain. Loftus had not appeared but the producer was apparently expecting him too – at any moment.

In the end, Phyllis had agreed to go to Will's place; we'd put her in a taxi via the back entrance of the building. I hated to send her off alone. She had looked like a lost bird: a feeble, bedraggled starling.

'She's in an awful state about it,' I said. 'God, Loftus is a shit.'

Antony sucked air through his lips. 'You can't believe everything you read in the press now…'

'What are you saying? That he's not already twice married? That he didn't also marry Phyllis?'

'I'm not saying anything. Don't be so touchy. We're all upset, you know. It's not exactly good timing.'

I had watched as Phyllis telephoned Will. It had felt so strange, knowing that he was on the other end of the telephone line, that if I chose to, I might reach over, take the receiver and hear his voice. *But that way madness lay. I had to let him go.*

'So where's Phyllis now?' Maud asked.

'She's at Will's place. I convinced her that Loftus wasn't showing and she relented. Maybe that was wrong of me, but if he does turn up, can you imagine? They can't play that one out in public.'

'Is she OK?'

'No, of course not.'

Maud couldn't sit still this morning. She kept pacing the Green Room, her wiry steel-grey hair in more than the usual disarray. She'd already told us the story of her sleepless night – the new make-up artist had been flapping about her, pulling her face to the light in an attempt to work out the right shade of concealer for the prominent dark circles that seemed to be getting darker each week, like slowly developing bruises – an allergy to media exposure.

'There's nothing you can do about it, Maud. Why don't you just sit down?'

'How can I sit down when I don't even know if the show's going ahead? I've worked myself to the bone for this and now the host decides to screw everything up.'

'He didn't plan for it to all come out today.' I had no idea why I was defending Loftus. 'I'm sure Vernon will show.'

I didn't blame Maud for her response. I felt the same, only my own agitation was internalised. It seemed to me that Maud was the most likely candidate to win, but in truth, none of us could second-guess the outcome. Maud's book, *High Wire* was a misery-memoir about her tragic upbringing in Cardiff and her later years as a performance artiste in the seventies and eighties. Maud had a gift for narrative and her prose put mine to shame. But I had never found a connection with her, finding her vain and highly-strung and prone to dramatic moments of self-doubt.

'What's happened to Loftus anyway?' Antony asked.

'Nobody can get hold of him,' I said. 'Apparently, he's not

275

answering his landline or his mobile and his agent has been trying to reach him all morning, but nothing doing. He was due at the studio an hour ago, but hasn't showed.'

'Vernon will make a bloody farce of it,' Antony said. 'You can't just change the main judge at the last minute. It'll be a complete disaster.'

Antony's book was a post-Cold War thriller set in Moscow and Washington, depicting the world of Artificial Intelligence and the struggle for technological supremacy. I had tried, several times, to make sense of it, but had failed. 'It won't be the same without Loftus,' he muttered again, under his breath. But as he spoke, he nearly choked. The door behind us opened – and who should walk in but the crinkle-faced legend that was Vernon Chandler.

'Right, you must be Antony,' he said, shaking Antony's hand, 'pleased to meet you.'

'It's an honour,' Antony said.

Bloody hypocrite.

'And Maud, excellent, good, good.' He was distracted by a speck of dust on the sleeve of his pristine suit. 'And Anna.' He scowled as if he found me the most displeasing of the bunch and turned to the make-up artist with a broad smile that was possibly as large as it was false. 'Right,' he said, 'I need to speak to the producer.'

I had grown up seeing Vernon's face on TV; to me he was like an old friend, yet this was the inequality of fame. What had I expected? That his face would light up on seeing me? Or was it, rather, that the absence of courtesy compounded the gulf in status? Vernon had looked right through me.

'At least it's going ahead,' Maud whispered. 'Just hold onto that. Tonight one of us will have a publishing deal.'

'Yes. I know.'

But I didn't find this idea even remotely cheering. I was beginning to wonder why I had allowed myself to become involved in this fiasco in the first place. Joel was right to doubt the whole enterprise. *Joel.* The memory of his body against mine had remained with me all morning; I had been walking around with a small thrill in the pit of my stomach, trying not to acknowledge it for fear that if I gave it too much attention, it might prove itself worthless.

I didn't want to be here. I just had to get through the evening. I had to grit my teeth and tolerate hair and make-up and blink my false eyelashes at the camera. The make-up artist had flashed a pair of tortoise-shell specs at me earlier; perhaps she hoped that if I wore the accoutrements of the ferocious intellectual, I might somehow convince the audience of my credentials. But I didn't care about the audience; I was thinking about Hilary. I hadn't been there when she needed me. I was to blame

If I were to survive the evening, I knew I would have to blank this out. I forced myself to imagine victory. I closed my eyes and pictured myself holding a copy of *The Modigliani Girl* in my hands. I imagined the little sticker on the cover: *Winner of TV's " Lit Factor"*.

I was nothing more than a sideshow.

'Anna?'

'I'm sorry?'

And Jeanne. What would Jeanne Hébuterne make of me? I had tried my best, to do her story justice. I had spent days in the library, tracing references, trying to find the truth of her relationship with Modi. But did that give me the right to peddle my story here? Did she not deserve better? An acknowledgement of her own talent?

'Can I have a word, Anna?' It was the PA again. She had been occupied with Vernon, but now she turned to me.

'Yes, of course.'

'In private.'

I stood up, but before I could find out what she wanted, we were interrupted. The Green Room door was flung open and there, in the doorway – smiling as if his life depended on it – was Loftus.

'OK,' he said. 'Why aren't you girls in costume?'

Vernon winced. His eyes narrowed, lizard-like; he looked Loftus up and down as if he were observing some inferior life form and discovered it to be extremely wanting. Loftus looked back at him and laughed with equal disdain. 'Let's get this show on the road,' he said.

32

'The test of literature is, I suppose, whether we ourselves live more intensely for the reading of it.' – Elizabeth Drew

I am standing in the wings, coiffed and perfected, waiting for the sound engineers to complete their checks. The Balmain dress is so tight, I feel corseted. All through the rehearsal I've felt oddly calm; something strange has happened, it's like stepping outside of myself, as if I'm not occupying this frock, this body at all.

Loftus is close by, deep in conversation with the PA. He knows that I've been crying and he can't look me in the eye. He's refusing to acknowledge there's a problem. As he passed me in the corridor, I smelt alcohol on his breath, but he's behaving much as he always does. The PA is still obsequious. He's widening his already-protruding eyes and peering without shame into the depths of her cleavage. She is either used to it or desperately ambitious because she's still speaking to him, as if she doesn't notice. But I keep thinking about Phyllis, her small, hunched frame in the back of the black cab, shrinking into the upholstery.

This is the man who has caused her so much anguish. I am here, playing his game, about to enter the arena of his revolting little circus. What does that make me, I wonder? Should I not just turn around and walk away?

'Hey!' I'm acting on a whim; I don't yet know what I'm about to do. I'm waving at the PA. There's no logic about my actions, only instinct. The PA appears relieved, as Loftus pats her on the shoulder and leaves.

'Everything OK, Anna?' she says. If she's glad to get away from him, she's not revealing that to me.

278

'Kind of. Sorry – you're new, aren't you?'

'I'm the new producer, yes. Been brought in to handle the crisis. I'm Ruth.'

The new producer?

'Ruth. OK. There's something I have to ask you.'

The idea is only forming as I speak. I can feel the words about to tumble out and almost can't believe they will be mine.

'Fire away…' she says, looking over her shoulder.

'The thing is… I've decided I can't take part.'

Now I have her attention. *Did I really say it? Have I lost my mind?*

Her face crumples into a display of blind panic, as if she's just witnessed an automobile accident.

'What are you talking about?'

'I'm dropping out.' *Stand firm.* I tell myself: 'Don't lose your bottle now. 'I don't want to do the show tonight.'

'I'm sorry,' she says, 'you can't do that.' Her face still betrays the fear that I'll do it all the same. Her eyes dart about the wings as if she might find a solution in the shadows. 'We've had 70,000 hits on the website today.'

'What's that got to do with it?'

'Look – everybody gets nervous. You've worked for months towards this.' She's pulling herself together, finding logical arguments to sway me. 'Fahy and Brown are practically eating out of your hand for God's sake. It's in the bag. You're the favourite.'

She was lying. She had to be lying. And even if I was, what matter? I was dining out on the story of a long-dead woman who would gain nothing from my fame. I was like the parasitical art-dealers who leapt on Modigliani's work the minute he was dead but never bought a single painting in his lifetime.

I shake my head. 'I don't think there are any guarantees here.' I'm thinking about Joel and his suggestion that I should do things the hard way, because it's possible, isn't it, *that the hard way is the right way?*

'Don't be an idiot,' Ruth says. There's a fly buzzing about her face and she swats it with the script she's holding – it panics and zigzags madly out of control across the set. 'You can't walk away from this opportunity. You might never have the chance again. The whole publishing world knows who you are and it's a tight-knit community, I tell you that. And think of the press too. If you stay, they'll be at your feet. If you walk out, they'll forget you in an instant. *The Modigliani Girl* might never see the light of day…'

'It doesn't feel right. I feel like a literary whore.'

'Oh grow up. There are thousands of struggling authors out there who would kill for the chance of being on this stage tonight.'

'With that drunken idiot?'

She flinches; but surely she's noticed he's been drinking? 'He'll pull it together. Believe me.'

'That's not the point. He's a shit. A total shit.'

Ruth sighs. 'You can agonise all you like about morals,' she said, 'but there is the small matter of your contract.' She smiles, as if to say *why didn't I think of that before?* "I think you'll find it pretty binding.'

I'm walking onto the stage and the crowd is now applauding. I think I might pass out and I long for a single reassuring face in the audience but the lights blind me.

The judges flank us, Loftus in his white suit, the ringmaster, navigating a perilous line towards his place on the podium. He's grinning so hard I think his mouth might crack open and the top of his head fall clean off. Meryl winces as he stumbles a little. *Has nobody thought to stop him going on?* Urmi Somayaji swishes elegantly across the stage, lifting her magenta sari to reveal her miniature feet. Antony has not escaped the sartorial madness. He's wearing a gold, embroidered waistcoat beneath his dinner suit and his hair has been absurdly coiffed. Maud is in emerald sequins and the show's host Helena Hyssop wears a gauzy, low-cut, white number that puts me in mind of a child's Halloween costume.

I wonder if Joel is in the audience; Hilary is surely there. I can see the cameras panning to my face, but nothing seems real suddenly. I feel like a small doll on a stage set. Didn't we make something like that once, Hilary and I? I had a suitcase full of dolls and dresses; the two of us would parade the tiny figures about the box, flexing their bendy plastic arms and legs into impossible poses, fingering the tiny glittering frocks, making them jump and preen.

Jumping. I'm smiling now – at least I think I'm smiling. Jeanne Hébuterne jumped – from a high window – pregnant. *How could she do that? How could Jeanne toss herself to the floor as if she and her unborn child were nothing more than a piece of garbage? It was not love, surely. It was a form of insanity.*

I can't hang on to a single thought. Helena is talking; people in the audience are applauding. But Phyllis – what about Phyllis? Crying on Will's shoulder most likely, on the sofa of my old living room. It was surely a betrayal, my being here. How could she see it any other way? I must smile, only smile, get through it. Make sense of it later. Nobody out there can see quite how much I despise myself for being here. *You've sold out, Anna Bright. Very soon you'll be a public commodity with the artistic integrity of an ant.*

I can see the VT running, on the other side of the podium, revealing highlights of the show to come. It's showing all the usual images of me, at the many parties I've recently attended, leaning towards various publishing-types, apparently engrossed in conversation. Again that sound: applause. But for what? How many of those who logged on to the website actually got past the pictures, soundbites and logos plastered everywhere and actually *read* our work? I think they are just voting for the dresses.

Breathe. Isn't that what they say, you just have to breathe in and focus on the "self" (if only I knew what the "self" was, I would do it). Sebastian is standing up now, leaping onto the stage, his long legs seeming to propel him up. He flicks his raffish blonde hair aside, clears his throat. Now there's a man who knows nothing of self-doubt. His voice is like molten sugar.

'Fahy and Brown are immensely proud to sponsor this competition. We know that the winner will represent all that is best in contemporary British fiction.'

He utters our names, each of us: Maud, Antony, and then me. But it's my turn now, as the VT rolls again. I'd almost forgotten this.

'Anna Bright talking about *The Modigliani Girl.*'

281

Watching the film, it's like watching somebody else. A woman walks beneath the arches of a church in South Kensington. (They should have flown her to Paris.) The audience is silent as a thin voice (my own) overlays the images. I'm reading from my novel and the screen dissolves to show two actors lying on a bed. It's supposed to be Modigliani and Jeanne on sardine-oil-soaked sheets. The man feigns near-death; the woman blind devotion. The man playing Modigliani does not look remotely Italian.

Then the screen dissolves to my face again, in interview:

'Her family couldn't imagine anything worse than her being the mistress of a failing artist,' I say. 'They did everything in their power to persuade her to leave Amedeo. But it was useless.' I shake my head; appear genuinely moved. 'Nothing they did had any effect on her passion. The thing was, she didn't care for their rigid conventions or their supposed morality. She was determined to pursue the man she loved even to the grave.' I pause then, take a breath. 'You have to remember, Modigliani was a man who failed to compromise. He would rather starve than take on commercial work and undermine his art. He sculpted in stone, even though he was tubercular and the dust made his condition worse. This was a man who once pushed his lover through a glass window in a public fight, without ever seeming to regret it.'

The scene fades but the studio camera is now upon me. I'm aware of it zooming closer, even before I recognise my own response to the VT. I'm crying and the camera is grateful for every single teardrop. Maud has an odd expression on her face; her jaw is slightly slack, she suspects me as a fake. If Joel is in the audience he might think I am ashamed. But in fact I am full of confusion. Beyond the studio lights my mother is watching too. She might have refrained from wearing her "mother of the bride" hat, yet my appearance here was surely her grand consolation prize. My Dad would like to have been here, she will say later. *Your Dad would have been proud.*

Yet I know I meant every word that I said on the VT. And it's possible I am simply seeing something for the first time: the fragility of artistic ambition; the impermanence.

282

The evening seems to go on forever, like a form of torture. When Helena Hysop finally approaches me, I wonder if I'll find a voice to speak. My throat feels constricted; my cheeks are burning beneath the make-up. I'm afraid that I might win.

'What would it mean to you if you won the *Lit Factor*?' Helena asks. She's not reading my mind. It's all any of us can think about now. It occurs to me that Helena is not really interested in my answer.

'I'm not sure it's all that important,' I say. *Wrong answer. That's the wrong answer.* 'What I mean is – what's important to me is the story here. I suppose if I can get people to see the indignity that artists faced at that time – and the limitations imposed on women artists in particular – then I've done my job. This is not just Jeanne's story. It's Modi's too. When you think of all the dealers who have profited over the years from his work, yet he died totally unacknowledged.'

'It's an odd choice of title, don't you think? *The Modigliani Girl*. Doesn't the word "girl" itself undermine your feminist agenda?'

Did she even listen to what I just said? I was the world's worst feminist. I could say whatever I liked and she wouldn't deviate from the script.

'The title's ironic,' I say. 'I thought people would get that.'

'Some people have said,' – she laughs – 'that you would have been better writing about Modigliani himself, attempting to unravel the nature of misunderstood genius. It's been suggested that Jeanne Hébuterne is nothing more than a figure on the sidelines of history; and that is how she should remain.'

'Modigliani has had more than enough books devoted to him.' I want to swear at her but I'm distracted by the judges. I hear something and glimpse at Loftus; he is engrossed in conversation with Urmi Somayaji. Their heads are close together but they appear to be involved in some kind of acrimonious debate.

'Jeanne Hébuterne was a product of her time,' I say. 'Her story reveals that when women become subservient to men, their own brilliance can be subsumed.'

I smile vacuously as my statement is met with rapturous applause from the audience and a small nod of approval from Sebastian.

Something is wrong with Helena. I can hear a small, tinny voice emanating from her earpiece. I watch her face closely for some hint of what's going on: her bottom lip trembles and she blinks her eyes harder, which does not disguise her distress. Our interview is over.

Tonight, on the sofas, Sebastian Brown of Fahy & Brown is Guest Judge. He sits us in an apparently cosy group, sipping water, nodding mutely. Sebastian talks about life after the competition. He speaks about artistic merit but he throws in references to foreign publishers, lunches, festivals. He glimpses at Maud frequently during his little talk. *He's grooming her for success*, I think. *It's impossible to compete with prose like hers. If this were purely judged on merit, her victory would be assured.* But soon the viewers will cast their votes. We will adjourn, then reappear; they'll drag it out for as long as they possibly can; there's a fortune to be made in commercial breaks. Soon I will be either catapulted to instant stardom or relegated to a footnote in literary history.

Beyond the stage, Loftus has stood up. He's approaching us, reaching his hand out for Helena's microphone. This didn't happen in rehearsal and Helena seems reluctant to relinquish it. Loftus appears to be swaying; more visibly drunk than he was earlier; either a delayed reaction or else that's not water he's been sipping.

'I am here tonight,' he says, his vowels running together, 'because I believe in literature.' He pauses, an actor who's forgotten his lines. He appears to be searching for an autocue, but there's none, only a director signalling frantically that he should shut up. 'I believe in these writers,' he manages finally. He gestures towards us, as if he expects us to speak. Again the silence yawns and nobody is willing to break it. Loftus clears his throat. 'I believe in the human spirit. And though I've been libelled by the press today, these stories won't break me, I tell you that…'

Helena has her hand to her earpiece. She's receiving emergency instructions.

'You see, I'm up here tonight for one reason – and one reason alone.' *Why isn't anybody stopping him?* He's pausing again; somebody should act. I watch and it's all happening in slow motion, a mischievous expression crossing Loftus's face. 'If I hadn't appeared, you would have had Vernon Chandler up here on the stage!' He breaks into laughter. 'Can you imagine anything worse than that, Ladies and Gentlemen?'

It's car-crash TV. I hear a few nervous laughs before everyone in the audience falls silent. We're live and there's nothing anybody can do about it. Sebastian has turned pale.

Urmi Somayaji surprises us all. She's followed Loftus onto the stage, half-tripping over her sari as she comes closer. She hooks her arm through Loftus's – just as well, who knows how long he'll be able to remain vertical without her? – and takes the microphone from him. 'Actually James,' she says, 'perhaps this would be a good moment for me to speak up.'

Thank heavens for that. Urmi has such serenity about her. If anyone can save the day it will be her.

'I have a question for Maud, actually,' she says.

Maud adjusts her posture, crosses her legs and tilts her head towards Urmi.

'There's no easy way to put this,' Urmi says, 'and this is something that was only drawn to my attention earlier this afternoon...'

I'm used to the studio lights now and I can make out people in the front row, their slight shifting movements revealing their increasing fascination with the unravelling events.

Urmi unzips a magenta silk bag that had appeared to be part of her sari – but she is now detaching it. From the bag, she draws out a book and opens it at a marked page. I watch with increasing fascination. Maud's expression changes: her eyes flicker, her lips tighten.

'I wonder if you are familiar with this book?' Urmi appears nervous but there's a hard fury beneath the nerves; I've never seen her like that. '*Flying High* – it was written in 1993, published, oddly enough by Fahy and Brown...'

Maud is silent. She's fixing Urmi with a direct stare and her expression has set, revealing nothing now.

'Perhaps, I could read you an extract?' Urmi says.

Maud appears to falter and it's sinking in already, the impact of these words. I can't believe Urmi is doing this.

'The storyline *is* very similar to that of *High Wire*,' Urmi said. 'The style of *Flying High* is less impressive, of course. The thing is, nobody can doubt the brilliance of your prose, but there are a few passages that do seem extremely similar.'

I hold my breath. If Somayaji is wrong, she's making a tremendous fool of herself. To do this, she must be certain of her ground. Has she planned this? Is it some big publicity stunt designed to detract from Loftus's own disgrace? Yet if she's right...

I shift my eyes to him, yet Loftus appears oddly relaxed, laughing quietly to himself, as if he no longer cares to create a literary genius at all. He's shaking his head as if the whole thing is some enormous joke. 'We won't tolerate plagiarism,' he says. 'It's unforgivable. I won't countenance it.' But he's chuckling; it's nothing but a game.

'How dare you...' Maud is spluttering. She can hardly get the words out. 'Of course it's not true.'

I feel for her now. There's no victory for me in this. They're ruining her career on live TV, with no proof, only their own suspicion. I want to speak up on her behalf but I have no information; my tongue is glued to the back of my throat.

'We need honest people,' Loftus says. The audience seems to draw a collective breath and their mutterings become louder. 'We're looking for an ambassador for this industry.'

'People-pleasers, you mean,' Maud says. 'I thought this was a professional set-up. You expect us to be performing monkeys!' She's ripping off her microphone, storming off the stage. 'I'm not anybody's monkey,' she says. 'Sod your show.' But now the mouthpiece has gone, hardly anybody hears her but me.

There's silence again now. Meryl raises an eyebrow at me, as if to say 'You've got this one in the bag, dear.' But all I can think about is Maud whose sobs spill from the wings; I'm thinking of joining her there but before I can move, Helena has stood up. She's shimmying to the front of the stage.

'Never a dull moment on the *Lit Factor*,' she says – and something about her light, unassuming voice is strangely reassuring. 'Now, only two contestants left…' She speaks with an authority that has me reeling. 'Who will win your vote? Don't forget to tune in for the results show, here at 10pm tonight.'

A huge beam lights up her face – her lips so full and glossy, her teeth white as china plates – and it's a smile that almost convinces me (and surely everybody else), that anything is possible.

33

'We are in the same tent as the clowns and the freaks – that's show business.' – Edward R Murrow

I did not have Maud down as a plagiarist. That term conjures up a petty, untalented idiot who steals the words of another who is far more capable. Yet Maud writes the most beautiful prose. Was it possible that her story was not her own but simply a lie?

The question bothers me as I walk off stage, wondering how this has happened and why. I can't hear Maud now; I want to look for her. But I can tell, almost instantly, that something else is wrong. Ruth's expression reveals this, even before I see them enter the wings: two uniformed police officers. So, this was the cause of the backstage panic. Loftus stops dead in his tracks.

'Did that really happen?' Meryl says. Her mind is still on Maud.

'I think so.' I'm trying to make sense of the police officers. Why isn't anybody mentioning them? They're just standing there, watching us.

'Urmi, what the hell was that about?' Meryl doesn't acknowledge them either. 'You can't do something like that without proof!'

'Oh dear, I didn't know what to do.' Urmi is shaking her head; as if that innocent gesture might excuse her for what she'd done. 'I told James earlier. Somebody passed that book to me this morning. I spent the afternoon reading it. There's no doubt about it. Whole passages that are almost identical. The storyline is a perfect parallel.'

'But why didn't you speak to me about it?' Ruth says. 'What did you think you were doing up there? Apart from anything else, it cut the programme short and now they're racing around trying to find

288

something to fill the gap. Helena, couldn't you have kept it running for a bit longer?'

'Thanks for the credit!' Helena, like me, is distracted by the police officers. 'I thought I was stunning under the circumstances.'

'I'm sorry. Perhaps it was stupid of me,' Urmi says.

'It'll probably be good for the ratings,' Ruth said.

'I didn't know that plagiarism was a crime,' Urmi continued.

'Don't be ridiculous. Where is Maud anyway?'

'I think Antony's looking for her,' Helena says.

'She's the least of our concerns,' Ruth replies.

Loftus is watching the police officers. They're looking at us, as if we're still on stage, as if this whole argument is a pantomime. Loftus is standing very upright but he's watching them from the corner of his eye, he's making small jerking movements with his head that reveals the effort of maintaining such perfect posture.

Now, at last, one of the officers steps forwards. His nose is pockmarked and swollen; his eyes are hard, like small pieces of grit.

'James Loftus,' he says. 'I'm arresting you on suspicion of fraud and bigamy. You do not have to say anything but it may harm your defence...'

Our argument is over. We're just beginning to register what is happening. There's a sense of rising panic amongst the rest of us but nobody speaks. We're all thinking the same thing – if Loftus is being arrested, what's going to happen to the results show? They can't arrest him now when he's right in the middle of a prime-time television event. I look towards Ruth, waiting for her to speak. Surely she can explain that it will be absolutely fine to arrest Loftus, but could they possibly, please wait until after the show? But she does nothing. She's just looking on, a casual observer, as Loftus struggles to contain himself.

'This is unacceptable,' Loftus says. 'Absolute idiocy. It's trial by press, that's what it is. You don't have a leg to stand on. Tell them, Ruth.'

'I'm afraid there's nothing I can do, James,' Ruth says. Her voice is deflated. 'I've already had a long conversation with the officer. They're not prepared to compromise. This is the law we're talking

289

about.'

'The law? What about the show? What about the fucking show?'

Nobody steps forward to help. Nobody speaks in his defence. I ought to feel pleased. This is justice for Phyllis after all. But as I turn to Loftus, some further involuntary spasm crosses his chest and he's retching. He's vomiting right in front of us.

'Oh God!' Ruth turns away.

'What are we going to do?' I say.

'Its OK,' she whispers. 'Vernon's back.'

'Don't all rush to help,' Loftus is bent double.

'Let me clean you up,' Urmi says. 'It's OK, officers. I'll bring him right along...'

Loftus bows his head as she escorts him to the bathroom.

'At least Vernon's a professional,' Ruth says. 'God knows we need one.'

'You're just going to let them arrest him?' Helena says. 'Right in the middle of the final?'

'You want me to interfere with the course of criminal justice?'

'Just an idea! How am I supposed to cope? Christ, I'm going to need a holiday to get over this show. Has anyone got any valium?'

Helena's glaring at me as if the whole thing is my fault and she marches towards the bathroom, accidentally slipping in the pool of vomit, then recovering and continuing as if nothing whatsoever has happened.

Vernon Chandler strides onto the stage, grabs the microphone and smiles as if he had been born for this moment. The audience falls to laughing and rapturous applause.

'Thank you!' he says, adjusting his bowtie, then throwing his arms wide open. 'Thank you indeed!'

In the front row, a member of the audience stands up and he's swiftly followed by others; before we know it, Vernon has a standing ovation just for being here. Nobody is looking at Helena now, which is just as well given the large vomit stain that marks her dress.

'Thank you!' He pauses. 'I knew you wouldn't be disappointed!'

There's more laughter and the sense of relief in the room is almost palpable. On the judge's podium, Urmi and Sebastian appear shell-shocked. Meryl however lets out a hoot of approval.

'Now, the votes have been close this evening…' Vernon says. No explanation of why he is here, nor of the fiasco that's just passed; no apology, only panache. I'm looking at him, wondering what it is about this man that people respond to. Is it just the grooming, the coiffed hair, the apparent wisdom suggested by the creases about his eyes? '…and I can reveal that there is only a 1% difference between our two final competitors,' he says. 'Maud Armstrong has chosen to step down but that still leaves us with two competitors, so keep your votes coming in. The lines close in one minute. Who do you want to be the winner of this first ever *Lit Factor?*'

He's moved to our side now. 'Antony Thornwood with *Silent Voices* or Anna Bright with *The Modigliani Girl.*' He's looking at me with an affection that was entirely absent when he met me earlier in the Green Room. I have a strong desire to slap him.

'While those last votes are coming in, let me introduce once again Mr Sebastian Brown who will publish the winning author.'

Sebastian bends down to retrieve something from beneath his desk: he holds a trophy aloft, an open bookcase, sculpted in bronze. I wonder what my Mum's thinking right now. I suppose she's out there rooting for me, but if Dad were alive today, would he want this, would he be proud? Perhaps he would, but that doesn't make it right. He wanted me to go to Cambridge too and I'd spent half a lifetime thinking I'd let him down somehow by failing. *How utterly stupid.* The idiocy of my own logic strikes me now. Was I really still living for his approval? Wouldn't his greatest desire simply be that I grow up and make my own decisions?

I glimpse at Antony, half-smile at him but he can't manage such civility. He has his eyes on the trophy and I know instantly that he wants it more than I do. He thinks that prize offers the answer to his dreams, the promise of eternal happiness. He sees the bestseller, the lunches at the Ivy, the royalty cheques, the adulation of his fans. He knows Maud's failure to play by the rules represents an opportunity and now, for him, it's all-out war.

I close my eyes. The lights are too bright and I no longer really know what I want.

'The lines are now closed. In a few moments, I'll be able to reveal the winner of the Lit Factor.'

Sebastian Brown is mounting the stage again. But what's he doing? My God, he's turning a little pirouette with the trophy. Has the world gone mad?

'Sebastian, Ladies and Gentleman!' Helena trills.

From stage left, a man in black emerges, holding a small white envelope.

'Ladies and Gentlemen,' Sebastian says. 'I think you'll all agree that we have had two remarkable competitors here, both writing very different books, both tremendously talented individuals. But as you know, we can only give the prize to one winner.' The man in black gives the envelope to Sebastian.

'I know I will feel privileged to work with either of these two writers,' Sebastian says.

The moment extends. I feel my own heartbeat. In the future, I might never stand alone at a party, wondering if anyone will speak to me. I might never know how it feels to be an unacknowledged artist.

'The winner of this *Lit Factor* competition is…'

Nor would I ever live in Montmartre and live on absinthe and pure air.

I fear that I will faint and miss the announcement. Vernon holds the silence, milking it for all that it's worth. Everything pivots on his words.

'…Antony Thornwood for *Silent Voices.*'

Antony is clasping his chest in shock and wonder. His mouth hangs open and there is a brief pause before relief gives way to unadulterated joy. He doesn't look at me as he steps up to receive his trophy. Glitter rains down from the studio ceiling. Small fragments of bright light that blind me. I'm trembling.

Helena flings her arms around me but I shrug her off. Meryl's heading towards me too as half the crowd roar their approval of this choice and Antony hold the trophy aloft between them. A fragment of glitter has caught in my eye and it hurts, it's making my eyes water. At the bottom of the stage staircase, I see my Mum and behind her, Lois and Hilary. They're coming on stage to comfort me, but I know they can't see what's really happening. They're walking towards me. Then Joel is there, he's so close.

'Oh pet,' Mum says, kissing me. 'You did really well.'

Joel's arm is about my waist and he's whispering in my ear.

'Thank God,' he says. 'Thank the bloody Lord.'

I think Mum overhears him because she's looking daggers at him, but I'm nodding and unexpectedly, I begin to laugh.

'Fancy a tin of sardines?' I ask.

I kiss him, very hard, as the glitter dislodges from my eye.

Epilogue

'It is better to allow our lives to speak for us than our words.'
– Mahatma Gandhi

As soon as I stepped onto the Tube platform, I saw the poster. It was one of those enormous ones that you can't miss as you're waiting for the train. I had to stop for a minute to stand and stare. Joel nearly tripped over me.

'I can't believe she's getting so much exposure,' I said.

'She might be getting exposure but you do realise the book is probably shite,' he said.

'How would you know? You haven't read it.'

'Is she still with Carl McGahan?'

'I imagine so,' I said. 'If those thigh length boots are anything to go by.'

A low rumble announced the arrival of a train. It drew into the station and obscured the poster. It was odd that it stung a little, even now.

The train was pretty empty for a Saturday. There were a few teenagers in our compartment, a dark-haired young woman with a baby and a middle-aged couple poring over a map of London. We sat down next to each other. Joel picked up his copy of *The Guardian* and scanned the front page.

'Glad I'm so interesting,' I said.

'Stop being demanding,' he replied and I laughed.

'OK, I'll put it down.'

'Sorry. I'm still feeling raw, after that reading.'

'Anna, it's nothing to do with your book. It's just a failure of publicity, that's all.'

'I know, it's just when I see Lucy ChickLit...'

'And Antony Thornwood... I know. I know... but you never really wanted that, did you?'

'I suppose I'm lucky to have a book out there at all. I'm lucky to have a deal, no matter how meagre.'

'What's all this sudden obsession with the marketplace? Don't you remember how *pleased* you were that you didn't win the *Lit Factor*?'

'I know. But only two people at last night's reading?'

'It doesn't mean anything. It's a damn good book, Anna. It's still very early for reviews. They don't always come out immediately. Sometimes it takes weeks.'

'I just wonder what it's all about sometimes, you know?'

'It's about the meaning you create in this world, Annie,' he said. 'That goes beyond whether it's noticed by the media.'

'What do you have against the media, suddenly? If it weren't for the media, you'd be out of a job.'

'But I write what seems important to me; if they print it, fantastic, but I'm led by my own instinct, not by their agenda.'

'Idealist!'

He smiled and I wondered then how long you had to be with somebody before their expressions became utterly ordinary and unremarkable, because I'd been with Joel for almost a year now and this particular expression of his still got me every time. I'd spoken with Hilary about this only a few days ago. '*It's not normal,*' she'd said. '*It's totally weird. I'd marry him, if I were you.*' But I told Hilary that I had no intention of marrying anybody right now. I was slightly worried that the minute marriage was mentioned, Joel might develop a strange proclivity to pornography or I might feel inclined to have a love affair with some undeserving idiot. I really couldn't cope with that right now. Things were hunky-dory exactly as they were.

Today, we were heading to Billericay for a family barbeque. It was Lois and Paul's wedding anniversary, which was about as close to a wedding as I wanted to get right now. I suppose it wasn't surprising that weddings were on my mind, as only yesterday I'd heard the news that Phyllis was engaged again. She had e-mailed to tell me that she'd met a wonderful psychiatrist in San Francisco and they were planning a huge white wedding in Hollywood in the "fall".

'Poor Loftus,' I said, half to myself.

'Loftus? Why are you thinking about him? He's out of jail now, isn't he?'

'Yes. But he doesn't know what he missed with Phyllis. You know, I think they were in love once, a very long time ago.'

'But love never lasts,' Joel said, though I knew that he just being provocative.

'I guess not. Love... words... they all vanish in the end.'

'That's pretty profound,' he replied. 'But isn't this our stop?'

'Bugger...'

We leapt up, just a little too late and missed it. We grabbed our seats again as a girl sat down opposite us. She was wearing a gorgeous vintage dress that Julia Claiborne would have killed for – pale cream with a rosebud design. She seemed a little irritated at our laughter. Her forehead creased in a frown and in an attempt to ignore us, she reached into her bag and took out a book. It was a shiny hardback, the cover featuring a woman with a pale, elongated face and red hair tied back in a chignon. I drew breath. *The Modigliani Girl* by Anna Bright.

Within minutes, she appeared absorbed; it was clear that she had forgotten us. We had become completely invisible. It was only the words that mattered.

THE END

Acknowledgements

This book was first conceived of in a meeting with my former agent Caroline Dawnay. My writer friends, Linda Buckley-Archer, Stephanie Chilman, Kate Harrison, Jacqui Hazell and Louise Voss offered regular encouragement and sound advice during the writing process. Novelist Louise Doughty gave wise editorial suggestions. Literary agent Broo Doherty read the manuscript several times and her knowledgeable input and belief in the book were instrumental in my completing the novel. I am immensely grateful to her. I would like to thank Stephanie Zia of Blackbird Digital Books for having faith in this novel and for seeing it through to publication. Without Stephanie the novel would still be in a drawer. Thanks also to the team at Blackbird in particular proofreaer Andrew Ives for his attention to detail and Mark Binner for his help with formatting.

My husband David Lewis kept me going by laughing aloud at the funny bits; and I thank my children Jack and Saskia for their love and comic genius.

About The Author

Jacqui Lofthouse began her career in radio production and media training. In 1992 she studied for her MA in Creative Writing at the University of East Anglia under Malcolm Bradbury and Rose Tremain. She is the author of four novels including *The Temple of Hymen* and *Bluethroat Morning*. Her novels have sold over 100,000 copies in the UK, the USA and Europe and have been widely reviewed.

If you enjoyed this book and would like to know more about becoming a **Reader Ambassador** for *The Modigliani Girl*, please email us at blackbird.digibooks@gmail.com and we'll let you know how you can become a valuable, visible, part of this book's journey to a wider audience.

Keep up to date with all Jacqui Lofthouse news and new titles, join the Jacqui Lofthouse Mailing List
http://bit.ly/1zNu0ng
(All email details securely managed at Mailchimp.com and never shared with third parties.)

Jacqui's blog: http://thewritingcoach.co.uk/
Facebook: https://www.facebook.com/jacquilofthouseauthor
Twitter: @JacquiLofthouse

More Books By Jacqui Lofthouse

The Temple of Hymen (Hamish Hamilton/Penguin 1995/1996)
Bluethroat Morning (Bloomsbury 2000)
Een Stille Verdwijning (De Bezige Bij 2005)

More Original Fiction From Blackbird Digital Books

The Dream Theatre (2011*)* by Sarah Ball
The Widow's To Do List (2013) by Stephanie Zia
That Special Someone (2014) by Tanya Bullock
The Road To Donetsk (2015) by Diane Chandler

http://blackbird-books.com
@blackbirdebooks
A publishing company for the digital age

We publish rights-reverted and new titles by established quality writers alongside
exciting new talent.

303

Printed in Great Britain
by Amazon